COMEBACK

Also available in Large Print from
G.K. Hall by Dick Francis:

Longshot
Straight
The Edge
Hot Money
Bolt
Break In
Proof
The Danger
Banker
Twice Shy
Reflex
Blood Sport
Odds Against

COMEBACK

Dick Francis

G.K. HALL & CO.
Boston, Massachusetts
1992

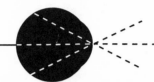

This Large Print Book carries the Seal of Approval of N.A.V.H.

Published in Large Print by arrangement with
G. P. Putnam's Sons.

G.K. Hall Large Print Book Series.

Printed on acid free paper in the United States of America.

Set in 16 pt. Plantin.

Library of Congress Cataloging-in-Publication Data

Francis, Dick.
    Comeback / Dick Francis.
        p. cm.—(G.K. Hall large print book series)
    ISBN 0-8161-5418-X (lg. print).—ISBN 0-8161-5419-8
      (pbk. : lg. print)
    1. Large type books. I. Title.
    [PR6056.R27C6 1992]
    823'.914—dc20   92-14133

With heartfelt thanks
to Jenny Hall
Veterinary Surgeon
and to
Peter Spicely
and Philip Grice
British Consuls

1

I'm Peter Darwin.

Everyone asks, so I may as well say at once that no, I'm not related to Charles.

I was in fact born Peter Perry, but John Darwin, marrying my widowed mother when I was twelve, gave me, among many other things, a new life, a new name and a new identity.

Twenty years rolled like mist over the memories of my distant childhood in Gloucestershire, and now I, Peter Darwin, was thirty-two, adopted son of a diplomat, in the diplomatic service myself.

As my stepfather's postings and later my own were all at the whim of the Foreign Office, I'd mostly lived those twenty years abroad in scattered three- or four-year segments, some blazing, some boring, from Caracas to Lima, from Moscow to Cairo to Madrid, housed in Foreign Office lodgings from one-bedroom concrete to gilt-decked mansions, counting nowhere home.

Friendships were transitory. Locals, left behind. Other diplomats and their children came and went. I was rootless and nomadic, well used to it and content.

"Look us up if you're ever in Florida," Fred Hutchings said casually, leaving Tokyo to be consul in Miami. "Stay for a day or so if you're passing through."

That "day or so," I thought wryly, was a pretty good indicator of the warmth of our feelings for each other: tepid to luke.

"Thanks," I said.

He nodded. We'd worked together for months without friction. He half-meant the invitation. He was trained in politeness, as we all were.

My own posting, when it came through nearly a year later, was surprisingly to England, to the Foreign and Commonwealth Office in Whitehall.

"What?" My stepfather in Mexico City chuckled with pleasure on the phone when I told him. "Private secretary! Well done! The pay's rotten. You'll have some leave first, though. Come and see us. Your mother misses you."

So I spent nearly a month with them and then set off to England via Miami, which was why, after a delayed flight and a missed connection, I found myself with twenty-four hours to kill and the echo of Fred Hutchings' invitation in my head. Why not, I thought, and on an impulse found his number from Enquiries, and phoned him.

His answering voice sounded genuinely welcoming and I pictured him on the other end of the line; forty, plump, freckled, eager, with a forehead that perspired under the slightest nervous pressure. The mildness of my liking for him flooded belatedly back, but it was too late to retreat.

"Great, great," he was saying heartily. "I'd ask you here for the night but the children aren't well. How about dinner, though? Get a taxi to The Diving Pelican on a Hundred and Eighty-sixth Street, North Miami Beach. I'll meet you there about eight. How's that?"

"Splendid," I said.

"Good. Good. Great to see old friends." He told me the address of the restaurant again, carefully. "We eat there all the time. Come to think of it"—his voice brightened enthusiastically—"two of our friends there are going to England tomorrow too. You'll like them. Maybe you'll all be on the same plane. I'll introduce you."

"Thank you," I said faintly.

"A pleasure." I could feel him beaming with goodwill down the wire. "See you then."

With a sigh I replaced the receiver, booked myself and my bags into the airport hotel for the night and in due course taxied as instructed to the rendezvous.

The Diving Pelican, less striking than its name, glowed dimly at one end of a dark row of shops. There seemed to be few other signs of neighborhood life, but the twenty or so parking spaces in front were full. I pulled open the outwards-opening door, stepped into a small entrance hall and was greeted by a young woman with a bright smile who said, "And how are you today?" as if she'd known me for years.

"Fine," I said, and mentioned Fred.

3

The smile grew wider. Fred had arrived. Fred, it seemed, was good news.

He was sitting alone at a round table spread with a cream lace cloth over a pink underlay. Stainless steel flatware, pink napkins, unfussy wineglasses, little oil lamps, carnation in a bud vase, the trappings of halfway up the scale. Not very large overall, the place was pleasantly packed. Not a pelican in sight, diving or otherwise.

Fred rose to his feet to pump my hand and the smiling lady pulled out a chair for me, producing a shiny menu and showing her molars.

"Great, great," Fred was saying. "Sorry I'm alone but Meg didn't want to leave the children. They've got chicken pox."

I made sympathetic noises.

"Covered in spots, poor little buggers," Fred said. "Like some wine?"

We ate our salads first in the American way and drank some reasonable red. Fred, at my prompting, told me about life in his consulate, mostly a matter, he said, of British tourists complaining of lost documents, stolen money and decamping boyfriends.

"They'll con you rigid," Fred said. "Sob stories by the dozen." With a sly gleam of amusement he looked at me sideways. "People like you, smooth two-a-penny first secretaries used to embassy life, you'd fall for the wet-handkerchief routine like a knockover. All half of them want is a free ticket home."

4

"You've grown cynical, Fred."

"Experienced," he said.

Always expect a lie, my stepfather had said right back at the beginning of my enlightenment into what his job entailed. Politicians and diplomats, he'd said, are liars until proved different. "You too?" I asked, dismayed, and he'd smiled his civilized smile and educated me. "I don't lie to you or your mother. You will not lie to us. If you hear me tell an untruth in public you will remain calm and keep your mouth shut and work out why I said it."

We got on fine from the start. I couldn't remember my natural father, who had died when I was a baby, and I had no hangups about anyone taking his place. I'd longed to have a father like other boys, and then suddenly there was this big stranger, full of jokes, who'd swept like a gale into our single-parent only-child existence and carried us off to the equator before we could gasp. It was only gradually, afterwards, that I realized how irrevocably he'd changed me, and how fortunate I had been.

Fred said, "Where have they posted you, after your leave?"

"Nowhere. I mean, England. Private secretary."

"Lucky old you!" There was a jealous edge to his voice at my promotion, all of a piece, I thought, with his gibe about two-a-penny gullible young men in embassies: and he'd been one himself in the past.

"Perhaps I'll get Ulan Bator after that," I said. Ulan Bator was the pits with everyone. It was heavily rumored that instead of a car there the ambassador got issued an official yak. "No one gets plums in a row."

Fred flicked me a rueful smile, acknowledging that I'd seen his envy, and welcomed our seafood fettucini with yum yum noises and a vigorous appetite. Fred had recommended the house speciality. I'd been persuaded, and in fact it was good.

Midway through, there was a small burst of clapping, and Fred, pausing with fork in the air, exuded pleasure.

"Ah," he said proprietorially. "Vicky Larch and Greg Wayfield. They're the friends I told you about, who are going to the U.K. tomorrow. They live just round the corner."

Vicky Larch and Greg Wayfield were more than friends; they were singers. They had come into the restaurant without fanfare through curtains at the far end, she dressed in a white sequined tunic, he in a Madras checked tailored jacket, both in light colored trousers. The only thing really surprising about them was their age. They were mature, one might perhaps say, and no longer slim.

I thought reprehensibly that I could have done without the embarrassment of having to applaud earnest elderly amateurs all the way back to England. They fiddled around with amplifying equipment and tapped microphones to make sure they were working. Fred nodded encouragingly to them and to me and happily returned to his pasta.

They got the equipment going and ran a tape: soft sweet music from old stage shows, well known, undemanding, a background to food. Greg Wayfield hummed a few bars after a while and then began to sing the words, and I looked up from my fettucini in surprise because this was no geriatric disaster but a good true voice, gentle, virile and full of timbre.

Fred glanced at my expression and smiled with satisfaction. The song ended, the diners applauded, and there was more tape. Then, again without announcement or fuss, the woman smoothed into a love song, the words a touch sad, moody, expressed with the catchy syncopated timing of long experience. Dear heavens, I thought with relief they're pros. Good old pros, having a ball.

They sang six songs alternately and finished with a duet, and then to enthusiastic clapping they threaded a way round the tables and sat down with Fred and me.

Fred made introductions. Half-standing, I shook the singers hands across the lace cloth and said with perfect honesty how much I'd enjoyed their performance.

"They'll sing again," Fred promised, pouring wine for them as if from long habit. "This is just a break."

At close quarters they looked as wholesome and old-fashioned as their act, he still handsome,

7

she with the air of a young chanteuse trapped in a grandmotherly body.

"Did you sing in nightclubs?" I asked her, as she sat beside me.

Her blue eyes widened. "How did you know?"

"Something about your phrasing. Intimate. Designed for shadowy late-night spaces. Something about the way you move your head."

"Well yes, I did clubs for years." She was amused, aware of me physically despite her age. Once a woman, always a woman, I thought.

Her hair was white, a fluffy well-cut helmet. She had good skin lightly made up and her only real concession to theatricality lay in the silky dark up-curling false lashes, second nature to her eyes.

"But I retired ages ago," she said, lowering the lids and raising them in harmless coquetry. "Had a bunch of babies and got too fat. Too old. We sing here just for fun."

Her speaking voice was English, without regional accent, her diction trained and precise. Under the mild banter she seemed serene, secure and sensible, and I revised my gloomiest views of the next night's journey. Flight attendants could be chatted-up another time, I supposed.

Greg said, "My wife would flirt with a chair leg," and they both looked at me indulgently and laughed.

"Don't trust Peter," Fred cautioned them ironically. "He's the best liar I know, and I've met a few, believe me."

8

"How unkind," Vicky said disbelievingly. "He's a lamb."

Fred made a laughing cough and checked that we all were in fact booked on the same flight. No doubt about it. British Airways' jumbo to Heathrow. Club class, all of us.

"Great. Great," Fred said.

Greg, I thought, was American, though it was hard to tell. A mid-Atlantic man: halfway accent, American clothes, English facial bones. Part of the local scenery in Miami, he had presence but not his wife's natural stage charisma. He hadn't been a soloist, I thought.

He said, "Are you a consul too, Peter?"

"Not at the moment."

He looked perplexed, so I explained. "In the British foreign service you take the title of your present job. You don't take your rank with you. You can be a second or first secretary or a consul or counselor or a consul-general or a minister or a high commissioner or an ambassador in one place, but you'll very likely be something different in the next. The rank stays with the job. You take the rank of whatever job you're sent to."

Fred was nodding. "In the States, once an ambassador always an ambassador. 'Mr. Ambassador' forever. Even if you've only been an ambassador to some tiny country for a couple of years and are back to being a dogsbody, you keep the title. The British don't."

"Too bad," Greg said.

"No," I disagreed, "it's better. There's no ab-

9

solutely clear-cut hierarchy, so there's less bitch-
ing and less despair."

They looked at me in astonishment.

"Mind you," Fred said to them with mock con-
fidentiality, "Peter's father's an ambassador at the
moment. Between the two of them they've held
every rank in the book."

"Mine are all lower," I said smiling.

Vicky said comfortingly, "I'm sure you'll do
well in the end."

Fred laughed.

Greg pushed away his half-drunk wine and said
they'd better get back to work, a popular move
with the clientele, always quick to applaud them.
They sang another three songs each, Greg finishing quietly with a crooning version of "The
Last Farewell," the lament of a sailor leaving his
South Seas love to go back to storms and war
at sea round Britain. Shut your eyes, I thought,
listening, and Greg could be the doomed young
man. It was a masterly performance; extraordinary. A woman at the next table brought out a
handkerchief and wiped away surreptitious
tears.

The diners, sitting transfixed over long-cooled
cups of coffee, gave Greg the accolade of a
second's silence before showing their pleasure.
Sentimental it might all be, I thought, but one
could have too much of stark unsugared realism.

The singers returned to our table, accepting
plaudits on the way, and this time drank their
wine without restraint. They were pumped up

with the post-performance high-level adrenaline surge of all successful appearances of any sort, and it would take them a while to come down. Meanwhile they talked with animation, scattering information about themselves and further proving, if it were necessary, that they were solidly good, well-intentioned people.

I'd always found goodness more interesting then evil, though I was aware this wasn't the most general view. To my mind, it took more work and more courage to be good, an opinion continually reinforced by my own shortcomings.

He had trained originally for opera, Greg said, but there weren't enough roles for the available voices.

"It helps to be Italian," he said ruefully. "And so few of any generation really make it. I sang chorus. I would have starved then rather than sing 'The Last Farewell.' I was arrogant, musically, when I was young." He smiled with forgiveness for his youth. "So I went into a banking house as a junior junior in the trust department and eventually began to be able to afford opera tickets."

"But you went on singing," I protested. "No one could sing as you do without constant practice."

He nodded. "In choirs. Sometimes in cathedrals and so on. Anywhere I could. And in the bathroom, of course."

Vicky raised the eyelashes to heaven.

"Now they both sing here two or three times

a week," Fred told me. "This place would die without them."

"Hush," Vicky said, looking round for outraged proprietorial feelings but fortunately not seeing any. "We enjoy it."

Greg said they were going to England for a month. One of Vicky's daughters was getting married.

Vicky's daughter?

Yes, she said, the children were all hers. Two boys, two girls. She'd divorced their father long ago. She and Greg were new together: eighteen months married, still on honeymoon.

"Belinda—she's my youngest—she's marrying a veterinary surgeon," Vicky said. "She was always mad about animals."

I laughed.

"Well, yes," she said, "I hope she's mad about him, too. She's worked for him for ages, but this came on suddenly a few weeks ago. So, anyway, we're off to horse country. He deals mostly with horses. He acts as a vet at Cheltenham races."

I made a small explosive noise in my throat and they looked at me inquiringly.

I said, "My father and mother met at Cheltenham races."

They exclaimed over it, of course, and it seemed a bit late to say that my mother and *stepfather* met at Cheltenham races, so I let it pass. My real father, I thought, was anyway John Darwin: the only father I could remember.

Fred, reflecting, said, "Didn't your father spend his entire youth at the races? Didn't you say so in Tokyo, that time you went to the Japan Cup?"

"I expect I said it," I agreed, "though it was a bit of an exaggeration. But he still does go when he gets the chance."

"Do ambassadors usually go to the races?" Vicky asked doubtfully.

"This particular ambassador sees racecourses as the perfect place for diplomacy," I said with ironic affection. "He invites the local Jockey Club bigwigs to an embassy party and they in turn invite him to the races. He says he learns more about a country faster at the races than in a month of diplomatic handshaking. He's right, too. Did you know they have bicycle parks at Tokyo racecourse?"

Greg said, "Er . . . uh . . . I don't follow."

"Not just car parks," I said. "Motorcycle parks and bicycle parks. Rows and rows of them. They tell you a lot about the Japanese."

"What, for instance?" Vicky asked.

"That they'll get where they want to go one way or another."

"Are you being serious?"

"Of course," I said with mock gravity. "And they have a baby park at the races too. You leave your infant to play in a huge bouncing Donald Duck while you bet your money away in a carefree fashion."

"And what does this tell you?" Vicky teased.

"That the baby park draws in more than enough revenue to fund it."

"Don't worry about Peter," Fred told them reassuringly. "He's got this awful quirky mind, but you can rely on him in a crisis.

"Thanks," I said dryly.

Greg asked a few things about our time in Japan. Had we enjoyed it, for instance. Very much, we both said. And did we speak the language? Yes, we did. Fred had been a first secretary in the commercial department, spending his time oiling the wheels of trade. My own job had been to learn what was likely to happen on the political scene.

"Peter went to the lunches and cocktail parties," Fred said, "drinking sake out of little wooden boxes instead of glasses."

The customs and cadences of Japan still flowed strongly in my head, barely overlaid by the month in Mexico City. It was always an odd feeling of deprivation, leaving behind a culture one had striven intensely to understand. Not exactly postpartum blues, but departing-from-post blues, definitely.

The diners in the restaurant had gradually drifted away, leaving the four of us as the last to leave. Vicky and Greg went off to pack up their equipment and as a matter of course Fred and I divided the bill between us to the last cent.

"Do you want it in yen?" I asked.

"For God's sake," Fred said. "Didn't you change some at the airport?"

I had. A habit. Fred took the notes and handed me some coins in return, which I pocketed. The Foreign Office was permanently strapped for cash and our basic pay came nowhere near the level of status and responsibility given us. I wasn't complaining. No one ever entered the diplomatic service to get mega-rich. Fred said he would run me back to the airport to save me having to pay for another taxi, which was good of him.

Vicky and Greg returned, she carrying a large white handbag aglitter with multicolored stones outlined in thin white cord and he following with a large squashy holdall slung boyishly from one shoulder. We all four left the restaurant and stood for a while outside the door saying goodnights, Vicky and Greg making plans to find me the following day.

On the wall beside the door a glassed frame held a sample menu flanked by two eight-by-ten black-and-white photographs of the singers, both taken, it was clear, a long time previously.

Vicky saw the direction of my eyes and made a small sad moue, philosophical with an effort. Her likeness, a striking theater-type glossy with her head and shoulders at a tilt, bright light shining on the forehead, stars in the eyes, tactful shadows over the beginnings of double chin, must have been from twenty years earlier at least. Greg's no-nonsense straight-ahead smile had few photographic tricks and was very slightly out of focus as if enlarged from a none-too-clear print. It too was an earlier Greg, thinner, positively masculine, strongly handsome, with a dark, now-vanished moustache.

Impossible to guess at Vicky's character from that sort of picture, but one could make a stab at Greg's. Enough intelligence, the complacency of success, a desire to please, an optimistic nature. Not the sort to lie about people behind their backs.

Final goodnights. Vicky lifted her cheek to me for a kiss. Easy to deliver.

"Our car's down there," she said, pointing to the distance.

"Mine's over there," Fred said, pointing the other way.

We all nodded and moved apart, the evening over.

"They're nice people," Fred said contentedly.

"Yes," I agreed.

We climbed into his car and dutifully fastened the seat belts. He started the engine, switched on the lights, backed out of the parking space and turned the car to the general direction of the airport.

"Stop!" I yelled abruptly, struggling to undo the hampering seat-belt buckle so easily done up.

"*What?*" Fred said, jamming foot on brake but not understanding. "What the hell's wrong?"

I didn't answer him. I got the wretched belt undone at last, swung open the car door and scrambled out, running almost before I had both feet on the ground.

16

In the passing beam of Fred's headlights as he'd turned the car I'd seen the distant sparkle of Vicky's sequined tunic and seen also that she was struggling, falling, with a dark figure crowding her, cutting half of her from my sight, a figure of unmistakable ill-will . . . attacking.

I sprinted, hearing her cry out shrilly.

I myself yelled "Vicky, Vicky" in an attempt to frighten off the mugger, but he seemed glued to her like a leech, she on the ground and kicking, he close on her, hunched and intent.

No sign of Greg.

I reached the man over Vicky, cannoning into him to knock him away. He was heavier than I'd thought and not easily deterred, and far from running from me he seemed to view me as merely another mug to be robbed. He jabbed a strong fist at my face, a blow I ducked from nothing but instinct, and I tried catching him by the clothes and flinging him against a parked car.

No success. He connected with a fist to my chest that left me breathless and feeling as if he'd squashed my heart against my backbone. The face above the fists was a matter of darkness and narrow eyes: he was shorter than I and thicker.

I was losing the fight, which made me angry but not much more effective. It was hostility I was up against, I thought, not just greed. Behind the robbery, hatred.

Vicky, who had crawled away moaning, sud-

17

denly rose to her feet as if galvanized and came up behind our assailant. I saw her eyes momentarily over his shoulder, stretched wide with fear and full of determination. She took aim and kicked at him hard. He hissed fiercely with pain and turned towards her and I in turn kicked him, targeting nowhere special but hitting the back of his knee.

Vicky had her long scarlet nails up, her fingers bent like a witch. There was bright red blood in splashes down her tunic. Her mouth was stretched open in what looked in that dim light like the snarl of a wolf, and out of it came a shriek that began in the low register and rose to a fortissimo scream somewhere above high G.

It raised the hairs on my own neck and it broke the nerve of the thief. He took a stumbling step to go round her and then another, and belatedly departed at a shambling run.

Vicky fell weakly into my arms, the fighting fury turning fast to shakes and tears, her triumphant voice roughened and near incoherence.

"God. Oh God . . . There were two of them . . . Greg . . ."

Headlights blazed at us, fast advancing. Vicky and I clutched each other like dazzled rabbits and I was bunching muscles to hurl us both out of the way when tires squealed to a stop and the black figure emerging like a silhouette through the bright beam resolved itself into the solid familiarity of Fred. The consul to the rescue.

Good old Fred. I felt a bit light-headed, and stupid because of it.

"Is she all right?" Fred was asking me anxiously. "Where's Greg?"

Vicky and I declutched and the three of us in unison looked for Greg.

He wasn't hard to find. He was lying in a tumbled unconscious heap near the rear wheel on the far side of what turned out to be his and Vicky's dark blue BMW.

There was a stunned moment of disbelief and horror. Then, crying out, Vicky fell on her knees beside him and I squatted down and felt round his neck, searching for the pulse under his jaw.

"He's alive," I said, relieved, straightening.

Vicky sniffed in her tears, still crying with distress. Fred, ever practical, said, "We'd better get an ambulance."

I agreed with him, but before we could do anything a police car wailed with its siren down the road and drew up beside us, red, white and blue lights flashing in a bar across the car's roof.

A big man in midnight blue trousers and shirt with insignia stepped out, bringing his notebook to the ready and telling us someone had just reported a woman screaming and what was it all about. Fast, I thought. Response time, spectacular. He had been cruising nearby, he said.

Greg began moaning before anyone could answer and struggled to sit up, appearing dazed and disoriented and startlingly old.

Vicky supported him round the shoulders.

Looking at her with pathos and pain and gratitude, he saw the blood on her tunic and said he was sorry.

"Sorry!" Vicky exclaimed blankly. "What for?"

He didn't answer, but one could see what he meant: sorry that he hadn't been able to defend her. It was encouraging, I thought, that he seemed to know where he was and what had happened.

The policeman unclipped a hand-held radio from his belt and called for the ambulance and then, with notable kindness, asked Vicky just what had occurred. She looked up at him and tried to answer, but the phrases came out unconnectedly and on jagged half-hysterical breaths, as if from splintered thoughts.

"Greg's wallet . . . well, they banged his head on the car . . . shadows . . . didn't see them . . . he was trying . . . you know, he was trying to take my *rings* . . . the plane tickets . . . my daughter's wedding . . . I'd've killed him . . ." She stopped talking as if aware it was gibberish and looked lost.

"Take your time, ma'am," the policeman said. "When you're ready."

She took a visibly deep breath and tried again. "They were waiting . . . behind the car . . . I could kill them . . . They jumped on Greg when he went round . . . I hate them . . . I hope they die . . ."

There were high-colored patches of extreme stress over her cheekbones and more strong flush

20

marks on her jaw and down her neck. Blood on her neck, also; quite a lot of it.

"You're doing good," the policeman said.

He was about my age, I thought, with a natural kindness not yet knocked out of him by the system.

"My ear hurts," Vicky said violently. "I could kill him."

I supposed we'd all noticed but not done much about the source of the blood on her tunic. One of her lobes was jaggedly cut and steadily oozing. She turned her head slightly, and the other ear shimmered suddenly in the car's lights, revealing a large aquamarine ringed by diamonds.

"Your earring," Fred exclaimed, fishing his pockets for a handkerchief and not finding one. "You need a bandage."

Vicky put a finger tentatively to her torn ear and winced heavily.

"The *bastard*," she said, her voice shaking. "The bloody bastard. He tugged . . . he just *ripped* . . . he's torn right through my ear."

"Shouldn't earrings come off more easily than that?" the policeman asked uncritically.

Vicky's voice, high with rage and shock, said, "We bought them in Brazil."

"Er . . ." the policeman said, lost.

"Vicky," Fred said soothingly, "what does it matter if they came from Brazil?"

She gave him a bewildered look as if she couldn't understand his not understanding.

"They don't have butterfly clips on the back,"

21

she told him jerkily. "They have butterfly *screws*. Like a nut and bolt. So they don't fall off and get lost. And so people can't steal them . . ." Her voice died away into a sob, a noise it seemed suddenly that she herself disapproved of, and she sniffed again determinedly and straightened her shoulders.

Hanging on to her courage, I thought. See-sawing towards disintegration, hauling herself back. Agitation almost beyond her control, but not quite.

"And another thing," she wailed, misery and anger fighting again for supremacy. "They stole my handbag. It's got my passport . . . and, oh *hell*, my green card . . . and our tickets . . ." A couple of tears squeezed past her best resolutions. "What are we going to *do?*"

The distress-filled plea was answered pragmatically by Fred, who said he wasn't consul for nothing and he'd get her to her daughter's wedding willy-nilly.

"Now, ma'am," the policeman said, uninterested in travel arrangements, "can you give a description of these two men?"

"It was dark." She seemed angry with him suddenly. Angry with everything. She said furiously, "They were dark."

"Black?"

"No." She was uncertain, besides angry.

"What then, ma'am?"

"Dark-skinned. I can't think. My ear hurts."

"Clothes, ma'am?"

"Black . . . What does it matter? I mean . . . they were so quick . . . He was trying to pull my rings off . . ."

She extended her fingers. If the stones were real they were worth stealing.

"My engagement ring," she explained. "Bastard didn't get it, thanks to Peter."

The urgent whipping siren of a dazzlingly lit ambulance split the night and paramedics spilled out purposefully, taking charge with professional heartiness and treating Vicky and Greg like children. The policeman told Vicky he would be following them to the hospital and would take a proper statement once her ear and Greg's head were fixed, but she didn't seem to take it in.

Two more police cars arrived fast with flashing lights and wailing sirens, disgorging enough blue-clad figures to arrest half the neighborhood, and Fred and I found ourselves with our hands on the car roof being frisked while explaining insistently that we were not in fact the muggers but instead the British consul, friends and witnesses.

The kindly original cop looked back fleetingly and said something I couldn't hear in the bustle, but at least it seemed to blunt the sharpest of suspicions. Fred loudly reiterated his identity as British consul, a statement he was this time asked in a bullish fashion to substantiate. He was allowed to fetch out an oversized credit card which announced—with photograph—his diplomatic status, thereby inducing a reluctant change of attitude.

Greg was on his feet. I took a step towards him and was stopped by a midnight blue arm.

"Ask him for his car keys," I said. "If his car stays out here all night it will be stolen."

Grudgingly the midnight blue presence yelled over his shoulder, and presently the information percolated back that Greg had dropped the keys by the car when he was attacked. Midnight-blue went to look, found the keys and, after consultation, gave them to Fred.

The uniforms seemed to be doing things at great speed which no doubt came from much practice and was a regular pace for such an occasion. Vicky and Greg were helped into the ambulance, which at once departed, followed immediately by the first policeman. Other policemen fanned out into the surrounding area to search for the muggers should they still be around and hiding. Fat chance, I thought.

One of the new bunch wrote down my name under Fred's and paused over the address I gave him: the Foreign and Commonwealth Office, Whitehall, London, England.

"Diplomatic immunity, like him?" He jerked his head in Fred's direction.

"I'll help if I can," I said.

He sucked his teeth a bit and asked what I'd observed.

I told him, in fair detail.

Had I seen this mugger at close quarters?

Well yes, I said, since he'd hit me.

Description?

24

"Dark-skinned."

"Black?"

I found the same difficulty as Vicky over the skin color.

"Not West Indian or African," I said. "Maybe Central American. Maybe Hispanic. He didn't speak. I can't tell you any better."

"Clothes?"

"Black." I thought back, remembering how I tried to throw him, refeeling the cloth that I'd clutched. "I'd say black jeans, black cotton sweatshirt, black sneakers. When he ran off he wasn't easy to see."

I made my guesses at his age, height, weight and so on but I couldn't remember his face well enough to be sure I'd recognize him in other clothes, in daylight.

Midnight-blue shut his notebook and produced two cards with his name on, one for Fred, the other for me. He would be grateful, he indicated, if we would present ourselves at his police station the following morning at ten A.M., and he gave us the impression that had it not been for the sheltering umbrella of the Foreign Office, the request would have been an order.

The scattered searchers returned without a mugger but with, surprisingly, Vicky's torn-out earring, which they'd found on the ground. Bagged and labeled, it was solemnly retained in police custody. There was no sign, it seemed, of a capacious white bejeweled handbag or Greg's wallet or his shoulder-slung holdall.

As fast as they'd arrived, the midnight-blues departed, leaving a sudden deafening silence in which Fred and I stood and looked at each other a touch dazedly, deciding what to do next.

The few curious local inhabitants faded back through their doors, their interest level in the noise and glittering red, white and blue illuminations having been remarkably low throughout, as though the circus were too familiar to bother with: though this, Fred commented ruefully, was supposed to be a quiet residential area.

"You'd better drive the BMW to the hospital," Fred said, "and collect them and take them home."

"Um . . ."

"I can't do it," he said reasonably. "I promised Meg I wouldn't be late. She's got her hands full . . . the children were crying because their spots are itching."

"Won't the hospital send them home in an ambulance?" I asked.

Fred looked at me pityingly. "This is not the National Health Service. This is pay-through-the-nose country."

"Oh, all right. Where's the hospital?"

He began to give me directions but shrugged finally and said I'd better follow him: so he led me to the entrance, pointed to it emphatically through his open window and, without pausing for more speech, zoomed away towards the chicken pox.

I found Greg and the friendly policeman sitting

glumly side by side in the waiting area, Greg looking drained and gray, the policeman glowing with health and watching the passing nurses in the same sort of way that I did, once I settled myself in the next seat.

"How are you feeling?" I asked Greg: an unnecessary question.

"Tired," he said, "but my head's all right. They say there's only a bruise. Got to rest a bit, that's all."

I nodded. "I brought your car," I said. "I'll drive you home."

He said limply, "Thanks."

Conversation lapsed. The ratio of middle-aged to nubile nurses proved to be ten to one. Disappointing.

After a long time Vicky reappeared, sitting in a wheelchair pushed by a (middle-aged) nurse and accompanied by a young doctor whose smudged white coat spoke of long hours on duty. Vicky, wearing a large white bandage like an earmuff above the bloodstained sparkling tunic, held a tissue to her mouth and had her eyes shut. Her face, cleaned of makeup, appeared lined and pudgy. The false eyelashes had been removed. The trouper persona was in abeyance; the grandmother alone inhabited the body.

The young doctor told Greg that his wife was fine, he'd stitched the ear under local anesthetic, it should heal without trouble, he'd given her painkillers, sedatives and antibiotics and she should come back later that day to have the dressing changed. Vicky opened her eyes and looked no better.

I glanced at my watch and found it was very nearly two o'clock. Time flies, I thought wryly, when one's having a good time.

The doctor departed and the policeman gently asked Vicky questions which she answered in a low voice without emotion. After a while he produced a card with his name on it and asked her and Greg to go to the police station at ten in the morning to complete their statements.

"You too," he said to me.

"Your pals have already given me a card." I showed it to him. He peered at it and nodded. "Same place, same time."

He said goodnight to us and left, his kindness, I saw, a habitual way of getting things done, not a deep compassion for each individual. Much better, all the same, than a brusque automatic universal disregard of sensibilities.

A nurse reappeared to push Vicky to the doorstep, but no further. Hospital care and hospital insurance stopped right there, she firmly said. We persuaded her merely to let me fetch the car to the door, rather than have Vicky walk to the car, a concession she made with impatience. Both Greg and Vicky were beyond caring.

They chose to sit together in the back of the car, and I asked for the most elementary instructions on how to get to their home, like which way out of the gate. It was amazing we ever reached the house, as Vicky closed her eyes again and kept them shut, and Greg kept drifting off to sleep, waking when I stopped and asking where we were. You tell me, I said.

I stifled the beginnings of irritation and drove with care and we did at last pull up in a semi-circular drive outside their front door. Greg fortunately still had the house keys in his pocket, and I didn't think it was exactly the moment to speculate aloud as to whether the thieves had acted on the knowledge, they must have found in their possession and come to rob and destroy while their victims were in the hospital.

Telling the couple to stay where they were for a moment, I got Greg to give me the key, and fed it into the lock with some foreboding. All was dark and quiet inside, however, and when I felt around and found the light switch, all was also revealed as undisturbed.

Feeling exposed to predators and half-ready for another attacking rush from the many surrounding bushes, I tried to hurry Greg and Vicky into the house without actually scaring them into paralysis, but they were agonizingly slow. It wasn't until we were all safely inside with the door locked behind us that I began in any way to relax.

They lived in a one-story house, most of the rooms flowing into each other without doors. No heating problems, of course, in South Florida. I went round checking that all the curtains were drawn, finding that the Wayfield taste in interior decorating ran to bright floral prints and mahogany.

Returning to find them both sitting in the chairs nearest the front door, as if their legs could take them no further—the life force at its lowest ebb—I suggested they make themselves a hot sweet drink before they went to bed. I, I said, would phone for a taxi.

They looked at me in horror.

"Oh no," Vicky said, near to tears. "Stay here. Please do. I hate to say it, but I feel so shaky and shivery. And I'm scared. I can't help it. They might come here. I've realized they must know our address."

Greg reached across for her hand and squeezed it. He didn't actually say he was scared but he too begged me to stay.

"You chased them off before," Vicky said. "They won't come if you're here."

I thought with longing of a quiet bed in the airport hotel but saw I couldn't abandon them to a panic-filled night. I'd known them for less than six hours: felt I'd been with them forever.

"I'll stay," I said, "but it wasn't I who chased them off. You," I said to Vicky, "you did it yourself with that brilliant scream."

I remembered her as she looked then, a white-haired witch with scarlet raking nails and brilliant eyes, the personification of all the dark female powers that had petrified men from prehistory.

"You were magnificent," I said: frightening, I might have added, if I'd wanted to admit it.

She brightened a little at the memory, a movement in the eyes. "It wasn't just the scream," she said. "It was the kick."

I asked in awakening understanding, "Where?"

She looked down at her shoes, high-heeled with sharply pointed toes.

"Where do you think?" she said. "I used to be a dancer too. High kicks. I was behind him. I aimed for just below the bottom of his spine. I was so angry I'd have killed him if I could." She looked up, a smile somewhere near, full of revengeful satisfaction. "I was right on target. It was a doozie, hard and straight. He had his legs apart, balancing himself to clobber you." She paused, then finished it with a nod. "I got him in the balls."

2

Two nights later I flew to England. Across the aisle Vicky and Greg slumbered peacefully, blanketed to their chins, heads together, babes in the wood.

"Peter, it wouldn't hurt you to put your journey off for one more day," Fred had said. "It isn't as if you've got anything to go *to*, especially. And Greg and Vicky are badly shaken by all this, you know they are."

Fred was at his most earnest, almost evangelical in his desire to do good. Rather, in his desire that I should do good. I thought of a T-shirt I'd once owned which read, "Stress is what happens when your gut says *NO* and your mouth says *YES I'D BE GLAD TO*"; and Fred asked me what I was smiling at.

"Nothing, really."

"Then you'll wait a day?"

"Yes, all right."

"Great. Great. I was sure you would. I told them I was sure you would. They can't possibly go tonight, you can see that."

We were in his office at the time, in the consulate in Miami, on the day after the mugging. The night had passed undisturbed by marauders but it had been an exhausted pair that had pottered round the kitchen in dressing gowns that morning to assemble much needed breakfasts. Vicky's ear was throbbing, Greg's forehead was dark with bruise and both were suffering from depression.

"All my credit cards . . ." Greg said wearily. "There's so much to *do.*" He picked up the telephone and passed on the bad news to the companies.

I thought of my bags sitting unattended in my unused room and phoned the hotel: no problem at all, I could pick up the luggage later but they would charge me for the past night regardless. Fair enough, I agreed.

Once they were dressed, I drove Vicky and Greg to meet Fred and keep the police appointment, a session that taxed the Wayfields' remaining stamina sorely. The only bright spot for Vicky was the return of her earring, though it would be a long time, she guessed, before she could wear it.

"I don't want to keep thinking of last night," she said vehemently during the interview, but the friendly policeman carried on asking friendly persistent questions nonetheless. Finally they let all four of us go, and Fred in his car led the rest of us in the BMW across town to his official domain.

The consulate proved to be a modest suite of offices high in a glass-walled tower. British firms and holidaymakers had clamored for it to be opened, but funding it, it was rumored in the service, Fred said, had meant closing its equivalent in some other place from where the tourist tide had ebbed.

Arriving on the 21st floor, we squeezed through tall doors into a small entrance and waiting area already filled by an indignant family who'd been robbed at Disneyworld and a man in a wheelchair who'd been brought in by the police as he couldn't remember where he was staying in Florida and had been found dazed and alone in the street repeating an English address.

Behind a glass partition, two good-looking young women, trying to sort everything out, welcomed the sight of Fred with relief.

"Bombproof glass, of course," Fred said to me, and signaled the girls to let us in through the electronic glass door. "Carry on," he said to them, which they did most competently, it seemed to me.

Beyond the antiterrorist door, the available space had been cleverly divided to allow for all the familiar sections of embassy life, but in miniature. Records room, cipher room, conference room, individual offices, large busy secretaries' room, kitchen, and a more spacious office with the best view for the man in charge.

This efficient layout was staffed by Fred himself, he said, along with the two super-secretaries and two vice-consuls, one of whom was involved in trade, the other, currently out on a job, in delicate areas like the unlawful movement of drugs.

Fred parked Greg and Vicky in a conference room just big enough for a round table surrounded by dining chairs and then, his forehead sweating, beckoned me into his private sanctum and shut the door.

"They won't be able to leave today," he said. "They" had become shorthand for Greg and Vicky. "Tickets, easy. But there's her passport, and she has to go to the hospital and she's only half packed, she said."

"And new locks for their house," I agreed.

"So you could stop another day and help them, couldn't you?"

I opened my mouth and shut it again and it was then that Fred had warmed to his persuasion.

Fred and I were of equal rank in the service, consuls and first secretaries both being (if one equated things to the army) like colonels.

As in the army, the next step up was the big one. First secretaries and consuls abounded, but counselors and consul-generals and ministers led towards the peak of the pyramid: there were at least six hundred consuls and probably more first secretaries around the world but only about a hundred and fifty ambassadors.

Fred looked out of his window at the wide spectacular view of palm trees, glittering blue sea and downtown skyscraper Miami and told me he'd never been happier.

"I'm glad, Fred," I said, meaning it.

He turned with a self-deprecating smile, his

plumpish body soft but his mind as agile as an acrobat.

"We both know you'll go higher than me in the end," he said.

I made disclaiming motions but he brushed them aside.

"But here," he went on, "for the first time ever, I'm in charge. It's a great feeling. Terrific. I just wanted to tell you. I can't tell many people. They wouldn't understand. But you do, don't you?"

I slowly nodded. "I've never really been totally in charge myself except now and then for a day or so. There's always someone to report to."

"This is much better." He grinned, looking almost boyish. "Think of me sometimes while you're scuttling round in Whitehall."

I thought of him as I sat in the jumbo with Greg and Vicky asleep across the aisle. I'd probably learned more about him in the last few days than in all the time in Tokyo, and certainly I liked him better. Being his own chief seemed to have sharpened the outlines of his character and smoothed away a lot of nervous mannerisms and maybe one day even the sweating forehead would remain dry.

Somehow or other he had persuaded me not only to travel to England with his distressed friends but to deliver them safely to their daughter in Gloucestershire. I was aware that if they'd been going to somewhere like Northumberland my response might have been different, but there had been a tug of curiosity about returning to the county of my childhood. Two weeks remained of my leave and I hadn't planned to do anything in them definitely except find myself somewhere in London to live. So to Gloucestershire—why not?

I rented a car at Heathrow when we arrived in the morning and drove the pathetically grateful Wayfields westward in the general direction of Cheltenham and the racecourse, Vicky having said that her daughter lived close to the track itself.

As Vicky hadn't been there before and my own memory was hazy I stopped a couple of times to consult the map provided with the car, but we arrived in the general area at about noon without getting lost and drew up at a garage to ask for final directions.

"The vets' place? Turn right, go past the fire station . . ."

The road ran through an uneasy mix of centuries, the mellow and old elbowed into the shade by aggressive shopfronts and modernized pubs. Not a village, more a suburb: no cohesive character.

"The vets' place" was a substantial brick building set back from the road, allowing enough parking space in front for not only several cars but a horsebox. A large horsebox, in fact, was parked there. Did vets no longer make house calls?

I stopped the rented car on a spare piece of tarmac and helped Vicky unwind to her feet. She was suffering already from jet lag, from a metabolism telling her she'd been awakened at two in the morning, never mind that it had said seven on the local clocks. There were dark smudges under her eyes and a sag in her facial muscles and an overall impression of exhaustion.

A white plastic shield on a headband neatly covered her repaired ear, but a lot of fluffy bounce had gone out of the white hair around it. She looked a tired old woman, and even the attempt at lipstick in the car as we neared our destination in no way disguised the true state of affairs.

The weather hardly helped. Straight from the warmth of Florida to a gray cold windy late February day in England was a shiversome enough transition for anyone: on top of their injuries, it was debilitating.

Vicky wore a dark green trouser suit with a white blouse, inadequate for the English out-of-doors, and had had no energy for brightening things with jewelry or gold chains. Simply getting onto the airplane had been enough.

Greg did his best to be her mainstay but, despite his protestations, it was clear that being knocked unconscious and helpless had shaken him to the foundations. He had left the humping of all the suitcases entirely to me and apologized six times for feeling weak.

I didn't in any way think that either of them should have snapped back like elastic. The muggers had been strong, purposeful enemies, and the single punch I'd taken had been like a jab from a pole. Moreover the police had depressed us all by their opinion that the muggers would not be discovered or caught: the savage hostility we'd felt from them wasn't unusual, it appeared. Vicky was more or less advised not to wear screwed-on earrings in future.

"To make it easier for them to rob me?" she asked with tired sarcasm.

"Better wear fakes, ma'am."

She'd shaken her head. "No fun, when you have the real thing."

Outside the vets' place, Greg extricated himself from the car and all three of us went over to the brick building and in through a glassed entrance door to a lobby. This brown carpeted space was furnished with two chairs and a counter for leaning on while one talked with the young woman in an office on the far side of it.

She was sitting at a desk and speaking on a telephone.

We waited.

Eventually she made some notes, disconnected, turned an inquiring face in our direction and said, "Yes?"

"Belinda Larch . . ." Vicky said tentatively.

"Not in, I'm afraid." The reply was crisp: not impolite exactly, but not helpful either. Vicky looked as if it wouldn't take much to bring her to tears.

I said to the young woman, "Perhaps you could tell us where we could find her. This is her mother, just arrived from America. Belinda is expecting her."

"Oh yes." She wasn't moved to any show of excessive welcome. "Supposed to have arrived yesterday, I thought."

"I telephoned," Vicky said miserably.

"Sit down," I said to her. "You and Greg sit on these two chairs and wait, and I'll find Belinda."

They sat. I'd been taking care of them for so long now that if I'd said, "Lie down on the floor," they might have done it.

"Right," I said to the girl. "Where do I find her?"

She began to answer with the same sort of underlying obstructiveness, and then saw something in my expression which changed her mind. Very prudent, I thought.

"Well, she's in the hospital section assisting the vets. You can't go in there. They're operating on a horse. I'm sorry, but you'll have to wait."

"Can you phone her?"

She started to say no, looked at the Wayfields, looked at me, and with raised eyebrows picked up the receiver.

The conversation was short but produced results. The girl put down the phone and drew a labeled bunch of keys out of a drawer.

"Belinda says she can't get out for an hour at least, but these are the keys of the cottage where her mother will be staying. She says to go there and she'll come as soon as she can."

"And where's the cottage?"

"The address is on that label on the key ring. I don't know where it is."

Thanks for very little, I thought. I escorted Greg and Vicky back to the car and sought directions from passersby. Most proved equally uninformed but I finally got a reliable pointer from a telephone repairman up a pole and drove away from the bustle, up a hill, round a bend and down the first turning on the left.

"It's the first house along there on the right," I'd been told from aloft. "You can't miss it."

I did in fact nearly miss it because it wasn't my idea of a cottage. No thatched roof and roses round the door. No quaint little windows or bulging whitewashed walls. Thetford Cottage was a full-blown house no older than Vicky or Greg.

I braked the car doubtfully, but there was no mistake: the words "Thetford Cottage" were cut into square stone pillars, one each side of imposing gates. I stopped, got out, opened the gates and drove through and stopped again on the graveled expanse inside.

It was a weathered gray three-story edifice built of stone from the local Cotswold hills, roofed in gray slate and painted brown round the windows. The one surprise in its otherwise austere façade was a roofed balcony over the front entrance, with a stone balustrade and a glimpse of long windows behind.

Vicky got out of the car uncertainly, holding on to my arm, blown by the wind.

"Is this the place?" she said doubtfully.

She looked around at the bare flower beds, the

leafless trees and bedraggled grass, her shoulders sagging ever more forlornly.

"Surely this isn't the place . . .?"

"If the key fits, it is," I said, trying to sound encouraging; and indeed the key did fit, and turned easily in the lock.

The house was cold inside with a deep chill speaking of no recent heating. We stood in a wood-floored hall looking around at a lot of closed doors and a polished wood staircase leading to undiscovered joys above.

"Well," I said, shivering myself. "Let's see what we've got."

I opened one of the doors purposefully, expecting vistas at least, and found it was a washroom.

"Thank God for that," Greg said with relief, eyeing the comforts within. "Excuse me, Peter." He brushed past me, went in and closed the door behind him.

"That's one of us satisfied," I said, moved nearly to a giggle. "Now let's find a fire."

A pair of double doors led into a large drawing room, another door into a dining room, a third into a small sitting room with armchairs, television and, the gods be thanked, a fire that lit with switches, not paper, wood and coal.

Turned on, it warmed up nicely and put on a show of flickering flames. Vicky subsided speechlessly into an armchair near it and sat huddled and shaking, looking ill.

"Back in a moment," I said, and made tracks up the staircase, looking for blankets or anything warm. All the doors upstairs were again closed. The first I opened revealed a bathroom. I must be a water diviner, I thought. The second held twin beds, unmade, the bedclothes neatly stacked on each.

Better than blankets: duvets. Royal blue, scattered with white daisies. I gathered the pair of them into my arms and negotiated the bare polished wooden stairs downwards, thinking that they were a skating rink for the unwary.

Vicky hadn't moved. Greg stood over her, looking helpless.

"Right," I said, handing them the duvets. "You tuck these round you and I'll see what's in the kitchen in the way of hot drinks."

"Johnnie Walker?" Greg suggested.

"I'll look."

I'd left all the hall doors open, though two were as yet unexplored. One led to a capacious broom, gardenware and flower-vase storeroom, the other to a cold antiseptic kitchen of white fitments round a black and white tiled floor. On a central table stood the first signs of recent human life: an unopened box of tea bags, some artificial sweeteners and a tartan-printed packet of shortbread.

The refrigerator was empty except for a carton of milk. The cupboards on inspection held, besides the normal clutter a large quantity of homemade marmalade, serried ranks of condensed soups and several stacks of tinned fish, mostly tuna.

I went back to Vicky and Greg, who now sat dumbly in royal blue scattered with white daisies.

"Tea bags or instant coffee?" I asked.

"Tea," Vicky said.

"Johnnie Walker?" Greg repeated hopefully.

I smiled at him, warming to him, and went on the quest. No alcohol, however, in the dining room cupboards, none in the kitchen, none in the drawing room. I made tea for both of them and carried it, along with the shortbread and the bad news, to the little sitting room.

"You mean, no drink *anywhere?*" Greg exclaimed, dismayed. "Not even beer?"

"I can't find any."

"They've locked it up," Vicky said unexpectedly. "Bet they have."

They, the owners, whoever they were, might have done so, I supposed, but they'd left their storeroom cupboards stocked and unprotected, and I hadn't come across any unopenable spaces.

Vicky drank her tea holding the cup with both hands, as if to warm them. The room itself by then was perceptibly warmer than the rest of the house and I began to think of roaming round switching on every heater I could find.

Action was frustrated by the arrival of a car outside, the slam of a door and the rapid entrance into the house of a young woman in a hurry. Belinda, one supposed.

We heard her voice calling "Mother?" followed by her appearance in the doorway. She was slim in stone-washed jeans topped by a padded olive green jacket. Pretty in a fine-boned scrubbed sort of way. Maybe thirty, I thought. Her light brown hair was drawn up into a ponytail that seemed more utilitarian than decorative and she looked worried, but not, it soon appeared, on her mother's account.

"Mother? Oh good, you got here."

"Yes, dear," Vicky said wearily.

"Hello, Greg," Belinda said briefly, going over to him and giving him a dutiful peck. Her mother got the same treatment in turn: a kiss on the cheek but no deeply loving welcoming hug.

"Well, Mother, I'm sorry, but I can't stay," she said. "I'd arranged to have yesterday free, but you being a day late . . ." She shrugged. "I have to go back. The horse died. They have to do a postmortem." She stared hard at her mother. "What's the matter with your ear?"

"I told you on the phone . . ."

"Oh yes, so you did. I'm so worried about the horse. . . . Is the ear all right now? By the way, we're getting married in church instead of the registrar's office, and we're having the reception here in this house. I'll tell you about it later. I have to go back to the hospital now. Make yourselves comfortable, won't you? Get some food in, or something. I brought some milk, etcetera, yesterday." Her gaze sharpened from vague to center upon myself. "Sorry, didn't catch your name?"

"Peter Darwin," I obliged.

"Peter," Vicky said forcefully, "has been our lifeline."

"Oh? Well, good. Nice of you to have helped them." Her gaze slid away, encompassing the room in general. "The Sandersons, who own the house, have gone to Australia for a couple of months. They're renting it to you quite cheaply, Mother, and I've engaged the caterers. . . . You always said you wanted me to have a proper wedding and I decided it would be a good idea after all."

"Yes, dear," Vicky said, accepting it meekly.

"Three weeks tomorrow," Belinda told her. "And now, Mother, I really have to run."

I abruptly recalled a conversation I'd had long ago in Madrid, with my father.

"A child who calls its mother 'Mother,' wants to dominate her," he said. "You will never call your mother 'Mother.' "

"No, Dad."

"You can call her Mum, Darling, Mater, Popsie or even silly old cow, as I heard you saying under your breath last week, but *never* Mother. Understood?"

"Yes, Dad."

"And why did you call her a silly old cow?"

Lying to him was fairly impossible: he always saw through it. Swallowing, I told him the truth. "She wouldn't let me go to Pamplona to run with the bulls because I'm only fifteen."

"Quite right. Your mother's always right. She's made a good job of you and one day you'll thank her. And never call her Mother."

"No, Dad."

"Mother," Belinda said, "Ken says we'll have dinner together soon. He meant it to be tonight, but with all this worry . . . I'll phone you later."

She gave a brief wave, turned and departed as speedily as she'd come.

After a short silence Vicky said valiantly, "She was a really sweet baby, very cuddly and loving. But girls grow up so independent . . ." She paused and sighed. "We get on quite well really as long as we don't see each other too much."

Greg gave me a sideways look and made no comment, though I saw that he felt much as I did about the offhand welcome. Belinda, I thought, was as self-centered as they come.

"Right," I said cheerfully, "we may as well get your cases in, and if you like I'll go to the shops."

A certain amount of bustle at least partially filled the emotional vacuum, and after a while Vicky felt recovered just enough to investigate upstairs. The large bed in what was clearly the Sandersons' own domain at least looked ready for occupation, though their clothes still filled the closets. Vicky said apathetically that she would unpack later the cases I'd carried up for her but meanwhile she was going to sleep at once, in her clothes, on the bed.

I left Greg fussing over her and went downstairs, and presently he followed, agitated and displeased.

"Belinda's a pain in the ass," he said. "Vicky's

crying. She doesn't like being in someone else's house. And I feel so helpless."

"Sit down by the fire," I said. "I'll go foraging."

When I came to think of it, I hadn't been shopping regularly for food in England since I'd been at Oxford, and not much then. I was more accustomed to eating what I was given: the sort of life I led was rarely domestic.

I drove back to the straggly suburb and bought all the essentials I could think of, and felt like a stranger in my own country. The inside layouts of shops were subtly different from my last brief visit four years earlier. The goods available were differently packaged. Colors were all brighter. Even the coins had changed shape.

I found I'd lost, if I'd ever really known, any clear idea of what things in England should cost. Everything seemed expensive, even by Tokyo standards. My ignorance puzzled the shop assistants as I was obviously English, and it was altogether an unexpectedly disorienting experience. What on earth would it be like, I wondered, for someone to return after half a century, return to the world of my parents' childhood, a time that millions still clearly remembered?

Every child had chilblains in the winter back then, my mother said; but I hadn't known what a chilblain was.

I collected some scotch for Greg and a newspaper and other comforts and headed back to Thetford Cottage, finding things there as I'd left them.

Greg, dozing, woke up when I went in and came shivering out into the hall. The whisky brightened his eye considerably and he followed me into the kitchen to watch me stow the provisions.

"You should be all right now," I said, closing the fridge.

He was alarmed. "But surely you're staying?"

"Well . . . no."

"Oh, but . . ." His voice deepened with distress. "I know you've done a lot for us, but please . . . just one more night?"

"Greg . . ."

"Please. For Vicky's sake. *Please.*"

For his sake too, I saw. I sighed internally. I liked them well enough and I supposed I could stay one night there and start my rediscovery of Gloucestershire in the morning, so again, against my gut reaction, I said yes.

Vicky woke at six-thirty in the evening and came tottering down the stairs complaining of their slipperiness.

Greg and I had by that time lowered the scotch level, read the newspapers from cover to cover and found out how the television worked. We'd listened to the news, which was all of death, as usual. Amazing how many ways there were of dying.

Belinda had not telephoned.

At seven, however, a car arrived outside and the daughter herself came in as before, managerial rather than loving. This time, however, she had brought her affianced.

"Mother, you met Ken two or three years ago, you remember."

"Yes, dear," Vicky said kindly, though she'd told me she couldn't bring him to mind. She offered him her cheek for a kiss, and after the fleetest of pauses received one.

"And this is Greg," Belinda said. "I suppose he's my stepfather." She laughed briefly. "Odd having a stepfather after all these years."

"How do you do?" Ken said politely, shaking Greg's hand. "Glad to meet you, sir."

Greg gave him an American smile that was all front with reservations hidden, and said he was sure pleased to be in England for the happy occasion.

Ken, at the moment, looked a long way from happy. Anxiety vibrated in his every gesture, not a simple nervousness at meeting his future in-laws but a much deeper, overriding bunch of worries, too intense to be covered.

He was tall, thin, sandy and wiry-looking, like a long-distance runner. A touch of Norwegian, perhaps, about the shape of the head and the light blue of his eyes. Fair hair on the point of thinning. I guessed his age at nearing forty and his dedication to his job as absolute.

"Sorry," Belinda said to me, not sounding contrite. "Can't remember your name."

"Peter Darwin."

"Oh yes." She glanced towards Ken. "Mother's helper."

"How do you do?" He shook my hand per-functorily. "Ken McClure," he said.

It sounded very familiar. "Kenny?" I said doubtfully.

"No. Ken. Kenny was my father."

"Oh."

None of them paid any attention but I felt as if I'd been kicked in the subconscious by sleeping memory. Kenny McClure. I knew about Kenny McClure—but what did I know?—from a long time ago.

He'd killed himself.

The knowledge came back abruptly, accom-panied by the curiosity I'd felt about it as a child, never having known before that people could kill themselves, and wondering how he had done it and what it felt like.

Kenny McClure had acted as veterinary sur-geon at Cheltenham races. I knew I'd driven round the track with him in his Land-Rover a few times, but I couldn't now recall what he'd looked like.

Ken had made an attempt at dressing for the occasion in a suit, shirt and tie but with one black shoe and one brown. Belinda had come in a calf-length blue woolen dress under the padded olive jacket and, having made the effort herself, was critical of Vicky, who hadn't.

"Mother, honestly, you look as if you'd slept in those clothes."

"Yes, dear, I did."

Belinda impatiently swept her upstairs to find

something less crumpled and Greg offered Ken some scotch.

Ken eyed the bottle with regret. "Better not," he said. "Driving, and all that."

A short silence. Between the two of them there was no instant rapport. Eye contact, minimal.

"Belinda told us," Greg said, finally, "that you've had some trouble with a horse today."

"It died." Ken had clamped a lid tight over his seething troubles and the strain came out in staccato speech. "Couldn't save it."

"I'm real sorry."

Ken nodded. His pale eyes turned my way. "Not at my best this evening. Forgotten your name."

"Peter Darwin."

"Oh yes. Any relation to Charles?"

"No."

He considered me. "I suppose you've been asked before."

"Once or twice."

He lost interest, but I thought that in other circumstances he and I might have done better together than he with Greg.

Ken tried, all the same. "Belinda says you were both mugged, sir, you and . . . er . . . Mother."

Greg made a face at the memory and gave him a brief account. Ken raised a show of indignation. "Rotten for you," he said.

He spoke with a Gloucestershire accent, not strong, but recognizable. If I tried I'd still be able to speak that way easily myself, though I'd lost it to my new father's Eton English soon after I had met him. He'd told me at once that I had a good ear for languages, and he'd made me learn French, Spanish and Russian intensively all through my teens. "You'll never learn a language as naturally as now," he said. "I'll send you to school in England for two final years to do the university entrance, but to be truly multilingual you must learn languages where they're spoken."

I'd consequently breathed French in Cairo, Russian in Moscow, Spanish in Madrid. He hadn't envisaged Japanese. That had been a quirk of Foreign Office posting.

Vicky and Belinda having reappeared, Vicky in red this time, Ken led the way in his car to a small country inn with a restaurant attached. He took Belinda with him and I again drove the rental car with Vicky and Greg sitting together in the back, an arrangement that led Belinda to conclude that "helper" meant chauffeur. She gave me sharply disapproving looks when I followed the group into the bar and accepted Ken's offer of a drink before dinner.

We sat round a small dark table in a corner of a room heavily raftered and furnished in oak. The level of light from the red-shaded wall lamps was scarcely bright enough for reading the menus and there was an overall warmth of atmosphere that one met nowhere else on earth but in a British pub.

Belinda stared at me from over her glass.

"Mother says you're a secretary. I can't understand why she needs one."

"No, dear," Vicky began, but Belinda made a shushing movement with her hand.

"Secretary, chauffeur, general helper, what does it matter?" she said. "Now that you're here, Mother, I can look after you perfectly well myself. I'm sorry to be frank, but I don't see how you justify the expense of someone else."

Greg and Vicky's mouths dropped open and both of them looked deeply embarrassed.

"Peter . . ." Vicky's words failed her.

"It's OK," I reassured her, and to Belinda I said peacefully, "I'm a civil servant. A private secretary in the Foreign Office. Your mother isn't paying me. I'm literally here just to help them over the few sticky days since they were attacked. I was coming to England in any case, so we traveled together. Perhaps I should have explained sooner. I'm so sorry."

An apology where there was no fault usually defused, things, I'd found. The Japanese did it all the time. Belinda gave a shrug and twisted her mouth. "Sorry, then," she said in my general direction but not actually looking at me. "But how was I to know?"

"I did tell you . . ." Vicky began.

"Never mind," I said. "What's good on this menu?"

Belinda knew the answer to that and began to instruct her mother and Greg. Ken's thoughts had been on a distant travel throughout, but he made a visible effort then to retrieve the evening from gloom, and to some extent succeeded.

"What wine do you like with dinner . . . um . . . Mother?" he asked.

"Don't call me mother—call me Vicky."

He called her Vicky easily, without the "um." She said she preferred red wine. Any. He could choose.

Vicky and Ken were going to be all right, I thought, and was glad for Vicky's sake. Belinda softened enough over dinner to put a glow on the thin beauty that had to be attracting Ken, and Greg offered a toast to their marriage.

"Are you married?" Ken asked me, clinking glasses with Vicky.

"Not yet."

"Contemplating it?"

"In general."

He nodded, and I thought of the young Englishwoman I'd left behind in Japan who had settled for a bigger fish in the diplomatic pond. The English girls on the staff of the embassies abroad were often the high-grade products of fashionable boarding schools, intelligent and good-looking as a general rule. Liaisons between them and the unmarried diplomats made life interesting all round but often ended discreetly, without tears. I'd said fond farewells in three different countries, and not regretted it.

By the time coffee arrived, the relationships among Greg, Vicky, Belinda and Ken had taken the shape they were likely to retain. Vicky, like a rose given water, had revived to the point of flirting very mildly with Ken. Ken and Greg remained outwardly cordial but inwardly stiff. Belinda bossed her mother, was reserved with Greg and took Ken for granted. A pretty normal setup, all in all.

Ken still retreated every five minutes or so for brief seconds into his consuming troubles but made no attempt to share them. He talked instead about a horse he'd bought two years earlier for peanuts to save it from being put down.

"Nice horse," he said. "It cracked a cannon bone. The owner wanted it put down. I told him I could save the horse if he'd pay for the operation but he didn't want the expense. Then, of course, the horse would have to rest a year before racing. All too much, the owner said. Put it down. So I offered him a bit more than he would have got from the dog-food people and he took it. I did the operation and rested the horse and put it in training and it won a nice race the other day, and now Ronnie Upjohn, that's the owner, won't speak to me except to say he'll sue me."

"What a pig," Vicky said indignantly.

Ken nodded. "Luckily I got him to sign a paper at the time, saying he understood an operation might save the horse but that he preferred to have it put down, so he hasn't a chance of winning. He won't sue in the end. But I guess I've lost a client."

Ronnie Upjohn, I thought.

I knew that name too. Couldn't attach any immediate information to it, except that it was linked in my vague memory with another name: Travers.

Upjohn and Travers.

Who or what was Upjohn and Travers?

"We're planning on running the horse here at Cheltenham in a couple of weeks," Ken said. "I'm giving it to Belinda and it'll run in her name, and if it wins it'll be a nice wedding present for both of us."

"What sort of race?" I asked, making conversation.

"A two-mile hurdle. Are you a racing man?"

"I go sometimes," I said. "It's years since I went to Cheltenham."

"Peter's parents met on Cheltenham racecourse," Vicky said, and after Belinda and Ken's exclamations of interest I gave them all a version of the facts that was not the whole truth but enough for the casual chat of a dinner party among people one didn't expect to get close to.

"My mother was helping out with some secretarial work," I said. "My father blew into her office with a question, and bingo, love at first sight."

"It wasn't at first sight with us," Belinda said, briefly touching Ken's hand. "Fiftieth or sixtieth sight, more like."

Ken nodded. "I had her under my feet for months and never really saw her."

"You were getting over that frightful Eaglewood girl," Belinda teased him.

"Izzy Eaglewood isn't frightful," Ken protested.

"Oh, you know what I mean," his fiancée said; and of course, we did.

Izzy Eaglewood, I thought. A familiar name, but out of sync. Something different. Eaglewood was right, but not Izzy. Why not Izzy? What else?

Russet!

I almost laughed aloud but from long training kept an unmoved face. *Russet* Eaglewood had been the name to giggle over in extremely juvenile smutty jokes. What color are Russet Eaglewood's panties? No color, she doesn't wear any. Russet Eaglewood doesn't need a mattress; she *is* one. What does Russet Eaglewood do on Sundays? Same thing, twice. We had been ignorant of course, about what she actually did. We called it "IT," and "IT" in fact applied to anybody. Are they doing IT? Giggle, giggle. One day—one unimaginable day—we would find out about IT ourselves. Meanwhile IT went on apace throughout the racing world, and indeed everywhere else, we understood.

Russet Eaglewood's father had been one of the leading trainers of steeplechasers: it had been that fact, really, that had made the scurrilous stories funniest.

The knowledge came crowding back. The Eaglewoods had had their stables at the end of our village, half a mile from our little house. Their horses clattered through the village at dawn on their way up to the gallops, and I'd played in

58

the stable yard often with Jimmy Eaglewood until he got hit by a lorry and died after three hushed weeks in a coma. I could remember the drama well, but not Jimmy's face. I couldn't clearly remember any of the faces; could dredge up only the sketchiest of impressions.

"Izzy Eaglewood ran off with a guitarist," Belinda said disapprovingly.

"Nothing wrong with guitarists," Vicky said. "Your father was a musician."

"Exactly. Everything wrong with guitarists."

Vicky looked as if defending the long-divorced husband from Belinda's jokes was an unwelcome habit.

I said to Ken, "Have you heard Vicky and Greg sing? They've lovely voices."

He said no, he hadn't. He looked surprised at the thought.

"Mother," Belinda said repressively, "I do wish you wouldn't."

"Wouldn't sing?" Vicky asked. "But you know we enjoy it."

"You're too old for it." More than a gibe, it was a plea.

Vicky studied her daughter and said with sad enlightenment, "You're embarrassed, is that it? You don't like it that your mother brought you up by singing in nightclubs?"

"Mother!" Belinda cast a horrified glance at Ken, but Ken, far from being shocked, reacted with positive pleasure.

"Did you really?"

"Yes, until time put a stop to it."

"I'd love to hear you," Ken said.

Vicky beamed at him.

"Mother, please don't go around telling everyone," Belinda said.

"Not if you don't like it, dear."

Shout it from the rooftops, I wanted to say: Belinda should be proud of you. Stop indulging your daughter's every selfish snobbish whim. Vicky's sort of love, though, forgave all.

Ken called for the bill and settled it with a credit card but, before we could rise to go, a buzzer sounded insistently somewhere in his clothes.

"Damn," he said, feeling under his jacket and unclipping a small portable telephone from his belt. "I'm on call. Sorry about this."

He flipped open the phone, said his name and listened; and it was obviously no routine summons to a sick animal because the blood left his face and he stood up clumsily and fast and literally swayed on his feet, tall and toppling.

He looked wildly, unseeingly, at all of us sitting round the table.

"The hospital's on fire," he said.

3

The vets' place was on fire, but actually not, as it turned out, the new hospital itself, which lay separately to the rear. All one could see from the road, though, was the entrance and office block totally in flames, scarlet tongues shooting far skywards from the roof with showers of golden sparks. It was a single-story building, square, extensive, dying spectacularly, at once a disaster and majestic.

Ken had raced off frantically from the restaurant alone, driving like the furies, leaving the rest of us to follow and thrusting Belinda into suffering fiercely from feelings of rejection.

"He might have waited for me."

She said it four times aggrievedly but no one commented. I broke the speed limit into the town.

We couldn't get the car anywhere near the vets' place. Fire appliances, police cars and sightseers crowded the edges of the parking area and wholly blocked the roadway. The noise was horrendous. Spotlights, streetlights, headlights threw deep black shadows behind the milling helpers and the flames lent orange halos to the firemen's helmets and shone on spreading sheets of water and on the transfixed faces outside the cordoned perimeter.

"Oh, God, the horses . . ." Belinda, leaving us at a run as soon as our car came willy-nilly to a halt, pushed and snaked a path through to the front where I briefly spotted her arguing unsuccessfully with a way-barring uniform. Ken was out of sight.

Great spouts of water rose in plumes from hoses and fell in shining fountains onto the blazing roof, seeming to turn to steam on contact and blow away to the black sky. The heat, even from a distance, warmed the night.

"Poor things," Vicky said, having to shout to be heard.

I nodded. Ken had enough worry beside this.

There were the thuds of two explosions somewhere inside the walls, each causing huge spurts of flame to fly outwards through the melted front windows. Acrid smoke swirled after them, stinging the eyes.

"Back, back," voices yelled.

Two more thuds. Through the windows with a searing roar like flame throwers, sharp brilliant tongues licked across the parking space toward the spectators, sending them fleeing in panic.

Another thud. Another fierce jet-burst of flames. A regrouping among the firemen, heads together in discussion.

The whole roof fell in like a clap of thunder, seeming to squeeze more flames like toothpaste from the windows, and then, dramatically, the roaring inferno turned to black gritty billowing smoke and the pyrotechnics petered out into a wet and dirty mess, smelling sour.

Ash drifted in the wind, settling in gray flakes on our hair. One could hear the hiss of water dousing hot embers. Lungs coughed from smoke. The crowd slowly began to leave, allowing the three of us to get closer to the ruined building to look for Belinda and Ken.

"Do you think it's safe?" Vicky asked doubtfully, stopping well short. "Weren't those bombs going off?"

"More like tins of paint," I said.

Greg looked surprised. "Does paint explode?"

Where had he lived, I wondered, that he didn't know that, at his age?

"So does flour explode," I said.

Vicky gave me a strange look in which I only just got the benefit of the doubt as to my sanity, but indeed air filled with flour would flash into explosion if ignited. Many substances diffused in a mist in air would combust. Old buddies, oxygen, fuel and fire.

"Why don't you go back to the car," I suggested to Vicky and Greg. "I'll find the other two. I'll tell them I'm driving you back to the house."

They both looked relieved and went away slowly with the dispersing throng. I ducked a few officials, saw no immediate sign of Belinda and Ken but found on the right of the burnt building an extension of the parking area that led back into a widening space at the rear. Down there, movement, lights and more people.

Seeing Ken briefly and distantly as he hurried in and out of a patch of light, I set off to go down there despite warning shouts from behind. The heat radiating from the brick wall on my left proved to be of roasting capacity, which accounted for the shouts, and I did hope as I sped past that the whole edifice wouldn't collapse outwards and cook me where I fell.

Ken saw me as I hurried towards him and stood still briefly with his mouth open, looking back where I'd come.

"Good God," he said, "did you come along there? It isn't safe. There's a back way in." He gestured behind him and I saw that indeed there was access from another road, as evidenced by a fire engine standing there that had been dealing with the flames from the rear.

"Can I do anything?" I said.

"The horses are all right," Ken said. "But I need . . . I need." He stopped suddenly and began shaking, as if the enormity of the disaster had abruptly overwhelmed him once the need for urgent action had diminished. His mouth twisted and his whole face quivered.

"God help me," he said.

It sounded like a genuinely desperate prayer, applying to much more than the loss of a building. I was no great substitute for the deity, but one way or another I'd helped deal with a lot of calamities. Crashed busloads of British tourists for instance, ended up, figuratively speaking, on embassy doorsteps, and I'd mopped up a lot of personal tragedies.

"I'll take Vicky and Greg back to the house, and then come back," I said.

"Will you?" He looked pathetically grateful even for the goodwill. He went on shaking, disintegration not far ahead.

"Just hold on," I said, and, without wasting time, left by the rear gate, hurrying along the narrow road there and getting back to the main road via an alley, finding that by luck I'd come out only a few steps from the car. Vicky and Greg made no objections to being taken home and left. They hoped Belinda would forgive them, but they were going to bed to sleep for a week, and please would I ask her not to wake them.

I glanced at them affectionately as they stood drooping in the polished hall of Thetford Cottage. They'd had a rough time, and when I thought of it, looking back, they hadn't seriously complained once. I said I'd see them in the morning and took the front door key with me at their request, leaving them to shut the door behind me.

Finding a way round to the back road, I returned to the vets place from the rear and smelled freshly again the pervading ashy smoke that stung in the throat like tonsillitis. The rear fire engine had wound in its hoses and departed, leaving one man in yellow oilskins and helmet trudging around to guard against the ruins heating up to renewed spontaneous life.

I took brief stock of what lay in the unburnt area: a new-looking one-story building with electric lights shining from every window, a row of stable boxes set back under an overhanging roof all empty, with their doors open, and a glass-walled thirty-yard passage connecting the burnt and unburnt buildings. That last was, extraordinarily, mostly untouched, only the big panes nearest the heat having shattered.

A good many people were still hurrying about, as if walking slowly would have been inappropriate. The first urgency, however, was over: what was left was the usual travail of getting rid of the debris. No bodies to go into bags this time, though, it seemed. Look on the bloody bright side.

As Ken was nowhere to be seen and a door to the new building stood open, I went inside to look for him and found myself in an entrance hall furnished as a waiting room with about six flip-up chairs and minimum creature comfort.

Everything, including the tiled floor and a coffee machine in a corner, was soaking wet. A man trying to get sustenance from that machine gave it a smart kick of frustration as if its demise after all else was insupportable.

"Where's Ken?" I asked him.

He pointed through an open door and attacked the machine again, and I went where directed, which proved to be into a wide passage with doors down each side, one of them open with light spilling out. I found Ken in a smallish office along there, a functional room already occupied by more people than the architect had intended.

Ken was standing by the uncurtained window, still trembling as if with cold. A gray-haired man sat gloomily behind a metal desk. A woman with a dirt-smudged face stood beside him, stroking his shoulder. Two more men and another woman perched on office furniture or leaned against walls. The room smelled of the smoke trapped in their clothes and it was chilly enough to make Ken's shivers reasonably physical in origin.

The heads all turned my way when I appeared in the doorway, all except Ken's own. I said his name, and he turned and saw me, taking a second or two to focus.

"Come in," he said, and to the others added, "He's a helper."

They nodded, not querying it. They all looked exhausted and had been silent when I got there as if sandwiched in shock between hectic crisis activity and facing the resumption of life. I'd seen a lot of people in that suspended state, starting from when I was twenty-three, in my first posting, and in a far-flung consulate with the consul away I had had to deal alone with a British-chartered airplane that had clipped a woody hillside after dark and had scattered broken bodies among splintered trees. Among other things I'd been out there at dawn trying to stop looters. Relatives then came to the city to identify what they could and to cling to me numbly for comfort. Talk about growing up fast. Nothing, since that, had been worse.

The man who had been kicking the coffee machine came into the office, passed me, and slid down to sit on the floor with his spine against the wall.

"Who are you?" he asked, looking up.

"Friend of Ken's."

"Peter," Ken said.

The man shrugged, not caring. "Coffee machine's buggered," he announced.

His eyes were red-rimmed, his hands and face dirty, his age anywhere from thirty to fifty. His news was received with apathy.

The gray-haired man behind the desk seemed to be the senior in rank as well as years. He looked round at the others and wearily said, "Suggestions?"

"We go to bed," the coffee machine man said.

"Buy a better computer," one of the other men offered. "When the records are saved on backup disks, in future store them in a vault."

"A bit late for that," said one of the women, "since all the records are burnt."

"The new records, then."

"If we have a practice," Ken said with violence.

That thought had occurred to the others, who went on looking gloomy.

"How did the fire start?" I asked.

The gray-haired man answered with deep tiredness. "We were having the place painted. We ourselves have a no smoking rule, but workmen with cigarettes . . ." He left the sentence unfinished, the scenario too common for comment.

"Not arson, then," I said.

"Are you a journalist?" one of the women demanded.

"No, definitely not."

Ken shook his head. "He's a diplomat. He fixes things."

None of them looked impressed. The women said that a diplomat was the last thing they needed, but the gray-haired man said that if I had any practical suggestions, to give.

I said with hesitation, "I would leave someone here all night with all the lights on."

"Well . . . why?"

"Just in case it was arson."

"It couldn't have been arson," the gray man said. "Why would anyone want to burn our building?"

One of the other men said, "They wouldn't get far trying to burn this hospital. We had it all built of flame-retardant materials. It's supposed to be fireproof."

"And it didn't burn," the woman said. "The fire doors held in the passage. The firemen poured tons of water on all that end . . ."

"And buggered the coffee machine," the man on the floor said.

There were a few wan smiles.

"So we still have our hospital," the gray-haired man told me, "but we've lost the pharmacy, the lab, the small-animal surgeries and, as you heard, every record we possessed. The tax situation alone . . ." He stopped, shaking his head hopelessly. "I think the going to bed suggestion was a good one, and I propose we adopt it. Also if anyone will stay here all night, please volunteer."

They'd all had too much, and no one spoke.

After an appreciable pause Ken said jerkily, "I'll stay if Peter will."

I'd let myself right in for it, I thought. Oh well. "OK," I said.

"Who's on call?" the gray-haired man asked.

"I am," Ken said.

"And I am," a dark-haired young woman added.

The gray hair nodded. "Right. Ken stays. Everyone else, sleep." He rose to his feet, pushing himself up tiredly with hands flat on the desk. "Council of war here at nine in the morning." He came round the desk and paused in front of me. "Whoever you are, thanks." He briefly shook my hand. "Carey Hewett," he said, introducing himself.

"Peter Darwin."

"Oh. Any relation to . . ."

I shook my head.

"No. Of course not. It's late. Home, everyone." He led the way out of the office and the rest drifted after him, yawning and nodding to me briefly but not giving their names. None of them expressed any curiosity, let alone reservations, about the stranger they were so easily leaving on

70

their property. They trusted Ken, I supposed, and by extension, any friend of Ken's.

"Where's Belinda?" I asked, as the last of them disappeared.

"Belinda?" Ken looked temporarily lost. "Belinda . . . went with the horses." He paused, then explained. "We had three horses out in the boxes. Patients. Needing nursing care. We've sent them to a trainer who had room in his yard. Belinda went to look after them." Another pause. "They were upset, you see. They could smell the smoke. And we didn't know . . . I mean, the hospital might have burnt too, and the boxes."

"Yes."

He was still faintly trembling.

I said, "It's pretty cold in here."

"What? I suppose it is. The firemen said not to turn the central heating on until we'd had it checked. It's gas-fired."

"Gas-fired in the office building too?"

"Yes, but it was all switched off. It always is at night. The firemen asked." He stared at me. "They made a point of shutting off the mains." The shakes came back strongly. "It's all a nightmare. It's . . . it's . . ."

"Yes," I said, "sit down." I pointed to the gray-haired man's padded chair behind the desk, the only remotely comfortable perch in sight.

Ken groped his way onto it and sat as if his legs had given way. He had the sort of long loose-jointed limbs that seem always on the point of disconnecting from the hipbone, the thighbone, the anklebone—the skeleton coming apart. The longish Norwegian head accentuated it, and the thin big-knuckled fingers were an anatomy lesson in themselves.

"Apart from the fire," I said, "what's the problem?"

He put his elbows on the desk and his head in his hands and didn't answer for at least a minute. When he finally spoke his voice was low and painfully controlled.

"I operate on horses about five times a week. Normally you'll lose less than one out of every two hundred on the table. For me, that means maybe one or at most two deaths a year. You can't help it, horses are difficult under anesthetic. Anyway," he swallowed, "I've had four die that way in the last two months."

It seemed more like bad luck to me than utter tragedy, but I said, "Is that excessive?"

"You don't understand!" The pressure rose briefly in his voice and he stifled it with an effort. "The word goes round like wildfire in the *profession*. People begin to snigger. Then any minute the public hears it and no one's sending horses to you anymore. They ask for a different vet. It takes years to build a reputation. You can lose it like *that.*" He snapped the long fingers. "I *know* I'm a good surgeon. Carey knows it, they all know it, or I'd be out already. But they've got themselves to consider. We're all in it together."

I swept a hand round the empty office. "The people who were here . . . ?"

Ken nodded. "Six vets in partnership, including me, and also Scott, the anesthetist. And before you ask, no, I can't blame *him*. He's a good technician and a trained veterinary nurse, like Belinda."

"What happened this morning?" I asked.

"Same thing," Ken said miserably. "I was putting some screws in a split cannon bone. Routine. But the horse's heart slowed and his blood pressure dropped like a stone and we couldn't get it back."

"We?"

"Usually it would have been just Scott, Belinda and me, but today we had Oliver Quincy assisting as well. And that was because the owner insisted, because he'd heard the rumors. And still the horse died, and I can't . . . I don't . . . it's my whole *life.* "

After an interval I said, "I suppose you've checked all the equipment and the drugs you use."

"Of *course* we have. Over and over. This morning we double-checked *everything* before we used it. Triple-checked. I checked, Scott checked, Oliver checked. We each did it separately."

"Who checked last?"

"I did." He said it automatically, then understood the significance of what I was asking. He said again, more slowly, "I checked last. I see that maybe I shouldn't have. But I wanted to be sure."

The remark and action, I thought, of an innocent man.

I said, "Mightn't it have been more prudent, in the circumstances, to let one of the other vets see to the cannon bone?"

"What?" He looked at me blankly, then understood my ignorance, and explained. "We're partners in a big general practice but we all have our own specialities. Carey and the two women are small-animal vets, though Lucy Amhurst does sheep and ponies as well. Jay Jardine does cattle. I do horses. Oliver Quincy is a general large-animal man working with both Jay and me, though he does mostly medical work and only minor surgery, almost never here in the hospital. Castrations, things like that. They're done on-site."

He had almost stopped shaking, as if the unburdening and explanations themselves had released the worst of the pressure.

"We're all interchangeable to some extent," he said. "I mean, we can all stitch up a gash whether it is a ferret or a carthorse. We know all the usual animal diseases and remedies. But after all that, we specialize." He paused. "There aren't all that number of surgeons like me in the whole country, actually. I get sent cases from other vets. This hospital has earned a reputation we can't afford to lose."

I reflected a bit and asked, "Have there been any over-the-top calamities in the dog and cat departments?"

Ken shook his head in depression. "Only horses."

"Racehorses?"

"Mostly. But a couple of weeks ago there was an Olympic-standard show-jumper—and that didn't die during an operation. I had to put it down." He looked into tormented space. "I'd done a big repair job on its near hind a week earlier where it had staked itself breaking a jump, and it was healing fine back at home, and then they asked me out to it as the whole leg had swelled like a balloon, and the tendon was shot to hell. The poor thing couldn't put its foot to the ground. I gave it painkillers and brought it here and opened the leg up, but it was hopeless . . . the tendon had disintegrated. There wasn't anything to repair."

"Does that happen often?" I asked.

"No, it damn well doesn't. The owner was furious, his daughter was in tears, there was a hullabaloo all over the place. They'd insured the horse, thank God, otherwise we would have had another lawsuit on our hands. We've had to insure ourselves against malpractice suits just like American doctors. You get some very belligerent people these days in the horse world. They demand perfection a hundred percent of the time, and it's impossible."

I had a vague feeling that he'd glossed over some fact or other, but decided it was probably to do with a technicality he knew I wouldn't understand. I wasn't in a position, anyway, to demand that he tell me his every thought.

The night grew colder. Ken seemed to have

retreated into introspection. I felt a great desire to make up for some of the sleep I'd missed. No one would come to set fire to the hospital. It had been a stupid idea of mine to suggest it.

I shook myself mentally awake and went out into the passage. All quiet, all brightly lit. I walked back to the entrance hall and checked that the departing vets had locked the front door when they left.

All secure.

Although wet, the entrance hall was distinctly warmer than the passage and the office. I put my hand on the wall nearest the burned building and felt the heat in it, which was of a comforting level rather than dangerous. The solid door to the glass-walled connecting passage was fastened with bolts and bore an engraved strip of plastic with the instruction "Keep This Fire Door Shut." The door's surface was warmer than the wall, but nowhere near to frying eggs.

A third door led from the entrance hall into a spartan roomy washroom and a fourth opened onto cleaning materials. No arsonists crouching anywhere.

Passing the defunct coffee machine, I went back to the office and asked Ken to show me round the rest of the hospital. Lethargically he rose and told me that the office we were in was used by whoever was operating in the theater for writing notes of the procedures used, together with drugs prescribed. The notes, he added with a despairing shake of the head, were then taken to the secretarial section and stored in files.

"Not in the computer?" I asked, flicking a finger at a monitor which stood on a table near the desk.

"In the main computer in the office, yes, but our secretary enters only the date, the name of the animal, owner, type of surgery and a file number. It takes too long to type in all the notes and, besides, mistakes creep in. If anyone wants to refer back, they just call up the file number and go and find their actual notes." He gestured helplessly. "Now all the files are bound to have gone. So has the computer itself, I suppose. This terminal is dead, anyway. So there will be no records anymore to prove that all the operations when the horses died were normal regular procedures."

I reflected that on the other hand if in fact there had been any departure from regular procedures, all records of that too had conveniently vanished. Yet I did believe in Ken's distress, otherwise what was I doing wandering round an animal hospital in the middle of the night looking for people playing with matches?

"What's absolutely *irritating,*" Ken said, "is that the architect we engaged for the hospital told us the office wasn't up to his standards of fireproofing. He said we should install heavy fire doors everywhere and frankly we didn't want to, they slow you up so much. We knew we'd simply prop them open. But there you are, he was right. He insisted on at least fireproof doors at each end of the connecting passage, and the firemen say those doors—and the length of the passage—saved the hospital."

"Why is the passage so long?"

"Something to do with what's under the ground. It wasn't suitable for foundations any nearer. So we had to have the passage or else run from building to building in the rain."

"Lucky."

"So it turned out."

"How old is the hospital?"

"Three or four years," Ken said. "Three and a half, about."

"And you all use it?" He nodded. "Not for minor things, of course. Often it's because of some sort of emergency. Dog run over, that sort of thing. There's a small-animal wing. Otherwise there are—were—the two small-animal surgeries over in the main building for vaccinations and so on." He paused. "God, it's all so depressing."

He led the way out of the office and into the central passage. The floors throughout were of black, gray-streaked vinyl tiles, the walls an unrelenting white. The hospital hadn't been designed, of course, to soothe human patient anxieties: severe practicality reigned along with the fire-retardant ethos.

Nothing was made of wood. Doors were metal everywhere, set into metal frames, painted brown. A row of three on the left-hand side were storerooms, Ken said. All the doors were locked. Ken opened them and we checked inside: all quiet.

On the right, past the office, lay another, much bigger, double room, one half housing X-ray developing equipment, the other, a movable X-ray machine on wheels. There was also a simple bed in there, with folded blankets, looking unused, and a closed door giving access from the car park for patients.

"We have to keep all these doors locked, including the office," Ken said grimly. "We've found things walking out of here when we're all busy in the theater. You wouldn't believe what some people will steal."

Looting was a built-in instinct, I thought.

Immediately beyond the X-ray room there was what should have been a heavy fire door blocking our way. It was present, but had been opened flat against the wall and held there by a substantial wedge. Ken saw me eyeing it and shrugged.

"That's the problem. We can't open these doors with our arms full of equipment. The firemen closed that door earlier, when they first came, but someone's opened it since. Force of habit."

Past the habit, there was an extra-wide door straight ahead. The passage itself turned right.

"That door," Ken said, pointing ahead, "is the entry to the theater area from this side. The passage goes round to an outside door."

He unlocked the theater door, pressed rows of switches to light our path, and led the way into a vestibule with doors on either side and another across the end.

"Changing rooms right and left," Ken said, opening the doors and pointing. "Then we go ahead into the central supply of gowns and gloves and so on. We'd better put gowns and shoe-covers on, if you don't mind, in the interests of cleanliness in the operating room."

He handed me a pair of plastic disposable shoe-covers and a sort of cotton overall, dressing in similar himself, and then supplied us also with hats like shower caps and masks. I began to feel like a hospital movie, only the eyes emoting. "Instruments and drugs are in here too," he went on, showing me locked glass-fronted cupboards. "This cupboard here opens both ways, from this side and from inside the operating room. The drug cupboard has two locks and unbreakable glass."

"A fortress," I commented.

"Carey took advice from our insurers as well as the police and the fire inspectors. They all had a go."

Ken pointed to a door in the left-hand wall. "That leads towards the small-animal operating room or theater." A door to the right, he showed me, opened to a scrub room. "You can go through the scrub room into the operating room," he said, "but we'll go straight in from here."

He pushed open double swing doors ahead—not locked, for once—and walked into the scene of his disasters.

It was unmistakably an operating theater,

though the wide central table must have been almost nine feet long with an upward-pointing leg at each corner, like a four-poster bed. There were unidentifiable (to me) trolleys, carts and wheeled tables round the walls, all of metal. I had an impression of more space than I'd expected.

Without ado, Ken skirted the table and went to the far wall where, after another clinking of keys, a whole section slid away to reveal another room beyond. I followed Ken into this space and found that the floor was spongy underfoot. I remarked on it, surprised.

Ken, nodding, said, "The walls are padded too," and punched his fist against one of the gray plastic-coated panels which lined the whole room. "This stuff is like the mats they put down for gymnasts," he said. "It absorbs shocks. We anesthetize the horses in here, and the padding stops them hurting themselves when they go down."

"Cozy," I said dryly.

Ken nodded briefly and pointed upwards. "See those rails in the ceiling, and those chains hanging down? We fasten the horse's legs into padded cuffs, attach the cuffs to the chains, winch up the horse and he travels along the rails into the theater." He pointed back through the sliding door. "The rails guide the horse right over the table. Then we lower him into the position we want. The table is mobile too, and can be moved."

One lived and learned, I thought. One learned the most extraordinary things.

"You have to support . . . er, to *carry* . . . the head, of course," Ken said.

"Of course."

He rolled the wall-door into place again and relocked it, then went across the spongy floor to another door, again padded, but opening this time into a short corridor which we crossed to enter what Ken called the preparation room. There was a clutter of treatment carts round the walls there, and more cupboards.

"Emergency equipment" he explained briefly. "This is reception, where the horses arrive." He stepped out of the shoe-covers and gestured to me to do the same, throwing them casually into a discard bin. "From here we go back into the corridor and down there into the outside world."

A gust of wind blew specks of ash in through the widening opening of the outside door and Ken gestured me to hurry through after him, relocking as usual behind us.

Each of Ken's keys had a colored tag with a stick-on label, identifying its purpose in the general scheme of things. Ken clanked like an old-time jailer.

Outside, we were still under a wide roof which covered a good-sized area in front of a row of four new-looking boxes stretching away to the left. All the box doors stood open, as I'd seen before, the patients having left.

82

"That's about it," Ken said, looking around. "We unload the sick animals just here and usually take them straight into reception. There's often not much time to lose."

"Nearly always horses?" I asked.

He nodded. "Occasionally cattle. Depends on the value of the beast, whether the expense is justified. But yes, mostly horses. This is hunting country, so we get horses staked and also we get barbed wire injuries. If we can't sew them up satisfactorily in their home stable we bring them here. Abdominal wounds, that sort of thing. Again, it depends on love, really."

Reflecting, I asked, "How many horses are there in your area?"

"Can't tell exactly. Between us we're the regular vets of, say, half a dozen or more racing stables, five riding schools, a bunch of pony clubs, countless hunting people, showing people, eventers, and people who just keep a couple of hacks about the place . . . oh, and a retirement home for old steeplechasers. There are a whole lot of horses in Gloucestershire."

"A whole lot of love," I commented.

Ken actually smiled. "It keeps us going, no doubt of it." The smile faded. "Up to now."

"Law of averages," I said. "You'll go months now without another death."

"No."

I listened to the hopelessness and also the fear, and wondered if either of those emotions sprung from facts he hadn't told me.

"There won't be anyone out here in the boxes," he said.

"We may as well look."

He shrugged and we walked along the row and found it indeed deserted, including the small feed and tack rooms at the end. Everywhere was noticeably swept and clean, even allowing for the fire.

"That's it, then," Ken said, turning back.

He closed and bolted the empty boxes as we passed them and, at the end, made not for the door into the treatment areas but to another set back to the left of it, which led, I discovered, into the offshoot of the black-tiled passage. From there, through uncurtained windows, one could look out to where the fire engine had been. A long line of pegs on the wall opposite the windows held an anorak or two, a couple of cloth caps and a horse's head collar. Pairs of green wellies stood on the floor beneath, with a row of indoor shoes on a shelf above.

Ken wiped his own shoes carefully on a mat and waited while I did the same, then opened yet another door, at which point we were only a few steps and a couple of turns away from where we'd started. Ken took the gowns back to the changing room and returned to comment on the silence everywhere in a building usually full of bustle.

I agreed that we could relax on the score of ill-intentioned intruders for the moment and rather regretted having offered an all-night service. Cold was a problem I hadn't given much thought to, and although it was by then nearing three o'clock, it would presumably get colder still before dawn.

"How about us borrowing those anoraks?" I suggested, "and wrapping ourselves in blankets."

"Yes, we could," he began to say, but was forestalled by the same muffled noise as in the restaurant, the chirp of his telephone on his belt.

He looked at me blankly for a second, but pulled out the phone and flipped it open.

"Hewett and Partners," he said. "Yes . . . Ken speaking."

I wouldn't have thought he could grow much paler, but he did. The shakes returned as badly as ever.

"Yes," he said. "Well . . . I'll come straightaway."

He clipped the phone back onto his belt with fumbling fingers and tried with three or four deep breaths to get himself back into control, but the pale blue eyes were halfway to panic.

"It's the Vernonside Stud," he said. "They've a broodmare with colic. The stud groom's been walking her round but she's getting worse. I'll have to go."

"Send someone else," I suggested.

"How can I? If I send someone else I've as good as resigned."

He gave me the wild unseeing stare of a courage-racking dilemma and, as if he indeed had no choice, unhesitatingly went down the passage and

85

into the drugs room where he rapidly gathered an armful of bottles, syringes and other equipment to take out to his car. His fingers trembled. He dropped nothing.

"I'll be gone an hour at least," he said, "that's if I'm lucky." He gave me a brief glance. "Do you mind staying here? It's a bit of an imposition . . . I hardly know you, really."

"I'll stay," I said.

"Phone the police if anything happens."

He set off fast along the passage in the direction of the coats-on-pegs and over his shoulder told me that I'd get no incoming calls to worry about because they'd be rerouted in the exchange to his own portable phone. Always their system for whoever was on duty at night.

"You can make calls out," he said, taking down an anorak, shaking off his shoes and sliding into wellies. "You'd better have my keys." He threw me the heavy bunch. "See you."

He sped out of the far door, letting its latch lock with a click behind him, and within seconds I heard his car start up and drive away.

When I couldn't hear him any longer I tried on the remaining olive green anorak, but it would have fitted a small woman like Belinda and I couldn't get it on. I settled for a blanket from the X-ray room and, wrapped to the chin, sat on the padded chair in the office, put my feet up on the desk and read an article in a veterinary journal about oocyte transfers from infertile mares into other mares for gestation, and the possible repercussions in the thoroughbred stud book.

This was not, one might say, riveting entertainment.

A couple of times I made the rounds again, but I no longer expected or feared to find a new little bonfire. I did go on wondering whether the office building had been torched or not, but realized that it was only because of Ken's general troubles that arson had seemed possible.

I read another article, this time about enzyme-linked immunosorbent assay, a fast antibody test for drugs in racehorses. It was the only reading matter of any sort in sight. I had a readaholic friend who would read bus timetables if all else failed. Hewett and Partners didn't use buses.

I eyed the telephone. Who could I call for a chat at three in the morning? It would be nine o'clock at night in Mexico City. A good time for the parents. Better not.

I dozed over an account of 3-D computer scanning of bone-stress factors in hocks and awoke with a start to hear someone rapping on the window with something hard, like a coin.

A face accompanied the hand, coming close to the glass, and a voice shouted, "Let me in."

He pointed vigorously in the direction of the rear door and as I went along the passage I remembered that he was the one who'd been kicking the coffee machine and so could be presumed to be on the side of the angels.

He came in stamping his feet and complaining of the cold. He held two large Thermos flasks and explained that in the rush he'd forgotten his keys.

"But not to worry, Ken said you were here."

"Ken?" I asked.

He nodded. "He's on his way back here with the mare." He thrust the Thermos flasks into my grasp and kicked off his boots, reaching up for a pair of indoor shoes on the shelf above the pegs. Slipping his feet into those, he took off his padded jacket. Then he said, "God, it's freezing in here," and put it on again. "Ken's phoning Belinda, and I'm to get the theater ready."

He was moving as he talked. "I hate these middle-of-the night emergencies." He reached the central passage. "I hate buggered coffee machines." He marched into the office, took one of the Thermoses back, unscrewed its inside top and used it as a cup. The coffee steamed out and smelled like comfort while he drank.

"Want some?" he asked, wiping his mouth on the back of his hand.

"Please."

He filled the container again and handed it to me carefully. Hot sweet instant; strong and milky. Better than champagne at that moment.

"Great," I said, screwing the emptied cap back on the Thermos.

"Right. I take it you know nothing about anesthetizing horses?"

"Nothing."

"Can't be helped. Are these Ken's keys? Good."

He picked up the bunch and exited rapidly. He was tall, wide-shouldered, dark-haired, roughly forty, and he moved jerkily as if there was far more explosive power available in his muscles than he needed.

I followed him into the passage and found him unlocking one of the storerooms.

"OK," he said. "Maintenance fluids." He went in and reappeared with several large plastic bags full of clear liquid. "Do you mind carrying these?" He didn't wait for an answer but pushed them into my care and dived back for more of the same, setting off down the passage at a great rate. Cursing under his breath, he unlocked the wide door leading to the vestibule and the theater.

"I hate all these doors," he said, stacking the bags of fluid inside the two-way cupboard that led into the operating room. He then hooked the door back against the wall. "Do you mind putting on a gown and shoe-covers?"

We donned the whole paraphernalia, and when we were clad he went backwards through the double swing doors into the theater itself and held one open for me to follow.

"Good." He bustled about. "Ventilator." He rolled one of the metal carts from against the wall to the head of the operating table. "Horses can't breathe very well on their own when they're under anesthetic," he said. "Most animals can't. Or birds, for that matter. You have to pump air into them. Do you want to know all this?"

"Carry on."

He flicked me a brief glance and saw I was genuinely interested.

"We pump the anesthetic in with oxygen," he said. "Halothane usually. We use the minimum we can, just a light anesthesia because it's so difficult for them."

He expertly linked together the tubes of the ventilator and plugged an electric lead into a socket in the floor.

"We went through all this ad infinitum yesterday morning," he said. "Checked every valve, checked the pump, checked the oxygen, which comes in from outside cylinders when we turn on this tap." He showed me. "Sometimes the heart starts failing and there's not a damn thing one can do about it. We've had our fair share of those recently." He stopped his narrative abruptly, as if remembering I didn't wholly belong there. "Anyway, I'm checking everything twice."

He darted in and out readying other things that he didn't explain and I stood around feeling that I ought to be helping, but out of ignorance couldn't.

There was the sound of a car door slamming outside. Scott—it had to be Scott, the anesthetist—lifted his head at the sound and rolled enough wall to one side to allow us access to the padded room. He crossed the spongy floor with his power-packed stride and unlocked the door to the corridor. With myself still at his heels (snapping off the shoe-covers) we went down there and emerged into the brisk air and found Ken in anorak and wellies letting down the rear ramp of a small horse-trailer that had been towed there by a Land-Rover.

"Scott, good," Ken said, letting the ramp fall with a clang. "I had to drive the damn thing myself. They've two mares foaling at this moment at Vernonside and no staff to spare. They're stressed beyond sense. This mare is dying on her feet and she's carrying a foal worth God knows what by Rainbow Quest."

He sped into the trailer to fetch his patient, who came lumbering backwards down the ramp looking sicker than I'd known was possible with animals. Heavy with foal, she was bloatedly fat. Her head hung low, her brown skin glistened with sweat, her eyes were dull and she was making groaning noises.

"She's full of painkillers," Ken said. He saw me standing there and in black distress said, "Her heart's laboring. She's swollen with gas and there's feedback up from her stomach. That means her gut's obstructed. It means she'll die probably within an hour if I don't operate on her, and quite likely if I do."

"You'd be safer with a second opinion," I said.

"Yes. I phoned Carey on my way back here, asking him to get someone, or come himself. He said to trust my own ability. And he said I'm the best horse surgeon in this area. I do know it, even if I don't usually say it."

"So you'll go ahead," I said.

"Got no choice, have I? Just look at her."

He handed the mare's leading rein to Scott, who said, "Belinda's not here yet."

"She's not coming," Ken said. "I couldn't find her. I phoned the trainer who's got our horses in his yard and he said he didn't know where she was sleeping and he wasn't going around at this hour looking for her."

"But . . ." Scott said, and fell silent.

"Yes. But." Ken looked directly at me. "What I want *you* to do is watch and make notes. A witness. Just write down what I tell you and what Scott tells you. Do you faint at the sight of blood?"

I thought of the broken bodies on the hillside.

"No," I said.

4

In the padded room, while Scott held her by the head collar, Ken, with sensitive fingers, found the mare's jugular vein and pushed into it what looked like a long hypodermic needle covered with plastic and an end connector that remained outside on the skin.

"Catheter," he said, removing the needle and leaving the plastic sleeve in the vein.

I nodded.

"Intravenous drip," he enlarged, fastening to the catheter a tube from one of the bags of fluid that Scott was busily suspending from the ceiling. "You have to keep the body fluids up."

He went briefly to the operating room, returning with a small syringeful of liquid which he injected into the mare's neck via the catheter.

"Half a cc of Domosedan," he said, spelling it for me as I wrote on a pad on a clipboard. "It's a sedative to make her manageably dozy. Mind you, don't get within reach of her feet. Horses kick like lightning, even in this state. Go behind that half-wall, out of reach."

I stood obediently behind a freestanding section of padded wall that allowed one to see the action while being shielded from trouble: rather like the shelter provided in bullrings for humans to escape the horns.

"What do you do with the syringe now?" I asked.

"Throw it away. It's disposable."

"Keep it," I said.

Ken gave me a pale blue stare, considered things, and nodded.

"Right."

He took the syringe into the operating room and put it in a dish on one of the tables round the walls. He wore what I did: his own shoes covered with disposable covers, green cotton trousers, short-sleeved green shirt, a lab coat over them, surgical mask dangling round his neck, a soft white cap like a shower cap over his hair.

Scott, in similar clothes, rubbed a hand down the mare's nose, fondling her ears and making soothing noises. Slowly some of the jangle loosened in her beleaguered brain, peace perceptibly creeping in until she was quiet and semiconscious on her feet.

Ken, watching her closely, had come back carrying a larger syringe in another dish. "Antibiotic," he said, injecting. He went away to pick up a third.

"This is ketamine hydrochloride," he said, returning and spelling it again for me. "Sends her to sleep."

I nodded. Scott shut the sliding door to the operating room: Ken temporarily disconnected the drip and with smooth skill injected the mare again through the catheter in her neck. Almost immediately the great body swung round in an uncoordinated arc, staggered, wavered and collapsed slowly sideways, one hind leg lashing out in a muscle spasm that spent itself harmlessly against the padding, the head flopping with a thump onto the spongy floor.

Dramatic, I thought; but routine, obviously, to Scott and Ken.

"Intubation," Ken said to Scott.

Scott nodded and passed an impressively large tube into the mare's mouth and down her throat.

"For oxygen and halothane," Ken told me briefly.

Scott opened the sliding door wide, went into the operating room with the syringe in the dish and returned with the padded cuffs for the mare's legs, and also bags to cover her feet.

Both men buckled these on, then pulled down the chains from the ceiling and linked them to the cuffs. Scott fetched a sort of canvas sling with handles for carrying the mare's head, and Ken without waste of time pressed buttons on a panel in the theater wall to activate the winch.

The chains wound back and hoisted the half-ton horse effortlessly into the air. Scott supported her head in the sling while Ken reconnected the drip. Then Ken pressed another button and a high rolling trolley moved slowly along the ceiling rails, taking the dangling body, intravenous fluid and all, into the theater.

The rails themselves positioned the patient directly over the table. Ken pressed buttons. The chains lengthened, letting down their burden inch by inch until the mare was lying on her back with all four legs in the air, her distended belly a brown rounded hump. Scott laid her head down gently and then helped Ken hitch the legcuffs to the four posts at the corners of the table so that her legs were comfortably bent, not stiff and straight. The two men worked without speaking, moving smoothly through a maneuver often repeated.

"Ventilator on," Ken said. "Gas on."

Scott fixed the tube in the horse's mouth to a tube from the ventilator, then pressed a switch and turned a tap, and the oxygen-halothane mixture began pumping with slow insistent rhythm into the mare's lungs.

Ken asked me briefly, "Do you understand all that?"

"Yes," I said.

"Good. Now I'm going to slide another catheter into her facial artery where it curves round the mandible. It will directly monitor her blood pressure. Normally Belinda would do this but today I'll do it myself."

I nodded and watched his deft fingers push a small tube into the mare's jaw and connect it to a metering machine rolled into place by Scott. Both he and Scott watched with clear anxiety the two lines which appeared on a monitoring screen, but it seemed that they were reassured, at least for the present.

"Final scrub," Ken said at length. He looked at me. "You'd better come and watch."

I followed him into the scrub room where he lengthily scrubbed his hands clean and dried them on a sterile towel. Then at his request I helped him put on a fresh sterile gown, tying the tapes for him. Finally he pushed his hands into sterile latex gloves.

"If this mare dies," Ken said, "I'm finished."

"Stop thinking about it."

He stood for a moment with all the strain showing in his eyes, then he blinked them a few times very positively and took a visibly deep breath.

"Come on, then." He turned away and went towards the theater, asking me to open the swing door for him so as not to contaminate himself.

He went first to where Scott stood, which was in front of the blood pressure screen, watching it.

"She's stabilized," Scott said, his relief evident, "and I've shaved her skin." There was indeed now a shaved strip all along the mountainous belly.

Ken said to me, "I need Scott to assist me. Will you stand by this screen? Watch it all the time. A horse's blood pressure is about the same as humans, ideally 120 over 80; but like humans, it drops under anesthesia. If it drops below 70 millimeters of mercury, we're in trouble and an alarm will go off. We should be safe between 80 and 90, where we are now. Watch that line there. And that counter, that's the heart rate. If there's

any change in either of them, tell me immediately."

"Right."

"Write down the time, the heart rate and the
blood pressure."

I nodded, and wrote.

He went round to the other side of the table
where Scott brought forward instruments on rolling carts and created what Ken called a sterile
area in the room. He and Scott between them
took disposable green cloths out of sterile pack-
aging and laid them all over the horse's abdomen,
leaving visible only a narrow shaved section on
top.

"All set?" Ken asked Scott, and Scott nodded.

It was the last moment that Ken could have
drawn back, but the commitment in his mind
had been made long before.

"Incision," he said, dictating to me while he
picked up a scalpel and with precision suited the
deed to the word. "Ten inches, beside the um-
bilicus."

I wrote fast what he'd said and switched my
gaze back to what he was doing. Scott, meanwhile, went off to scrub.

"Watch the blood pressure," Ken said fiercely,
not even raising his eyes. "Don't watch me, watch
the monitor between writing."

I watched the monitor, which remained steady.
I still couldn't help taking fascinated second-long
glances at a process I'd expected to be horrifying,
but wasn't in the least. For one thing, there was

little smell, when I'd somehow been prepared for stench, nor, with retractors, clamps, forceps and swabs, even a great deal of bleeding.

"Cutting along the linea alba," Ken said, continuing his running commentary. "That's the central fibrous ridge between muscle groups. If you cut through there into the abdominal cavity you get little bleeding." He looked at Scott, who had returned, and without being asked Scott held out a long rubber sleeve-glove which he pulled on over Ken's right hand and arm up to the armpit. "Watertight," Ken explained to me briefly, "and of course sterile, for going into the abdomen."

What I hadn't begun to envisage were the extraordinary contents of an equine tum. From out of the quite small incision popped a large ridged bit of intestine and in its wake Ken slowly began to pull a loop of vast tube ten or more inches in diameter, seemingly endless, pink, bulbous and glistening. My eyes, I suppose, were equally huge with astonishment.

"Watch the screen," Ken said. "This is the colon, now distended by gas. The equine colon's not held in place by connecting tissue like in humans, it just zigzags free. Half of all cases of twisted gut are colon trouble." He pulled out at least another yard of the enormous tube and gave it to Scott to support in a green cloth while he felt around in the cavity it had come from.

"The mare's less than a month from foaling," he said. "It's a good-sized foal." He was silent for a moment or two, then said unemotionally, "If she collapses and I can't save her, I'll deliver the foal here and now by cesarean section. It might have a chance. It's got a good strong heart-beat."

Scott glanced at him quickly and away, knowing, I thought, a good deal more than I did about the risks of such a procedure.

From time to time, as the drip bag emptied, Scott replaced it with a full one from the two-way cupboard, asking me to fetch it for him and to throw the empty one away.

"Screen?" Ken asked me after each change.

"Same," I said.

He nodded, intent, slowly feeling his way round the internal organs, his eyes in his fingertips.

"Ah," he said finally. "Here we are. God, what a twist." He brought some part I couldn't see up into his own vision but still just inside the mare and made an instantaneous decision to cut out the tangled obstruction altogether.

"Eyes on the screen *all the time*," he instructed me sharply.

I obeyed him, seeing his actions only in peripheral vision.

Supplied with instruments by Scott, he worked steadily, attaching clamps, clipping, removing tissue, swabbing, stitching, making occasional noises in his throat but otherwise not talking. Time passed. Eventually he took two clamps off and watched the results unwaveringly.

"Monitor?"

"Steady."

He murmured to himself and finally looked up. "All right. The obstruction's excised and the gut repaired. No leaks." He seemed to be fighting down hope he couldn't help. "Ready to close up."

I glanced at the great length of huge intestine looped over Scott's arm and couldn't see how on earth they were going to stuff it all back into the body cavity.

As if reading my mind Ken said, "We'll empty the colon." Scott nodded. Ken asked me to fetch an open trash can which stood against one wall and to position it near him beside the table. Next he wanted me to slot a tray into the table, rather like tray-tables in airplanes. A colon tray, he said.

He nodded his thanks. "You're a nonsterile area," he said almost cheerfully. "Go back to the screen, will you?"

He straightened the colon until part of it was on the tray and over the trash can, then swiftly made a slit, and he and Scott began systematically to squeeze out all of the contents.

This time it did smell, but only like a stable yard, quite fresh and normal. For some reason I found myself wanting to laugh: the process was so incredibly prosaic and the can so incredibly full.

"Monitor," Ken said severely.

"Steady."

Scott washed the now empty, flabby and lighter

tubing with fluid, and Ken, in a fresh gown and gloves, stitched up the slit he'd made in it; then, carefully folding it into zigzags, he returned the large gut to its rightful position inside. He did a quick, half-audible checklist on the abdomen, almost like a pilot coming in to land and, still with deftness and care, fastened the incision together in three layers, first the linea alba with strong separately knotted stitches, then the subcutaneous tissue with a long single thread, finally closing the skin with a row of small steel staples, three to an inch. Even the stapler came separately packed, sterile and throwaway, made mostly of white plastic, handy and light.

After the briefest of pauses, when he'd finished, Ken pulled his mask down and gave me a look of shaky triumph.

"She's made it so far," he said. "Scott, gas off."

Scott, who had put a lid on his odorous trash can and rolled it away, had also been round to the ventilator to turn off the halothane.

"Blood pressure?" Ken asked.

"No change," I said.

"Ventilator off," Scott said. "Disconnect the catheter?"

Ken nodded. "She's got a strong heart. Write down the time," he said to me, and I looked at my watch and added the time to my notes.

"Ninety-one minutes from incision to finish," I said.

Ken smiled with the professional satisfaction of star work well done, the doubts and shakes in abeyance. He lightheartedly peeled off the green sterile cloths from the mare's round body and threw them into a trash can.

He and Scott unclipped the mare's legs from the bedposts. Then the hoist, with Scott supporting her head, lifted her up off the table. In reverse order she rolled along the rails and through the sliding door into the padded room, where Ken brought over an extra panel of padding and placed it on the floor. The hoist lowered the mare onto that until she lay on her side comfortably, her legs relaxing into their normal position.

Scott removed the padded cuffs from her legs and put a rope halter on her head, leading the rope through a ring on top of the half-wall so that someone standing behind the wall could partly control her movements and stop her staggering about too much.

"She'll take twenty minutes or so to wake up slowly," Ken said. "Maybe in half an hour she'll be on her feet, but she'll be woozy for a good while. We'll leave her here for an hour after she's standing, then put her in the stable."

"And is that it?" I asked, vaguely surprised.

"Well, no. We'll leave in the stomach tube to make sure nothing's coming back up the wrong way, like it was before—reflux, it's called—and because we can't give her anything to eat or drink for at least twelve hours, we'll continue with the intravenous drip. Also we'll continue with antibiotics and a painkiller-sedative and we'll monitor her heart rate, and tonight if everything's OK we'll take out the stomach tube and try her with a handful of hay."

Hay, after all that, seemed like bathos.

"How long will you keep her here?" I asked.

"Probably a week. It knocks them over a bit, you know, a major op like that."

He spoke with earnest dedication, a doctor who cared. I followed him back into the operating room and through to the vestibule, where he stripped off all the disposable garments and threw them into yet another bin. Scott and I did the same, Ken walking back immediately to take a continuing look at his patient.

"He won't leave her," Scott said. "He always wants to see them wake up. How about that coffee?"

He strode off towards the office to return with the Thermoses and all three of us drank the contents, watching the mare until movement began to come back, first into her head and neck, then into her forelegs, until with a sudden heave she was sitting sideways, her forelegs bearing the weight of her neck and head, the hind legs still lying on the padding.

"Good," Ken said. "Great. Let's get behind the wall now." He suited the action to the word and took hold of the steadying rope.

The mare rested in the same position for another ten minutes, and then, as if impelled by instinct, staggered onto all four feet and tottered a step or two, weaved a bit at the end of the rope and looked as if she might fall, but stayed upright.

I supposed she might have been feeling sore, disoriented and in her own way puzzled, but she was clearly free of the terrible pain of the colic.

Ken said, "Thanks," to me and rubbed his eyes. "You gave me confidence, don't know why."

He handed Scott the rope and left him watching the mare, jerking his head for me to follow him back into the operating room.

"I want to look at something," he said. "Do you mind if I show you?"

"Of course not."

He went over to the table where the dishes still lay with the spent syringes in them: not three dishes now, but four. The fourth contained a large unidentifiable bit of convoluted bloody tissue with flapping ends of wide tube protruding, the whole thing pretty disgusting to my eyes.

"That's what I took out of the mare," Ken said.

"That? It's huge."

"Mm."

I stared at it. "What is it?"

"A twisted bit of intestine, but there's something odd about it. Wait while I get some gloves, and I'll find out."

He went and returned with clean gloves, and then with strong movements of fingers and a spatula he slightly loosened the fearsome knot in which one loop of intestine had tightened round another like a noose, throttling the passage of food altogether. Incredibly, there seemed to be a thread wound in among the tissue: pale strong thread like nylon.

Frowning, Ken spread some of the cut edges apart to look at the contents, astonishment stiffening in his face.

"Just look at this," he said disbelievingly, and I peered through his hands into the gap he was holding open and saw, with an astonishment beyond his own, a three-inch-diameter semicircular needle, the strong sort used for stitching carpet.

He spread open another few inches and we could both see that the needle was threaded with the nylon. The needle, passing round and round in the intestine, had effectively stitched it into the knot.

"We have this happen from time to time with cats and dogs," Ken said. "They swallow sewing needles that have fallen to the floor and literally stitch themselves together. I've never known it in a horse. No needles carelessly dropped in their vicinity, I suppose." He looked at it, fascinated. "I don't think I'll take it out, it's more interesting in situ." He paused, thinking deeply. "It's a real curiosity and I'll organize photos of it for our records and maybe veterinary magazines, but to do that I need to keep this in good condition, and bugger it, the fridge was in the other building, in the path lab there. The lab was by the rear door. We didn't go to the expense of another lab in the hospital. I mean, there was no point."

I nodded. I said, "What if you take it home?"

"I'm not going home. After I've set up the mare's drip I'll catch quick naps on the bed in the X-ray room. I do that sometimes. And I'll watch the monitor until Belinda arrives."

"What monitor?" I asked.

"I hope to God it still works," he said. "It's connected to a monitor in the main building as well." He saw I was going to ask the question again, and answered it. "There's a closed-circuit television camera in the intensive-care box, the nearest stall this end, with a monitor in the office here and another at the main reception desk. Well, there used to be. It's so we can check on the patient all the time without forever going out there."

I looked at the cause of the mare's troubles.

"I could put that in the fridge at Thetford Cottage," I said briefly, "if we labeled it conspicuously not to be touched."

"Christ." His pale face crinkled with amusement. "All right, why not."

He carefully wrapped the piece of gut, and in the office tied on a luggage label with a cogent message to deter curiosity in future parents-in-law.

The television circuit, when he pressed switches without much hope, proved in fact to be working, though there was nothing at present on the screen but night and a section of barred window in the empty stall.

"If only tomorrow was that simple," he said.

I slept at Thetford Cottage for four hours as if drugged and was awakened by a gentle persistent tapping on the bedroom door. Rousing reluctantly, I squinted at my watch and managed a hoarse croak, "Yes?"

Vicky opened the door with apology and said Ken had phoned to ask if I would go down to the hospital.

"Not another emergency, for God's sake." I sat up, pushed my fingers through my hair and looked back with awe at the night gone by.

"It's some sort of meeting," she said. "I didn't want to wake you but he said you wouldn't mind."

She had taken off the ear-shield and had washed her hair, which was again white and fluffy, and she looked altogether more like Vicky Larch, singer.

"Are you feeling better?" I asked, though it was obvious.

"Much," she said, "though still not right, and Greg's the same. It's going to take us days. And I don't like this house, which is ungrateful of me."

"It's unfriendly," I agreed. "A personality clash."

"And boring. Did you put that 'don't touch on any account' parcel in the fridge?"

"Yes," I said, remembering. "It's some horse innards." I explained about the burnt lab and Ken's need for them to be stored.

"Ugh," she said.

She went away and I tottered into some clothes, jet-lagged myself if the truth were told. The face in the bathroom mirror, even when newly shaven, had tired, brownish-green eyes below the usual dark hair and eyebrows. Teeth freshly brushed felt big behind stiff facial muscles. I pulled a face at my familiar real self and practiced a diplomatic expression to take to the meeting.

Diplomatic expression? Air of benign interest with give-away-nothing eyes. Habit-forming, after a while.

Vicky in the kitchen had made me coffee and hot toast. I drank the coffee, kissed her cheek and took the toast with me for the drive to the hospital, crunching gratefully all the way.

Chaotic activity filled the rear car park. A towing truck was trying to maneuver a Portakabin into a space already occupied by cars whose drivers were reversing all over the place to get out of the way. There were animals weaving in and out, mostly on leads, and people with anxious expressions or open mouths, or both.

I backed out of the mêlée and left the rented car in the road outside, walking in and being accosted by an agitated lady carrying a large cloth-covered birdcage who told me her parrot was sick.

Fighting down a laugh, I said I was sorry about that.

"Aren't you one of the vets?" she demanded.

" 'Fraid not."

"Where am I supposed to take my parrot?" I managed the diplomatic expression but it was a close-run thing.

"Let's try that door over there," I suggested,

pointing to the visitors' entrance in the hospital. "I expect you'll find an answer there."

"This fire's very inconvenient," she said severely, "and I do think they might have phoned to save me the journey."

"The appointment book was burned," I said.

She looked startled. "I didn't think of that."

From the rear, the main visible legacy of the flames was great black licks of soot above the frames where the windows had been and daylight itself showing in the openings because the space inside was open to the sky. There was still a lingering smell of doused ash, sour and acrid, leaving a taste in the mouth.

I steered the sick-parrot lady into the entrance hall, which had a chaotic quality all of its own with cats and barking dogs sitting on people's laps all round the walls and the center filled by Carey Hewett in a white medical coat arguing with a fire officer, one of the women vets trying to sort out patient priority, yesterday's receptionist stolidly taking names and addresses and a large man in a tweed suit demanding Carey Hewett's attention.

Abandoning the parrot and all else, I threaded a way along to the office, which was almost as full, though not as noisy.

The television monitor, I noticed at once, showed the mare standing apathetically in the box, her head a mass of tubes and tapes and leather straps with buckles. Poor old thing, I thought, but at least she was alive.

The people in the office weren't those of the night before. A motherly lady sat behind the desk answering nonstop inquiries on the telephone. "Hewett and Partners . . . Yes, I'm afraid the news of the fire is correct . . . if it's urgent, we'll send Lucy today, otherwise we'll have a clinic running again by Monday . . . Not urgent . . . would you care to make an appointment?"

She was calm and reassuring, holding the disorganized practice together. Around her appeared to be an assortment of administrators, one audibly making a list of the most urgently needed replacements, another, a plaintive-looking man, demanding impossible details for insurance purposes of what had been lost.

Belinda was there, but not Ken. She noticed my arrival after a while and a spasm of annoyance crossed her thinly pretty face. The hair was scraped back, as before. No lipstick.

"What are you doing here?" she wanted to know. "Can't you see we're busy?"

"Where's Ken?" I asked.

"Asleep. Leave him alone."

I wandered out of the office and down the passage towards the operating theater. The door of the X-ray room stood ajar: I looked in there, and there was no Ken asleep on the bed.

The access door to the operating suite was locked. I made the turns instead towards the anorak-and-wellies rear entrance and let myself out into the stable area, and there I found Ken lean-

ing on the half-door of the first of the boxes, looking in at his patient.

He was drooping with tiredness, the line of his
shoulders and neck a commentary on the limits
of muscle power: at what point, I wondered, did
they literally stop working?

"How's she doing?" I asked, reaching him.

He knew my voice without turning his head.

"Oh, hallo. Thanks for coming. She's doing
fine, thank God."

She looked, of course, anything but fine to me.
The intravenous drip led from a bag at the ceiling
into her neck, another tube led out of one nostril,
and there was a muzzle over her nose (to stop
her dislodging everything else).

"Her owner's coming," Ken said. "Carey says
he's upset."

"Understandable."

Ken shook his head wearily. "Not about her
colic. About me. He'd heard the rumors. Apparently he told Carey he should have got a different surgeon."

"He'll have to change his mind."

"He'll take a look at her and he'll see her like
this. He demanded I be here to talk to him, so
I wanted you along for backup. Hope you don't
mind?"

"A witness you wanted and a witness you've
got."

He finally turned his head my way and openly
studied my face.

"You've no obligation," he said.

"I'm interested," I said truthfully. "How old are you?"

"Thirty-four, just," he answered, surprised. "Why?"

I'd thought him a good deal older, but it seemed tactless to say so. It was the elongated bone structure and the intimations of thinning hair that added the years; the opposite, I knew, of my own case, where people doubted my professional seniority as a matter of course.

"I'm thirty-three, almost," I said as a quid pro quo, and after a moment, acknowledging the implicit as well as the factual information, he suddenly held out his hand to be shaken. The bond of mutual age was an odd one, but definitely existed. From that moment Ken and I, though not yet close friends, all the same became a team.

A good deal of bustle appeared to be going on behind us across the car park. The Portakabin had finally been positioned to everyone's satisfaction and the tow truck disconnected. People were carrying flipped-up flip-up chairs from a van to the cabin, followed by trestle tables and a portable gas heater.

"Instant office," Ken said, but it was more like instant clinic, as it was the animals with their owners who presently straggled across from the hospital, not the secretaries and administrators.

"Oliver Quincy and Jay Jardine are both out on calls," Ken said, watching them. "Scott's gone home to rest. Lucy's out with some sheep. I'm dead on my feet. That leaves Carey himself and

113

Yvonne Floyd to deal with that lot, and we ought to have a nurse helping them, but she left in a huff last week." He sighed. "I suppose I shouldn't complain, but we have too much work."

"How about Belinda?" I asked. "She's here, I saw her."

He nodded. "She brought the other three horses back this morning." He gestured along the row. "Two of them go home today anyway. Belinda's looking after this mare chiefly, though I expect Carey will want her over with him."

Belinda appeared at that moment to check on her charge, giving me an irritated glance which made Ken frown.

"Peter doesn't belong here," Belinda said, "and we don't need him."

"I'm not so sure. Anyway, I asked him to come."

Belinda bit off whatever rose into her mind to say and with compressed lips she opened the mare's door and went in. Over her shoulder, as if only then remembering, she said, "Carey wants you in the entrance hall more or less five minutes ago."

Ken gave her a fonder smile than I could have managed and set off round the outside of the building, taking it for granted that I would go with him.

Emptied of the cats, dogs, parrot and assorted owners, the entrance hall now held only Carey Hewett himself, the argumentative fireman, the woman vet, the receptionist and the bulky man in the tweed suit. Carey Hewett in his white coat seemed to be carrying on a multidirectional conversation, addressing a sentence to each in turn, a gray-haired pivot of calm within fringes of hysteria.

"Yvonne, do the best you can. Use the drugs from my car. Use anything from the hospital drugs cupboard. We've new supplies coming this afternoon. No, of course we don't know any reason for it to burn down. Your mare came through the operation very well. Yvonne, better get moving or we'll be here until bedtime . . . Oh, Ken, there you are."

His gaze moved past Ken to me and paused for a second or two while he remembered. Then he gave me a nod and made no comment about my presence, probably because of the other voices talking in his ears.

The fireman gave up and went away. The two women walked over towards the Portakabin with a bravely resigned air of being thrown to the lions, and the large importunate man finally held the field alone, swinging round to stare hard at Ken.

"Are you Ken McClure?"

Ken said he was.

Carey Hewett forestalled the large man as he drew breath and said to Ken, "This is the mare's owner, Wynn Lees."

Wynn Lees.

Again the extraordinary fizz of memory. I knew

a lot about Wynn Lees, if it was the same person. The Wynn Lees of twenty-five years ago had been a cautionary tale freely used by my mother to scare me into good behavior. "If you hang out with that Gribble gang, you'll grow up to be like Wynn Lees." "If you smoke at your age . . . if you're cruel to insects . . . if you steal . . . if you play truant . . . if you throw stones at trains (all of which things I'd done) . . . you'll grow up like Wynn Lees."

The present-day Wynn Lees had a fleshy obstinate look on his heavy face, the cheeks broken-veined from wind and weather, the head thrust forward on a thick neck. A bull of a man with no razor brains, he was saying belligerently to Ken, "You had no right to operate on my mare without my say-so, and I certainly didn't give it."

Carey Hewett said patiently, "She'd be dead now if it weren't for Ken."

"He had no permission," Lees insisted doggedly.

"Yes, I did," Ken said.

"Whose?" Lees demanded.

"Your wife's."

The Lees mouth dropped again. "My wife wouldn't do that."

Ken explained. "The stud groom had your phone number. He stood beside me while I tried it. Your wife answered."

"When was that?" Lees interrupted.

"About a quarter past three this morning."

"She couldn't have answered. She takes sleeping pills."

"Well, she did answer. The stud groom will tell you. She said you weren't at home and she didn't know where you were. I explained the mare had colic and needed an emergency operation. She asked how much it would cost, and I told her, and the stud groom himself told her it was the only way to save the mare's life and the life of the foal. She said to go ahead."

Wynn Lees looked more shaken than seemed sensible by his wife's wakefulness, and belatedly came around to acknowledging his debt to Ken.

"Well, if my wife said . . . and the mare's apparently all right . . . well then, no hard feelings."

I didn't think the half-apology anywhere near good enough and nor, I sensed, did Ken, though from professional circumspection he swallowed it. Carey Hewett definitely relaxed inwardly and said he understood the operation had gone exceptionally well.

"How do you know?" Lees demanded, his truculence resurfacing like a conditioned reflex as though even the simplest statement was for him a cause of suspicion and challenge.

"I've read the notes," Carey said.

"What notes?"

"Ken prudently asked his friend here to attend and take detailed notes of the whole procedure. There's no room for doubt. From start to finish the operation was impeccable."

"Oh." Lees looked momentarily balked. "Well, I need to see my property."

"Certainly," Carey said pacifically. "Come this way."

He took the owner out of the front door into the car park and turned left towards the stable. Ken and I followed, but halfway there I put my hand briefly on his arm and slowed him down a pace or two, to leave a gap wide enough for privacy.

"What is it?" Ken asked.

"Don't trust Wynn Lees."

"Why not? I mean, he's obnoxious, that's all."

"No, not all. Don't trust him. And don't tell him what you found in the horse's gut."

"Why ever not?"

"In case he already knows."

Ken gave me a stare of total astonishment but by then we were approaching the mare's box and within earshot of Lees himself.

Lees was as shocked by the mare's appearance as Ken had predicted but Carey tried to reassure him, and Belinda, who was still there, slapped the mare's rump energetically and told him the old girl was doing fine. Lees shrugged a couple of times and displayed none of the joy he should have felt at the life preserved. Not a good dissimulator, I thought. No good for the Foreign Office.

"Will the foal be born normally?" he asked.

Carey said, "Ken?" and Ken gave it as his opinion that he couldn't see any reason why not.

"Only a very skillful surgeon," Carey said,

118

"could have performed such an operation successfully so late in the gestation period."

Ken showed no embarrassment at the accolade. He knew his worth. False modesty didn't occur to him. His great fear earlier had been that he had somehow taken leave of his ability, and I guessed he had satisfactorily demonstrated to himself, as well as to Carey, that he hadn't. To me, of course, his impressive performance had indicated something quite different, but then I had by training a nasty suspicious mind.

"I expect the mare's insured," I said neutrally.

I got swift glances from all three men, but it was Lees's attention that sharpened on my presence.

"Who did you say you were?" he demanded. "It's none of your business if she's insured."

"No, of course not," I agreed. "Just a random thought."

Carey said to me in mild rebuke, "You can't put a price on a Rainbow Quest foal," and Lees opened his mouth, thought better of it and closed it again.

Instead he said to Ken, "Did you find any reason for the colic?"

I didn't look at Ken. After the briefest of pauses he said, "Colic's usually caused by a kink in the gut. If it persists, as it did in this case, you have to operate to straighten it. Sometimes, like in your mare, the gut's so badly knotted that the twisted piece is literally dying, and you have to cut it out."

"It says in the notes," Carey nodded, " 'Twisted portion of gut removed.' "

The notes had ended with the mare's reawakening. I hadn't recorded the discovery of the needle and thread, meaning to add it later and not by then believing anyway that the notes were of great importance, once the mare had lived.

"What did you do with the excised bit?" Carey asked.

"It's in refrigeration," Ken said, "in case anyone wanted to see it."

"Revolting!" Lees exclaimed. "Throw it away."

Carey nodded his assent and Ken promised nothing one way or the other.

Wynn Lees turned away from the box and, in what I interpreted as acceptance of things as they were, asked Carey to supervise the mare's convalescence.

Ken said nothing. Carey gave him an apprehensive glance and appeared grateful for his restraint. He told Lees that Ken, of course, was in charge of the mare but that he, Carey, would be available for consultation at all times. Lees still gave Ken an intense darkling look, transferring the end of it to me. I gave him back a grade-one benign blandness and with satisfaction watched him shrug and write me off as of no significance.

He took his leave of Carey with minimum effusiveness, ignored Ken altogether, acted as if he hadn't seen Belinda in the first place, and marched across to drive away in a polished Roller.

Carey watched the departure with an unreadable expression of his own and, thanking Ken for his forbearance, took Belinda off towards the Portakabin. She went, looking back a few times over her shoulder in disapproval, not liking Ken to form even a transient link with anyone but herself. She would spend a miserable life, I thought, if she tried to build too many stockades.

Ken, unaware, said, "Why don't you trust Mr. Lees?"

"He acts as if he wanted the mare dead."

Ken said slowly, "You could look at it that way, I suppose. Do you mean . . . for the insurance?"

"Can't tell. It sounded as if he *had* insured the mare, but it would be a matter of which did he need most, the insurance money or the livestock."

"The mare and foal," Ken said without hesitation, as they would have been his own absolute priority. "And he doesn't need the money, he was driving a Rolls, don't forget. I can't believe anyone would deliberately scheme to kill a horse by feeding it something to block its gut, because that's what you're saying, isn't it?"

"You're not that naive," I said.

"Then I don't want to believe it."

"That's not the same thing."

"It's true," he said thoughtfully, "that I've never known a horse to swallow a needle before."

"Could you get a horse to swallow anything if it didn't want to?"

"Oh yes. Pack it in something round and slippery that would dissolve in the stomach or beyond, and then practically throw it down the horse's gullet, feeding some nuts or something very desirable to the animal immediately after. They used to give medicines that way. Horses can't vomit. Once they've swallowed something, it's for keeps."

"Our Mr. Lees," I said, "never dreamt that his wife would wake up and OK the op."

"No." Ken smiled. "That was a shock, wasn't it? She sounded far from having taken a sleeping pill. I'm pretty sure she had a man with her. I heard his voice."

We enjoyed the thought of Lees the cuckold: serve him right.

Ken yawned and said that as he was technically off duty he would go home for food and sleep. "On call tonight, free tomorrow afternoon. I've promised to take Belinda to the races tomorrow. Care to come?"

"Belinda wouldn't want me."

"What? Rubbish. See if Vicky and Greg would come too. Stratford-upon-Avon. Shakespeare and all that, just up their street. We could all go in my car. Why not? It's settled." He smiled and yawned again. "I like Vicky. Great old girl. I've drawn a winner in the mother-in-law stakes, don't you think?"

"You have," I agreed.

"Bloody lucky. Greg's unreal, though. Clothes, not much else."

Rather a good summing up, I thought. "He can sing," I said.

"So can blackbirds." Ken's eyes glimmered. "We'll never come to blows, Greg and I, but I can't take him down the pub for a jar."

"Talking of jars . . ."

Ken looked at his watch and yawned. "They'll still be open. What about it? Pie and a pint?"

"You're on."

This civilized plan however was delayed by a fireman in full gear who came ambling round the corner to ask if the boss was around as they wanted to show him something "out front."

Ken fetched Carey from the Portakabin and the three of us trudged after the firemen back up the driveway I'd run down the night before. I put my hand on the brick sidewall in passing: it was still warm to hot but no longer barbecue.

The scene "out front" was reasonably orderly, with most vehicles parked out on the road and the car parking space given only to one police car and one large glittering fire appliance. There were also six firemen in fireproof suits and three or four policemen in navy blue with checked bands on their peaked hats.

Seeing Carey Hewett arrive, one of the firemen came to meet him, followed immediately by a policeman. A small amount of handshaking took place, followed by an equal amount of head-shaking as a prelude to the news that in the firemen's professional opinion, the fire had been set.

Carey looked blank.

123

"Arson," the fireman said bluntly.

"I understand," Carey said, "but I just can't believe it. What makes you think so?"

The fireman explained in a healthy Gloucestershire voice that it was still too hot in there—he gestured to the gutted walls—to look at everything carefully, but they had found some big bottles of cleaning fluid. Spot remover, that sort of thing.

This time not only Carey looked blank.

"Highly inflammable," the fireman explained. "It always says so on the bottle."

"I expect we'd have spot remover," Carey said dazedly, "but I've no idea what's in the cleaning cupboard."

"Ah, but this was three bottles, all empty. And you know what? If our chum had simply smashed the bottles to get at the contents, we might not have noticed, but these bottles had no caps on. And they weren't in any cupboard, we found them because they were in the big front room which, according to one of your young ladies, was where the two secretaries worked, and what mostly burned in there was paper, which doesn't hold the heat so much. A bit of the roof fell at an angle against the wall in there, which gave us access, luckily."

"I don't follow you," Carey said.

The fireman gave the knowing look of one often confronted by villainy.

"We're experts, see, sir, at fires. Our chum made a common mistake in not screwing the caps back on. You'd be surprised how many times we find petrol cans with no caps. Firebugs are always in such a hurry they forget the caps. Then there's the paint. You were having the place painted inside, right? And some of the woodwork was being varnished?"

Carey nodded.

"Well, sir, there's paint tins in there with the lids off, same with pots of varnish, and good workmen don't leave empties about and certainly they don't leave lids off pots that've got paint in still."

Carey said bemusedly, "Someone said tins of paint had exploded."

"It looks like it." The fireman nodded. "But as far as we can tell just now, those tins were all together, like, where the painters stored them, not lying round in your office."

"In my office?" Carey repeated. "Do you mean in my own office? I don't understand."

"Your young lady drew a plan for us." The fireman put a hand inside his tunic and brought out a tattered paper, holding it open for Carey to peer at. "Isn't that where your own office was? In the front left-hand corner?"

Carey studied it for a few seconds, through his glasses. "Yes, that's about right. I suppose . . . is there any chance of anything being left in there to salvage?"

The fireman shook his head. "Not a lot."

Carey said forlornly, "I was making some notes for a book."

The fireman observed a decent interval of silence in face of such a disaster and then said they would know more by the next day, when they'd been able to sift the rubble, but meanwhile they'd have to inform Carey's insurers that arson was suspected.

"We're insured against arson," Carey said dully. "We can rebuild and restock, but no amount of insurance can bring back my records. All those years of work . . ."

He broke off, looking tired and depressed. It wasn't his life's work, exactly, that had gone up in smoke, but the evidence of it had. I tried to imagine what a void like that would be like, but no one could, really, who hadn't suffered it.

Carey, the elder statesman of the practice, looked gray, spent and sad, standing dispiritedly in the small chilly breeze that had sprung up to ruffle our hair and sting in our noses.

5

The journey to Stratford-upon-Avon races was short enough for Belinda to remain civil, even if not cordial, in my direction. She made no more remarks about my presence being unnecessary and seemed temporarily to have accepted that I would be part of the scenery for as long as I stayed around; and I'd been at pains to mention that I'd have to be reporting for work in London pretty soon.

"When?" Ken asked bluntly.

"I'll have to phone on Monday. They'll give me a date then."

"I was hoping . . ." He stopped for a moment, glanced at me over his shoulder and went on, "How about a spot of detective work?"

"What about?" Belinda asked.

"This and that."

"Ken!" She was reasonably exasperated. "If you mean the things that have been going wrong in the practice, well, Peter can't begin to understand them in veterinary terms, can he? Far less explain them."

"There was the fire, dear," Vicky murmured.

"Yes, Mother, but the police will see to that."

Belinda, sitting in the front passenger seat next to Ken, had come dressed in a chestnut leather skirt, big white sweater, knee-high boots and leather overcoat. She looked slender and pretty, her hair falling free to her shoulders, her mouth softened with color. Ken patted her knee from time to time in appreciation.

I sat between Vicky and Greg in a bit of a crush in the back, uneasily rubbing hams with Greg and receiving mildly coquettish knee contacts from Vicky. She herself wore intense red to dramatize her white hair, and apart from a small bandage on her ear, seemed back to normal in vitality, though complaining she kept going to sleep when you wouldn't expect.

I checked on the mare's health; Belinda knowledgeably answered my inquiry. "No sign of reflux, so we removed the stomach tube last night. This morning she's eating hay and drinking normally. So far, perfect." She gave Ken an admiring glance, confident in her love.

Ken himself looked slightly less haunted, as if he'd put the worst of the anxieties on hold, and appeared determined that his passengers should enjoy the day, to the extent of making a slow sightseeing detour through Stratford with glimpses of the theater and swans and a plethora of black and white Tudor timbering, some of it actually genuine.

Inside the racecourse, the five of us split naturally apart, Greg and Vicky going off in search of lunch, leaving me on my own to wander about and enjoy the first steeplechase meeting I'd been to in years.

Cheltenham racecourse had been my child-hood playground, my familiar backyard. My mother's "help with secretarial work" had been full-time employment in the racecourse manager's office: her pay our livelihood. In school holidays, while she labored at her desk, I was allowed by the manager to go almost everywhere on the course and in the buildings, "as long as he isn't a nuisance" being the only proviso. As being a nuisance meant instant banishment to my grand-mother (a tyrant) to spend endless boring days under her beady eye in her musty little bungalow, I endeavored to be the opposite of a nuisance with fervent diligence, and on the whole suc-ceeded.

Race days had been magic (and the cause of my truancy) and until John Darwin came along I had taken it for granted that one day I would be one of the jockeys rocketing over the jumps. I stood beside the fences entranced while the great horses thundered through the birch; I lis-tened to the jockeys cursing during races and practiced the words myself under the bedclothes; I read sporting newspapers, watched meetings on the box, knew the names and fortunes of every steeplechase horse, trainer and jockey in the busi-ness; fantasized eternally about being top jockey and winning all the top races, particularly the big one at home, the Cheltenham Gold Cup.

Two minor impediments damped the realistic prospects, though not the dreams. First, I had no pony of my own and could only snatch infrequent opportunities to ride at all, still less put in the concentrated practice I needed and longed for. Second, I faced the implacable determination of my mother that I shouldn't achieve my aim.

"It's in my blood," I protested at ten, having just come across that exciting-sounding phrase. "You can't say it isn't."

"It may be in your blood, but look where it got your father."

It had got my father into his grave. The man who'd sired me, whom I knew only from photographs, had been a jockey over jumps for one short year. Four winners to the good, he had ridden out as usual one morning with the string of horses, trotting along the road to the exercise gallops. His mount, they said, had shied at a bird flying out of a hedge: he himself was flung out of the saddle and into the path of a passing car and was already dead when the other lads dismounted to help him.

There were no headlines, none of the fuss that would have happened had he been killed in a race. My mother still kept the small paragraph from the local paper, yellowed by age, which gave the briefest details. "Paul Perry, 21, aspiring jump jockey, died last Tuesday morning on Baydon Road, Lambourn, as a result of an accident involving the racehorse he was riding and a passing car. Neither the horse nor the driver was injured. Perry leaves a widow and an infant son."

The widow, barely twenty herself, was sustained through months to come by the charitable Injured Jockeys' Fund, a marvelous organization which eventually found for her, a trained secretary, the job at Cheltenham racecourse. Very appropriate, everyone said: a neat and useful solution. The Perry kid—myself—could grow up in his father's footsteps, in his father's world.

The benign thinking behind all this washed over me at the time without my realizing how much I owed to it, but it wasn't until I returned to England as Peter Darwin to try for Oxford that I understood why my memories of early childhood were chiefly happy. Whenever I gave anything to charity from then on, it was to the Injured Jockeys' Fund.

At Stratford, coming back to my long-dead father's world after a gap of twenty years, it seemed in some ways as if time itself had stood still. Up on the number boards many of the jockeys' names were as they'd always been, yet these had to be the sons and daughters of the pack I'd idolized. In the race card, the same thing with trainers, though in this case, as I progressively discovered, many were indeed the same old brigade.

J. Rolls Eaglewood, for instance, identified as he stood with his runner in the parade ring before the first race, was an old man with a walking stick on which he leant heavily. J. Rolls Eaglewood, father of Russet-of-the-no-panties, was undoubtedly the same man, and was also related no doubt to Izzy, Ken McClure's onetime love.

I wouldn't have recognized him: his name alone

remained stuck in a remote neural pathway, lighting up when one pressed the right button, a name associated not with a face but with power and threat.

Only the horses themselves were wholly unfamiliar, including their breeding; too many horse generations had turned over like pages. Many owners, however, were recognizably the same, witnesses to enduring pleasure and faith.

I looked through the race card for Ronnie Upjohn, the owner threatening to sue Ken for daring to win with an Upjohn castoff, but he had no runner that day.

Upjohn . . . and Travers. Upjohn and Travers.

They ran together in my mind like Abbott and Costello, but definitely without the laughs.

I turned away from the parade ring and began to thread a way through the throng to a good watching place on the stands. The racegoing crowd had changed not at all: there were perhaps fewer hats and more open-necked shirts, but the same manufacturers of overcoats and padded jackets were clearly healthily in business. The faces scurrying to beat the odds bore the same calculating anxiety, the bookmakers shouted from under the same fictitious nameboards, the snatches of overheard conversation exactly echoed the voices of a quarter century ago.

". . . Blew up turning into the straight . . ."

". . . Couldn't ride in a cart with a pig net over it . . ."

". . . Honest as a corkscrew . . ."

". . . It's a bloody disgrace . . ."

". . . The handicapper murdered him . . ."

I smiled to myself and felt like an alien returned to a loved- and-lost planet, and through not looking where I was going almost cannoned into two short men in navy overcoats, who happened to be Japanese.

I apologized in English. They bowed to me, unspeaking. I went on up to the stands.

The two Japanese, standing below and to the left of me in the area outside the weighing room, looked bewildered and lost, and I had a feeling I'd met one of them before, though a quick run-through of the government officials I'd usually worked with brought no enlightenment. I shrugged, looked away, watched the runners canter down to the post.

The jockey riding for J. Rolls Eaglewood wore purple and white and remained unexcitingly in midfield throughout, the uneventful contest being won by the hot favorite, pulling up.

The crowd, roaring approval, streamed down from the stands to collect their winnings and, once the dust had settled, I glanced to where the Japanese had been standing.

They were still there, still looking lost, though they had by now been joined by a young woman who was trying to talk to them by signs. Black round heads together, the two men consulted each other earnestly and bowed a few times to their companion, but it was obvious that no one was understanding anything much.

The impulse to help was ingrained, I supposed. I strolled down from the stands and stopped a pace or two from the young woman who, at close quarters, looked impatient as well as harassed.

I said, "Can I perhaps be of service?" Good old Foreign Office lingo.

She flicked me the briefest of glances which would have stopped Casanova and said with crisp disapproval, "Not unless you speak Japanese."

"Well, yes, I do. That's why I asked."

She turned her full attention my way and metaphorically clutched the offered lifebuoy as one seeing escape from drowning.

"Then please," she said, "ask them what they want. They want something and they can't seem to be able to tell me what."

I bowed to the Japanese and asked them the question. The extent of their relief at hearing their own language was almost comical, and so was their answer. I bowed and pointed out to them what they wanted, and they hurried away, bowing sketchily as they went.

The young woman watched open-mouthed, crossly.

"They wanted the loo," I said. "They were bursting."

"Why for God's sake didn't they say so!"

"With sign language?" I asked.

She stared at me, then melted inside and began to laugh.

"Thanks, then," she said. "What are you doing for the rest of the afternoon?"

"I'll be around, watching the races."

"Can I send up smoke signals?"

"I'll look out for them," I promised.

"I was supposed to bring three of them," she said, talking easily, promoting me to instant friend. "The third one speaks English. I've been showing them round London for three days and this morning Mr. Kamato, he's the English speaker, had the squits. The other two didn't want to miss seeing Stratford, and if you've ever tried explaining Anne Hathaway's cottage with your hands you'll understand the morning I've had. They're perfectly charming and they think I'm retarded."

"Are they businessmen?" I asked.

"No, they're part of the Japanese Jockey Club."

"Ah," I said.

"What do you mean, ah?"

"I think I've met one of them before."

"Really. Where?"

"In Japan. I used to work there."

She gave me a bright assessing look and I in turn noted the small mouth, the huge blue eyes and the thick frizzed blond-streaked brown hair chopped off straight all round at earlobe level, except for an eyebrow-length fringe. The overall effect was slightly zany-doll, but the Japanese were wrong, the mind inside was no toy.

"I work for the British Jockey Club," she said. "I arrange things for visiting bigwigs. Transport, hotels, tourist traps, all that sort of thing. A general nanny."

I could think of worse things than having my path smoothed by her.

"I'm Peter," I said.

"Annabel."

First names only meant no commitment beyond that afternoon but made a temporary sharing of her work load possible. The unspoken signaling was like a formal dance, I thought, with advances, retreats and do-si-dos. No one at that stage was going to break step.

We waited for the return of her charges.

"They are supposed to be watching these races from the directors' room," she said, "but they wanted to mix with the crowds. We had drinks up there."

"Japanese feel at home in crowds."

She said casually, "What did you do in Japan?"

"Worked for the Foreign Office."

She wrinkled her nose. "As a career?"

"Mm."

"I suppose you know the famous definition of a diplomat?"

I knew. Everyone in the foreign service knew. I quoted, "An honest man sent to lie abroad for his country."

She smiled. "And do you?"

"Sometimes."

"The Foreign Office stirs up more trouble than it's worth."

"Who's that a quote from?"

She looked startled, then a shade defensive. "My father, as a matter of fact."

136

I didn't comment or argue. Every dogmatic opinion had a basis somewhere in truth, and there had been times when British along with other ambassadors had given wrong signals to would-be aggressors, indicating that opposition to intended tyranny might be slight or even nonexistent. Both the Kaiser and Hitler had reportedly felt aggrieved when the supposedly acquiescent British Lion had awoken and roared.

Ambassadors from every country could get things wrong and often did: it depended both on their orders from home and on the information they'd been locally fed. My exact job in every posting had been to try to find out what was really going on behind the scenes in our host country and to keep my superiors up to date. In consequence, I went to local parties and dinners, and gave them myself, with the sole object of gathering and checking rumors, of learning who had leverage, who had ideals, who was ill with what, who was sleeping with whom, who was on drugs, who drank, who beat their wives, who was up-and-coming, who was gullible, who was greedy, who could be bought or blackmailed, who would be likely to crack or resign, whose information could sometimes be trusted, whose never, whose professed friendship might be genuine, whose not.

At that game I'd become fairly adept but it was impossible to get it right every time. Then, too, even if an ambassador were primed with impeccable inside dope, there was no guarantee the government back home would believe it or act in accordance. Hair-tearing in ignored embassies could reach epic proportions. No country on earth was exempt.

The Japanese Jockey Club came back and bowed several times, expressing especial pleasure when I said I recognized one of them. He apologized for not having immediately recognized me in turn. We went through a lot of platitudes and bowing. Finally I asked them if there were anything else I could achieve for them, and they said with visible eagerness that they would like hot weak tea with no milk and no sugar and—in a decorous shaft of humor—a Japanese tea ceremony to go with it. I, who had watched countless tea ceremonies and enjoyed them, asked if Miss Annabel could stand in, even though without kimono and obi. Their oriental eyes smiled. They said gravely that they would be delighted. I asked if they would like to return to the directors' room for the purpose, but it seemed they would not.

I said to Annabel, "They're thirsty. They would like weak tea, no milk, no sugar. They would very much like you to get it for them down here."

"Is that all they said?"

"Not really. In Japan there are traditional tea ceremonies as part of the entertainment some days at race meetings. I think they're homesick."

"I suppose," she said, "you wouldn't come with me?"

"Might consider it. Where's the tearoom?"

We tracked down the required liquid and over

the cups held a three-way conversation slowly. After that, as I took my temporary leave, Annabel said, "Why do you bow to them more than they do to you? It's un-English."

"They are older. They are Jockey Club and we are on a racecourse. They feel reassured, I am not humbled."

"You are one crazy diplomat and can come to my rescue anytime."

I smiled at her and got a vivid smile back. Promising, I thought. She read my expression accurately, curled her little mouth and shook her head.

Still promising, nevertheless.

She took her charges at their gestured request into the Tattersalls enclosure to see the bookmakers at close quarters, and I watched them from the stands as the runners cantered down for the next race. She was taller than the two men, and the combination of two black and one frizzy blond heads was very easy to follow. They moved slowly from bookmaker to bookmaker, pointing at the odds chalked on the boards until in the end one of the men produced some money which Annabel offered to a bookie. The bet was struck, the ticket given. The trio went up into the Tattersalls stands behind the ranks of bookmakers and watched the race from there.

Greg and Vicky appeared at my side and tiredly said it was all very interesting, wasn't it? I diagnosed a slight case of boredom but Vicky said it wasn't boredom but the dearth of places to sit down. They had bet and lost in the first race, but at least the third race brought them a win, which sent them off to collect in less depression.

I didn't see Ken and Belinda at all and found later they'd walked down the course to be nearer the jumps. Annabel brought the Japanese to stand by the parade ring rails to watch the next lot of runners walk round and, far more from enjoyment than obligation, I joined them.

They were all pleased, the men almost effusively so: I'd become their dearest buddy in the West. They hoped I could tell them which of the horses in front of us would win the next race as they'd had to tear up their tickets after the last.

Sort out the fittest-looking had long been my policy, thanks to my adopted name, so I watched the parade and pointed to a load of lean glossy muscle striding round phlegmatically with its head down. The Japanese bowed their thanks and hurried back to the bookies, who were a novelty for them, they said, and Annabel asked why I had picked the horse I had.

"It looks well," I said.

"So you know about horses?"

"I wanted to be a jockey, once."

She looked up at my height. "There have been six-foot jockeys, I suppose."

I nodded. "But you might say I grew out of it in other ways."

"What ways?"

"Total lack of opportunity."

"I was a pony freak," she said, nodding, "and one fine day there was more to life than riding."

She wore black and white all over: black boots and thin legs, checked skirt, white turtleneck, black short coat and a huge fluffy white scarf with black pompom fringes. She looked at times sixteen and at times double that and had an overall air of competence, when not hurling herself against language barriers.

"Do you live in London?" I asked.

"Fulham Road, if you can call that London. And you?"

"Homeless."

I got a disillusioned stare worthy of the remark. "Does that mean a grating in Trafalgar Square?"

"Are there any good gratings down Fulham way?"

She answered with a look which said games had gone far enough, and I thought to myself that, if I didn't start searching soon for somewhere to lay my head, a nice warm grating where hot air vented up from subterranean tunnels would have its attractions. I'd slept rough in the capital several times in my student days: guessed I was too old for it now.

The Japanese came back happily waving tickets and we all went up on the stands to watch the fittest. He survived to the last hurdle and there turned end over end in a flurry of legs.

I apologized. They said it wasn't my fault. The horse got up and galloped riderless past the stands, looking ready to go round twice more

141

without panting. The Japanese put their useless tickets in their pockets along with their dashed hopes and decided that for the next race they would like to walk down to the fences, as they had seen other people do. I was ready to say I'd go with them when I spotted Ken walking alone slowly, looking at his race card, stopping in indecision.

"I'll be here when you come back," I said hastily in two languages, "but I have to speak to someone. Please, please excuse me."

I left them in midbow and reached Ken before he moved off, slowing to a stop at his elbow.

"I want to talk to you," I said.

"Fire away." He lifted his gaze briefly from the race card.

"Alone and uninterrupted."

"But Belinda . . ."

"If you want me to do anything useful, I need some of your time."

"All right." He made up his mind. "How about the bar?"

The bar turned out to be worse than useless because as we reached the door we came face-to-face with J. Rolls Eaglewood, who was on his way out, limping along with his walking stick.

"Afternoon, sir," Ken said. I hoped his tremble was detectable by me alone: I felt his panic flow across like a breeze. His impulse to turn and run couldn't have been clearer.

J. Rolls stopped dead, fixing a dire glare on Ken's face. "You killed my horse," he said.

Ken shook his head weakly. "He died. We couldn't save him."

"Sheer bloody incompetence, and I won't put up with it any longer."

Eaglewood at close quarters, though thin, gray-haired and with age-freckled skin, still generated the power and threat I associated with his name. His voice held the rasp of one long used to instant obedience, and he could and did score several patriarchal points over a vet less than half his age.

"I've put up with you this long because of my granddaughter's infatuation with you," he said, "and out of respect, too, for your father's memory, but I've had to tell Carey that you're never to attend my horses again or I'll be transferring my business to another firm of vets, and I'd be sorry to do that after all these years, as I told him, but this slaughter has got to stop."

Ken miserably made no attempt at defense. Eaglewood gave him a brief fierce nod, gestured to him with his stick to get out of the way, and stumped off out of earshot.

"You see?" Ken said, shaking and as pale as ever. "I can't even blame him. The horse that died on Thursday morning—with the split cannon bone—came from his stable."

"It sounded as if it might not have been the first disaster."

"You're right, it wasn't. Another of his died on the table about a month ago while I was doing respiratory-tract surgery. And one died in its own box . . ." His voice took the by-now familiar note of desperation. "I don't do anything wrong, I'm always careful. They just *died.*"

"Mm. Well, why don't you give me a complete chronological list of all the things that have ended badly? Also the names of all the owners and trainers and anything special or particular about them? If you're sure what you did was OK, we have to find another explanation."

"What explanation?"

"Villainy, wouldn't you think?"

"But it's impossible. That's the trouble. I've checked everything over and over again. Gone over everything in my mind. I can't sleep . . . And what's the *point* of killing them?"

I sighed. "Let's start with the list."

"I'd need my notes." He broke off freshly appalled. "All my notes are *burnt.*"

We'd moved away from the door to the bar and stood in the area outside the weighing room. Several people, I'd noticed, gave Ken sidelong glances, but I thought it might have been only because of his visible distress until I later heard Eaglewood spreading his opinions far and wide. " . . . ruining a good old firm . . ." and " . . . three of mine dead . . . can't go on." At what point, I wondered, did opinion become slander?

"What you've got to do," I told Ken, "is stop worrying what you did wrong and start wondering how you would have set about killing the horses that died. Think about a needle and thread

144

in a broodmare's gut. Think, in fact, of all the ways you know to commit equine murder."

"But I . . ." His voice tailed off indecisively.

"Knowledge isn't guilt," I said. "Knowing where to shove a dagger between the ribs doesn't mean you've done it."

"But if you know how, then it *might* have been you."

"So you do know ways."

"Well . . . every vet does."

I looked at his long unhappy face with its troubled light eyes and understood his unwillingness to part with information that might sound like confession. It was the same hesitation I'd noticed on the night of the fire. I would get him to tell me in the end, I thought, but the sooner the safer, on the whole.

Over his shoulder I saw Belinda making her way purposefully towards us and regretted not being hidden away in the depths of the bar.

"Think out the list," I urged Ken. "Meet me early tomorrow at the hospital. Alone."

"How early?"

"Eight?"

"Well . . ." He turned to see what I was looking at. Belinda had six paces to go. "All right," he said. "Eight."

"Eight what?" Belinda asked, overhearing.

"Number eight in the next race," I explained.

Ken closed his eyes.

"What's the matter?" Belinda asked.

"Nothing." He opened his eyes again, smiling

145

at her and fishing around for his wallet. "Go and put a fiver on number eight for me, there's a darling. You know I don't like people to see me bet."

"Eight hasn't a hope," she said.

"All the same . . ."

"All right, but you're mad."

She walked off towards the Tote windows and Ken at once said, "Why don't you want Belinda there too, in the morning?"

"You'll tell me more and clearer on your own. I can ask her later for her impressions."

He thought it over. "You're probably right. And you're a shocking liar."

"I thought I was quite good."

"I mean, you shocked me. So fast."

"Years of practice."

"That's pretty shocking too."

When Belinda returned we climbed the stands to watch the race and to everyone's blank surprise number eight came in first. The stunned crowd received the no-hoper's victory in silence, and Belinda stopped Ken's wide grin in its tracks by announcing a shade defiantly that she hadn't put his fiver on eight but on the favorite instead.

"People have been divorced for less," Ken said, just about managing civility.

"Number eight was useless," Belinda insisted. "I wanted you to win."

Number eight paid a fortune on the Tote, which caused a further chill between the betrothed. I left them fuming over the problem and

146

made tracks for Annabel as she brought her retinue back to the paddock.

After twenty minutes apart we greeted each other as old friends. The expedition to the closer action had raised heartbeats, it appeared, and also quite clearly the spirits. The two Japanese talked animatedly between themselves about what looked fittest for the next race and Annabel and I looked at each other with a lot of unspoken questions.

When she finally asked, it was solely a search for information.

"Who," she said, "were you talking to when we came back? A tall thin man with fair hair and a tetchity girl."

"Tetchity?"

She shrugged. "Whatever."

"Ken McClure and Belinda Larch. The wedding is three weeks today."

She frowned, but not at that news. "Is he a vet?"

"Yes, he is."

"Friend of yours?"

"I met him the day before yesterday, and yes, to that extent, he is."

I waited a bit, and she said, "I owe you for your help. I wouldn't want you to make a mistake in getting too friendly with that vet. They were talking about him upstairs."

"Who upstairs?"

"The directors and stewards. One of them was, anyway. He pointed him out to the others as they stood by the window having a drink before lunch.

He said your friend would soon be disbarred from practicing, or some such phrase, as he was killing horses left right and center and was dishonest, sneaky and a disgrace to his profession."

"As strong as that?"

"Stronger, if anything. There was a lot of hate in it."

"Really?" I was interested. "Who was he?"

"I was introduced to about eight people very fast and I was trying to present our chums here"—she pointed to her charges—"so I can't remember his name, but I think he might have been one of the stewards."

"Let's see," I said, and turned my race card back to page one, and there to my confusion found in the list of stewards the name I'd searched all the inner pages for in vain.

R. D. Upjohn, Esq.

"Ronnie!" Annabel exclaimed. "I still can't remember his last name, but they called him Ronnie." She studied my face. "Mean something to you?"

I told her why Ronnie Upjohn hated Ken Mc-Clure. "Ken made him look a fool. Some men can't bear it."

She listened with pursed mouth to the saga of the preserved castoff that went on to win and said, "I understand the spite and envy over the one that was saved, but how about the ones that died? It wasn't only Ronnie who'd heard about them, some of the others were nodding."

"What does this Ronnie look like?" I asked.

"You're changing the subject!"

"I don't know why the horses died, and nor does Ken. We're working on it. Could you point out Ronnie Upjohn, by any chance?"

She shook the mop of hair. "Stewards at race meetings all look alike."

"That's what people say about the Japanese."

"Oh no," she said instantly. "I'd know my three anywhere." She looked at her watch. "I really ought to take these two back upstairs, where all good little VIPs belong. Would you mind suggesting it?"

They went, it seemed to me, with polite resignation: they were having more fun down in the crowds with the doll of a girl. For me too, unexpectedly, the fizz went out of the hour with their departure, and I said to myself, "Well, well, well, Peter my boy, take it easy, she'll have half London in tow, and besides that, you know nothing about her except the way she looks and talks . . ." And who really needed more? Everything had to begin *somewhere,* after all.

I rejoined Greg and Vicky on the stands and learned they'd at length found two seats in the bar and had stayed there for an hour making one gin and tonic last forever and watching the races on closed-circuit television. They had backed two winners on quick forays to the Tote and had won a lot on number eight. "My birthday's the eighth of the eighth month," Vicky said. "Eight's always my lucky number." They'd quite enjoyed themselves after all, they said.

Belinda, looking glum, came to ask them dutifully if they were managing all right and was infuriated to be told of their winnings on number eight.

"The wretched animal's useless," she protested, "and Ken's kicking up the most ridiculous fuss."

"Why, dear?" Vicky asked, perplexed.

"He gave me money to back eight for him and I put him on the favorite instead, and you'd think I'd lost him the crock of gold the way he's going on."

"He's under a lot of pressure," Greg said gently. "You can see he is."

"He's proud and he's stubborn," Belinda said, "and he's not speaking to me." There was a sudden thin glitter of tears along her lower eyelids. She tossed her head as if to disclaim them and blinked hard, sniffing.

Vicky, looking relieved at this sign of emotion in her bossy daughter, said prosaically, "He'll get over it."

Belinda said, "I offered to give him the wretched money he would have won. He says that's not the point. Well, if it's not, what is?"

"The point is his ego, dear," Vicky said. "You questioned his decision. Worse still, you overrode it. That's what's the matter with him, not the loss of his money."

Belinda looked at her mother in wide-eyed silent astonishment, and I thought that it might even have been the very first time in her adult life that she'd really listened to what her mother said. After a long pause her gaze slid from Vicky to me, and a good deal of acerbity returned to her expression.

"And you," she said, not liking me, "what do you say about it?"

"I'd say," I said without emphasis, "that he's too used to you obeying him without question in the course of your work."

She gave me much the same stare that she'd bestowed on her mother.

"I wanted what was best for him," she said.

And to prove your judgment superior, I thought, but knew better than to say it.

She changed the subject as if to defend her self-esteem from more analysis, and said, "We all want to know who that weird-looking woman is you've been talking to all afternoon."

"We all" being Belinda's euphemism for "I am consumed by curiosity," Greg and Vicky looked mystified. They hadn't noticed Annabel, obviously.

"What woman?" Vicky in fact asked artlessly.

"She works for the Jockey Club," I said. "She escorts foreign official visitors. Today the visitors are Japanese. I helped her with translation, that's all."

"Oh." Belinda shrugged. "Extraordinary of the Jockey Club to employ someone who dresses like that at the races."

"Do point her out to me," Vicky said.

Annabel however stayed out of sight until after

the last race, when she came down from above and shepherded her charges towards the exit. She saw me hovering there (I was already keeping Ken and the others waiting) and came to my side with a small-mouthed grin.

"Ronnie Upjohn is that man there ahead of us, the one with the woman in the orange coat." We walked on together out into the car park, followed by the two Japanese. "I couldn't talk to him much, he was in and out all the time, and I was stuck with our friends, but he seems fairly ordinary. Dogmatic, of course. He thinks jockeys get away with murder, but who doesn't?"

"Who doesn't get away with murder, or who doesn't think jockeys do?"

"Take your pick."

We arrived at a big car with a chauffeur waiting to carry away the very important Japanese. I bowed in farewell to the two men, keeping an eye on the departing orange coat.

"Go chase him," Annabel said, "if you must."

I smiled at her blue eyes. "I'll phone you," I said.

"Do that."

She followed her charges into the car and closed the door, and without delay I hurried after the orange coat as fast as I could without drawing stares.

The coat stopped beside a large gray car and the man, Ronnie Upjohn, unlocked the car doors. He then opened the trunk, took off his hat, binocular case and overcoat and laid them inside.

The orange coat, removed, followed. I had time to arrive and see Upjohn clearly before he folded himself into the car, and when he did, it was into the front passenger seat, not behind the wheel. The orange-coat lady, now in gray with pearls, was the driver.

Ronnie Upjohn was sixtyish and basically unremarkable. I had to tick off features mentally to have any chance of knowing him elsewhere. Hair, gray. Forehead, medium height, lined. Eyebrows, medium bushy. Eyes, slightly drooping at outside edges, lids folded from age. Nose, large, a bit bulbous. Moustache, medium size, brownish. Mouth, firm. Jaw . . . I gave up. There wasn't anything memorable about his jaw. Moreover, he was by then inside the car and could be seen only through glass.

I turned away and started walking towards Ken's car across the main car park and found him standing with his arms folded, leaning on the car's roof and watching my antics with astonishment.

"Did you know who you were following?" he asked incredulously. "That was Ronnie Upjohn."

"I certainly hope so," I said.

"But why?"

"I wanted to put a face to the name." I paused. "Apart from acting as a steward, what does he do?"

"Owns a few horses." Ken thought it over. "He's something in finance. In an office. I don't exactly know. He's semiretired, I think. No lack of money. Probably inherited money: he has that feel. He's not overshrewd, I wouldn't say."

"He's doing you no good just now," I said.

Ken sighed. "No one is." He stood upright and prepared to get into the car. "And I gave Belinda a right bollocking, and it wasn't as if I even knew the name of number eight, let alone believed it would win, and I upset her something dreadful and now I'm in the shit."

I shook my head. "Not really. All you have to do is pat her knee."

I'd grown accustomed to him looking at me as if I'd taken leave of my senses, but on the drive home he did in fact wordlessly pat Belinda's knee, and she burst into tears, which resolved the quarrel instantly.

That evening, when they'd all gone out, I ate cheese on toast and drank some wine and telephoned my mother.

My parents had long ago set up a system for my calls to them from round the world which was, basically, if I would call, they would pay. I had myself only to get through and give them the number I was speaking from, and they would then call back. That way, I had to pay only for a maximum of three minutes though we might talk for an hour. My father had dryly remarked that it was the only way for them to make sure I was alive.

I counted out the money for three minutes to

Mexico City and left it in an envelope by the phone in Thetford Cottage, and in short order, striking lucky, was talking to my mum.

I pictured her on the other end of the line, as beautiful as ever. She'd always had what I had grown to recognize as style, an inborn quality that had made the transition from efficient secretary to ambassador's wife look simple, a deserved progression. I listened with a familiar sense of security to her light voice, elegant and very young, ageless.

"Wynn Lees?" she repeated in disbelief after she'd phoned back. "Why on earth do you want to know about Wynn Lees?"

Explaining took a fair amount of her money and left her both amused and alarmed.

"It's fascinating you've got to know Ken McClure, but you seriously don't want to get mixed up with Wynn Lees, darling. He won't have changed his spots."

"Yes, but *why?*" I asked. "What did he do that was so awful?"

"Heavens, it was all so long ago."

"But you used to tell me that if I didn't mend my ways I'd grow up like Wynn Lees, as if it was the worst fate in the world, and all I can dredge up about him is a vague impression that he went to prison."

"Yes, he certainly did."

"Well, what for?"

"For cruelty to horses."

"For *what?*" I was stunned.

"The first time, it was for cruelty to horses. It happened long before you were born, when Wynn Lees was about twenty, I suppose. He and another youth cut off a horse's tongue. I think they did it about six times before they were caught. I didn't know about it until we moved to Cheltenham, and by that time Wynn Lees was over thirty and had been to prison again, but the second time was for fighting. Good heavens, I haven't thought about this for years. He was a horrible man. He used to come to the office sometimes because at that time he lived on the far side of the racecourse, though he went off to somewhere like Australia afterwards. He used to complain about the boundary fencing and I couldn't stand him. He'd be talking about wire and all I could think about were those horses dying because they'd had their tongues cut out. People used to say he'd paid for it and it was wild oats and all in the past, but I think people's pasts are *them,* and if it was in him to do that at twenty it's still in him at fifty or sixty, even if he wouldn't actually *do* it now, if you see what I mean. So if he's back in England, don't cross him, darling, just don't."

"I'll try not to," I promised. "Who did he fight?"

"What? Oh . . . gracious . . . I can't remember. He'd not long come out of prison when we arrived in Cheltenham. You couldn't work on the racecourse without hearing about him all the time. Let me think . . . Oh yes!" She chuckled suddenly. "It wasn't just for fighting. He'd attacked some man with a rivet gun and shot staples into him through his jeans. Stapled the jeans to the man. It sounds funny now but I think he'd accused the man of laying his girlfriend behind his back and he was making sure he wouldn't be able to take his trousers down again."

"For God's sake!"

"Mm. I do remember now. The man with the staples in him had to go to hospital to get them taken out and they were mostly in the most painful of places, it was said, and touch and go whether he'd ever lay anyone again, let alone Wynn Lees's girlfriend."

"Why didn't I ever hear about this?"

"Well, darling, you may have done but not from me. I wouldn't have told you. You were a baby at the time of the stapling. I can tell you though that you didn't like Wynn Lees, at all. You used to hide if he came into the office if you were there. It was absolutely instinctive. You couldn't bear him. So I used him as a bogey-man without frightening you with what he'd actually done. I thought that the cutting off of horses' tongues would give you nightmares. I certainly wouldn't tell any child something like that even now, though no child grows up these days without knowing the world is full of horrors."

"Thank you for not telling me," I said. "I'd have hated it."

"You're a fairly rewarding child, now and then."

Pat pat on the back. And why not? We'd always been friends.

"OK," I said, "let me try you with some more names. How about Ronnie Upjohn?"

"Upjohn . . ." Her voice was negative, without recognition.

"Upjohn and Travers," I said. "Who were Upjohn and Travers?"

"My darling, I haven't a clue. You were at school with a boy called Travers. That's what you used to call him, Travers, which was his surname. He used to come and play with you sometimes. His mother bred Siamese cats."

"I don't remember"

"It's a long time ago. A world away."

"I'm here in it now, in that world."

"So you are. Isn't it odd?"

"Yes," I agreed slowly. "It is."

"Who else have you met? Anyone else?"

"J. Rolls Eaglewood. The same man, but old and with a walking stick."

"J. Rolls!" She laughed. "I don't suppose you remember Russet."

"No panties," I said.

"That's just the sort of thing you *would* remember."

"I remember Jimmy being killed."

"Poor boy. A nice kid."

"J. Rolls has a touch of the tyrants," I said.

"Always had. Ruled his yard like iron, and our village too. So the old monster's still training. . . . He would never hear a word against

Russet. He sacked his jockey just for laughing at a joke someone made about her. There was the heck of a fuss. What happened to Russet?"

"I don't know yet. There's a granddaughter now, called Izzy. She was Ken McClure's girlfriend for a while." I paused. "Mum, did you ever know why Kenny McClure killed himself?"

After a brief silence she said, "Depression, I suppose. It was a dreadful shock at the time. He was always popular. He used to take you round the course in his jeep. I never believed the rumors."

"What rumors?"

"Something to do with drugs. With ordering the wrong drugs. Some dreadful drug. That's all it was, a rumor. People trying to explain why he would kill himself when he was so well liked, and a good vet. It was really upsetting."

"How did he kill himself?"

"Shotgun. Blew his head to pieces. Darling, don't make me remember, it made me feel ill for days at the time. Just thinking about it now brings it all back."

"Sorry."

The strength of her reaction surprised me. I'd never speculated about her lovelife because as far as I knew it was nonexistent between husbands. But at twenty-something, a widow and as striking as her photos bore witness, she must, as I now saw, have been at least ready and available for love. She'd been actively waiting, I thought, for a John Darwin.

Always alarmingly able to interpret my silences, my perceptive mother said, "Kenny was married. It wasn't right for him to leave his wife and children. We both agreed on that. So it didn't last very long. It was over years before he killed himself. I saw him often, but we were just friends. Is that what you wanted to know?"

"I think so, yes."

"I'd prefer you didn't tell your friend Ken."

I smiled down the wire. "OK, I won't."

"He was a nice man, darling."

"I trust your judgment."

"You know," she said tentatively, "if you can help Ken in his troubles, it would be sort of fitting. Don't let him do what his father did. I would have given anything to know what was troubling Kenny . . . to have stopped him. But he never told me . . . we were no longer so close . . . so help his son for me and Kenny, will you?"

I was extraordinarily moved. Parents were full of the most amazing surprises.

"I will help him," I promised, "if I can."

I went along to the hospital at eight the next day determined to dig everything I could out of Ken, but instead of a quiet private chat early on a Sunday morning I found the whole place seething with activity.

A police barrier denied entry to the rear car park, which was itself full of police cars, with and without flashing lights.

An arm of the law also prevented my entry on

foot. Across the tarmac I could see Carey Hewett in his by-now familiar state of distress. I'd never seen him otherwise. Ken, in the same group, showed strain in every muscle.

"You can't go in, sir," the law said.

I shouted "Ken!" which he heard. He lifted his head, waved and walked over.

"God knows what's happening," he said. "The fire service were apparently here all day yesterday with the insurance people, sifting through the mess looking for absolute proof of arson."

"And did they find it?"

"They didn't say. But what they did find was a *body.*"

6

"Whose body?" I asked automatically.

"No one knows," Ken said. "Carey's just got here, a minute after I did."

We talked across the barrier, the policeman saying that I, as an unauthorized person, couldn't be let in.

"I authorize him," Ken said persuasively. "I work here and I need him."

The policeman wavered, took a quick look around, saw no senior officers or disapproval, and let me pass as if not quite noticing I'd taken the crucial step. I went across with Ken to join the group round Carey Hewett, who looked at me unseeingly and didn't question my being there.

He wore Sunday-morning casual clothes of checked shirt and maroon sweater, not his usual neat collar and tie under a white lab coat. Some of his air of authority was lost in consequence, and on top of that he looked a bewildered and worried man. He hadn't had time to shave, I guessed, seeing the dusting of gray beard, nor probably to have had breakfast, as he looked peaked and hungry. This last shock on top of what he had lost had noticeably aged him.

"I don't understand how anyone could have

been in the building so late on Thursday," he was saying. "Everything was locked as usual when we left. And everyone has been accounted for. If anyone was in the building it wasn't one of our people."

"Could have been the arsonist," one of the men in the group said. "It's been known for people to be trapped in their own fires."

He was a plainclothes policeman, I gradually discovered, though no one made clear introductions after my arrival and I never heard his name. Carey's tolerance of my presence gave me credence and in fact he mentioned later that he was quite glad Ken had a friend to support him, wishing ruefully that he had someone to lean on himself.

It appeared that a police pathologist was at that moment inside the burnt-out shell, but extreme care was having to be taken with shoring up all outer and inner walls as parts of the structure could be pushed over by the palm of a hand. I gathered gradually that the body had been found in the general area of what had previously been the pharmacy and had been burned beyond any chance of easy recognition. Even its sex hadn't yet been determined.

"They apparently found the body last night," Ken told me as an aside, "but the light was fading and as the place is so unsafe they decided to leave things alone until they could see what they were doing by daylight. So they posted police guards and came back this morning not long before I got here. What a bloody *mess!*"

"It could be worse," I said.

"How do you mean?"

"It might have been one of you in there. One of you might have disturbed the arsonist and been bumped off for your pains."

"I suppose so." The thought didn't especially alarm him. "There's often one of us around here at night when we've got patients in the boxes. Scott was in and out all day yesterday looking after the mare, and I came three times to check on her. Belinda and I both came by when we got back from Stratford and again last thing before bedtime. We saw the police here both times but I thought it was just because the building is dangerous." He paused briefly. "Scott should be back here at any minute."

"So the mare's doing all right?"

"Fingers crossed."

We left the group and went over to look at the two patients. They both seemed half asleep, standing quietly, alive and recovering.

"What's wrong with this one?" I asked of the one next door to the mare.

"He had wind troubles. Couldn't get air down to his lungs under pressure because one side of his larynx is paralyzed. Quite common in big horses. I put in a suture to hold that side of his larynx permanently open so he can breathe better when he's blowing hard. He could have gone home yesterday but his trainer's shorthanded and wanted him to stay in our care until tomorrow. He's been no problem, thank God."

"You operated on him here in the hospital?"

"Sure."

"Full anesthetic?"

"Yes. It's a fairly long procedure, fifty minutes or so. I did him on Wednesday morning. He'd been scheduled for the op for a couple of weeks. It wasn't an emergency."

"Have the horses that died all been emergencies?"

He thought briefly and shook his head. "One died out here of heart failure after a successful operation to remove a knee chip. Simple routine thirty-minute arthroscopy. I took out a chipped-off piece of bone from his knee."

"He died out here?"

Ken nodded. "It was a valuable colt. We took extra-special care. Scott stayed here all night after the op checking him regularly and watching the monitor. One minute he was all right. Next minute, dead."

"That couldn't have been your fault."

"Tell that to the owner. The horse was *here*. That was the trouble."

"Did Scott actually see him fall?"

"No, I don't think so. To be honest, I think Scott went to sleep, though he swore blind he didn't. But it's hard to stay awake here all night when there's nothing happening. And he'd been working all day, too. He was awake when I left him, which was when I checked the horse at about eleven. Scott phoned me in a panic about five, but I reckon the colt had been dead an hour

165

or so by then. We did an autopsy, but," he shrugged, "we found nothing amiss. His heart had just stopped."

"Is that common?"

"Not really. More common after a hard race. They sometimes die in the racecourse stables afterwards."

"Did you make out that list?"

"Haven't had a minute." He withdrew his attention from the patient that hadn't died and seemed as ambivalent as ever about the ones that had.

"What did you do wrong?" I said.

He opened his mouth with shock and closed it again.

"Nothing," he said unconvincingly.

"Something must have been wrong."

He made a movement of his head like the beginning of a nod, and then thought better of it.

I said, "Why don't you just tell me?"

He gave me a lengthy unhappy look and shrugged his shoulders.

"The first one," he began tentatively, his long face miserable, his mind still not totally committed, "I thought afterwards . . . maybe I'd missed . . . but it seemed so illogical . . . and anyway, it wouldn't have been that that killed him, it would have worn off anyway in the end . . ."

"What, Ken? What would have worn off?"

"Atropine," he said.

I could see why Belinda was so sure I wouldn't be able to sort out the veterinary puzzle. Atropine, to me, was merely a word I'd heard before and never bothered to look up.

"Is that a poison?" I asked.

His doubt of me echoed my own. He said patiently, "It's poisonous. It's belladonna. But it has its uses. It relaxes things. Stops spasms."

"Stops the heart?"

He shook his head. "Enough of it in a horse could cause ileus."

I looked at him.

"Sorry. It could stop movement in the gut. That's what ileus means. So with enough atropine, the gut would stop working and become distended with fluid and gas and cause unrelenting pain, and you'd have no option but to take the horse to surgery. But you wouldn't find any obstructions or kinks or twists. You could get rid of a lot of the gas . . . empty the colon like I did with the mare, and so on . . . and close up, and the gut would start working again normally when the atropine wore off. Only that's not what happened. They both died under anesthesia."

"Both?"

"I can't be sure . . ."

Irritatingly at that point, Scott yelled across to Ken from the gateway to come and tell the policemen to let him in past the barrier. Ken obligingly went over and returned not only with Scott but with two others of the vets, Oliver Quincy and Lucy Amhurst, living proof that bad news traveled like lightning even before breakfast on Sundays.

167

"You know Peter, don't you?" Ken asked his two colleagues, bringing them across to the boxes, and they nodded to me uninterestedly and focused only on who it was who had died in the fire.

Oliver Quincy had been tipped off to the body's existence by a friend of his in the police. He had immediately phoned everyone else in the practice and, sure enough, almost before he'd finished saying so, another two arrived, Jay Jardine and Yvonne Floyd; they were followed closely by Belinda, alerted by Yvonne, not Ken, to her annoyance.

Once I'd sorted out who was who, I had no difficulty: the vets were easily distinguishable from each other, in contrast to the anonymity of Ronnie Upjohn the day before.

They moved by consensus in through the main door, Scott, Belinda and I following, and came to form a conference in the office, fetching along the chairs from the entrance hall to accommodate the behinds. Carey Hewett alone remained outside with officialdom: his partners said it couldn't be helped and held their palaver without him.

Lucy Amhurst demanded to know what was going on, which no one, of course, could tell her. "We've enough dead horses for a glue factory, we've arson and we've a body. It's not bloody funny."

She was a positive, middle-aged, no-nonsense person with strong clean nails, a stocky countrywoman's body and years of goodwill to pony clubs in her eyes.

She sat in the desk chair as if by right and seemed to be accepted by the others as having seniority of tenure if not of age. She fixed a rather headmistressy gaze on me and said, "Excuse me, we know you're a friend of Ken's and have been helping him, and I know Carey accepts you, but I think you might explain a bit more who you are. We don't know you, do you see? We don't necessarily want strangers overhearing what we have to say among ourselves."

"I absolutely understand," I said neutrally. "I'll certainly leave if you would prefer it. But, um, I could perhaps help you in some way to find some answers."

"Are you a private detective?" She frowned, not liking the idea.

"No. But detective work is what I do, more or less, all the time. I'm employed to find things out."

"He's a civil servant," Belinda said flatly. "Some sort of secretary."

As usual, the British had no idea of civil service ranks. Someone had once asked the Commissioner, the austere top-of-the-heap mandarin who himself appointed other mandarins to top jobs, at what hotel he worked and how could he be sure of hailing a taxi. The vets didn't exactly ask my speed in shorthand and typing but pigeonholed me in that capacity.

"A snoop," Jay Jardine said disapprovingly.

Lucy Amhurst gave me a judicial inspection. "We can't afford anything extra at this point."

"This would be a freebie for Ken and Belinda."

A twitch of a smile moved her mouth. She looked round at the others with authority. "Well, if he's a good snoop, why don't we accept his offer? We do need some answers, God knows. If he doesn't come up with anything, we'll be no worse off."

There were shrugs. No one had passionate views. I quietly stayed and no one raised the subject again.

Jay Jardine, the cattle man, was thin, short, self-assertive and a fairly recent graduate from veterinary college. His conversation bristled with futuristic technology to the point where some of his colleagues asked for enlightenment. He was the youngest of the group and, it seemed to me, the least liked.

"Carey's dragging his feet," he complained. "We have to have lab space. You know we do. I phoned him yesterday evening again but he's still done nothing. I said I would do it myself but he says to leave it to him."

"He has a lot on his mind," Lucy Amhurst said.

"There are three or four facilities I can think of that would be willing to rent us space. If I don't get lab space we'll lose clients, can't he see that? I've already got to repeat a lot of tests and no one's pleased at the delay. Carey's too old to cope with all this, that's obvious."

The others protested up and down the scale from outrage (Lucy) to anxiety (Yvonne Floyd).

"He's sixty, isn't he?" Yvonne said worriedly.

She was young enough, as I was, to think sixty unimaginably ancient, but my father at fifty-six was only four years off the compulsory retiring age for the Foreign Office, and he, as I knew well, was still at the top of his exceptional mental powers. It wasn't so much simple age that was at the bottom of Carey's possible indecisiveness, I thought, but emotional fatigue at having lost so much. More people in my admittedly limited experience had become ill or rudderless under extreme loss-stress than had bounced all the way back with a curse at fate.

Yvonne Floyd, thirtyish, wore a wedding ring and emphasized her femininity with a luxuriant mass of almost black hair from which artful tendrils curved forward onto her cheeks and neck. Even so early, even in spite of the disturbing reason for the summons, she wore lipstick and eyeliner and a skirt with a black lace-edged underslip which showed when she crossed her legs.

Oliver Quincy hardly took his eyes off the legs, though whether from lust or absentmindedness I wasn't quite sure. Of all in the room, his response to calamity was the most relaxed. Though he, as the other vet occupied with horses, might have been most expected to share Ken's intense worries, he was the only one to try a joke.

"What four animals do women like most?"

"Shut up, Oliver," Lucy said. "We're not in the mood."

"It's funny," he insisted. "It will cheer us all up."

He was a brown-haired roly-poly sort of man in early middle age with a more comforting aura than the others: a better bedside manner, one might say, which must have encouraged the owners of his patients.

"A woman's favorite animals," he said carefully, "are a mink in the closet, a jaguar in the garage, a tiger in the bed—and a jackass to pay for it all."

I thought it hilarious, but no one laughed.

"I heard it last week," Lucy said.

Belinda said crossly, "How can you joke with some poor person lying dead over there?"

"That poor person probably scored an owngoal."

Belinda and Oliver didn't get on, I saw, and reckoned it was because of her habitual jealousy of anyone sharing Ken's time.

Yvonne said anxiously, "What will happen if the whole partnership falls to pieces?"

Everyone glanced at her and away, as if they'd all had the thought and hadn't wanted to express it.

Lucy after a pause said sturdily, "We've got the Portakabin. We can buy new supplies. The building's insured. We're all still alive. We've still got the hospital. Carey said all that himself. Of course the partnership won't fall to pieces."

"If it does," Oliver said easily, "I'm hiring."

"What do you mean?" Lucy asked.

"I'm talking *Quincy* and Partners," he said. "I'm the oldest of us here. We all need our jobs. We know all our clients. If Carey bows out, we go on as before, but without him. With me, instead, as senior partner."

"He won't bow out," Lucy said, upset.

Smart Jay Jardine said, "We can bow him out. Tell him he's too old, he's lost our confidence. It's a great idea."

"It's a lousy idea," Ken protested. "Carey built up this practice. It's *his.* "

"It's normal," Oliver said. "The young herd always gets rid of the old bull."

"The old man won't stand for it," Scott said forcefully. "You'll see."

"You're a good nurse," Oliver told him. "You'll have to choose to stay, or go."

"We're all staying with Carey," Scott asserted.

Oliver's mild-seeming gaze moved from Scott's face to Ken's. "Quincy and Partners," he said, "can't be doing with a discredited surgeon. Sorry, and all that."

There was a blank silence, then Lucy said with nervousness, "Is this another of your jokes?"

Oliver might have laughed uproariously and told them he'd had them all on the hop, but he didn't.

"Who owns the hospital?" I asked.

The heads all turned my way, surprised at my speaking as much as by my question.

"Who owns the burned building?" I added. "Who gets the insurance money?"

"The bank," Lucy said doubtfully. "Mostly."

"The bank," agreed Ken. "They advanced the money to build both blocks. They hold the mortgage. All of us vets pay towards it every month out of our salaries."

"Carey organized it all years ago," Lucy said. "I was the only one of us with him then. When I first joined, he ran the practice out of his own house but then his wife died and he wanted to move. . . . Why do you ask?"

"I just wondered if anyone benefited especially if the whole place burned down."

They thought about it, but one could see that it was basically caring for sick animals they were interested in, not finance. Even Oliver Quincy had an air of not having planned his insurrection in terms of cash.

Lucy took heart from his silence. "We'll have to ask Carey," she said with satisfaction. "He's still in charge."

The seeds of doubt had been sown though: one could see the eventual end of Carey's road writ plain on Quincy and Jardine, writ tentatively on Yvonne Floyd, writ unbelievingly on Lucy Amhurst and wretchedly on Ken. The words had been spoken and couldn't be retracted, and might work on them like dry rot, disintegrating their partnership from within.

Ken's prospects looked appalling. I understood clearly what he had seen all along. Carey's loyalty to him couldn't last forever, and the others of necessity would ditch him. With such an ignominious departure hanging over him, no one at all reputable would take him on.

I thought of the Foreign Office "in" joke of defining total unacceptability as "turned down by Lagos." Every country had the right to turn down a diplomat's posting to it. Absolutely no one ever chose to go to Lagos, as Lagos ran Ulan Bator close in career nonadvancement. Lagos had to take what it could get. To be offered to Lagos and *turned down* meant the ultimate in rejection and loss of face. Job prospects thereafter, nil.

Into the silence in which his five partners variously reviewed their futures, Carey himself put his gray head.

"Oh, there you all are," he said, unreceptive to the atmosphere. "The police want to see you over in the Portakabin. They've set up some sort of incident room in it although I told them we'd need that space for clinics tomorrow morning."

His voice sounded tired. His manner looked defeated. I wondered how he would have acted if he'd known of the disaffection among his ranks: wondered if it would have stiffened him or caused complete collapse. No sensible way of finding out.

He, his partners and his nurses traipsed across the tarmac, Ken last. I walked beside Ken, slowing him down.

"The police will probably chuck me out," I

said. "I'll wait for you back in the office if they do. This is all getting serious. You must tell me things without reservation."

"It was always serious," he objected.

"Terminal then."

He swallowed, his sharp Adam's apple making an up-and-down journey in his long pale neck.

"All right," he said.

Belinda looked back to us, waited and tucked her arm through Ken's. To do her justice, she was still unfalteringly linking her star to his, believing in him absolutely.

We went into the Portakabin where a constable was taking names and asking everyone to sit on the flip-up chairs lining the walls. I gave my name and sat down like everyone else and stayed quiet for as long as possible.

The senior policeman in charge, middle-aged, local accent, air of sober reliability, still without a name as far as I was concerned, said he was interested in knowing who had left the main veterinary building last on Thursday, before the fire.

Yvonne Floyd said that when she left at seven only Carey, working in his office, had remained.

"Seven?" asked the law. "Was that your normal time?"

"We hold small-animal clinics on Mondays and Thursdays from five to seven. I do Thursdays."

The policeman looked at the lace-edged slip and the long crossed legs and quite likely decided to buy a dog. He slid his eyes away reluctantly and sought confirmation from Carey.

Yes, Carey agreed wearily. Thursday had been a long bothersome day. The painters had been underfoot. A horse had died during an operation. He'd helped Yvonne with the clinic because they were short of a nurse, and then he'd had a good deal of telephoning and paperwork to see to. He hadn't left until after eight. At that time he'd checked into every room to make sure he was the last, then he'd let himself out and locked the front door from the outside. He'd then walked back to the hospital, which was locked but had a light on in the office, and had gone on along to the stable boxes where he'd found Scott checking on the three inmates there. He'd said goodnight to Scott and driven home.

"And after that, sir?"

Carey looked nonplussed. "Do you mean, what did I have for dinner? Things like that?"

"No, sir, not exactly. I meant, when did you find out that your place was on fire?"

"Oh, I see. The people who live over the shoe shop across the road, they phoned me. They said they'd already called the fire brigade."

The policeman nodded as if he'd heard that already and asked which of us was Scott.

Scott identified himself, broad-shouldered, lean, the power machine.

"Scott Sylvester, qualified veterinary nurse."

"Large animals," Carey supplemented.

"Did you see anyone around the place, sir, after Mr. Hewett left?"

Scott said it had all been quiet. He'd settled

177

his charges for the night and gone to the Red Lion just along the road for a few beers. It had been a rotten day, with the horse dying. Around closing time, someone had come into the pub and said the vets' place was on fire, so he'd belted back to help and found the fire department had got there first.

The policeman asked how many people had keys to the burned building.

"We all do," Carey said. "Also the senior secretary has some, and so do the cleaners, of course."

The policeman took a patient breath. "When do the cleaners come in?"

"Eight o'clock every weekday."

"And er . . . had they arrived when you left?"

"What?" Carey said, briefly puzzled. "Oh no. They come at eight in the morning, not at night."

The policeman made a note, which I speculated might be a memo to ask the cleaners if any of their number was missing. Vets' pharmacies held salable drugs: a thieving cleaner might even have been issued with a shopping list. But a thief after drugs didn't necessarily explain the fire.

Carey said, "I suppose it's impossible to tell if someone broke in through a window?"

The policeman nodded. "Can you tell me if the internal doors were locked, sir?"

"Just the pharmacy and the path lab," Carey said, shaking his head. "We might close the other

178

internal doors, but we very seldom locked them. When I left on Thursday, only the pharmacy and path-lab doors were locked."

"Would they be spring locks, sir, or mortise?"

Carey looked blank. "Mortise, I think."

"Would you have keys with you now, sir?"

Carey nodded and produced a bunch as substantial as Ken's, if not even larger. Carey's too were labeled, and on request he identified the right keys to the policeman.

"Mortise locks," the policeman said, nodding.

"What difference does it make?" Carey asked.

"You see, sir," came the patient explanation, "when wooden doors and frames burn away, the lock itself often doesn't. It falls to the floor and the heat may not melt it, you understand?"

Everyone nodded.

"The investigators now in your building have found a lock they think is lying in the position of the pharmacy door. It's a mortise lock, and it is in the *open* position."

The significance of this information landed like lead in the communal consciousness, though no one said anything.

"We'd like to borrow your keys, sir, to find out if they have the right lock."

Carey silently handed over the keys. The senior policeman handed them to his constable, showing him the key in question and telling him to take it over to the investigators, to wait there, and finally bring the keys back. The constable took the bunch and went away and the senior policeman then asked how many people had a key to the pharmacy.

"We all do," Carey said, sighing.

"Including the senior secretary, sir?"

Carey nodded.

"And the cleaners?"

Carey said defensively, "We have to keep the place spotless. And each cabinet has its own lock, of course. The secretary and cleaners don't have keys to those."

"Glass-fronted cabinets, sir?"

Carey nodded.

"The investigators say there was a great deal of melted glass in that area. The room was totally gutted. The roof obliterated anything remaining, when it fell. The firemen have been pumping tons of water out of the ruins. There seems to be no chance of identifying anything in the pharmacy, which means we can't identify what's missing, if anything is. We just ask you, all of you, to make a list of what you know was in the pharmacy, so that if any of it turns up in other hands, we can proceed further with our enquiries."

"It's hopeless," Lucy protested.

"Please try."

I thought of a quick way to get at least some of the answers, but decided I would tell Carey later. If I drew attention to myself at that point, I thought, I could be turned out pretty fast, and it was definitely more interesting to be present.

Lucy asked, "Is it true this body was in the pharmacy?"

"In that area," the policeman confirmed.

"What do you mean, area?"

The policeman seemed to add up the pros and cons of answering but finally said that some of the internal walls had crumbled under the weight of the roof. The pharmacy, as a four-sided room, no longer existed.

"Oh God," Lucy said.

Jay Jardine asked, "How badly was the body burned?"

"An examination is still proceeding, sir."

"How long will it take you to find out who he is?" Jay Jardine again.

"We can't tell, sir." A brief pause. "Some bodies are never identified."

"But what about missing people?" Lucy asked.

"Vagrants, the homeless, runaways, migrant workers, madam, people like that never turn up on lists of missing people."

"Oh."

"And I'd like to ask all of you," the policeman said, "whether you know of anyone who holds a grudge against any or all of you. Have you dismissed anyone recently? Have you received any hate mail? Has anyone threatened you? Have you been engaged in any litigation? Have you in the course of your work come across anyone who holds you responsible for a pet's death? Do you know anyone you might think of as unbalanced or obsessed?"

"Wow," Yvonne said. "That covers half the human race."

Oliver Quincy looked at Ken and said to the policeman, "We've had several horses die in the hospital recently and the owners are screaming."

"Details, sir?"

Carey took over, explaining the difficulties of equine anesthesia. The policeman wrote notes.

"Have any of those owners threatened you, sir?"

Carey shook his head.

Ken said forcefully, "If it had been those owners, it would have been the hospital they would have burned, and the body in it would have been mine."

No one laughed.

"Did they threaten you, sir?" The policeman consulted his list. "Kenneth McClure, equine surgeon?"

"Right. And I've received no threats. Not that sort of threat, anyway."

"What sort, sir?"

"Oh, just that they'll never send a horse into my care again, that sort of thing."

The policeman seemed to think that sort of threat more violent than Ken did, but then Ken was no doubt right: if he had been the target, it would have been he and the hospital under the torch.

The policeman flicked through his notes and after a pause asked Carey, "When you left the premises, sir, and checked the pharmacy door, was it already locked?"

"Yes," Carey said. "I told you."

"So you did, sir. But what I mean is, who actually locked it? Was it you yourself who locked it earlier?"

Carey shook his head.

"I locked it," Yvonne said. "I locked it as usual after the clinic."

The policeman glanced at the legs and suffered a spasm of regret, then pulled himself together, sighed and rubbed his fingers down his nose.

"And who locked the laboratory?"

"Probably I did," Jay Jardine said. "I had some tests in there that I didn't want to be disturbed." He laughed without mirth. "I suppose there's nothing left of those, either?"

"Very unlikely, sir." The policeman cleared his throat. "At what time were you last on the premises?"

Jay Jardine stared and took offense. "Are you suggesting that *I* set fire to the place?"

"I'm trying to establish a pattern, sir."

"Oh." Jardine still looked annoyed. "I locked up when I left at about four. I was called out to a sick cow. Anything else?"

"I'd like to make a list of where you all were during the evening." The policeman turned to a fresh page in his spiralbound notebook. "Starting with Mr. Hewett, please sir."

"I told you, I left after eight and went home."

"How far away is home, sir?"

"Are all these questions necessary?" Carey protested. "You surely can't think one of *us* started the fire?"

"We can't tell who started it, sir, but we'd like to eliminate as many people as possible."

"Oh, I see. Well, I live five minutes away."

"By car?"

"Of course by car."

"And you spent the evening with your wife?"

The policeman, not insensitive, observed the mental wince of everyone there and was ready for Carey's reply.

"My wife's dead."

"Very sorry, sir. You were alone, then, sir?"

"I suppose so. I got some supper, played some music, read the newspaper. I don't think of it as being alone, but if you mean was anyone else there, no, they weren't."

The policeman nodded, made a note and continued to the next name on his list.

"Mrs. Amhurst?"

"Miss," Lucy said.

The policeman gave her a slow reconnoitering look as if establishing a base against which to test her answers. A good detective, I thought, and very experienced.

"Thursday evening, madam?" he asked economically.

She answered straightforwardly, without Jardine's umbrage. "I left here soon after lunch as I had about four calls to make in the afternoon. The last was to some sheep up on a hill above Birdlip. I suppose I left there at dusk, say before seven, and then called on a basset hound I'd had in surgery in the morning. He was all right. I

184

had a drink with the owners and went home. Didn't look at the time."

"Do you live alone, madam?"

"My sister lives with me, but she's away on a cruise."

"So that evening . . . ?"

"Same as Carey. I suppose, though, in my case instead of music I watched some television." She forestalled his next question humorously. "Don't ask me what program I watched, I've no idea. I'm afraid I've a habit of falling asleep in my chair after a long day."

"How far away from here do you live, madam?"

"A mile and a quarter. In Riddlescombe."

I looked at her with interest. Riddlescombe was the village where I'd lived with my mother, where the Eaglewoods still held sway. I hadn't realized it was quite so near to the outskirts of Chelten-ham. Distances seemed greater, I supposed, to children.

The policeman consulted his list.

"Mrs. Floyd?"

"Yes," Yvonne said, uncrossing the spectacular legs and crossing them the other way. "Like I told you, I went home at seven."

"And home is?"

"Painswick Road. About a couple of miles from here. My husband was away on business but the kids were in."

"Er . . . how old are your children?"

"They're not mine. They're my husband's. Fif-teen and sixteen. Boys. They listen to pop music and chew gum, hey man." Her impersonation in the last few words brought the first cracking smiles of the morning.

"And could they vouch for you, madam?"

"*Vouch* for me?" She gave him a comical grin. "They were doing their homework. How anyone can do homework with a million decibels battering their eardrums beats me, but they get fidgety in silence. They have a room each. Just as well. I always go up and tell them when I get in. They give me a wave. We get on pretty well."

"So you went downstairs, madam, I'm guessing, and cooked some food and spent the evening more or less alone?"

"I suppose so. Read the day's letters and a magazine. Watched the news. Then Oliver phoned and said this place was on fire, so I hopped upstairs and told the boys why I'd be going out. They'd got their videos going by then but of course they wanted to come too but I wouldn't let them, it was already late and they had tests the next day. I told them to go to sleep. My name was shit."

The policeman didn't bother to smother his smile and made the briefest of notes.

"Oliver Quincy, large animals?" he asked next.

"That's me," Oliver said.

Oliver got the same contemplative inspection as Lucy.

"Sir, your evening?"

"Oh, well, I was bloody tired. We'd had that

damned horse die and we'd had all sorts of post-mortems, the real thing and endless checks of the equipment and we couldn't come up with anything wrong. But I was knackered by the end, we all were. I was supposed to be going to the rugby club annual dinner but I couldn't face the monkey suit and the speeches and the din, so I drove out to a pub and had a couple of pints and some bar food."

"Did you pay with a credit card, sir?"

"No. Cash."

"Are you married, sir?"

"My wife goes where she likes and so do I."

There was something in his voice that belied the comfort-giving exterior, that belonged more to the ruthlessness with which he angled to supplant Carey.

"How did you hear the building was on fire, sir?"

"I phoned him," Carey said. "He was a long time answering but he was the first I'd tried to reach. I think of Oliver as my second-in-command. It was natural to get to him first and ask him to phone everyone else."

None of them met any eyes. A real case of *et tu Brute* in the making. Poor old Carey.

"The phone was ringing when I got home," Oliver confirmed, still not looking at his Caesar. "I phoned Yvonne, Lucy and Jay and told them, but got no answer from the others."

"I was in the pub," Scott said.

The policeman nodded, looking at his list.

"Mr. McClure?" he asked.

"I took my fiancée, Belinda here, and her parents, out to dinner. Peter was with us too."

The policeman again reviewed his list.

"Belinda Larch, qualified veterinary nurse? Peter Darwin, general assistant?"

We both silently nodded.

"And you three were together all evening, with Miss Larch's parents? In a restaurant?"

"Right," Ken said. "We were just about to leave when Lucy phoned me there."

Lucy nodded. "When we all got here I realized Ken was missing. I remembered he was on call, so I phoned his portable phone from the hospital office. Does all this matter?"

"Some things matter, some don't," said our philosopher policeman. "We can't tell yet." He consulted the list. "Mr. Jay Jardine?"

Jay alone resented the questions. "I told you."

"Yes, sir. Could you go on from after the sick cow?"

With unsuppressed irritation, in snapping tight-mouthed syllables, Jay said he'd gone home and had a row with his live-in girlfriend. She'd stormed out to cry on her best friend's shoulder. So what?

So nothing, it seemed. His answer got written down without comment and it appeared the present session of questions had come to an end. The constable conveniently returned at that moment with Carey's keys, speaking quietly into his senior officer's ear so that probably only

Carey himself, who was nearest, could over-hear.

The senior policeman nodded, turned and handed the bunch to its owner. Then, glancing round our expectant faces, he said matter-of-factly that the pharmacy key did fit the lock in question. As no one had expected it wouldn't, the news fell short of uproar. Carey, looking worried, said he *thought* he'd checked the door was locked, but he'd had so much else on his mind that now he couldn't swear . . .

"But I *did* lock it," Yvonne said. "I'm sure I did. I always do."

"Don't worry too much about it, madam. It's quite easy to get duplicate keys cut and, frankly, between you, you already have so many keys in use here that I doubt if any would-be intruder would have much difficulty in borrowing and re-producing the whole bunch."

Into a moderately stunned silence he poured a little professional advice. "If you're thinking of rebuilding, sir, I would definitely consider electric locks. No one can pop into the nearest hardware shop to copy that sort of key."

He had to leave with his constable and Carey stood and went with them, leaving a roomful of thoughtfulness behind.

"I did lock it," Yvonne repeated doubtfully. "I always do."

"Of course you did," Oliver said. "It's typical of Carey not to know whether he checked it or not. That's just what I mean. He's past it. The sooner

189

we tell him, the better." He stood up, stretching. "There's no point in waiting about here. I'm off to play golf. Who's on call?"

"Carey is," Lucy told him, "and Ken."

Oliver said without humor, "Then let's hope it is a quiet Sunday."

He walked purposefully out of the Portakabin, followed immediately by his chief admirer, Jay. Everyone else stood and in varying degrees of unsettlement moved in their wake. Scott, his internal dynamos whizzing again after the short inactivity, announced he was spending the day by the lake stripping down the engines of his speedboat in preparation for the waterskiing season, and marched briskly out of the rear of the car park. We heard the roar of his engine starting, and presently saw his strong figure riding a motorbike past the entrance.

"Does he always ride a bike?" I asked.

"He hasn't a car," Ken said.

Lucy said tolerantly, "He pumps iron, he's got pectorals you'd hardly believe, he's as physical as they come."

"He's a good nurse," Ken said to me "You saw him."

I nodded.

"Loyal to Carey, too," Lucy went on approvingly. "I couldn't live the way he does, but he seems happy enough."

"How does he live?" I prompted.

Yvonne answered. "In a caravan park. He says he hates permanence. He's kind though.

We took our boys to his lake one day last summer and he spent hours teaching them to ski."

Lucy nodded. "Such a mixture."

"Unmarried?" I asked.

"A chauvinist," Belinda stated, and the other two women nodded.

"We may as well all go home," Yvonne said. "Oliver was right, we can't do any more here."

"I suppose not," Lucy agreed reluctantly. "It's all dreadfully upsetting."

The two women walked together to the gate. Belinda urged Ken to come with her to Thetford Cottage because her mother was a disastrous cook and she, Belinda, had said she would do the Sunday lunch for everyone.

"You go on, darling," Ken said, "I just want to go over a few things with Peter."

She went with bad grace, disliking it, delivering a parting shot about us not being late. Ken waved to her lovingly and walked purposefully ahead of me into the office.

"Right," he said, settling into the chair behind the desk and stretching for a note pad to write on. "No secrets, no reservations, and don't use what I tell you against me."

"Not a chance."

He must have heard more commitment in my voice than he expected, because he looked briefly puzzled and said, "You've known me less than three days."

"Mm," I agreed, and thought about his father and my mother, and the promises I'd made her.

7

"Chronologically," Ken said, "if we're counting horses that've died when I wouldn't expect them to, the first one was months ago, last year, September, maybe. Without my notes I can't be certain."

"What happened?" I said.

"I got called out to Eaglewood's at six one morning. The head lad phoned me. Old man Eaglewood was away for the night and the head lad was in charge. Anyway, he said one of the horses was down and extremely ill, so I went over there and he was by no means exaggerating. It was a three-year-old colt that I'd been treating for a strained tendon, but otherwise he'd been perfectly healthy. But he was lying on his side in his box in a coma, with occasional tremors and twitches in his muscles, obviously dying. I asked the head lad how long he'd been like that but he didn't know. He'd come in early to feed as usual, and found him in that state but with stronger spasms in the muscles."

"What did you do?" I asked.

"I didn't know what was wrong with him, but he was too far gone to be helped. I just took some blood samples for analysis, and put him out of his misery."

"And what *was* wrong with him?"

Ken shook his head. "Everything in his blood was just about within normal limits though the blood sugar was low, but . . ." He stopped.

"But what?"

"Well, there were other things. It had been a good colt before the tendon injury. A winner several times over. Even if the tendon had mended decently it would have been surprising if he'd been as good again. I asked the head lad if he'd been insured, because you can't help wondering, but he didn't know. I asked old man Eaglewood later, but he said it wasn't my business. Then before he died, the colt's heart rate was very high and there was swelling round his eyes."

He paused. I said he would have to explain.

"He looked as if he'd been suffering for quite a while before I got there. I began to think about poisons, about what would cause spasms, high heart rate and coma. I thought a specialist lab's blood analysis would tell us, but it cost a lot and showed nothing. But horses don't die like that, I mean, not in the normal course of events. I talked it over with Carey several times and in the end he asked Eaglewood himself about the insurance, but it seemed the owner actually hadn't insured the colt at all."

"But you weren't really satisfied?"

"Well, I mean, it was a mystery. I began thinking how the colt had behaved before the head lad found him, I mean, maybe for several hours alone in his box during the night. What he'd been like before he got to that final state. I wondered if he'd had seizures, perhaps like epileptic fits. The tremors at the end might have been just the last twitches of something absolutely terrible. I hate horses to suffer. . . . If that colt had suffered the way I was imagining, and if it was the result of poison, I thought I'd never stop before I got whoever had done it prosecuted." He shrugged. "I never did get anyone prosecuted because there was no way of knowing who'd done it, but I woke up one morning with the answer in my head, and I'm certain that that colt was deliberately killed even if there wasn't an obvious reason for it."

"So what killed him?" I asked, fascinated. "Insulin," he said, "though I can't prove it."

"*Insulin?*"

"Yes. Well horses don't get diabetes, except so rarely it's almost never. You wouldn't give horses insulin for anything. If you gave a horse a big overdose his blood sugar would fall catastrophically and he would go into hypoglycemic shock, with convulsions and then coma, and death would be inevitable. It fitted the symptoms of the colt. I began looking for mentions of insulin in veterinary case reports, but there isn't much anywhere about normal insulin levels in horses. As they don't get diabetes, there isn't the need for research. But I found enough to know better what to look for next time in the blood chemistry—if there is a next time. And I found that in America three or four racehorses had almost certainly been killed that way for the insurance.

I showed Carey the case reports and we both told Oliver what I thought so that he would be on the lookout, but we haven't come across it again."

"It *must* have been for the insurance," I said, pondering.

"But Mr. Eaglewood said it wasn't insured."

"Did he own the colt himself?"

"No. As a matter of fact it belonged to the man who owns the mare. Wynn Lees."

I drew in a breath sharply enough for him to wonder why, and he sought for and found an explanation.

"I suppose it *is* a coincidence," he said. "But the mare didn't die."

"But for you, she would have."

"Have you still got that bit of gut?" he asked.

"I transferred it into the freezer," I said.

"Oh." He nodded. "Good."

"How much do you know about Wynn Lees?" I asked.

"Nothing much. I'd never met him before Friday morning. Why did you tell me not to trust him?"

I thought briefly about letting him know, but decided not to. Not yet. I might find a more oblique path. There were more ways of revealing truths than marching straight up to them, and if one could get a truth revealed without disclosing one's own hand in it, it gave one an advantage next time around.

Ken waited for his answer.

"Instinct," I said. "Natural antipathy. Hostile vibes. Call it what you like. He gave me the shivers."

There was enough truth in all that to be convincing. Ken nodded and said the man had had much the same effect on himself.

After a moment I said, "Is your mother still alive?"

"Yes, she is. Why do you ask?"

"I don't know . . . I just wondered if she'd had a chance yet of enjoying Greg and Vicky being here. They'd have a lot to talk about, with the wedding just ahead. And I'd like to meet her, too."

He looked at me in dawning dismay. "Why in hell haven't I arranged it? I must be mad. But there's been so much on my mind. How about today, for lunch?" He stretched a hand out to the phone. "I'll ask the old lady at once."

"Check with Belinda first, I should. Er. . . to make sure there's enough food."

He gave me a sideways glance but saw the wisdom of asking Belinda first. It was actually Vicky who answered and who received the suggestion with enthusiasm, who said it was a lovely idea and that she would tell Belinda it was fixed. Ken disconnected with a smile and redialed, reaching his own parent and evoking a more moderate response. Ken was persuasive, his mother slowly let herself be persuaded. He would pick her up, he promised, and take her home afterwards, and she would be quite safe.

"My mother's not like Vicky," he said, putting

down the receiver. "She likes things planned well in advance. I mean, at least days in advance, if not weeks. She thinks we're hurrying the wedding, but the truth is she's been against me marrying *anyone.*" He sighed. "She'll never make friends with Belinda. She calls her Miss Larch half the time. Parents!"

"Do you remember your father?"

"Only vaguely. I was ten when he died so I ought to remember him clearly, but I don't. I know him from his photographs. I know he played with me and was fun. I wish . . ." he paused, ". . . but what's the point of wishing? I wish I knew why he died."

I waited without movement, and he said, "He killed himself." It was clearly still a painful thought. "The older I get the more I want to know why. I wish I could talk to him. Silly, isn't it?"

"No."

"Anyway, it explains a lot about my mother."

"I'll remember," I said. I looked down at his note pad on which he'd written the single word "insulin." "How about if you let me write the notes while you talk?"

He pushed the pad and pen across gladly. I turned to a new page and after a bit of thought he began again on the saga.

"The next one I can't explain was soon after Christmas. That was the one I thought had been given atropine."

"What sort of horse?" I asked, writing.

"Racehorse. A hurdler. Trained by Zoe Mack-intosh out past Riddlescombe."

"*Zoe* Mackintosh?"

"Quite a lot of women train," Ken said reasonably.

Sure, I thought, but Mackintosh in my shadowy memory was a man.

"Is she a trainer's daughter?" I asked.

Ken nodded. "Her father, old Mac, he's still there, but his memory's going. Zoe holds the license and does what she wants when he isn't looking. He's a cantankerous old man and he's always breathing over her shoulder. She still employs Hewett and Partners because she's known Carey all her life—he and Mac are great buddies—but she's been huffy to me about the dead horses, and I can't blame her."

"More than one?"

"Two. And I'd swear they were both given atropine. After the second one, I tackled Zoe about it and she practically threw me over her left shoulder. Very muscular lady, our Zoe. But it does no good to have her going round implying I'm crazy as well as incompetent, which she does."

I thought it over.

"Were both these horses owned by the same person?" I asked.

"No idea."

"And were they insured?"

"I don't think so. You'd have to ask Zoe or the owners, and frankly, I'm not going to."

"You're scared of her!"

"You haven't met her."

"What were the horses' names?"

"What a question! I'm always told their names but I can't remember them after I've finished treating them. Well, seldom. Only if they're in the top rank. I attend hundreds of horses in a year. They're filed under their names in the computer—well, they were—but to jog my own memory I write them down as, say, 'Three-year-old filly, white socks, herring-gutted,' then I know at once which horse I'm referring to."

"Describe the atropine horses."

"The first one, a bay four-year-old gelding, large white blaze down its nose. The second one, a five-year-old gelding, chestnut, two white socks in front, white face."

"OK." I wrote down the descriptions. "How did they die?"

"Colic cases, both times the same. We had the colon out on the table, like you saw, and I was palpating—that's feeling—the smaller intestines for obstructions, and not finding any, and without warning their heart started to fail and their blood pressure dropped disastrously. The alarm signal went off and we'd lost them. Hopeless. But, like I told you, it does sometimes happen, so I didn't think much about the first one."

"How many have died like that now?"

"Four in eight weeks." He swallowed. "It should be impossible."

"Exactly the same way?"

"Yes, more or less."

"How do you mean, more or less?"

"They weren't all colic operations. Like I told you, the last one was putting screws in a split cannon bone, and before that there was the respiratory tract, a tieback like the one here now. Those two were both Eaglewood's as I told you at Stratford."

"Um," I said, looking at my increasingly chaotic notes. "Do you remember in which order they happened?"

"Well . . ." He thought. "Put the insulin colt first, even though he didn't die here in the hospital."

"OK."

"Then Zoe Mackintosh's four-year-old."

"Right."

"Then . . . Eaglewood's respiratory tieback."

"OK," I said. "Do you ever do tubing? I remember being fascinated as a child that you could put a tube through into a horse's trachea so that it could breathe better, with a plug like a bath plug that you can put in and out of its neck—in for rest, out for galloping!"

"Not often. It's still done here sometimes, but you can't run tubed horses in America, and it will end here soon."

"And here, once upon a time, a tubed horse with the plug out galloped into a canal and drowned?"

"Ages ago," he nodded, smiling. "In the Grand National. It forgot to turn at the Canal Turn and made a proper balls of it."

"Derby Day II in 1930," I said, from the depths.

He was startled. "How the hell do you know that?"

"I've an endless memory for trivia." I said it as a joke, but realized it was more or less true. "And trivia," I said apologetically, "means 'three roads' in Latin. Wherever three roads met, the Romans put up notice boards with the news on. Little bits of information."

"Jeez," Ken said.

I laughed. "Well, after the respiratory tieback, what next?"

He thought for a good while. "I suppose the next one was Nagrebb's show-jumper. The horse that staked itself, that I told you about. It splintered one of the jumps while they were schooling it at home, and when I went there it was still in the field with a sharp piece of wood a foot long driven into its near hind above the hock. There was blood pouring down its leg, and it was fearfully agitated and trying to wrench itself away from the two people holding its head collar. One of them was a groom and the other was the girl who rode it and she was in tears the whole time which didn't help the horse. Horses react to fear with fear. I think they can smell it. They're very receptive. Anyway, she was afraid he would have to be put down, and her father was jumping around yelling at me to *do* something, which upset the horse too. Between them, they'd wound it up into such a state that the

201

first thing I had to do was tranquilize it and wait until it calmed down and that wasn't popular either. In the end I got old man Nagrebb to take his daughter into the house as I could manage well with just the groom. So after that I pulled the stake out of the leg and inspected the damage, which was considerable but mainly muscular, with a few severed blood vessels but not the main artery or vein. Well, I did a clean-and-repair job and closed the skin with strong sutures. Staples, like you saw me use on the mare, aren't adequate for that sort of wound. It looked neat enough. I told the Nagrebbs the leg would be swollen and hot for a bit but with antibiotics it should heal satisfactorily, and I would take the sutures out after a week. They wanted me to promise the leg would be as good as new but how could I? I didn't know. I rather doubted it myself but I didn't tell them that. I said to give it time."

He paused, thinking back. "Well, then, as I told you, the leg was healing OK. I went out there several times. I took out the sutures. End of case. Then a day or two later, I got a panic call and went and found its lower leg and fetlock up like a balloon and the horse unable to put his foot to the ground. So we brought him here and I opened the leg because I was worried that infection had got into the tendon sheath and, like I told you, the tendon had literally disintegrated. There was nothing to repair. I'd never seen anything so bad. I got Carey to come and look at it because I thought Nagrebb would take his word for it better than mine, because of course we had to put the horse down and it was this famous show-jumper. Nagrebb had insured it, so we told the insurers the horse couldn't be saved. They agreed to the lethal injection, which I gave. Then shortly after that, old man Nagrebb started complaining that I must have somehow damaged the fetlock and tendon myself when I repaired the stake wound but I know for certain I hadn't."

He stopped again and looked at me earnestly. "I'm going to tell you something because I promised I'd tell you everything, but you're not to think me raving mad."

"You're not raving mad," I said.

"All right. Well, you might say I brooded about that horse, about why its tendon disintegrated and, well, there is something that would make that happen."

"What?" I asked.

"Some stuff called collagenase." He swallowed. "If you injected, say, two cc's of collagenase into a tendon you would get that result."

"How, exactly?"

"It's an enzyme that dissolves collagen, which is what tendons and ligaments are made of."

I stared at him. He stared apprehensively back.

"You are not raving mad," I repeated.

"But you can't just go out and *buy* collagenase," he said. "It's supplied by chemical companies but it's only used in research laboratories.

It's pretty dicey stuff. I mean, it would dissolve human tendons too. You wouldn't want to ram a needleful into your wrist."

I felt like saying Jeez myself.

"You can buy it freeze-dried, in small bottles," Ken said. "I looked it up. You reconstitute it with one cc of water. You'd only need a small needle."

Jeez again, I thought.

"What do you think?" he asked.

I thought he might possibly be in great danger, but all I said was, "Go on to the next one."

"Don't forget," he said, "that in between all those I saw dozens of other horses, racehorses, hunters and so on, that were quite all right. For every horse that died here, I operated on many others without incident. We get quite a few referrals from other veterinary practices, and none of them died. Telling the dead ones all at once makes it sound as if they were one after the other without interval."

"I'll remember."

"OK. Then the next one that died was the one out in the intensive-care box, that I told you about this morning."

I nodded. He seemed to have finished with that one, but I asked, "Who owned it?"

"Chap called Fitzwalter. Decent sort of man. Took it philosophically and didn't blame me."

"And do you have reservations, or do you think that that one did die of natural causes?"

He sighed heavily. "I took some of the colt's blood for testing, though he'd been dead too long

204

really. The results came back negative for any unexplained substance."

I studied his pale worried face.

"Even if the tests were negative, do you have even a faint suspicion?"

"I suspect it because it happened."

That seemed reasonable enough for the circumstances.

"And straight after that, the second Mackintosh horse came in, and it died on the table exactly like the first one." He shook his head. "It wasn't until after that second one that I thought of atropine. Because the pupils were dilated, you see. I thought I might have missed that the first time, or not seen the significance, anyway, because at that point there wasn't any *reason* to be suspicious."

"No." I sighed.

"Then last Thursday, the day you came, we lost the Eaglewood horse with the cannon bone. Just the same. Failing heart and diving blood pressure. I took blood samples before we began that operation and Oliver took more when the horse was beyond saving, but we'll never know the results of those as they were in the fridge in the path lab. I was going to send them to a professional lab for analysis."

"Was there anything—anything at all—different in the two Mackintosh operations from the one I saw you do on the mare? Apart from not finding any physical obstructions, I mean?"

"Nothing, except naturally that it was Scott

and Belinda who were with me, not you. Belinda runs the room, Scott does the anesthetic. We always work that way."

"Just the three of you?"

"Not always. Any of the others might come in. Lucy assists with ponies, sometimes. Oliver's often helping. I've assisted Jay with cows and bulls. Carey keeps an eye on things generally. He can turn his hand to anything if he has to, though nowadays he does small animals only. Yvonne, for all her glamour, is a neat delicate surgeon, a pleasure to watch. I've seen her put car-struck dogs and cats back together like jigsaw puzzles. Even a pet rabbit, for one little boy. She micro-stitched its half-severed leg back on. It was hopping around later." He paused. "The hospital has been our pride and joy, you see. Not many vets' practices have such good facilities. It's brought us a lot of outside work."

"Go back to last Thursday morning," I said. "By then all of you were apprehensive over almost every operation, right?"

He nodded mutely.

"So you checked everything twice. You had Oliver there. You were operating on a leg, not an abdomen. Go through it all in your mind, right from when the horse arrived. Don't skip anything. Go slowly. I'll just wait. Take your time."

He raised no objections. I watched him think, watched the small movements in his facial muscles as he passed from procedure to procedure.

Watched him shake his head and frown and finally move his whole body in distress.

"Absolutely nothing," he burst out. "Nothing, except—" He stopped, indecisively as if unconvinced by what he was thinking.

"Except *what?*" I asked.

"Well, Oliver was watching the screen, like you were. I glanced over a couple of times. I can't swear to it but I think now that the trace on the electrocardiograph—the line that shows the heartbeat—had changed slightly. I didn't stand and watch it. Perhaps I should have done, considering. But then of course the trace did change anyway because the heart wasn't working properly." He frowned heavily, thinking it over. "I'll have to look a few things up."

"Here?" I asked, looking round the bare office.

"No, at home. All my books are at home. And thank God they are. Carey kept all his in his office so that we could all use them for reference if something cropped up we weren't sure of. What the fire didn't ruin, the water will have done." He shook his head. "Some of those books are irreplaceable."

"Very bad luck," I said.

"There's no saying the troubles are over, either."

"Particularly not with an unknown body lying around. "

He rubbed a hand tiredly over his face. "Let's go along to Thetford Cottage."

"OK. But Ken . . ."

"What?"

207

"Until they find out whose body it is, well, don't go down any dark alleys."

He stared. He didn't seem to have worried in the least about the body or seen it as any warning to be careful.

"It was the arsonist," he protested.

"Maybe. But why was he setting fire to the place?"

"I've no idea. No one has."

"It sounds to me as if the arsonist himself didn't know he was going to start a fire until just before he did it."

"Why do you think that?"

"Cleaning fluid. Paint. They happened to be there. If you intended to set fire to a building would you rely on breaking into it and finding inflammable liquids just lying around?"

He said slowly, "No, I wouldn't."

"So just take care."

"You scare me, you know."

"Good."

He studied my face. "I didn't expect you to be like this."

"Like what?"

"So . . . so *penetrating.*"

I smiled lopsidedly. "Like a carpet needle! But no one remembers everything all the time. No one sees the significance of things all at once. Understanding what you've seen comes in fits and starts and sometimes when you don't expect it. So if you remember anything else that you haven't told me about the dead horses, well, tell me."

"Yes," he said soberly, "I will."

Vicky did her best to charm Ken's mother—Josephine—but in truth they were incompatible spirits. Vicky, spontaneous, rounded, generous, essentially young despite the white hair, was having to break through to a defensive, plainly dressed angular woman in whom disapproval was a habit.

Belinda, taking refuge in the kitchen, was knocking back a huge bloody mary (to settle her nerves and stop her screaming, Ken said, mixing it for her) and in consequence seemed more human.

Greg and I batted some conversation around without saying anything worth remembering and eventually we all sat down to roast lamb with potatoes, peas, carrots and gravy, the sort of meal I'd almost forgotten existed.

It wasn't very difficult, once everyone had passed, poured and helped the food and was safely munching, to introduce the subject of Ken's brilliant work on the colicky mare being met with suspicion and ingratitude from its owner.

"A most extraordinary man," I said. "Wynn Lees, his name is. I didn't like him at all."

Josephine McClure, sitting next to me, raised her head from the forkful she'd been about to eat and paid attention.

I went on. "He showed no fondness for his mare. He didn't seem to care about her. It almost seemed as if he wanted her dead."

209

"No one could be so heartless," Vicky exclaimed.

Josephine McClure ate her forkful.

"Some people are born heartless," I said.

Ken recounted the story of his having got permission to operate from Wynn Lees's wife. He chuckled. "He said she couldn't have spoken to me in the middle of the night because she always took sleeping pills."

Josephine McClure said tartly, "Anyone married to Wynn Lees would take sleeping pills as a matter of course."

God bless you, dear lady, I thought, and in an amused chorus with the others, begged her to enlarge.

"Ken," she said severely, "you didn't tell me you'd done any work for Wynn Lees. That name! Unforgettable. I thought he'd gone to live abroad. Stay away from him."

Ken said, bemused, "I didn't know you knew him."

"I don't know him. I know *of* him. That's not the same."

"What do you know *of* him?" I asked in my most persuasive voice. "Do tell us."

She sniffed. "He tortured some horses and went to jail."

Vicky exclaimed in horror, and I asked, "When?"

"Years ago. Probably forty years ago. It was a frightful scandal because his father was a magistrate."

Ken looked at her open-mouthed. "You never told me any of that."

"There's never been any reason to. I haven't heard his name for years. I've never given him a thought. He'd gone away. But if your man was heartless to his mare, it must be the same person come back again. There can't be hundreds of people called Wynn Lees."

"You have a good memory," I said.

"I pride myself on it."

"Ken's also been having a spot of trouble with Ronnie Upjohn," I said. "Do you know any scandal about *him?*"

"Ronnie Upjohn?" She frowned slightly. "He used to know my husband. It's very stupid of him to complain about Ken winning with that horse. Ken told me about it."

I said tentatively, "Is he in business? Does he have a partner?"

"Oh, you mean old Mr. Travers? No, that was Ronnie's father's partner."

I held my breath.

Josephine cut up some meat and fed herself a mouthful.

"I've lost you," Ken said. "What are you talking about?"

"Old Mr. Travers," his mother said acidly, "was a frightful lecher."

Vicky looked captivated by the contrast between Josephine's censorious manner and the pithiness of her words. Vicky would have given "lecher" a laugh. Josephine was serious. Greg, smiling, was maybe thinking that dried-up old Josephine needn't fear the attentions of lechers: yet she had been a happy wife once and there were still vestiges of that young woman, though her mouth might be pursed now and bitter.

"Upjohn and Travers," I said.

"That's right." She went on eating unemotionally.

"What sort of business was it?" I asked.

"I don't know: Something to do with finance." Her voice said that finance to her was a closed book. "Ronnie Upjohn's never done a day's work in his life, as far as I know. His father and old Mr. Travers were rolling."

"You know so much about all these people," I said admiringly. "How about the Eaglewoods?"

"Oh no, not the Eaglewoods," Belinda said.

Josephine gave her future daughter-in-law a sharp glance and made a breathtaking statement. "I suppose you're an advance on that Izzy girl."

Belinda, although agreeing, looked astonished. Backhander though it might be, she had received a compliment.

"What was wrong with Izzy Eaglewood?" I asked Josephine.

"Her mother."

Vicky choked on some peas and needed her back patted.

When order had been restored I said, "What was wrong with Izzy Eaglewood's mother?"

Josephine compressed her lips but couldn't resist imparting knowledge. Now wound up, she would run and run.

She said, "Izzy's mother was and is a tart."

Vicky was fortunately not eating peas. She laughed delightedly and told Josephine she hadn't enjoyed a meal so much for ages. Josephine's pale cheeks faintly flushed.

"Hold on a bit," Ken protested. "It's not Izzy's fault what her mother is."

"Heredity," Josephine said darkly.

"Who is Izzy's mother?" I asked neutrally.

"Russet Eaglewood," Josephine said. "Such a silly name. Izzy is illegitimate, of course."

"Leave it," Ken begged her. He looked at me rather wildly. "Change the subject, can't you?"

I said to Josephine obligingly, "How about Zoe Mackintosh?"

"Who? Oh yes. Should have been born male. She's never made sheep's eyes at Ken as far as I know."

"I didn't mean . . ." I shook my head and left it. "I meant, are there any nice scandals about her or her family?"

"Her old father's going gaga, if you call that a scandal. He always was a villain. They said he would take a commission from bookmakers for telling them when a hot favorite of his wouldn't win."

"Do go on," said Vicky fervently.

"The Jockey Club could never prove it. Mackintosh was too slippery. I heard he lost a lot of his money a few months back in a property crash.

You wouldn't think people could lose money in property the way the cost of houses goes up, but a lot of people around here did. I don't feel sorry for them, they shouldn't have been so greedy."

"What happened?" I asked.

"I don't know exactly. A neighbor of mine lost everything. He said never guarantee a loan. I remember him saying it and I remember what he said. He's had to sell his house."

"Poor man," Vicky said.

"He should have had more sense."

"Even millionaires can make that mistake," I said.

Josephine sniffed.

"How about the Nagrebb family?" I asked her.

"She's the show-jumper, isn't she? I've seen her on television. Ken looks after their horses."

"And, um, Fitzwalter?"

"Never heard of him." She finished her plateful, put her knife and fork tidily together and turned to Ken. "Isn't that man Nagrebb," she asked, "the one who got into trouble for training show-jumpers cruelly?"

Ken nodded.

"What did he do?" I asked.

"Rapped their shins with a pole, while they were jumping, to teach them to lift their legs higher," Ken said. "Difficult to prove. Show-jumpers are always rapping their legs, like hurdlers. Nagrebb's horses always had lumps and contusions on their shins. They're better these days, since he got a stiff warning."

Belinda said, "Nagrebb's daughter swore he didn't do it."

Ken smiled. "She does everything he tells her. She rode the horses while he hit their legs. She wants to win, and Daddy provides the wherewithal, and there's no way she's going to blow the whistle on him."

"A wicked world," Vicky said sadly.

Some degree of evil is the norm, my father had told me. Wholly good people are the aberration. What's aberration? I'd said. Look it up in the dictionary, then you'll remember it. Aberration, a deviation from what is common and normal. See the world as it is, he'd said, then see what good you can do in it. Lie abroad for your country. The inconsequential thoughts ended on the reflection that I, like Nagrebb's daughter, had been molded by a father's cast of mind.

When the lunch party broke up I left Thetford Cottage and drove to Riddlescombe village to see how much I remembered. I'd had only vague pictures in my mind but it was a revelation how much was vividly familiar as I drove down the long straggly main street.

The post office, the garage, the pubs; all were still there. Time hadn't swept away the cottages or changed the stone houses. The pond I'd thrown stones into had shrunk as I had grown, and a small tree in whose bark I'd carved P.P. now spread limbs that would be shady in summer. I parked the car and walked, and remembered who had lived where and who had died and who had run away.

It was like walking back into a lost land that had existed for twenty years in mothballs. Henley's, the all-purpose shop, still sold violent colored sweets and plimsolls and horror comics. Graffiti still shocked the prim in the bus shelter. Notices threatened bigger fines for litter. Volunteers were needed for rebuilding the games pavilion. The village, unlike the supermarket, was territory still well known, though the red telephone box had vanished and there was a bright new medical center where the old doctor's house had been.

Untouched by centuries, let alone twenty years, stood the tiny ancient church to which I'd gone on Christmas mornings and not much oftener. Surrounded still by a low stone wall, a patch of grass, haphazard yews and weathered gray anonymous gravestones, it remained as always an expression of hope against hope for the life everlasting.

I supposed that in these days of normal evil it would be locked between services and I walked up its crunchy gravel path without expectation, but in fact the old latch clicked up with a familiar hollow cluck under my thumb and I pushed open the heavy wooden door to smell the musty mixture of hymn books, hassocks and altar flowers that I'd thought was the presence of God when I was six.

An elderly woman, straightening the pile of hymn books, looked round as I entered and said, "You're too early. Even-song's three hours yet."

Perhaps I could just look round, I suggested, and she said she saw no objection, if I was quiet. I could have ten minutes. After that she was leaving and would be turning out the lights.

I sat in a pew and watched her busy about the little turrety pulpit, running a duster over the brass rails of what I used to think of as a Punch and Judy stage, where the vicar popped into view from the chest up and read sonorous incomprehensible poetry that echoed richly off the walls.

Prayer now, I supposed, was what was really called for, but I had lost the habit and seldom felt the need. If there were spiritual sustenance within those walls, for me it lay in timelessness and silence which couldn't be achieved in the ten minutes.

I wandered to the rear of the church and read again the small brass plaque still fixed high up inconspicuously.

Paul Perry. Years of birth and death. Rest in Peace.

My mother had persuaded the vicar to let it be put there, even though Paul Perry had lived in Lambourn. My mother had blown a kiss every Christmas Day to the plaque, and although on this return I didn't do that, I did wish him well, that very young horseman who'd given me life.

I thanked the old woman. There was an offertory box by the door, she said. I thanked her again and paid my dues to the past, and walked on down the road to the bungalow where we had lived.

It looked small, of course, and in the prosperous village still seemed a poor relation. The paint was old, the garden bare but tidy, the front gate, that I'd swung on, missing altogether. I paused outside and wondered whether or not to try to go in, but it would all be different inside and I would have to start explaining, and in the end I turned back with the old memories undisturbed and strolled again to the car.

I decided, before I left, that I'd go up to the end of the village, to the Eaglewood stables, and although Sunday afternoon was a taboo time for visiting racing stables I left the car outside and wandered in, hoping, if anyone should see me from the windows, to look like a lost tourist, harmless. A brief nostalgic look round was all I intended—to see if I could better remember the long-dead Jimmy.

In fact I got no more than six paces into the yard before being challenged with an authoritative "Yes? Can I help you?"

I swiveled. The voice came from a thin, fortyish woman in jeans and sweater who was up a stepladder fixing onto a stable wall a painted sign, bright white letters on newly varnished wood, saying "Don't Feed the Horses."

"Er," I said, improvising, "I'd been hoping to talk to Mr. Eaglewood."

"What about?"

I cleared my throat. "About insurance." The first thing that came into my head.

"This is an absolutely ridiculous time to do any such thing. Also we have all the insurance we need." She regarded the sign with her head on one side, nodded to herself and came down the ladder. Another two signs, identical, were propped against the wall at its foot.

"About insuring the horses," I said, beginning to see a purpose.

"Go away, will you? You're wasting your time."

A chilly little breeze cooled the thin February sunshine and swirled her thick tawny hair across her face. Pushing it away, she was self-assured in her good looks. Her vitality and natural magnetism generated a force field all of their own. She was instantly, to me at least, attractive.

She tried to pick up the ladder with one hand and both signs with the other, and I caught one of the signs as it was sliding out of her grasp.

"Thanks," she said briefly. "Perhaps you wouldn't mind carrying it for me, though it won't get you anywhere except over there to the opposite wall."

With a smile I followed her across the yard to where two hooks were screwed into the old brick wall at just above head height. She planted the ladder, went up a few rungs and maneuvered the sign she was carrying until two hoops on its back engaged onto the two hooks. Once the sign hung flat against the wall she gave it the formal nod of approval and descended to the concrete underfoot.

She held out her hand for the sign I was still holding.

"Thanks," she said. "I can manage now."

"I'll take it to where you want to put it."

She shrugged, turned, and went off through an arch into a further, smaller yard beyond, and immediately I went through there I knew where the hay was stored and how to get through a tiny trapdoor into a roof space, and how to look down on the lads without their knowing that Jimmy and I were up there, spying on them. They never did anything worse than pee in the boxes; it was simply the secret of our presence that had absorbed me and Jimmy.

The third Don't Feed the Horses, also, was hung on prepositioned hooks in an easily seen place.

"School parties come here once a term on projects," she explained. "We try to stop the little buggers handing out sweets to the inmates. For one thing, they can get their fingers bitten off, as I always warn them. They think it's clever not to listen." She gave me a head-to-toe glance which felt like a moving X ray through flesh and spirit. "What sort of insurance?"

"Insuring the horses against death."

She shook her head. "We don't do that. It's a matter for the owners."

"Perhaps Mr. Eaglewood . . ."

"He's asleep," she interrupted. "And I'm the

220

business manager. I run the finances. When the owners want to insure their horses we put them in touch with an agent. It's no use you talking to Mr. Eaglewood. He leaves all such things to me."

"Then . . . you couldn't tell me if Mr. Wynn Lees insured the colt that died here in a coma last September?"

"*What?*"

I didn't repeat the question but watched a hundred speculations zip through her mind.

"Or," I said, "did the owner of the horse that died during respiratory operation insure him beforehand? And—er . . . how long before the operation in which he died last Thursday did that horse split its cannon bone?"

She stared at me speechlessly as if not believing what she was hearing.

"Ken McClure is in a lot of trouble," I said, "and I don't think it's of his own making."

She found her voice, which came out more with plain curiosity than anger.

"Just who are you?" she said.

"A friend of Ken's."

"A policeman?"

"No, just a friend. The police rarely investigate the apparently normal deaths of horses."

"What's your name?"

"Peter Darwin."

"Any relation to Charles?"

"No."

"Do you know who I am?" she asked.

221

I suggested slowly, "Mr. Eaglewood's daughter?"

I kept every vestige of a smile out of my face but she must have known her reputation.

"Whatever you've heard of me," she said severely, "revise it."

"I have."

She seemed fairly satisfied, and in any case I'd spoken the truth. I hadn't expected the brains.

"If you know Ken, you know he had a fling with my daughter," she said.

"He's fond of her," I said.

She shrugged philosophically. "Izzy threw herself at him, poor little bitch. She's only seventeen, half his age. He treated her decently enough. She just grew out of it."

"He won't hear a word against her . . . or you."

She tested that for cynicism, but seemed pleased enough.

"It's windy out here," she said, "and the lads will be along any minute for evening stables, making a racket. My father will be walking round. Why don't you and I go inside where we can talk quietly?"

Without waiting for my assent, she set off with the ladder to return it to a shed, and then led the way not to the big looming main house but to a small separate two-story wing where she lived alone, she said.

"Izzy's gone off on a music course. She's much too impressionable. I expect hourly to hear she's met the perfect man. There's no such thing as a perfect man."

Her taste in interiors ran to antique woods and classic fabrics, ultraconservative, cool color temperature; warm central heating. On the walls, original oils, mostly of horses. Overall, a relaxed accustomed prosperity.

She offered me an armchair and sat in another on the opposite side of the fireplace, her blue-clad legs crossed, a telephone and an address book on a small table at her elbow.

"There's no way I'm going to talk to Wynn Lees if I don't have to," she said. "We don't train for him anymore and I won't have him in the yard. I can't understand why my father agreed to train the colt for him in the first place, knowing his reputation. But the colt died of seizures, didn't it? Or at least, Ken had to put it down."

"Ken said that colt wasn't insured. Do you know if the other two were?"

"I never heard so." She lifted the telephone receiver, looked up a number, pressed a succession of buttons, and spoke to the owner of the respiratory-tract horse, asking about insurance. He seemed warm and friendly, and apparently the horse was not insured.

She repeated the conversation with the cannon-bone owner, with the same results.

"There were three days between the horse splitting its cannon bone and the operation," she said. "It was a stress fracture in a race. He seemed all right afterwards but the following day he was hopping lame. Ken came out with a portable X ray and told us the bad news. My father discussed it with Ken and Carey and they both thought the leg could be screwed and the horse saved. The owner agreed to go ahead with the expense because the horse was still an entire and could be sent to stud if he didn't get back his racing form. So those two horses just simply died in the hospital. They weren't insured. My father and everyone else believes Ken was careless, if not plain negligent."

I shook my head. "I've watched him do a difficult and critical operation on a broodmare, and I know he couldn't be careless or negligent. He's punctiliously careful every inch of the way."

She sat for a while thinking it over.

"Are you *seriously* saying," she asked, "that someone somehow engineered these two deaths?"

"Trying to find out."

"And Ken can't suggest how?"

"Not yet."

"But if it wasn't for insurance, what was the purpose?"

I sighed. "To discredit Ken, perhaps."

"But *why?*"

"He doesn't know."

She looked at me broodingly. I thought she'd known a lot of lucky men, if the tales were true.

"Of course," she said finally, "someone else besides the owner could have insured those horses."

How?" I asked.

"We had an owner once who wouldn't pay the bills. In the end, he owed us a worrying amount. He wasn't doing well in his business and couldn't find the money. His best asset was the horse we were training for him, and eventually we could have claimed the horse against the bills, but we would have had to have sold it to get the money and my father thought he might win the Grand National and didn't want to part with him. Do you follow?"

"Yes," I said.

"Well, he was due to run in a preliminary race and you know what it's like, horses can have accidents, and I was uneasy, so the day before the race I insured him for more than enough to cover what the owner owed us—and this is the point, I didn't tell the owner I'd done it."

"And did the horse die?"

"Not in the race. He won it. He was killed in a motorway crash coming home."

I made a sound of sympathy.

She nodded. "Nothing could give us the horse back. The owner was astounded when I told him I'd done the insurance. I did it in his name and I suppose he could legally have taken all the money and not paid us after all, but he was honorable, just broke, and he gave us what he owed. But I *could* have insured the horse and never told him and pocketed all the money myself."

I took a slow deep breath. "Thank you," I said.

"The insurers," she said, "might just possibly check that the name on the policy was the name of the registered owner, but even that's not certain, but they would never phone every owner to make sure the owner knew about and intended the insurance."

"Never, anyway," I said, "unless they'd grown suspicious."

"We haven't had any enquiry from any insurance company ever about proof of ownership."

"Well," I said, stirring, "I can't thank you enough."

"Like a drink?"

I listened carefully for overtones, for undertones, but there weren't any.

"That would be great," I said.

"Scotch or wine?"

"Either."

She rose fluidly, went over to a tray of bottles on a table and returned with two glasses full of deep tannin-rich Bordeaux. A wine to match the woman, I thought: good staying quality, earthy, mature, great body.

"How long have you known Ken?" she asked, sitting down again.

I thought "four days" might be inappropriate so I said merely, "I've known his fiancée's mother longer," which was accurate though not honest.

"Belinda!" my hostess said in wonderment. "That bossy nurse. She's the last one I'd have picked for him."

"She's not too bad."

She shrugged. "As long as they're happy."

I drank some wine. "They mentioned something about a boy who lived here long ago. Jimmy, wasn't it?"

Her face softened and she spoke with regret. "My little brother." She nodded. "A proper little tearaway, he was."

I willed her in silence to go on and after a moment she did. "Always larking around with a boy from the village. They got into trouble for throwing stones at trains and a policeman in uniform came to tick Jimmy off, and the next day he was hit by a lorry and died later without regaining consciousness." She smiled affectionately. "Funny how some things still seem like yesterday."

"Mm."

"I was ten years older than Jimmy. My father had always wanted a son and he's never got over it." She shook herself suddenly. "I don't know why I'm burdening you with this."

"I asked."

"So you did."

I was tempted to tell her I was the boy from the village but I still thought the anonymity of Peter Darwin, diplomat, might give me more chance of unraveling Ken's troubles, so I let the moment go by. She asked me in time what I did for a living, and I told her, and she asked about Japan and its ways.

"Everything possible's made from wood and paper," I said, "because trees grow and regrow. They are a frugal, orderly nation who continuously repress emotion from lack of space to scream and shout. Their houses are tiny. They work unremittingly hard. It's a male-dominated society and golf runs Shinto close as the observed religion."

"But you speak with respect."

"Oh yes. And with liking. I've left many friends there."

"Will you go back there to live?"

"If I'm sent."

She said with adult amusement, "Do you always meekly go where you're sent?"

"It's a condition of the service and to me it's normal, so yes, I go."

"I'd hate it. I grow roots in hotel rooms after one night."

She refilled our glasses and went on talking, switching on table lamps and drawing curtains as the light faded. I thought I had better leave and didn't make any move to, nor did I detect any "that's enough" maneuvers in her manner.

It's a wise man, I thought, who knows when he's being seduced.

Towards the end of the bottle came decision time. She'd made no overt suggestion, though by then all sorts of possibilities hung almost visibly in the air. I mentally ran through various forms of verbal invitation and came up with the least maudlin, the least lustful, the most humorous, the easiest to refuse.

Into a long smiling silence, lolling back in the armchair, I said casually, "How about a bonk, then?"

She laughed. "Is that Foreign Office standard phraseology?"

"Heard all the time in embassies."

She'd long had the intention and I hadn't mis-read her.

"No strings," she said. "Passing ships."

I nodded.

"Upstairs," she said economically, taking my glass.

So Russet Eaglewood and I enjoyed a lengthy no-strings bonk.

It was all true, not a panty in sight.

8

The next morning, Monday, I went down to the hospital to meet Ken in the office and found he'd been called out to deal with an acute laminitis.

This information came from Oliver Quincy, who had taken up the position he most coveted, the padded chair behind the desk.

"After that," Quincy said, "there's a wind op on Ken's schedule and this afternoon a referral from another practice, as long as they don't back out, so whatever you want will have to wait until after the next disaster."

He wasn't especially friendly: the comforting bedside manner wasn't to be switched on and wasted on the declared ally of the man he intended to oust.

"What's your gripe against Ken, actually?" I asked.

"You know perfectly well. He fucks it up."

"He's a good surgeon."

"Was." He stared at me judiciously. "You've seen him operate just once. You know nothing. You're no judge. He shouldn't have let the cannon bone die last Thursday."

"You were there. Could you have prevented it?"

"Of course not. Not my case. I wouldn't interfere in anyone else's case."

"Why do you think the horse died?"

He went on staring and didn't answer. If he knew, he wasn't telling. If he'd known how to stop it, he hadn't told Ken. I didn't much like his company so wandered back into the car park and stood for a while watching the comings and goings of a full-blown small-animals' session in the Portakabin.

Belinda was working there: I caught sight of her in her white lab coat as she came occasionally to the doorway, helping people with armfuls of cat or dog to maneuver up and down the steps.

The police had put a barrier across the back of the burned building, warning off foolhardy sightseers. Far away down the side drive I could see the unceasing activity of serious officialdom, still pecking away in search of guilt.

Over by the stable boxes, Scott was seeing to the unloading from a horse trailer of a skittish horse with flaring nostrils and tossing head, a horse full of vim and vigor looking not in the least ill. A groom with him led him into one of the empty boxes, bolting him in but leaving the top half of the door open. The horse's head appeared there immediately to watch the activity outside.

I strolled over as the trailer plus groom drove out of the car park and asked Scott if the broodmare was still progressing.

"Doing well," he said. "Her owner's with her at this moment.

231

"He's not?" I said, alarmed.

Scott said, shrugging, seeing no danger, "He has every right. She's his property."

The top half of the mare's box was also bolted back, and I went to it without delay and looked in.

Wynn Lees was standing there looking critically at the mare's big belly, his own pelvis thrust forward in such a way as to give him a big belly of his own. He saw the light change with my arrival in the doorway and turned inquiringly my way, his fleshy face already set in a scowl.

He barely remembered me from Friday morning except as some sort of assistant. He raised in me the same hackles as always.

"Get Carey to come here," he said truculently. "I'm not satisfied with this."

I turned away and asked Scott for Carey's whereabouts. Over in the Portakabin for the clinic, Scott said, so I went over there and delivered the message.

"What does he want?" Carey asked, walking back with me.

"He said he wasn't satisfied."

"He's a confounded nuisance, coming here like this."

He went into the mare's box but all I could hear of the conversation were remarks concerning the continuation of antibiotics, the removal of the staples and the approaching birth of the foal. After a short while both men came out not looking overly fond of each other, the one to leave in his Rolls, the other to go back to his invalids.

232

Scott and I looked over the door at the mare, who seemed quiet and unconcerned, and Scott decided to move her along the row to the far-end box, to leave the intensive-care box free for the new patients. I walked along with him as he led the great pregnant creature and asked another question.

"Last Thursday," I said, "when the cannon-bone horse died, did you notice anything you wouldn't expect in the trace on the screen? The electrocardiograph trace, I mean."

"Nothing I hadn't seen before. Nothing to worry about."

"Um . . . would you have seen it often before?"

"Often enough. Look"—he sounded aggrieved—"is Ken trying to say it was my fault the horse died? Because I'll tell you straight, it wasn't."

I said soothingly, "Ken says you're a very good anesthetist."

"And anyway, Oliver was watching the screen as well as me, you know."

"Mm."

I thought back to my own stint in front of the screen. I'd been concerned only about the regularity and power of the heartbeats, not about the exact shape of the trace. Unless it had changed to a row of Donald Ducks I wouldn't have noticed, and by the sound of things, if there had been any change at all, it had been subtle enough not to have registered even with Ken until I'd jogged his memory long afterwards.

Scott led the mare into the box and bolted the bottom half of her door and before I could think of anything else to ask him a small plain white van swirled into the car park and pulled up with a jerk. Scott gave it a disparaging look and strode muscularly over to greet the driver.

"Took your time, didn't you?" he said.

"Now you look, mate . . ." The driver hopped out belligerently. "My life's one long emergency call and I like a bit of appreciation."

Carey in his white lab coat hurried out of the Portakabin again as if he'd been waiting for this minute and gave the van driver all the appreciation he felt was his due.

"Good. Good. Well done," Carey was saying, going round to the van's rear doors. "Take it all into the office in the hospital. We'll unpack and distribute from there."

The van, it appeared, contained replacements for essentials destroyed in the burned pharmacy. It reminded me of the previous morning in the Portakabin and I went a few paces and offered Carey my suggestion for making the "lost" list that the policeman had wanted.

"I just thought," I said diffidently, "that if you asked all your suppliers to send duplicate invoices going back over, say, six months or whatever time you thought sensible, you'd have a pretty accurate inventory, allowing for daily or weekly usage."

He looked at me vaguely for long enough for me to begin to wonder if the marbles were indeed leaking away, but then his gaze sharpened and came alive with understanding.

"Good idea. Yes. A comprehensive list from the wholesalers and no need for us to rack our brains. I wasn't sure what you meant, at first. Well done. Get Ken to see to it, will you?"

He bustled off after the driver, who was carrying armfuls of boxes into the hospital, and I thought ruefully that Ken wouldn't thank me for the extra work. I followed him into the office and found Scott there, inspecting and carefully checking off each arriving box against a delivery note running to several pages.

Oliver Quincy's contribution to the activity was practically nil. He was waiting, he grumbled, for the appearance of worm powders as he couldn't go on his morning's first errand without them. Once they'd been identified and marked present, he took what he needed and departed, and Carey gave his back view a look of puzzled disappointment.

Ken himself returned at that point, blowing in with a gale of enthusiasm for the renewed supplies.

"Did the wind-op horse come?" he asked.

"Out in a box," Scott nodded.

"I thought they might cry off."

Carey cleared his throat. "I'm afraid I told him . . . I mean, I had to promise the owner I would . . . er . . . attend the procedure."

Ken demanded, "Do you mean, do the op yourself?"

"No. No. Just assist." From his voice, though, it had been a close-run thing.

Ken swallowed the insult to his ability as just another bitter pill in his mounting troubles and asked me to be there as well to take notes.

Scott looked surprised, Carey said it wasn't necessary, Ken stuck his toes in. "Will you?" he said to me, and I said, "Yes," and it was fixed.

Lucy Amhurst came in on a search for the new drugs and gave me a nod of friendly acceptance.

"How's the sleuthing?" she asked.

"Brick on brick," I said. "Slowly."

"What sleuthing?" Carey asked.

"Surely you remember?" Lucy said. "We gave him the go ahead yesterday morning to see what he could do for Ken. Oh no," she exclaimed, "you weren't there, of course." I guessed she was herself remembering the anti-Carey conversation, as her cheeks went slowly red. "We didn't see any harm in letting Peter find out whatever he could if it would help Ken."

"No, that's fine." Carey nodded. "I agree." To me he said, "Go ahead. Do what you can. An amateur detective!"

"He's a civil servant," Lucy said.

"A snoop," Scott added, using Jay Jardine's word.

Carey raised an eyebrow at me in amusement, said he hoped the drains were up to snuff and went back to his dogs and cats, telling Ken to let him know when he was ready to operate.

"Drains?" Scott asked, mystified, after he'd gone.

Red tape," I said.

"Oh."

Lucy, the wise woman, suggested Ken and Scott store the drugs somewhere safe, then took what she herself needed and followed Carey.

"Do you keep a list of who takes what?" I asked.

"We do normally," Ken said. "We have a book. Had." He sighed. "We all keep a stack of things in our cars, as you know. I'd never be sure at any given moment what I had."

He decided to put everything on the shelves in one of the storerooms as the drugs cupboard wouldn't hold everything, and I helped him and Scott carry the boxes across and arrange them in logical order.

I wanted Ken's undivided attention for an hour, but didn't get it. He sat in the padded chair and insisted on writing his notes on the steeplechaser with laminitis that he'd just visited.

"Funny thing," he said, pausing and looking up at me, "they say the horse was quite all right yesterday."

"What about it?" I asked.

"It reminded me . . ." He stopped, frowning, and went on slowly. "You're making me see things different."

Do get on with it, I thought, but prodded him more gently. "What have you thought of?"

"Another of Nagrebb's show-jumpers."

"Ken." Some of my impatience must have shown because he gave his shoulders a shake and said what was in his mind.

"One of Nagrebb's show-jumpers had laminitis . . . that's an inflammation of the lamina, which is a layer of tissue between the hoof wall and the bone of the foot. Sometimes it flares up and the sufferers hobble around, other times they seem perfectly all right. The condition makes them stiff. If you get the animal moving, exercising, the stiffness wears off, but it always comes back. So, anyway, one of Nagrebb's horses developed it and Nagrebb was annoyed I couldn't cure it. Then one day last autumn he called me out, and there was this same jumper in the field literally unable to move. Nagrebb said he'd left the horse out all night as it was warm enough, and in the morning he'd found him in this extreme stage of laminitis. It wasn't just in his two forefeet, as it had been, but in all four. Like I said, the poor animal simply couldn't move. I'd told Nagrebb not to give him too much grass as that always makes it worse, but he'd put him in the field anyway. I said we could try to save the horse, though frankly his feet were literally falling apart and it was a very poor prognosis. Nagrebb decided to put him out of his misery and called the knackers at once. But now, thanks to you, I wonder . . . but even Nagrebb wouldn't do that . . . but then there's that tendon . . ."

"*Ken!*" I said.

"Oh, yes. Well, you see, you could *give* a horse laminitis pretty easily."

"How?"

"All you'd need to do is put a tube down into its esophagus and pour a gallon or so of sugar solution into its stomach."

"What?"

He anticipated the question. "Several pounds of sugar dissolved in water to make a syrup. A huge amount of sugar or any carbohydrate all at once would result in very severe laminitis not many hours later."

God, I thought. No end to the villainous possibilities.

"The opposite of insulin," I said.

"What? Yes, I suppose so. But the insulin colt was Wynn Lees's at Eaglewood's."

"You said it would be pretty easy to put a tube down into a horse's esophagus," I remarked. "Not for me, it wouldn't."

"Child's play for Nagrebb. He could do it with a twitch. A twitch is . . ."

Yes, I nodded, I knew. A twitch was a tight short loop of rope attached to a short length of pole and twisted round the soft end of a horse's nose and upper lip. Held by that, any horse would stand still because it was painful to move.

"If he did it," I said, "there's no way of finding out." Ken nodded gloomily. "And what would be the point?"

"Insurance," I said.

"You keep on about insurance."

239

I brought a couple of folded sheets of paper out of my pocket and said I wanted to show him some lists.

"No, not now. Later. I simply want to do these notes before the op. I shouldn't have wasted all this time. Show me the lists later, OK?"

"OK." I watched him scribble for a bit and asked if I could use the telephone, if he didn't mind. He pointed to it for acquiescence and I got through to the Foreign Office, reversing the charges.

It took a while to reach the right desk. I was reporting my presence in England, I said. When did they want me to darken the Whitehall doorway?

"Ah." Papers were audibly shuffled. "Here we are. Darwin. Four years in Tokyo. Accrued and terminal leave, eight weeks." A throat was cleared. "Where does that put you?"

"Three weeks today."

"Fine." Relief at the precision. "Let's say . . . er. . . three weeks today, then. Splendid. I'm making a note."

"Thank you very much."

"Not at all."

Smiling, I put down the receiver. They'd given me a fortnight longer than I expected, which meant I could go to Cheltenham races, held during the last of those weeks, without dereliction of duty.

Ken had finished his notes.

"One more quick one?" I asked, lifting the phone.

"Sure. Then we'll get started."

I asked Enquiries for the Jockey Club and I asked the Jockey Club for Annabel.

"Annabel?"

"In public relations."

"Hold on."

Remarkably, she was there.

"It's Peter," I said. "How are the Japanese?"

"They leave today."

"How about dinner tomorrow in London?"

"Can't do tomorrow. How about tonight?"

"Where will I find you?"

She sounded amused. "Daphne's restaurant, Draycott Avenue."

"Eight o'clock?"

"See you," she said. "Got to rush." The phone disconnected before I could even say goodbye.

Ken looked at my expression. "Two bits of good news in one morning! Like a cat that's tipped over the goldfish." With awakening alarm he went on, "You're not leaving, though, are you?"

"Not yet." His alarm remained, so I added, "Not if there's anything I can do."

"I rely on you," he said.

I could have said that to me what I was doing was like walking through a fog of confetti looking for one scarlet dot, but it would have increased his worries. I thought he wouldn't have minded much if his patient hadn't turned up that morning because in spite of his success with the broodmare he was again looking pale and apprehensive.

241

The operation however went smoothly from start to finish. Carey watched intently. I watched and took notes. Scott and Belinda moved expertly as Ken's satellites and the prancing horse, fast asleep, got its larynx firmed and widened to improve its breathing.

From behind the safe section of wall, we watched him wake in the recovery room, Scott holding the rope-through-the-ring to steady him. He staggered to his feet looking miserable but most decisively alive.

"Good," Carey said, going off to the office. "I promised to phone the owner."

Ken gave me a glance of rueful relief, and he and I stripped off our gowns and left Scott and Belinda to clear the theater again ready for the afternoon stint, while also checking on the patient continually.

"You all work hard," I commented.

"We're understaffed. We need a couple of dogs-bodies. Would you like a permanent job?"

He didn't expect an answer. We went into the office where Carey was giving his thumbs-up report and after Carey had gone he finally said it was time for my list.

I brought it, much creased from folding, out of my trousers pocket, smoothed it down on the desk and added to it one more line. We sat in the chairs side by side and I explained what he was seeing.

"The list on the left of the page," I said, "is of the owners and trainers whose horses have died with question marks, to say the least. The middle column is the various ways they may or may not have died. The list on the right is . . . well . . ."

Ken looked at the list on the right and protested immediately, as it named all his partners plus Belinda and Scott.

"They're not involved," he insisted.

"All right. Look at the first and second columns, then, OK?"

"OK."

I'd written in table form:

Wynn Lees/ Eaglewood	Colt with insulin	Put down in stable
Wynn Lees/ Vernonside Stud	Broodmare/needle	(Alive)
Mackintosh	Colic from atropine?	Died on table
Mackintosh	Colic from atropine?	Died on table
Eaglewood	Respiratory tract	Died on table
Eaglewood	Cannon bone	Died on table
Fitzwalter	Chipped knee	Died in intensive care
Nagrebb	Show-jumper/ dissolved tendon	Put down on table
Nagrebb	Show-jumper/ laminitis	Put down in field

243

"Whew," Ken said thoughtfully, reading to the end.

"Are there any others?"

"Not that I can think of." He paused. "We had one that broke its leg thrashing around when it came out of the anesthetic after a successful colic operation. You've seen two satisfactory awakenings. They're not always so peaceful. We had to put that horse down."

"All the horses that died on the table," I pointed out, "could have been there by appointment." I forestalled his objection. "If two were given atropine, their time was chosen. They weren't random emergencies."

"No, I suppose not."

"The respiratory job had been booked in well in advance," I said, "and that cannon bone was fractured three days before you screwed it."

"How do you know?" he asked surprised. "I thought he'd done it the day before."

"It was a stress fracture in a race last Monday."

"How do you know?" he repeated, mystified.

"I . . . er . . . drifted up to Eaglewood's stable yesterday afternoon and asked."

"You did *what?*" Didn't old Eaglewood throw you out?"

"I didn't see him. Someone in the stable yard told me."

"Great God."

"So all the deaths on the table very likely had a common premeditated cause, and it's up to you to work out what."

"But I don't know." His despair surfaced again. "If I knew I wouldn't be in this mess."

"I think you probably do know in some dark recess or other. I've great faith that one of these days a blinding light will switch on in your brain and make sense of everything."

"But I've thought and thought."

"Mm. That's where the third list comes in."

"No."

"It has to," I said reasonably. "Do any of Lees, Eaglewood, Mackintosh, Fitzwalter or Nagrebb have the knowledge to accomplish all this? Has any of them had the opportunity?"

He silently shook his head.

"The knowledge," I said, "is veterinary."

"Let's stop this right away."

"It's for your own sake," I said.

"But they're my friends. My partners."

Partners weren't always friends, I thought. He was still raising barriers against belief: a common enough mechanism encountered perennially in embassies.

I didn't want to antagonize him or force him into destructive self-analysis. He would come to things in time. Understanding, as I'd grown to see it, was often a matter of small steps, small realizations, small sudden visitations of "Oh, yes." As far as Ken's problems were concerned I was still a long way from the "Oh, yes" stage. I hoped that perhaps we might reach it together.

"Incidentally," I said, "you know the pharmacy list the police want?"

He nodded.

"Carey agrees it would be a good idea to ask your suppliers for copies of their invoices for six months back or maybe more. He asked me to ask if you would do it."

He predictably groaned. "One of the secretaries can do it."

"I just thought," I said diffidently, "that if you did it yourself, you could get the invoices sent back to you personally."

"What for?"

"Um . . . just suppose, for instance . . ." I came to it slowly. "Just suppose someone here had ordered something like . . . collagenase."

The pale eyes stared as if they would never blink. After a long pause he said, "That wouldn't come from our regular wholesale suppliers. It would have to come from a chemical company dealing with research reagents for laboratory use only."

"Do you deal with any of those companies for the laboratory here?"

"Well, yes, we do."

A silence settled.

He sighed heavily. "All right," he said at length. "I'll write to them. I'll write to all I can think of. I hope they all come back negative. I'm sure they will."

"Quite likely," I agreed, and hoped not.

The afternoon's operation, with Carey coming in tired but vigilant and myself taking notes, passed off without crisis. The more accustomed I became to the general theater routine, the more impressed I was by Ken in action: his long-fingered hands were steady and deft, his whole oddly articulated height taking on an economical grace where one might have expected gangling clumsiness. His self-doubts seemed to evaporate every time once he had a scalpel in his hand and I supposed that that really was to be expected, because the doubts were thrust upon him from outside, not generated within.

He closed the incision with a neat row of staples and the hoist once again lifted the big inert body by its feet to transport it to the padded recovery room. Everyone followed and waited in safety behind the breast-high partition while the patient staggered and lunged back to consciousness, to stand in dumb and no doubt sore bewilderment.

"Good. Good," Carey said again, sighing nevertheless. "Nothing wrong with that."

He still looked overtired, I thought, still gray. He seemed to be functioning in irregular spurts of energy, not, like Scott, with inexhaustible stamina.

As if to confirm my impression, he rubbed a hand over his face and round his neck, easing out stiffness, and said, "I've asked Lucy to be on call instead of me. That makes Lucy and Jay tonight. Let's hope it's a quiet one. I'm going home."

Ken and I went with him along to the office where he phoned the referring vets to tell them their horse was recovering normally. In his voice there was only a taking-it-for-granted tone; no hint of excessive relief. Oliver Quincy, who'd been writing notes all afternoon while monitoring the closed-circuit television to check continually on the well-being of the morning's patient, said grumpily it was about time he was relieved.

"Jay's been spelling me," he protested, "but this isn't my job. It's Scott's or Belinda's."

"We must all muck in," Carey said, seeing no difficulty. "Where's Jay now?"

"Taking what he wants of the new drugs. Yvonne and Lucy have been in doing that as well. I got them to write down what they took."

"Good. Good," Carey said.

Oliver gave him an unfriendly glance which he didn't notice, and said that as he had two calls to make on his way home, he'd better be going. Jay put his head in briefly with much the same message, and they left together, thick as thieves.

Ken began writing his own professional notes to supplement those I'd taken and through the window I watched Carey go out to his car and drive away. I borrowed the phone again and got through to Vicky, telling her I was going to London and not to be scared if she heard me coming back in the early hours, or even later. Thank you, dear, she said. She sounded bored, I thought.

Ken looked up from his task. "All right for some," he said.

"You've got yours on the doorstep."

He grinned. "Is Annabel the girl at Stratford?"

"She is."

"You don't waste time."

"This is just a reconnaissance."

"You know," he said unexpectedly, "I can't imagine you getting drunk."

"Try harder."

He shook his head in friendly evaluation. "You wouldn't want to lose that much control."

He surprised me, and not just because he was right.

"You've only known me since Thursday," I said, repeating his own reservations.

"I basically knew you in half an hour." He hesitated. "Funny, that. Vicky told me the same."

"Yeah," I said. "An open book." I smiled and prepared to go. "See you tomorrow."

"See you."

I left the hospital and walked across the car park to the car. I would be early for the planned meeting: I'd have time for buying newspapers with accommodation ads. I'd get to know how difficult it would be to find somewhere to live, and how expensive.

Belinda came out of the hospital and went into the intensive-care box briefly to get it ready for the new incumbent. Leaving the first door wide open, she then took a look in the next box, where the morning's patient stood, and after that , went along for a routine peek at the mare. I watched her trim capable figure and wondered if time and motherhood would soften or harden her caring instincts. Some nurses grew gentle, some unsym-pathetic. A tossup, I thought.

She unbolted the mare's door and went in, and came tearing out at high speed yelling, "Ken. Ken." She ran into the hospital and I thought, Oh, God, no, and went over to the end box to see.

The big mare lay on her side.

There were no heaving breaths, no agitation in the limbs. The head lay floppily. The liquid eye looked gray, opaque, unseeing.

The mare was dead.

Ken came at a run, stricken. He fell on his knees beside her and put his ear to her brown body behind the shoulder, but one could see from his face that there was nothing to hear.

He sat back on his heels as moved and dev-astated as if she'd been a child, and I saw and understood his dedicated love of horses and the solicitude he unstintingly lavished on them with-out any thought or possibility of thanks.

I thought of the courage he'd dredged up to operate on that mare. Thought of the extreme skill he'd summoned to save her life while be-lieving he was risking his own future. Felt im-potently angry that so much holy nerve, so much artistry had gone to waste. In a way missing be-fore, when I'd only heard about murdered horses but hadn't seen one, I felt personally engaged in avenging them. It was no longer just for Ken and to please my mother that I'd do my utmost to pierce the fog, but now too for the horses themselves, the silent splendid victims with no defense against predatory man.

"She shouldn't have died," Ken said numbly. "She was out of danger."

It was a fraction too soon, I judged, to say I disagreed. Danger, in that place, wore many faces.

He smoothed his hand over the brown flank, then rose and knelt again, this time by her head, lifting the drooping eyelid, opening the mouth, peering down her throat.

"She's been dead for some time," he said. He stood up wearily and trembled as of old. "We'll never survive this. It's the absolute end."

"It's not your fault."

"How do I know? How does anyone know?"

Belinda, in the doorway, said defensively, "She was all right at lunchtime. When we brought the wind-op gelding out here I came along and checked, and she was eating hay, quite all right."

Ken was only half listening. "We'll have to have a postmortem," he said dully. "I'll see if I can get any blood." He walked away disjointedly towards his car and after a while returned with a case containing syringes, bottles and a supply of rubber gloves from the well-stocked trunk.

"I phoned the knackers on the car phone," he said. "They're coming to fetch her. I told them we'd need to do a postmortem at their place, and I'll have to get Carey and any number of outside vets to be there, and I don't think I'm going to do the postmortem myself. I mean . . . I can't. And as for what Wynn Lees will say . . ."

His voice stopped; the shakes didn't.

"He was here this morning," I said.

"Dear God."

I described what I'd seen of Wynn Lees's visit. "The mare was all right when he left. Scott moved her along to the end box afterwards and she was fine. You ask Carey."

Ken looked down at the corpse. "God knows what Carey will say about this."

"If he's got any sense he'll start thinking about poison."

It was Belinda who protested that I was being melodramatic, not Ken.

"But last time," he said, taking the idea in his stride, "when the Fitzwalter horse dropped dead out here, all the tests we could think of were negative. No poison. It cost us a lot in specialist lab fees, and all for nothing."

"Try again."

Without answering, he pulled on a pair of gloves and tried with several syringes to draw blood from various areas in the mare's anatomy.

"How did you say you would give a horse atropine?" I asked.

"Inject it or scatter it on its feed. But this isn't atropine."

"No, but test its feed anyway."

He nodded. "Makes sense. Water, too. Belinda, see if you can find two glass jars with tight lids.

There ought to be some specimen jars in the cupboard under the drugs cupboard."

Belinda went off without question, accustomed to being given orders in the line of duty. Ken shook his head over his task and muttered about the speed with which blood started decomposing after death.

"And the foal," he said with a deep sigh. "Such a *waste.*"

I said, "What are we going to do with that needle you cut out of her gut?"

"God knows. What do you think? Does it matter anymore?"

"It does if Wynn Lees ever mentions it."

"But he hasn't."

"No," I agreed, "but if he shoved it down her throat he must be *wondering* . . . He might just ask, one day."

"All it would prove would be that he did want the mare dead and did his best to kill her, and he might be prosecuted for cruelty, but I wouldn't put any bets on a conviction. Every vet in the kingdom would testify that cats and dogs swallow sewing needles and stitch their guts into knots."

He began to label the phials containing the pathetic samples of blood.

"I'll divide each sample into two and send them to two different labs," he said. "Double check."

I nodded.

"Also we'll take umpteen sections of tissue from her organs at the postmortem, and I tell you, there will be no results, like before, because we don't know what to look for."

"You're such a pessimist."

"With reason."

He produced from the bag a large rectal thermometer and took the internal temperature, explaining it helped to indicate the time of death. Horses, because of their body mass, retained heat for hours and the result could be approximate only.

Belinda returned with two suitable jars into which she put and labeled samples of water from the half-empty bucket and hay from the half-empty net. There was no doubt that the mare had drunk and eaten from those sources.

Scott came fast on Belinda's heels and couldn't contain his feelings, a mixture of disbelief, rage and fear of being held responsible, as far as I could see.

"I put her in the box. I even gave her new water and fresh hay and she was right as rain. Peter will tell you. There's just no way she could be dead."

No one bothered to say that, one way or another, she was.

Ken stripped off his gloves, finished packing the samples, snapped the case shut and stood up to his six foot four.

"Who's looking after this afternoon's patient?" he said. "Scott, go and check at once. Belinda, set up the drip in the intensive-care box. We can move him out here soon, then Scott can oversee him all evening. He's not to be left alone, even if

I have to sit on a chair all night outside his door." He gave me a wild look, still shattered for all his surface decisiveness. "I'll have to tell Carey."

I went with him into the office and listened to the fateful phone call. Carey on the other end received the news not with screeching fury but with silence.

"Carey?" Ken said anxiously, "did you hear what I said?"

It appeared that he had heard and was speechless.

Ken told him he'd talked to the knackers; told him he wanted an outside vet to do the postmortem; told him Peter suggested they look for poison.

That last sentence produced a sharp reaction which I couldn't quite hear but which surprised and embarrassed Ken. He skipped on hurriedly to his opinion that the mare had been dead at least two hours when Belinda found her. Two hours, he said, clearly having done some thinking, meant a possible or probable period when he (Ken) and Carey and Belinda and Scott and Peter had all been together in the theater, engaged in a long operation. Who knew, he said, what had been going on outside?

There was a lengthy issue of scratchy noises of disapproval from the telephone until finally Ken said, "Yes. Yes, OK," and slowly put down the receiver.

"He won't believe anyone deliberately killed the mare. He says you're panicking." Ken looked at me apologetically. "I suppose I shouldn't have told him what you think."

"It doesn't matter. Is he coming here?"

He shook his head. "He's going to fix the post-mortem for tomorrow morning and he's going to tell Wynn Lees, which is one chore I'm very relieved to get out of."

"Wynn Lees might know already."

"Jeez," Ken said.

I scorched the tires to London not even in time for my appointment and with no chance of newspapers. I solved the problem of my sketchy if not nonexistent knowledge of most of London by stopping at a multistory car park as soon as I was off the M.40 motorway and letting a taxi find Draycott Avenue and Daphne's restaurant, which it achieved irritatingly slowly.

Annabel efficiently had arrived on time. I was seventeen minutes late. She was sitting primly at a table for two, a single glass of wine before her.

"Sorry," I said, taking the opposite chair.

"Excuses?"

"A dead horse. A hundred miles. Dearth of taxis. Traffic."

"I suppose that will do." The small mouth curved. "What dead horse?"

I told her in some detail and no doubt with heat.

"You care," she said when I'd finished.

"Yes, I do. Anyway . . ." I shook my head dismissing it, "did the oriental chums get off all right?"

She said they had. We consulted menus and chose, and I took stock of the surroundings and of herself.

She'd come dressed again in black and white: black skirt, loose harlequin black and white top with big black pompoms for buttons down the front. The cropped frizzy hair looked fluffy from recent washing and she wore gentle eye makeup and pale pink lipstick. I didn't know how much was normal to her or how much she'd done for the evening's benefit, but I definitely liked the result.

As at Stratford she effortlessly established a neutral zone around herself, across which she would be friendly to a point. The amusement in her big eyes was like a moat, I thought, dug for the deterrence of over-the-top attentions.

The narrow restaurant was packed and noisy, the waiters hurrying precariously holding big trays head high.

"Lucky to get a table," I commented, looking round.

"I booked."

I smiled. Effective public relations. "I've no idea where I am," I said. "In terms of London, I mean."

"Just off the Fulham Road, less than a mile from Harrods." She considered me, her head on one side. "Are you really looking for somewhere to live?"

257

"Three weeks today," I said, nodding, "I start work in Whitehall. What should I do if it's not to be a grating?"

"Are you rolling?"

I laughed. "I've got a huge promotion in career terms at half the income I had before."

"Impossible."

I shook my head. "In Tokyo I had more than my salary again in cost-of-living supplements, entertainment allowances, free food and the use of a car. Over here, zilch. Severe drop in living standards, one might say. Over there I had diplomatic immunity if I got a parking ticket. Here, too bad, no immunity from anything, pay the fine. Britain, incidentally, is the only country in the world that doesn't give its diplomats diplomatic passports. There's a whole lot of no featherbedding."

"Poor dears."

"Mm. So I need somewhere to lay my head, but not too many frills."

"Will you share?"

"Anything, for a start."

"I could put out a few feelers."

"I'd be grateful."

She ate snails, adept with the tongs. I, still uncertain of my way in my own country, had settled for safe old pâté and toast.

"Do you have a last name?" I asked, eating.

"Nutbourne. Do you?"

"Darwin. As in, but not descended."

"You must always be asked."

"Pretty often."

"And, um, is your father, say, a bus driver?"

"Does it matter?"

"It doesn't *matter*. It's just interesting."

"He's another diplomat, then. And yours?"

She chewed the last snail and put the tongs and fork down neatly.

"A clergyman," she said. She looked at me carefully, waiting for a response. I guessed that was why she'd brought up occupations in the first place, to tell me that fact, not to worry about my own background.

I said judicially, "Some perfectly good people are clergymen's daughters."

She smiled, the eyes crinkling, the pink mouth an upturning arc. "He wears gaiters," she said.

"Ah. That's more serious." And so it was. One trod softly around a bishop if one were a sensible little private secretary with good prospects in the Foreign Office, and especially around one who thought the Foreign Office did more harm than good. One didn't take any bishop's daughter lightly. It explained everything, I thought, about the touch-me-not aura: she was vulnerable to gossip and wouldn't incur it needlessly.

"My father's an ambassador," I said, "to be fair."

"Thanks," she said.

"It doesn't mean we can't turn cartwheels naked in Hyde Park."

"It does," she said. "The virtues of the fathers are visited on the children, just like sins. Millstones aren't in it."

"They don't always deter."

"They deter me," she said flatly, "for my own sake, as well as Dad's."

"Why did you choose the Jockey Club?" I asked.

She smiled vividly. "The old boy network heard of my existence and proposed it. They blinked a bit when they saw my clothes and still gulp politely. Otherwise we get on OK because I know what I'm doing."

We progressed to Dover soles and I asked her if there was anyone in the Jockey Club who was a specialist in fraudulent insurance claims on dead horses.

She looked at me soberly. "You think that's what's been happening?"

"Almost certainly, unless we have a fixated psychopath on the loose."

She thought it over. "I'm pretty good friends with the deputy director of the security service," she said. "I could ask him to meet you."

"Could you? When?"

"If you'll just wait until I've finished my dinner, I'll phone him."

Sleuthing took a step back while Annabel Nutbourne carefully cleared every particle from the fish bones and left a skeleton as bare as an anatomy lesson.

"Do you have suitors in droves?" I asked.

She flicked me an amused glance. "Only one at a time."

"How about now?"

"Don't they teach you diplomacy in the Foreign Office?"

The gibe was earned, I supposed. Where was the oblique approach that I'd practiced so often? A cool honeypot could make an instant fool of a healthy drone.

"Heard any good sermons lately?" I asked.

"It's better to be a buffoon than a lout, I suppose."

"Do I say thanks?"

"If you have any sense." She laughed at me, malice absent. There were fewer insecurities, I thought, beneath that confident exterior, than one met normally. I was more accustomed to drying eyes than being teased by them.

I thought of Russet Eaglewood, whose insecurities couldn't be guessed at and whose reputation had passed into legend. A selfish, generous, passionate, passive, devouring, laughing lover she'd been by turns, and Annabel might be all of those things if the time were right, but I didn't think I would loll back in my chair that evening and say, "How about a bonk, then?" to Miss Nutbourne.

She chose cappuccino coffee with nutmeg on top for us both and after that, while I paid the bill, she made the phone call.

"He says," she reported, "no time like the present."

"Really?" I was as surprised as pleased. "How lucky he's in.

"In?" She laughed. "He's never in. He just has

a telephone growing out of his ear. I've ordered a taxi."

Efficient transport, she said, was part of her job.

The deputy director of the security service of the Jockey Club met us in the entrance hall of a gaming club, and signed us in as guests. He was big in a useful way, broad shouldered, heavy topped, flat bellied, with long legs. The watchful eyes of his trade made me speculate on a police past, upper ranks.

"Brose," Annabel said, rubbing his arm in greeting, "this is Peter Darwin. Don't ask him, he isn't." To me she said in introduction, "John Ambrose. Call him Brose."

He shook my hand; nothing indecisive about that, either.

"Do you understand blackjack?" he asked me.

"Twenty-one? More or less."

"Annabel?"

"The same."

Brose nodded and led us through swing doors into a wide stretch of gaming room where life was lived on green baize under bright low-slung lights. Slightly to my surprise it was noisy, and the stakes, I was relieved to find, weren't immediately ruinous. Brose steered us to a deserted blackjack table without a croupier and told us everything comes to him who waits.

"Order lemonade," he said. "I'll be back."

He set off into the busy throng of punters who were determinedly putting little pieces of plastic where they believed their luck was, and we could see him from time to time leaning over people's shoulders and speaking into their ears.

"You wouldn't believe it," Annabel said, "but what he's doing is putting the fear of God into a lot of seamy characters from the racecourse. He goes round the clubs keeping tabs on them and they hate it. He says anyone sweating over losing is ripe for trouble, and besides that he gets told things on the quiet that put crooks out of business and keep racing at least halfway honest."

"Did he literally mean lemonade?"

"Oh, I expect so. He doesn't drink alcohol and he has to account for everything he spends here. We wouldn't rate champagne."

We settled for fizzy water instead and in time a few more people came to sit at our table where eventually a croupier appeared, broke open new packs, shuffled forever, pushed the cards to a wheezy fat man to cut and then fed them into a shoe.

Most of the newcomers had brought chips with them. Annabel and I each bought twenty and played conservatively and in short order she'd doubled hers and I was down to two.

"You'll never win taking a card on fifteen," Brose said in my ear. "The odds are against it. Unless the dealer turns up a ten or facecard, stick on twelve and bet the house will go bust."

"That's not exciting," I said.

"Nor is losing."

I took his advice and the house went bust three times in a row.

"I've time for a drink," he said. "Want to talk?"

He led us to a railed-off corner section where at small tables hollow-eyed unfortunates sat drowning their mortgage money. A waitress without being asked brought Brose a glass of citron pressé which he dispatched in a long smooth swallow.

"The air's kept dry here," he said. "Have you noticed? It makes everyone thirsty. Very good for trade. What is it exactly you want to know?"

I explained about Hewett and Partners' troubles with horses, though not in great detail except for the mare.

"She was carrying a foal by Rainbow Quest," I said. "Her owner's a weird man . . ."

"Name?" Brose interrupted.

"The owner? Wynn Lees."

Brose grunted and his attention sharpened. "There can't be two of them."

"It's the same man," I assured him.

"What's weird about him?" Annabel asked.

Brose said, "He's a pervert. Not sexual, I don't mean. Cruel. He should never be allowed near horses. He got chucked out of Australia, our bad luck."

I explained about the colic operation and told him about the needle, and I described the circumstance of the mare's death that afternoon.

"And these vets don't know what she died of?"

"Not yet, no. But why kill her? The foal was valuable, so was she."

He looked at me with disillusion. "You think Wynn Lees did it?"

"He was there in the morning, but she was alive when he left."

He summoned a refill lemon with a raised finger and an unexpectedly sweet smile. The waitress brought his drink purring.

"I'll tell you," he said at length. "I'd lay you odds the foal was not by Rainbow Quest."

"Vernonside Stud said it was.

"Vernonside Stud would believe what they were told. They're sent a broodmare with her name on her head collar, right? So that's what they call her. She doubtless has papers with her, all in order. In foal to Rainbow Quest. Why doubt it?"

"OK then," Annabel repeated. "Why doubt it?"

"Because she's died the way she has." He paused. "Look, you own a decent broodmare, you send her to Rainbow Quest. She seems to be in foal and you take her home and put her in a field, very pleased, but somewhere along the line she slips it. It's often difficult to detect when that happens, but at some point you realize that all you have now is a barren year. But suppose an idea pops in your brain and you go out and buy some other unknown mare in foal to some obscure stallion. Well, now you have a mare in foal at about the right stage of gestation and you insure it as if it's your mare in foal to Rainbow Quest. If anyone checks, then yes, the visit to Rainbow Quest is fully documented. She goes to Vernonside Stud to have the foal because she's down for one of their stallions next. You have to act as a normal owner would. At that point she's ready for the chop, poor beast, which is what she's got." He paused to drink. "These days paternity can be proved without doubt. If I were the insurance company, I'd make sure. Pity your vets didn't take tissue from the foal. Even though it's dead, they might still have got results."

"They still could," I said. "The postmortem's tomorrow morning. I'll tell them."

"What do you do with the real decent mare?" Annabel asked, fascinated.

"Ship it to some of your shady mates down under."

I said, "How do we find out which company carried the insurance? If, of course, you're right."

Brose wasn't hopeful. "You've got a problem there. There aren't exactly thousands of underwriters who'll take on horses, but any of them could. The non-marine syndicates at Lloyd's will insure anything from a kidnap ransom to a wet church fête. You ask them, they'll name you a price."

"Perhaps one could send them all a cautionary letter."

"You'll get yourself in trouble doing that." Brose shook his head. "What's your priority in all of this?"

"Um . . . to stitch Ken McClure's reputation together again and prove the horses' deaths weren't his doing."

"Difficult," he said.

"Is it impossible?" Annabel asked.

"Never say anything's impossible. Unlikely's better."

"We also," I said, "have the vets' main building destroyed by arson with an unknown body in it."

Brose listened impassively, Annabel open-mouthed, to the extent of Hewett and Partners' problems.

"Carey Hewett, the senior partner, looks older by the hour. All the partners are tied together in a common mortgage on the burned building, but falling apart in loyalties. All their records were burned, including the backup disks for the computer. Their chief remaining asset, the hospital, is gradually being boycotted by clients frightened by Ken operating on their horses. After today's disaster, that will accelerate. There isn't much time left for putting things right."

Brose pursed his lips. "I take it back. Impossible is the right word."

"It would be really helpful," I said, "if you could give me a list of unidentifiable poisons.

"If you can't identify them," Brose said, "you can't prove they were administered."

Annabel raised her eyebrows. "So they do exist?"

"I didn't say that," Brose said.

"As good as."

"Do they exist?" I asked.

"If they did," Brose answered, "and Annabel, I'm not saying that they do, then that's the sort of thing I'd not let out into common knowledge. What I will tell you is that all poisons are hard to find and identify if you have no general idea of what to look for."

"Ken said that too," I agreed.

"He's right." Brose stood up. "I'll just wish you luck. Keep me posted on Wynn Lees." He thought briefly and changed his mind. "Suppose I come to Cheltenham one day? It's not strictly a racing matter as such, but I might be able to suggest a few things."

"Terrific," I said, very pleased.

"Check with Annabel," he said, "and tomorrow I'll look at my diary."

He patted Annabel on her rag-doll hair, nodded to me amiably and ambled off to instill fear into a few more unsuspecting wrongdoers.

Annabel held up her fistful of chips and said she felt like multiplying them, so we found a table with spaces and spent a fast hour in which she doubled her stake again and I lost my lot.

"You gamble too much at the wrong time," she said, taking her half ton of plastic to the cashier to be changed back to spendable currency. "You should have listened to Brose."

"I had fun for my money."

She put her head on one side. "That sounds like an epitaph."

"I'll settle for it," I said, smiling.

We went back to the outer world where gambling was real and went in a taxi (Annabel phoned for it) to the house she shared in Fulham. The cab stopped outside and the driver waited resignedly to take me towards the M.40.

She thanked me for the dinner. I thanked her for Brose.

"I'll phone you," I said.

"Yes, do that."

We stood on the pavement for a few moments. I kissed her cheek. I'd got that right, it seemed, from her little nod.

"Good luck with everything," she said. "It sounds as if you and the vets need a miracle."

"A miracle would be fine."

Instead, we got a nightmare.

9

Vicky had left a note on my pillow.

"Ken asks you to go to the hospital at nine A.M."

With a groan, as the night had already half gone, I set my alarm, crawled under the daisy duvet and fell over black cliffs into sleep.

I dreamed of horses dying, their deaths somehow my fault. Awakening, I was relieved to shed the guilt, but a sense of unease remained and it was with a feeling of oppression I returned to the hospital.

At first sight everything seemed relatively normal, even if gloomy under a scurrying cloudy sky. Cats and dogs went on arriving at the Portakabin. Lucy in a white coat gave me a wave as she crossed from the hospital. I went in through the rear door and found Ken in the office, pale and seething.

"What's the matter?" I said.

"Three referrals have canceled for later this week. All breathing improvements. We need outside fees to keep the hospital going. They've all heard about the mare and they're now in a full-scale panic. On top of that I sat here until three this morning checking on yesterday's patients, then Scott took over. He promised blind he wouldn't go to sleep. So I came back ten minutes ago, and guess what? No Scott. He's sloped off somewhere for breakfast. It isn't my fault we haven't had the coffee machine mended."

"How are the patients?"

"All right," he said grudgingly, "but that's not the point."

"No," I agreed. "When's the postmortem on the mare?"

He looked at his watch. "Carey said at ten. I suppose I'd better be there. Carey's called in a fellow from Gloucester to do it and he's more a butcher than a surgeon. The last person I'd have chosen. So I'll have to be there in case he does something diabolical." Irritation and stress were plain in his voice. "I wondered if you would mind finishing these letters to the pharmaceutical companies so that they can go out today. I was doing them last night." He picked up a folder and slid out a bunch of papers. "With the computer down I've had to get the names and addresses of some of the firms off the bottles and packets, if they're not supplied by the wholesalers who came yesterday. I've sent their letter already. Well, anyway, I wrote a general letter and at least our copier here is working, so I've made enough copies for every firm I could think of."

He pushed them across the desk towards me, along with another sheet of paper with the names and addresses.

"While I'm out, could you type in a company

271

name at the top of each letter, and also do the envelopes? I know it's a ghastly chore but it was you who suggested it."

"Mm," I agreed. "All right."

"Thanks a lot."

"I've got another suggestion," I said.

He groaned.

"Take a tissue sample from the dead foal to do a test for paternity."

He stared. I told him Brose's theory.

"To activate the insurance," I said, "the mare had to die. You inconveniently saved her life the first time, so someone had another go. If Brose is right, he, she, or they couldn't afford to have the foal born. Death had to occur before that, and as they probably didn't know exactly when the foal was due, they had to hurry."

"It gets worse," Ken said.

"You'd have to get a tissue sample from Rainbow Quest as well," I said.

"Not difficult. Tissue matching is expensive, though. So is searching for poison, incidentally. Specialist labs cost the earth."

"So you do think it was poison?"

"Well, it wasn't electrocution. She wasn't suffocated by a plastic bag. She didn't choke. I couldn't see any stab wounds. She shouldn't have died . . . something stopped her heart."

Yvonne Floyd, coming into the office, overheard Ken's last words.

"Nerve gas?" she suggested ironically.

"So easy to get hold of," Ken said.

"Smoke inhalation from a smoldering sofa?"

"I bet it wasn't," Ken said, actually smiling. "Only trying to help."

Her presence lightened things always. She said she had an emergency dog case on its way in and had come over to ready things for the small-animal theater.

"I'll need both Scott and Belinda, ideally."

"Yes," Ken said. "They're around."

"Great."

She looked great herself in her white lab coat: white gleaming teeth, bright eyes, cloud of black hair.

She said, "Belinda's asked me to be her matron of honor."

"What?" Ken said, puzzled.

"At your wedding, nitwit. Sort of married bridesmaid."

"Oh." He looked as if he'd forgotten the wedding altogether.

"I suppose you've got a best man?" she teased.

"Er . . ." Ken said. "I've left everything to Belinda. It's her day."

"Really, Ken"—she was mildly exasperated—"you have to find your own best man."

His gaze fell on me. "How about it?"

"You must have other friends," I said. "Long-time friends."

"You'll do fine," he insisted, "if you will."

"But Belinda . . ."

"She's coming round, changing her mind about you," Ken said. "She'll be all right. Say you will."

"OK."

Yvonne was pleased. "That's better. Don't forget your clothes, Ken. Or buttonholes."

"Oh God," he said. "At a time like this, who can think of *buttonholes?*"

Yvonne smiled affectionately. "Life goes on," she said. "We'll all come out of this all right, you'll see."

She went out of the office and turned in the direction of the theater.

"Terrific surgeon," Ken said.

"Terrific legs."

"Yes, I suppose so." He was unmoved. After a pause he began to say, "What are we going to do?"

There was a crash of a door slamming back against a wall and a clatter in the corridor and a groan.

"What's that?" Ken said alarmed, rising to his feet.

I being nearest to the door was first through it, Ken on my heels. Yvonne was coming towards us, weaving and stumbling, her eyes stretched wide, one hand clamped over her mouth. We went towards her to help her and she shook her head violently, tears coming into her eyes and her knees buckling.

"Yvonne," Ken exclaimed, "for God's sake, what's the matter?"

She took her hand away as if going to tell us and instead vomited violently onto the passage floor.

She leaned weakly against the wall, crying, her stomach heaving, looking as if she would pass out at any second. Ken and I moved instantly, one to each side of her, stepping round the vomit, to give her support.

She shook us off and, unable to speak, pointed with a wild sweep of an arm towards the theater. Ken gave me a wide-eyed frightened glance and we went fearfully along there to see what had caused such an extreme reaction. It was the door to the vestibule that had crashed against the wall: it was still open. We went through and into the supply room and tried the door to the small-animal section, but it was locked. We pushed on through the swing doors leading to the big main operating room.

What we saw there brought me perilously near fainting myself.

Scott lay on the long equine operating table, on his back, his arms and legs in the air. Round each ankle and each wrist was buckled a padded cuff. Each cuff was attached to a chain, each chain came down from the hoist. He had been lifted onto the table like a horse.

He was dressed as always in blue jeans and sweater, and he still had shoes and socks on, and his wristwatch.

One might have thought it a joke, but there was about that energetic hard-muscled body an unaccustomed absolute stillness, a silence as lonely as the cosmos.

Ken and I stood one on each side of him,

looking down on his face. His head was tipped back, his jaw jutting up. His eyes were unnervingly half-open, as if he were watching and waiting for our help. His mouth was closed. He was white.

"Christ," Ken said under his breath, very pale.

I swayed. Told myself fainting was out of the question.

Scott's mouth had been securely fastened shut by a neat row of staples. Small silvery tacks. Nine of them.

The faintness ebbed. I'd seen a great many dead bodies before: it wasn't the fact of death but the barbarity that disturbed so radically. I swallowed and closed my teeth and breathed shallowly through my nose.

Ken said "Christ" again and turned towards the controls of the hoist.

"Don't touch it," I said.

He stopped and turned back. "You're right, of course. But it's wrong to leave him like that."

I shook my head. We had to leave him like that, and the one person who wouldn't care was Scott himself.

"We must get the police," Ken said dully.

"Yes. And help Yvonne, and make sure no one else comes in here."

"God."

A stapler was lying on the floor near my feet. I left it alone. There were no lights on: only daylight through frosted glass skylights. Everything looked clean and tidy, ready for work. It didn't matter anymore, I thought, that we had gone without shoe-covers into that sterile environment.

We went back into the corridor and along to Yvonne, who was kneeling on the floor, her head against the wall. Ken squatted down beside her. She turned to him and clung, sobbing.

"He was . . . so good . . . to my boys."

There were worse epitaphs. I went on past them into the office and picked up Ken's bunch of keys which were on the desk. The labels were all smudged from much use, but I found "Theatre vestibule" and took it along the passage to see what it fitted.

Yvonne and Ken were standing. He was giving her his handkerchief, not especially clean, to wipe her ravaged face. He watched me go by with unseeing eyes, his mind, I guessed, like my own, unable to cast out the sight in the theater.

The vestibule door, I supposed, was covered with everyone's fingerprints, but all the same I slotted the key into the lock without adding any more and found that the tongue turned easily. Using the key alone I closed and locked the door and then went round the corners, along the passage and out into the welcome fresh air.

The outside door leading to the large-animal reception room was closed. I sorted through the bunch for the key and fed it into the hole. I turned it to unlock the door, but nothing happened. Tried the other way: the bolt clicked audibly across. That made the whole theater area safe from casual eyes, but everyone had keys . . . it was all a disaster.

I turned back to the office, skirting the thin splashy patch of vomit. Ken, his arm round Yvonne, was helping her to the washroom off the entrance hall. I found a large piece of paper, wrote DO NOT ENTER on it, grabbed a roll of sticky tape and returned to the outside door. Even Oliver, I thought, sticking it on firmly, might obey that notice, or obey it at least long enough to come into the office to discover why it was there.

Returning to the office, I wrote a second notice and stuck it to the vestibule door, again without leaving finger marks. Then Ken came back from the entrance hall and together in the office we stood for a silent second simply looking at the telephone.

"It's going to be terrible," he said.

"Mm."

He sat in the chair behind the desk and picked up the receiver. "Yvonne says Carey isn't here yet. He was calling in before the postmortem. Don't you think we should wait for him?"

"No, I don't think so."

"What do I say, then?" he asked numbly. "How can I say it?"

"Just say who you are, where you are, and that there's a man dead here. Speak slowly, it saves time."

"You do it." He gave me the receiver. "I feel sick."

I did it at dictation speed. Someone would

come, they said. In the pause before the police arrived Carey himself turned up wanting to know why the don't enter notice was on the outside door.

"I didn't know there was one," Ken said wearily.

"I put it there," I said.

He nodded, understanding.

"Why?" Carey asked.

I found it difficult to tell him. While I did, he went even grayer. Ken gave him the desk chair and asked if he would like some water. Carey put his elbows on the desk and his head in his hands and didn't reply.

The telephone rang and because it was next to my hand I answered it.

"This is Lucy. Who's that?" a voice said.

"Peter."

"Oh. Is Yvonne there?"

"Er . . . where are you?"

"In the Portakabin, of course."

I remembered that the old building's number had been rerouted to a swaying wire connected to the temporary accommodation. The partnership's slender attachment to the well-organized past was about to be stretched to the limit.

"Yvonne's here," I said, "but not feeling well."

"She was perfectly all right fifteen minutes ago."

"Lucy, when you can, come over here."

"I can't possibly. Belinda and I are knee deep in distemper jabs. Anyway, will you tell Yvonne her run-over dog has arrived outside our door here, but the poor thing's already dead. Ask her to come and talk to the owners, they're very upset."

"She can't come," I said.

She finally heard the calamity note in my voice.

"What's the matter?" she asked, her own alarm awakening.

"Get rid of the dogs. I'm not telling you on the phone, but it's catastrophic."

After a brief silence, she simply replaced her receiver and a moment later I saw her through the window coming down the Portakabin steps and hurrying across to the entrance hall. She appeared in the office doorway prepared to be annoyed with me for frightening her.

One look at Carey's bent head, at Ken's extra pallor, at my own signs of strain, convinced her that fear was reasonable.

"What is it?" she asked.

I said, as the other two were mute, "Scott's dead."

"Oh no!" She was horrified. "On his motorbike? I always told him he'd do himself in one day on that machine. Oh, poor man."

"It wasn't his bike," I said. "He's here, in the theater, and it looks . . . well, it looks as if someone's killed him."

She sat down abruptly on one of the chairs, her mouth open in protesting shock.

"Yvonne found him," I said. "She's in the washroom. She could do with your help."

Strong sensible Lucy rose to her feet again and went on the errand.

Through the window, I saw Oliver Quincy arrive in his mud-spattered white car which he parked next to mine.

"Why don't the police come?" Ken asked fretfully.

The police, I thought, would take everything over. My glance fell on the folder of letters Ken had pushed my way in a long-ago different time-zone, and on impulse I picked it up and took it out to my car, meeting Oliver as he locked his own.

"I'd better warn you . . ." I said slowly. He interrupted brusquely.

"Warn me about what?"

"Ken and Carey can tell you," I said. "They're in the office."

"Not *another* dead horse?"

I shook my head. He shrugged, turned away, and went into the office through the rear door, throwing an inquiring look at the don't enter notice as he passed it. I stowed the folder of letters in the trunk and locked it, and turned to follow Oliver just as a police car drove into the car park.

It stopped outside the entrance hall and the same plainclothes policeman as before emerged from it, followed by the same constable. They looked around briefly and went in through the hospital's front door, and I decided to go back that way myself.

Lucy and Yvonne were coming out of the wash-room together, both looking sick and shaky, as if Lucy's imagination had been as strong an emetic as Yvonne's actual experience. They sat unhappily on two of the chairs each with a tissue to wipe her face, each sighing, both staring into space.

"The police have come," I said.

"I left Belinda coping with the whole Porta-kabin," Lucy said, sniffing and swallowing. "I'll have to go back." She stood up slowly as if suddenly older. "We'll finish there as fast as we can." She went out to the car park with little of the brave determination of four days ago.

"I ought to help her," Yvonne said with difficulty, "but I can't."

"Much better to sit here for a bit."

"You saw him, didn't you?"

I nodded.

"How could anyone do that?"

A question without answer.

"However will I sleep?" she said. "I can't get him out of my mind. I think of him water-ski-ing, so expert and strong, so *alive*. And now like this . . ."

Jay Jardine in his self-assertive way strode pos-itively into the entrance hall from up the central corridor and came to a halt at the sight of us.

"What the heck's going on?" he demanded. "There's dog sick all over the passage and that bloody rude policeman in the office told me to come along here and wait. Why is he here again?

282

Have they finally pinned a name on our corpse in the ashes?"

Yvonne groaned quietly and closed her eyes.

"For Christ's sake"—he was irritated—"what's the matter?"

I told him.

He stared. Then he sat down, leaving a chair between himself and Yvonne. He said only, "Too bad."

The understatement of the day, I thought.

Jay said, "The coffee machine's still buggered, I suppose."

We all looked at it across the hall. The first words I'd heard Scott say, I remembered, were "the coffee machine's buggered." Poor Scott. There was still no coffee, nor likely to be any.

For a while, as we sat in limbo, there was little commotion, as if the stillness in the theater had spread through the whole hospital. We could hear no voices from the office. We couldn't ourselves find much to say. Time passed.

Eventually two more plainclothes police cars came to a halt outside the entrance door, the first spilling out its human contents, the second remaining closed. A thickset man with the broken-veined complexion of a farmer ambled without great speed into the entrance hall, followed by an elderly man with a too-big suit, heavy black-rimmed glasses sliding down his nose, and the black top-opening bag of old-fashioned doctors.

The farmer type asked briefly, "The office?"

"Down the passage, first on the right," Jay told him.

He nodded and went down there, and things began to happen, though none of them joyful. The second police car contained a photographer and other specialists who after a while followed their master under Jay's direction.

Ken came the other way, jerky, disjointed. "They've gone into the operating room," he said. "Come outside, Peter. I need air."

I went with him, looking at my watch. Nine-fifty. The morning had seemed a week long already. The air was brisk and cold.

"Did you remember the postmortem?" I asked.

"Carey did. He phoned them to go ahead without us." He took a deep breath as if sucking life from the air, as if empty.

I said, "Did you, um, ask him to get some foal tissue?"

He raised his eyebrows. "I forgot it. Does it matter now?"

"Maybe more than before. You never know."

"Oh God." He pulled his radiophone off his belt, looked up the number in a small pocket address book, and got through to the knackers. He told someone who seemed to have no problem understanding that he wanted properly labeled tissue samples and, as if struck by a thought, he added that he also wanted one of the foal's ears and the tail and some of the mare's mane.

"Why on earth the ear and tail?" I asked as he put the phone away.

"Hair," he said succinctly. "You can get perfect DNA identification from hair, and of course hair doesn't decompose. To prove the foal's paternity you'd need its own hair, its dam's hair and its sire's hair. Or any tissue, really. You get the mare's DNA pattern, then you subtract that from the foal's pattern. What's left in the foal's DNA will be a match with the sire. It's a long expensive process but a genetic match is absolute proof."

I looked up at the gray sky. "Suppose whoever killed Scott left a hair on him?"

"Better if Scott fought and scratched. Murderers and rapists can be convicted by their scratched-off skin under their victim's fingernails. It's an exact science now."

"Mm." I half smiled. "That works if you have a suspect."

We watched the cat and dog brigade come and go.

"Will the police close us down?" Ken asked.

"God knows."

"The second-wave policeman who came," Ken said, "he's a detective superintendent. The first lot wouldn't do anything until he'd got here, not when I described the state Scott was in. A blatant piece of buck-passing, it looked to me."

"Prudent and proper, more like."

"You're used to a hierarchy," he said. "I'm not."

The Hewett and Partners setup was a sort of mini-hierarchy in itself I thought, but didn't press it. Instead I asked Ken if he owned a typewriter of any sort.

"Whatever for?"

"The letters. The envelopes. I can't use the office, it's full of police."

"Oh, yes. Are we still going on with the letters?"

"We are indeed."

He thought briefly. "I've an old battered portable at home. Would that do?"

"Sooner the better," I said, nodding. "Where do you live?"

"We can't go now, though," he protested. "The police told me to wait."

"They haven't told *me* to wait," I said. "Give me directions and keys and I'll pick up the typewriter and come back. Then I can get on with the letters as soon as possible."

"But what will I say . . . ?"

"If anyone complains, say I was hungry. I'll bring back some croissants or something."

"There's actually a decent bakery two doors from where I live."

"Fine."

He gave me his house keys and told me where to find the typewriter, and as the dog and cat cars were still on the move I had no problem driving with them out of the car park. I'd have had more difficulty in getting in again without a sick animal as passenger if Ken, looking out for me, hadn't hurried across and told the policemen on gate duty that I belonged.

Ken's typewriter was by then locked in the

trunk, along with a packet of large envelopes and a sheet of stamps. I carried several big pâtisserie bags into the hospital and scattered sustenance all round, which everyone ate hungrily while protesting they had no appetite. Carbohydrates, as ever, were the easiest of sedatives. I ate two Danish pastries myself and even Yvonne gratefully chewed and said she felt better. Ken sat beside her and fell on my offerings ravenously.

"You weren't supposed to leave the premises, sir," the familiar constable said reprovingly as I went along to the office.

"Sorry. Have a doughnut?"

He eyed the sugar-coated temptation with obvious longing but said he was on duty. No one else made any comment on my excursion. All the same if I'd been disposing of vital evidence, I thought.

Carey ate a piece of sticky almond ring distractedly as if his brain wasn't quite aware of what his mouth was doing. He was still sitting in the same chair, still looking near collapse. Oliver eyed him like a predatory lion but meanwhile made do with double the cake. Jay Jardine, now in the office, stuffed down two doughnuts in quick succession and sucked the sugar off his fingers.

The door to the theater vestibule, I'd noticed, was shut and still bore my don't enter sign. I didn't want to think about what was going on behind it. I was just glad that I didn't have to deal with it.

Carey, Oliver and Jay were taciturn, each busy with their own thoughts. I returned to the more congenial company of Yvonne and Ken and time inched by as through the glass entrance doors we watched the flow of dogs diminish and finally dry. Lucy and Belinda, locking the door behind them, came down from the Portakabin and walked towards us across the tarmac.

Halfway, they stopped, their heads turning towards the gate. They stood unmoving, watching, then finally completed the traverse.

Lucy had tears in her eyes, coming into the entrance hall.

"They've taken him away," she said. "They backed an ambulance right up to the large-animal reception door. We couldn't see anything, thank God."

Oliver and Jay came along the passage with messages. Carey had gone into the operating room at the police's request to tell them if anything struck him as being out of its ordinary place. Yvonne would please wait in the office for the police to ask her questions. They, Oliver and Jay, and also Lucy, could go out on their scheduled calls. Belinda—Oliver shrugged—could presumably do what she liked, they'd had no instructions about her one way or the other. Ken and Ken's friend should stay in the entrance hall. No one could enter or use the theater until future notice. Someone, Oliver said finally, should take a mop to the muck on the floor.

It was Lucy, predictably, who cleaned the passage, sweeping aside Yvonne's objections and Ken's and my halfhearted offers.

The crowd in the entrance hall broke up and scattered about its business until only I remained. Ken and Belinda were alone at the stables checking on their horse patients. Yvonne was in the office with the door closed, reliving what she longed to forget. She came out crying, awkwardly accompanied by the constable.

"They want to see you next," she said, gulping and wiping her eyes. "They say I can go home but I'm due to attend some damned dog-lovers' lunch and lecture on the care of puppies. How can I?"

"Best if you do, perhaps. Make this morning seem unreal."

"Sir. . ." the constable said, gesturing towards the office.

"Yes." I gave Yvonne a hug. "Go to the lunch."

I left her trying to achieve a wan rain-washed smile and went where required, faithfully followed by the no-doughnut policeman.

The farmer-lookalike was standing by the window, head back, inspecting the cloud cover. He turned at my arrival and announced himself as Detective Superintendent Ramsey of the Gloucestershire police. His voice matched his appearance; an outdoor country intonation, a canny poacher on the side of the gamekeepers.

He checked a list. "You are Peter Darwin, employed here as a general assistant?"

"Not employed," I said. "Unpaid helper."

He raised his eyebrows, clicked open a pen and made a note.

"Are you employed elsewhere, sir?" The pen was poised.

"I'm on leave from the Foreign Office."

He gave me a brief reassessing glance without pleasure, then wrote down the information and asked me what sort of unpaid help I'd been giving.

I told him that several horses had died in the hospital, that Ken McClure, my friend, was worried about it and that I was trying to help him find out why they'd died.

"And, sir, have you succeeded?"

I said regretfully, "No."

"How long have you been trying?"

"Since last Thursday."

He pursed his lips and shook his head slightly, forgiving me, it seemed, for not having achieved results in five days. He made another note, then looked up and began again.

"Do you think the deaths of the horses and the death of the anesthetist are connected?"

I frowned. "I don't know."

"Do you think the deaths of the horses and the burning of the main building are connected?"

"I don't know."

"Have you discussed any theories with anyone, sir?"

"I think it may not be safe to discuss theories round here."

His eyes narrowed sharply. "You saw Sylvester's body, I understand."

"Yes." I swallowed. "How did he die?"

"All in good time," he said blandly. "When you were in the theater, did you touch anything?"

"No."

"Are you positive, sir?"

"Absolutely positive."

"Did you see anything of note? Except Sylvester, of course."

"There was a surgical stapler on the floor near the operating table."

"Ah . . . you know surgical staplers by sight?"

"I've seen Ken use one."

He made another note.

"Also," I said, "I think all the doors were unlocked, which isn't usual. I went round outside to check the outer reception door, which is where the sick animals enter, and it was unlocked. I put the key in the hole and locked it to prevent anyone just walking in there and seeing Scott . . ." I paused. "And when Ken and I went into the theater, the door to the padded room was open, and so was the one from there to the corridor and the reception room."

He made a note. "And was it you who put up the notices and locked the door between the passage here and the theater?"

I nodded.

"So after you locked the doors, no one went in there?"

"I don't know for sure," I said slowly. "Everyone has keys."

"Do you have keys?"

"No. I used Ken McClure's."

"Where were you, sir, between nine last night and nine this morning?"

I almost smiled, the inquiry being classic. I said calmly, "I went to London, to a private dinner. I was in the company of the Jockey Club's deputy director of security from eleven until two, then I drove back here to Cheltenham and went to bed. I'm staying with Ken McClure's fiancée's parents about a mile from here."

He made short notes. "Thank you, sir."

"When did he die?" I asked.

"You don't expect me to answer that."

I sighed. It had to have been after three, when Ken had left Scott in charge. Everyone's alibi would be the same and as hazy as mine: home in bed.

Superintendent Ramsey asked how long I would be staying with Ken McClure's fiancée's parents.

"It's in the air," I said. "Several more days, I should think."

"We may need to speak to you again, sir."

"Ken will know where I am, if I leave."

He nodded, made one more note, thanked me in general and asked the constable to invite Ken to the office. As I went out into the passage, Carey and the policeman from Sunday, whose name I still didn't know, were coming out of the theater vestibule. Carey walked heavily, gray head bowed, deep in distress.

He walked towards me unseeingly and turned into the office.

"There's nothing out of place," he said leadenly to Ramsey. The Sunday policeman followed Carey into the office and closed the door, and I and the constable left the hospital by the rear and found Ken and Belinda doing nothing much but leaning on the closed lower halves of the stable doors, aimlessly watching their patients recover.

"Your turn with the top brass," I said to Ken. He looked depressed.

"I'm going back to Thetford Cottage," I said. "I'll be there if you want me."

Belinda said, "I'm staying here with Ken."

I smiled at her and after a second she smiled back, the wattage not blinding but an advance nevertheless.

Vicky and Greg were out when I reached the house. They had solved the boredom factor to some extent by making an arrangement to be driven on demand by a taxi firm, neither of them feeling confident enough to rent and drive a car themselves. "The taxi drivers know where to go," Vicky had said. "They tell us what to do and see."

I let myself in, took Ken's typewriter and the folder of letters up to my bedroom, and set to work.

Ken's letters, each made on the partnership writing paper and personally signed with his own sprawling signature, explained the police's need-to-know request for the pharmacy's burned contents and asked for the firm's cooperation. The letter was all right as far as it went, I thought, but as a candidate for the "sometime or other" tray it got full marks. I slotted the first copy into the machine, typed in the first name on the address list at the top and rolled down to the bottom, below Ken's signature, to add an extra paragraph.

"This matter is of extreme urgency," I wrote, "as the police are concerned that certain dangerous, unusual and/or illegal substances may have been stolen prior to the arson, and may have passed into the general community. Please would you treat this request *with the utmost urgency* and send copies of all relevant invoices back by return of post in the stamped addressed envelope provided. Hewett and Partners expresses its profound appreciation of your kind and rapid participation."

In Japan I'd have scattered a few "respectfuls" around, but respect didn't seem to go down well with British commerce, as various mystified Japanese businessmen had told me. Bowing, too, for instance, produced not a contract but a squirm. In Japan it was the host who gave a gift to his guest, not the other way round. The opportunities for mutual embarrassment were endless.

I lavishly stamped a page-size envelope for the return information, addressing it to Hewett and Partners at Thetford Cottage (temporary office). The resulting missive looked official and commanding enough, I hoped, to get results.

Then I folded the letter and return envelope together, enclosing them in a business envelope addressed to the pharmaceutical firms. Without a copier or even carbons (which I hadn't thought of) it took me a fair while to type the extra paragraph on every letter and complete the task, but when they were all done I drove to the post office in the long shopping street and sent the whole inquiring bunch on its way.

Back in Thetford Cottage I made up on an hour's sleep and then on the off-chance phoned Ken's portable number.

He answered at once, "Ken McClure."

"Where are you?" I asked. "It's Peter."

"On my way to a dicky tendon. What do you need?"

"I thought we might go and see the Mackintoshes . . . or the Nagrebbs."

He drew in an audible breath. "You do think of vicious ways of passing the afternoon. No thanks."

"Where do I find them?" I asked.

"You don't mean it?"

"Do you or don't you want your reputation back?"

After a silence he gave me directions. "Zoe Mackintosh is a tigress and her old man's in dreamland. I'll meet you outside there in, say, fifteen minutes."

"Fine."

I drove through Riddlescombe and stopped on a hillside looking down on the Mackintoshes' village. Slate roofs, yellow-gray Cotswold stone walls, winter trees not yet swollen in bud. Charcoal and cream sky, heaped and hurrying. Sleeping fields waiting for spring.

The sense of actual deja vu was immensely strong. I'd come over these hills before and seen these roofs. I'd run down the road where I now sat in the car. Jimmy and I, laughing ourselves sick over an infantile joke, had chucked off our clothes and splashed naked in the stream going down to the valley. I couldn't see the stream from where I sat but I knew it was there.

Near the appointed time for meeting Ken, I started the engine, released the brake and rolled down the hill. I still couldn't see the stream. Must have muddled the places, I thought, but I'd been so certain. I shrugged it away. Memory was unreliable enough after a week: hopeless after twenty years.

Ken met me at the entrance to the drive to a long gray house with gables and ivy. I'd been there before. I knew the patterns on the folded-back wrought-iron entrance gates.

"Hi," I said prosaically, getting out of my car.

"I hope you know what you're doing," he said with resignation, looking out of the driver's window of his own car.

"Often," I said.

"Oh God." He paused. "Zoe knows my car. She'll attack me.

"Get in mine, then, coward."

He climbed out of his car and folded his length in with me and put an arresting hand on mine when I moved to put the car in gear.

"Carey says he's resigning," he said. "I thought I'd better tell you."

"That's unthinkable."

"I know. I believe he does mean it, though. And he's all that holds us together.

"When did he say he was resigning?"

"In the office. You know, after you left, when I went along there? Carey was there with that superintendent."

I nodded.

"Carey had more or less collapsed. When I went in, the policeman was giving him a glass of water. Water! He should have had brandy. The moment he saw me he said he couldn't go on, it was all too much. I told him we needed him, but he didn't answer properly. All he said was that Scott had worked for the practice for ten or more years and we'd never find an anesthetist like him."

"And will you?"

He made a shrugging gesture that involved not just his shoulders but his neck and head.

"If Carey disbands the partnership," he said, "because that's what will happen if he resigns, we'll have to start again.

"And to start again," I pointed out, "you need a clean slate. So we walk up the drive here and jerk the bell-pull."

His long head turned slowly towards me.

"How do you know about jerking the bell-pull?"

I couldn't answer. I hadn't realized when I was speaking that I was drawing on memory.

"Figure of speech," I said lamely.

He shook his head. "You know things you couldn't know. I've noticed before. You knew my father's name was Kenny, that very first evening. How did you know?"

After a while I said, "If I do any good for you, I'll tell you."

"That's all?"

"That's all."

I started the car, drove in through the gates and stopped in a circular graveled area short of the house. Then, alone, I got out of the car and I walked along the last piece of driveway and jerked the bell-pull, which was a wrought-iron rod with a gilded knob on the end. I knew, before I heard them, what the distant chimes would sound like inside the house.

I couldn't remember who should be opening the door, but it certainly wasn't the woman who did. Of indeterminate age, she was sandy-colored with dry curly hair, fair eyelashes, and noticeable down on her upper lip and lower jaw. Thin and strong, dressed in jeans, checked shirt and faded sweater, she made no attempt at personal show but was not unattractive, in an unconventional sort of way. She looked me up and down, and waited.

"Miss Zoe Mackintosh?" I asked.

"I'm not buying anything. Good afternoon." The door began closing.

"I'm not a salesman," I said hastily.

"What then?" The door paused.

"I'm from Hewett and Partners."

"Then why didn't you say so?" She opened the door wider. "But I didn't send for anyone."

"We're . . . er . . . working on the question of why two of your horses died in our hospital."

"Bit late for that," she said crisply.

"Could we possibly ask you a few questions?"

She put her head on one side. "I suppose so. Who's we?"

I looked back to the car. "Ken McClure's with me."

"Oh, no. He killed them."

"I don't think so," I said. "Couldn't you please listen?"

She hesitated. "He told me some rubbish about atropine."

"What if it wasn't rubbish?"

She gave me a straight uncompromising inspection, then made up her mind at least to hear the case for the defense.

"Come in, then," she said, stepping back. She looked across to the car and said grudgingly, "I told Ken he'd never set foot in here again, but he can come too."

"Thank you."

I made a beckoning arm movement to Ken but he approached warily and stopped a full pace behind me.

"Zoe . . ." he said tentatively.

"Yes, well, you've brought a devil's advocate, I see. So come in and get on with it."

We stepped into a black and white tiled hallway and she closed the door behind us. Then she led the way across the hall, down a short passage and into a square room crowded with office paraphernalia, racing colors, photographs, sagging armchairs and six assorted dogs. Zoe scooped several dogs off the chairs and invited us to sit.

In an obscure way I thought the interior of the house was somehow wrong: it didn't smell the way it should, and there was an absence of sound. Zoe's room smelled of dogs. I couldn't get back past that, the way one can't remember a particular tune with a different one bombarding one's eardrums.

"Have you lived here long?" I asked,

She raised her eyebrows humorously, glancing round at the clutter.

"Doesn't it look like it?" she said.

"Well, yes."

"Twenty-something years," she said. "Twenty-three, twenty-four."

"A long time," I agreed.

"Yes. So what about these horses?"

"I think they and several others died as a result of insurance swindles."

She shook her head decisively. "Our two weren't insured. Their owners don't let us forget it."

I said, "Horses can be insured without the owner or the trainer knowing."

Her eyes slowly widened in memory. "Russet Eaglewood did that once. Good job she did."

"Yes, she told me."

Ken gave me a hard stare.

Zoe reflected. "So you went to see her about the Eaglewoods' dead horses?"

"Yours and theirs died in the same way."

Zoe looked at Ken. I shook my head. "Not his fault."

"Whose then?"

"We're trying to find out." I paused. "The horses all died in the hospital, except perhaps one . . ."

"How many died?" she interrupted.

"Eight or nine," I said.

"You're kidding!"

Ken protested, "You shouldn't have told her."

"One death could be put down to your carelessness," I said. "Perhaps even two. But *eight* unexplained deaths? Eight, when you are an expert surgeon? You've been carrying the can for someone else, Ken, and sensible people like Miss Mackintosh will realize it."

The sensible Miss Mackintosh gave me an ironic glance, but all the same looked on Ken as victim not villain from then on.

"To get the horses to the hospital, after they'd

301

been insured, of course," I said, "they had to be made ill. Which is why we'd like you to concentrate hard on who had any opportunity to give your horses emergency-sized colic by feeding them atropine."

Instead of answering directly she said, "Did the Eaglewood horses have atropine?"

"No," I said. "They had appointments."

She turned a gasp into a laugh. "Who *are* you?" she asked.

"Peter. Friend of Ken's."

"I'd say he's lucky."

I gave her the ironic look back.

"All right," she said. "After Ken said that, even though I was furious, I did think about it. To be frank, any one of our lads would have fed their mothers to the horses for a tenner. A doctored apple? A quick agreement in the pub? Too easy. Sorry."

"Worth a try," Ken said.

A buzzer rasped loudly into the pause. "My father," Zoe said briefly, rising. "I'll have to go."

"I'd very much like to meet your father," I said.

She raised fair bushy eyebrows. "You're five years too late. But come if you like."

She went out into the passage and we followed her back into the hall and in through double doors to a large splendid drawing room whose far wall was glass from floor to ceiling. Just outside the glass was a mill wheel, a huge wooden paddle wheel, more than half of it visible, the lower part below floor level. It was decoration only; there was no movement.

"Where's the stream?" I said, and remembered what was wrong about the house. No musty smell of everlasting water. No sound of the mill wheel turning.

"There isn't one. It dried up years ago," Zoe said, crossing the floor. "They mucked around with the water table, taking too much for a bloody power station. Dad," she finished, coming to a halt by a high-backed chair, "you've got some visitors."

The chair made no reply. Ken and I walked round to the front of it and met the man who had been Mac Mackintosh.

10

McIntosh was small and wrinkled, an old dried apple of a horseman. Set in the weather-beaten face, his startlingly deep blue eyes looked alert and intelligent enough, and it was only gradually one realized that the thoughts behind them were out of sequence, like a jumbled alphabet.

He was sitting facing the immobile wheel, looking through it, I supposed, to the field and hedge beyond. There was an impression that he'd sat there for a long time; that he sat there habitually. The arms of the chair, where his thin hands rested, had been patched and repatched from wear.

He said in a high scratchy voice, "Have you forgotten evening stables?"

"Of course not, Dad," Zoe said patiently. "They're not for another half hour."

"Who's that with you? I can't see faces against the light."

"Good afternoon, Mr. Mackintosh," Ken said.

"It's Ken McClure," Zoe informed him, "and a friend of his."

"Peter," Ken said.

"I thought you said Ken," Mackintosh complained testily.

"I'm Peter," I said.

Zoe reintroduced everyone with clarity but it was doubtful if the old man grasped it, as he kept looking at me with bewilderment every few seconds.

"You said," he told Zoe, "that only Carey would come."

"Yes, I know I did, but I've changed my mind. Carey will still come to play cards with you but Ken is back looking after the horses." To us she quietly added, "They've played cards together for years but it's a farce these days. Carey just pretends now, which is good of him."

"What did you say?" Mackintosh asked crossly. "Do speak up."

"Where's your hearing aid, Dad?" Zoe asked.

"I don't like it. It whistles."

Ken and I were both standing in front of him, between him and the window, and it seemed to displease him that he couldn't see the whole wheel, as he kept moving his head to look round and beyond us. Ken must have sensed the same thing, because he turned sideways as if to minimize the obstruction.

The backlight from the window fell on half of Ken's bony face, the rest being still in shadow, and Mackintosh sat up sharply in his chair and stared at him joyfully.

"Kenny!" he said, "did you bring the stuff? I thought you were . . ." He broke off fearfully confused. "Dead," he said faintly.

"I'm not Kenny," Ken said, moved.

305

Mackintosh flopped back in the chair. "We lost the money," he said.

"What money?" I asked.

Zoe said, "Don't bother him. You won't get a sensible answer. He's talking about the money he lost in a bad property investment. It preys on his mind. Every time anything worries him or he doesn't understand something, he goes back to it."

I asked Ken, "Is that what your mother was talking about?"

"Josephine?" Zoe involuntarily made a face. "She always enjoys a good disaster. Sorry Ken, but it's true." To me she added, "Dad lost a small fortune, but he wasn't alone. The scheme looked all right on paper because you didn't have to invest any actual cash and it should have been a good return. Dozens of people guaranteed slices of a huge loan to build an entertainment and leisure center between Cheltenham and Tewkesbury, and it did get built, but the location and the design of it were all wrong and so no one would use it or buy it and the bank called in all the loans. I can't bear to look at the damn thing. It's still unfinished and just rotting away, and half my inheritance is in it." She stopped ruefully. "I'm as bad as Dad, rabbiting on."

"What was it called?" I asked.

"All our money," Mackintosh said in his high voice.

"Porphyry Place," Zoe said, smiling.

Ken nodded. "A great white elephant, except

306

a lot of it's dark red. I pass it sometimes. Rotten luck."

"Ronnie Upjohn," Mackintosh said gleefully, "got his comeuppance."

Zoe looked resigned.

"What does he mean?" I asked.

"Ronnie Upjohn is a steward," she explained. "For years he kept reporting Dad to the Jockey Club and accusing him of taking bribes from the bookies, which of course Dad never did."

Mackintosh shrieked with laughter, his guilt plainly a satisfaction.

"Dad!" Zoe protested, knowing, I saw, that the charges were true.

"Ronnie Upjohn lost a packet." Mackintosh shook with delight and then, under our gaze, seemed to lose the thread of thought and relapse into puzzlement. "Steinback laid it off at a hundred to six."

"What does he mean?" I asked Zoe again.

She shrugged. "Old bets. Steinback was a bookie, died years ago. Dad remembers things but muddles them up." She gave her father a look compounded of affection, exasperation and fear, the last, I guessed, the result of worry over the not-too-distant future. She and Russet Eaglewood had that in common: daughters holding together the crumbling lives of their fathers.

"As you're here," Zoe said to Ken, "would you like to look round at evening stables?"

Ken's pleased acceptance pleased Zoe equally. My mission of reinstatement seemed to have suc-

ceeded with her as with Russet. The world, however, remained to be conquered.

"Come on, Dad," Zoe said, helping her father
to his feet. "Time for stables."

The old man was physically much stronger
than I'd somehow expected. Short, and with
slightly bowed legs, he moved without hesitation
and without stooping, heading straight down the
big room in evident eagerness. The three of us
followed him out into the tiled hall and passage,
and down past the open door of Zoe's room. She
put her head in there and whistled, and the six
dogs came bounding out, falling over their own
feet with excitement.

This enlarged party crammed into a dusty
Land-Rover outside the back door and set off
down a rear roadway which led to a brick-built
white-painted stable yard a quarter mile distant.
From a single-story white house at one side, the
head lad had emerged to join us, and I attended
the ritual of British evening stables in an invited
capacity for the first time ever.

It seemed familiar enough. The slow progress
from box to box, the brief discussion between
trainer, lad and head lad as to each horse's well-
being, the pat and the carrot from the trainer,
the occasional running of the trainer's hand down
a suspect equine leg. Ken discussed the inmates'
old injuries with Zoe, and old man Mackintosh
gave the head lad an unending stream of instructions which were gravely acknowledged but which
sounded to me contradictory.

At one point I asked Zoe which boxes had been occupied by the two atropine colics.

"Reg," she said to the head lad, "talk to my friend here, will you? Answer any question."

"*Any?*" he queried.

She nodded. "He's on the side of the angels."

Reg, small and whippy like Mackintosh himself, gave me a suspicious inspection and no benefit of any doubt. Reg, I thought, might be on the side of the devil.

I asked him anyway about the boxes. Reluctantly he pointed and identified them: numbers 6 and 16. The numbers were painted in black on the white wall above the door of each box. Nothing else to distinguish them from all the others.

Reg, carrying the bag of carrots, was handing them to Zoe and her father at each box and didn't want me getting in the way.

"Do you know anyone called Wynn Lees?" I asked him.

"No, I don't."

The answer was immediate, without pause for thought.

Old Mackintosh, taking a carrot, had also heard the question, and gave a different answer.

"Wynn Lees?" he said cheerfully in his high loud voice. "He tacked a man's trousers to his bollocks." He laughed long and hard, wheezing slightly. "With a rivet gun," he added.

I glanced at Ken. He was going rigid with shock, his mouth open.

"Dad!" Zoe protested automatically.

"True," her father said. "I think it was true, you know." He frowned, troubled, as the memory slid away. "I dream a bit, now and then."

"Do you know him, sir?" I asked.

"Who?"

"Wynn Lees."

The blue eyes sparkled at me. "He went away . . . I expect he's dead. Six is Vinderman."

"Come on, Dad," Zoe said, moving along the row of boxes.

He said mischievously, as if reciting a nursery rhyme, "Revised Edition, Wishywashy, Pennycracker, Glue."

Zoe said, "They don't want to be bothered with all that, Dad."

I asked him lazily, "What comes after Glue?"

"Faldy, Vinderman, Kodak, Boy Blue."

I smiled broadly. He laughed happily, pleased.

"They're the names of horses he used to train long ago," Zoe said. "He forgets the names of today's." She took his arm. "Let's get on, the lads are all waiting."

He went amenably, and we came to a horse that Zoe said had been much stronger and tougher since he'd been cut. For cut, read castrated, I thought. Most male steeplechasers were geldings.

"Oliver Quincy did it," Zoe said.

Ken nodded. "He's good at it."

"He came out several times, did three or four of them. Dad likes him."

Ken said neutrally, "Oliver can be good company when he chooses."

"Oliver?" Mackintosh asked. "Did you say Oliver?"

"Yes, sir. Oliver Quincy."

"He told me a joke. Made me laugh. I can't remember it."

"He does tell jokes," Ken agreed.

Oliver's joke had fallen flat on Sunday morning: "what four animals did a woman like most." My mother would love it, I thought.

We came to the last box. "Poverty," Mackintosh said, feeding a carrot to a chestnut with a white star. "How's he doing, Reg?"

"Coming along fine, sir."

"Is she still in season?" Zoe asked him.

Reg shook his head. "She'll be fine for Saturday."

"What's her name?" I asked. "Shall I bet?"

"Metrella," Zoe said, "and don't. Well, thanks, Reg. That's all. I'll be down later."

Reg nodded and Zoe swept everyone back into the Land-Rover except for the dogs, who bounded home at varying speeds in the wake.

Zoe invited us halfheartedly to go in for a drink and didn't mind when we declined.

"Come again," Mackintosh said warmly.

"Thank you, sir," Ken said.

I looked along the sweep of the fine mellow frontage, the mill wheel out of sight round the far end, the old stream gone forever.

"Splendid house," I said. "A piece of history. I wonder who lived here before."

"As it's been here two centuries, I can't tell

you everyone," Zoe said, "but the people Dad bought it from were a family called Travers."

Ken wanted to talk not about the Mackintoshes but about his session with the Superintendent, which had pressing priority in his mind. When we reached his car we sat on for a while in mine and he told me what had gone on in the office after I'd left.

"Superintendent Ramsey wanted to know if there were any surgical gloves missing. I ask you, how could we know? We buy them by the hundred pairs. We order more when we get low. Carey told him to stop asking, no one knew."

"You and Carey were both there?"

"Yes, for a while. I told Ramsey we had several sizes of gloves. Yvonne uses size six and a half. Mine are much bigger. He asked dozens of questions. What are the gloves made of? Where do we buy them? How often do we count them? Where do we dispose of them? I asked him if he'd found any used gloves lying about, but he wouldn't say."

While he drew breath I said, "What *are* they made of, then?"

"Latex. You've seen them often enough. Each pair is packed in its own sterile packet. You've seen me throw them in the bin. I mean, sometimes I might use three pairs during one operation. It always depends. So then he started on gowns, caps and masks. Same thing, except not so many sizes. We throw them away. We throw the packets away. All we could pretty well swear to was that there were no lab coats missing, because those aren't disposable, they go to the laundry. Ramsey said wasn't it extravagant to throw so much away. He has no understanding of sterile procedure. He'd never heard of shoe-covers. After that army of doctors, police and photographers had marched through the operating room, any hope of deducing who'd been in there would have vanished, I would have thought."

"Mm."

"And why should he think anyone would need to be sterile to commit murder?"

"You told me yourself."

"What do you mean?"

"So as not to leave any personal telltale litter on Scott. No hair, no skin, no fluff, no nothing."

He blinked. "Do you really believe that?"

"I don't know, but I'd guess they didn't find any fingerprints on the stapler, and took it from there."

"It's all ghastly," he said.

"What else did they ask?"

"They asked if I thought Scott had killed the horses."

"Mm."

"What do you mean, mm? He couldn't have done." He was indignant at my response. "He was a *nurse.*"

"And an anesthetist."

"You're as bad as the police."

"It's always been a possibility," I said reasonably. "I'm not saying he killed them, I'm saying he had the ability and the opportunity. Just like you."

He thought it over. "Oh."

"Maybe he found out who killed them," I said.

Ken swallowed. "I didn't believe you when you said things were dangerous. I mean killing horses is one thing but killing a man is different."

"If you have the means to kill without trace, that's dangerous."

"Yes, I see."

"And Scott is the second person dead here."

"The second? Oh, you mean the arsonist?"

"Everyone forgets him," I said. "Or her, of course."

"Her?"

"How about the nurse who left in a huff?"

"Surely the police checked on her!"

"Yes, I expect so," I reflected. "How about us going to see Nagrebb?"

He hated the idea. "Nagrebb's bad enough but his son's worse."

"I thought you said he had a daughter."

"He has. Two sons and a daughter. One of the sons is also a show-jumper and he's the meanest bastard that ever sat in a saddle."

"That's saying something, with Wynn Lees about."

"You'll be wanting to see *him* next!"

"Actually, no, I don't think so."

"You've a vestige of sense left, then."

"Well," I said, "who trained the Fitzwalter horse?"

"He trained it himself. He holds a permit."

"Does he?" I didn't know why I should be surprised. Many owners of steeplechasers trained their own horses. "I thought you said it was a colt."

"Yes, it was. A three-year-old colt. It had run and won on the Flat as a two-year-old, and Fitzwalter bought it because he likes to get them going and run them as three- and four-year-old hurdlers and then put them over fences a bit later on."

"What's he like?"

"Fitzwalter? Opinionated, but not too bad as a trainer. If you're thinking of going to see *him*, I don't mind coming with you. He took it quite well when his horse died."

"Where does he live?"

"Five miles or so. Do you want me to phone, to see if he's home?"

"We might as well."

"He hasn't stopped employing me, though. I mean, you don't have to persuade him, like the others. And how did you tame Zoe so quickly? She was positively putty. Not a claw in sight."

"I don't know. I thought her attractive. She probably saw that."

"Attractive!"

"In a way."

"Astounding. Anyway, Fitzwalter engages us on a sort of contract basis, and it's still in operation."

"Good, then can you drop in without his calling you out specifically?"

He nodded. "I often pop in if I'm passing."

"Let's pop, then."

He consulted the small address book, phoned, got an affirmative answer, removed himself from my car to his own and led the way through country lanes and up a winding hill to a bare upland and a gray stone house. The house, unremarkable, stood next to about three acres of smashed and rotting cars, a jumbled rusting dump of old dreams.

We turned off the road into a straight drive which led past the house and ended by a small open-ended stable-yard that looked as if it had been constructed from old sheds, a barn, a garage or two, and a henhouse.

"Fitzwalter's a scrap metal merchant," Ken said unnecessarily as we got out of the cars. "At weekends, that pile of junk is buzzing with crowds looking for parts, wheels, valves, seats, pistons, he sells anything. Then he compresses the picked carcasses and ships them to be melted down. Makes a fortune."

"An odd mixture, scrap metal and horses," I said.

Ken was amused. "You'd be surprised. Half the kids pot-hunting at horse shows and gymkhanas are funded this way. Well, OK, not half, but definitely some."

In the yard, doors were open, lads carried buckets: evening stables were in full swing.

Fitzwalter, whom Ken called and introduced simply as Fitz, came out of a garage-like stall and greeted us with a wave. He wore patched corduroys streaked blackly with oil and a big checked rough wool shirt. No jacket, despite the chill in the air. He had straight black hair, dark eyes and tanned skin, and was thin, energetic and perhaps sixty.

"You should see him at the races," Ken said under his breath as we walked into the yard to join him. "He has his suits made. Looks like a city gent."

He looked more like a gypsy at that moment, but his voice was standard English and his manner businesslike. He excused himself from shaking hands as they were covered with sulfanilamide powder, instead wiping them casually on his trousers. He seemed pleased enough to see Ken and, nodding to include me, asked him to just take a quick look at the rash inside his mare's stifle.

We walked to the box he'd come out of, which proved to contain a pair of enormous chestnut hindquarters and a flicking tail. Presumably she also had a head and the usual front half, but they were out of sight beyond. Ken and Fitz sidled unconcernedly past the kicking area, but I stayed further back, out of reach.

Unable to hear the professional consultation within, I watched instead the activity out in the yard and listened to the clink and clank of the buckets.

I had no feeling here of familiarity. Memory held a blank.

"Try Vaseline instead," Ken was saying, coming out. "Keep the rash moist for a while instead of trying to dry it up too soon. She's looking well otherwise."

He and Fitzwalter moved across the expanse of packed earth and dead brown weeds and headed for the barn. In there, I discovered, following, were two roomy stalls strong enough for cart-horses but each containing a good-looking narrow bay horse tied to the wall by its head collar.

Ken and Fitzwalter looked at each in turn. Ken ran his hand down the legs. A good deal of nodding went on.

"How many horses do you train?" I asked Fitzwalter interestedly.

"Six at present," he said. "It's the busiest time of year, you see. I've room for seven, but we lost one a while back."

"Yes, Ken told me. Bad luck."

He nodded and asked Ken, "Did you ever find out what hit him?"

"No, 'fraid not."

Fitzwalter scratched his neck. "Good little colt," he said, "pity he had a chipped bone."

"Did you have him insured?" I asked sympathetically.

"Yes, but not for enough." He shrugged easily. "Some I insure, some I don't. Most times the premium's too high so I don't insure. I risk it. With him, well, he was expensive when I bought him so I took some cover. Not enough, though. Win some, lose some."

I smiled noncommittally. He was perhaps lying, I thought.

"Decent insurance company, was it?" I asked.

"They paid up, that's the main thing." He laughed briefly, showing his teeth, and led the way out of the barn. "I'm running the five-year-old tomorrow at Worcester," he said to Ken. "What about a blood count to see if she's in good shape?"

"Sure," Ken said, and returned forthwith to his car for the necessaries of collecting a blood sample, telling Fitzwalter he would borrow a neighboring vet's lab for the count. "Ours went up in smoke," he said, "if you remember."

Fitzwalter nodded and thanked him and offered drinks, but we again declined. He looked at Ken speculatively, as he had been doing on and off all along, and came to a decision.

"One of my lads," he said, "told me a rumor that I really can't believe."

Ken said, "What rumor?"

"That you had one of your people murdered this morning." He inspected Ken's face and got his answer. "Who was it? Not Carey!"

"Scott Sylvester, our anesthetist," Ken said reluctantly.

"What happened?"

"We don't know," Ken said, shying away from describing Scott's state. "It'll be on the news . . . and in the papers."

"You don't seem much worried," Fitzwalter said critically. "I was expecting you to tell me. When you didn't, I thought it couldn't be true. How was he killed?"

"We don't know," Ken said uncomfortably. "The police are trying to find out."

"I don't like the sound of it."

"It's devastating," Ken agreed. "We're trying to go on as normal but frankly I don't know how long we'll be able to."

Fitzwalter's dark eyes looked into the distance, considering. "I'll have to talk to Carey," he said.

"Carey's very upset. Scott had been with us a long time," Ken said.

"Yes, but *why* was he killed? You must know more than you're saying."

"He was dead in the hospital when we arrived this morning," Ken told him. "In the operating theater. The police came and took him away and asked us questions, but so far we don't have any answers and the police haven't told us what they think. It's all too soon. We'll know more tomorrow."

"But," Fitzwalter insisted, "was he shot? Was there blood?"

"I don't think so," Ken said.

"Not a shotgun?" Ken shook his head.

"Suicide?"

Ken was silent. I said for him, "It wasn't suicide."

Fitzwalter's attention sharpened on me for the first time. "How do you know?"

"I saw him. His wrists and ankles were tied. He couldn't have killed himself."

He accepted my positive tone. "Who are you, exactly?" he asked.

"Just a friend of Ken's."

"Not involved in the practice?"

"Only visiting."

"A vet?"

"Oh, no," I said, "far from it."

He lost interest and turned back to Ken. "I think it's extraordinary you didn't tell me first thing."

"I try to forget it," Ken said.

He could try, but it was impossible. I would never forget Scott's head. The memory had been coming back in flashes of nausea all day. It must have been the same for Ken.

Fitzwalter shrugged. "I think I only met the man that time when the colt died. I reckoned he'd dropped off to sleep and not been watching properly, but it's unlikely he could have saved him anyway. That's the man, isn't it?"

Ken nodded.

"Well, I'm sorry."

"Thanks," Ken said. He sighed deeply. "When it was just dead horses, life was simpler."

"Yes, I heard you had an epidemic."

"Everyone's heard," Ken said despondently.

"And a fire and another body. I don't see how Hewett and Partners can survive."

Ken didn't answer. The oftener anyone strung the disasters together the more impossible became the prospects. Even a quick solution to everything might not avoid the wreckage, and a quick solution lived in cloud-cuckoo-land.

"Time to go," I said, and Ken nodded.

"How do we stand?" he asked Fitzwalter. "You and I."

Fitzwalter shrugged. "I need a vet. You know the horses. I'll phone Carey. I'll see what can be worked out."

"Thanks very much."

Fitzwalter came halfway with us to the cars.

"Anytime you want to scrap that old Ford," he told Ken, "I'll give you a price."

Ken's car rattled with age and use but he looked indignant.

"There's miles in the old bus yet."

Fitzwalter gave him a pitying shake of the head and turned away. Ken patted his old bus affectionately and folded his gangly height into it behind the wheel. We were both supposed to be returning to Thetford Cottage but it seemed he had as little eagerness as I.

"How about a pint?" he said. "I haven't eaten all day and I feel queasy and I frankly can't talk to Greg for more than five minutes without rigor mortis."

His last words disturbed him after he'd said them. Scott was everywhere in our minds.

"I'll follow you," I said, and he nodded.

As the day darkened, we passed by the tangled metal dump, went down the winding hill and through the country lanes and ended in a quiet old pub where only the chronically thirsty were yet propping up the bar.

I couldn't face beer and settled for brandy in a lot of water, realizing I also hadn't eaten and was feeling more not less unsettled.

"It's hopeless, isn't it?" Ken said, staring into his glass. "Talking to Fitz, I could see it. You give me hope sometimes, but it's an illusion."

"How old is Nagrebb?" I asked.

"Not Nagrebb. I'm not going there."

"Is he sixty or more?"

"He doesn't look it, but his son's over thirty. What does it matter?"

"All the owners or trainers of the dead horses have been men of sixty or more."

He stared. "So what?"

"So I don't really know. I'm just looking for similarities."

"They all know me," Ken said. "They've got that in common."

"Do they all know Oliver?"

Ken thought it over. "I don't suppose he's met Wynn Lees. He probably knows the others. They all know Carey, of course."

"Well, they would. But other things . . . is there anything else that links them?"

"I can't see the point really," he said, "but I suppose anything's worth a try."

I said, "We have a cruel-to-horses pervert, a gaga old man, a scrap metal dealer, an unscrupulous show-jumping trainer, the old tyrant father of Russet Eaglewood and a steward."

323

"What steward?"

"Ronnie Upjohn."

"But his horse *lived.*"

"He's the right age."

"It's nonsense," Ken said. "You'll never get anywhere that way. A quarter of the population's over sixty."

"I expect you're right." I paused, then said, "Did they all know your father?"

He gave me a slightly wild look but didn't shirk the question.

"Old Mackintosh obviously did," he said. "Wasn't that odd? I didn't know I looked so like him as all that."

"Who else?"

"I don't know. He was a vet in this area, so I expect he knew most of them."

"And of course he knew of Wynn Lees."

"But it couldn't matter now, after all this time."

"Just fishing around," I said. "Do they all know each other?"

He frowned. "Eaglewood knows Lees and Mackintosh and Fitzwalter and Upjohn. Don't know about Nagrebb. The three trainers all know each other well, of course. They meet all the time at the races. Nagrebb's in a different world. So is Wynn Lees."

"And all this started since Wynn Lees came back from Australia."

"I suppose it did."

Wholly depressed, we finished our drinks and drove to Thetford Cottage. Belinda, looking

324

tired, had already told Vicky and Greg about Scott, so we passed a long subdued evening without cheer. Vicky offered to sing to raise our spirits but Belinda wouldn't let her. She and Ken left at ten and the rest of us went to bed in relief.

In the morning I went back to the hospital, drawn as if by a magnet, but there was nothing happening. The Portakabin doors were shut. The car park, usually overfilled, was half empty. There were two police cars by the hospital but no barrier to keep other cars out.

I parked near the front entrance and went in and found Ken, Oliver, Jay and Lucy all sitting glumly silent in the office.

"Morning," I said.

They couldn't raise a greeting between them.

"Carey's closed the practice," Ken said, explaining the general atmosphere. "He got the secretary to phone all the people with small-animal appointments to cancel them. She was doing it in the Portakabin when we arrived. Now she's in there answering the phone and telling people to find other vets."

"I didn't think he would do this to us," Lucy exclaimed. "He didn't even ask us."

"He hasn't the right," Oliver said. "It's a partnership. He can resign from it if he likes—and the sooner the better—but he can't just put us all out of work like this."

Jay said, "It isn't as if any of these disasters

touched my cattle. I'm going to phone all my clients and tell them I've set up on my own."

"Sometimes you need the hospital," Ken said.

"I'll rent the theater when I need it."

"Good idea," Oliver said.

I didn't bother to point out that as they jointly owned the hospital and each paid a share of the mortgage, it might not be as simple as they thought to disengage from it. Not my business, though.

"Is Carey here?" I asked.

They shook their heads. "He came. He told us. We were speechless with shock. He left."

"And the police? Their cars are here."

"In the theater," Lucy said. "Don't know what they're doing."

As if on cue, the police constable appeared in the doorway and asked the vets to go with him to join the Superintendent. They trooped out and followed him up the passage and I might have tried to tack on unobtrusively, but the telephone on the desk gave me a better idea and I phoned Annabel at the Jockey Club instead.

"Oh, good," she said when I announced myself, "I didn't know how to reach you. Some people I know need a new sharer in their flat. Are you interested?"

"Fervently," I said.

"When can you come?"

"This evening," I said.

"Can you pick me up at my house at six?"

"I'll be there and I'm highly grateful."

"Have to go now. 'Bye."

" 'Bye," I said, but she'd already gone. I put down the receiver thinking that life wasn't all doom and gloom after all.

Almost immediately the phone rang again and after a moment or two, as no one ran back from the theater, I picked it up and said "Hewett and Partners, can I help you?" just like Ken.

A voice on the other end said, "This is the Parkway Chemical Company. We need to speak to Kenneth McClure about a letter we received from him this morning."

I said, "I'm Kenneth McClure." Lie abroad for your country . . . !

"Fine. Then I'm answering your query. I'm the sales manager, by the way. Condolences on your fire."

"Thanks. It's a mess."

"Will you be needing replacements for what you've lost?"

"Yes, we will," I said. "If you can send us the past invoices, we can make up a new shopping list."

"Splendid," he said. "You will remember, though, won't you, that there are some substances we can't put in the post? Like last time, you'll have to send someone to collect it."

"OK," I said.

"Last time, according to our records, your messenger was a Mr. Scott Sylvester. He's been vouched for, but if you send anyone else he'll need full identification and a covering letter from your partnership laboratory. Even Mr. Sylvester will need identification. Sorry and all that, but we have to be careful, as you know."

"Yes," I said. "Could you give us the copies of the invoices as soon as possible?"

"Certainly. We're getting them together at this moment. They'll go off today."

"Could you also send us a copy of the delivery note that I'm sure you gave Scott Sylvester when he collected from you?"

"Certainly, if you like."

"It would help us restore our records."

"Of course. I'll assemble it straightaway."

"Thank you very much indeed."

"No trouble. Glad to help." He put the phone down gently and I stood thinking of the possible significance of what he'd told me.

Scott had personally collected at least one substance that couldn't be sent through the mail. It might be harmless. It might be anything. I'd wanted to ask the sales manager exactly what Scott had carried, but he'd talked as if I knew, and I hadn't wanted to make him suspicious. In the morning, or whenever the reply fell through the letterbox at Thetford Cottage, we would find out. Patience, I sometimes thought, was the hardest of virtues.

I reached Annabel's house on time at six and she opened the door to my ring.

The clothes this time were baggy black silk trousers and a big top that looked as if it were made of soft white feathers. She'd added silver boots, wide silver belt and silver earrings and carried a black swinging cape to put on to keep warm. Her mouth was pink and her eyes were smiling. I kissed her cheek.

"We may as well go straight on in your car," she said. "The people are expecting us."

"Fine."

She told me on the way that they were offering a bed-sitting room but I'd have to accept cleaning and breakfast.

"They say they have to be able to get you out if they don't like your habits. They don't want any legal hassle."

"You've lost me."

"The rent acts, of course."

I was unclear about the rent acts and got a brief lecture on how it was currently impossible to evict undesirable tenants unless the landlord cleaned for them and preferably provided food.

"Count me in enthusiastically for cleaning and breakfast," I said. "Suits me fine."

The flat itself was in an ancient mansion block, on the fourth of six floors and approached by a creaky old lift. The inhabitants were a bearded professor and his intimidated wife. The room they offered was large and old-fashioned with a view of nearby roofs and fire escapes. I didn't like it much, but it was at least a foothold. We agreed on terms and I gave them a check for a deposit, and Annabel and I descended to the car.

"It's not awfully good," she said doubtfully. "I hadn't seen it before."

"It's a start. I'll look around later for something else."

It had the virtue at least of being within two miles of Annabel's house, and I hoped I might be crossing those two miles frequently. The bishop's daughter already had me thinking in such heavy unaccustomed words as permanent, forever and commitment, and common sense told me it was far too soon for that. It had always been too soon; common sense had ever prevailed. Common sense had never come to grips with an Annabel.

"Six-forty," she said, looking at her outsize black watch. "Brose has fixed up someone for you to meet if you want to. It's about insuring horses."

"Yes, please," I said with interest.

"Brose says this man always drinks in a hotel bar near the Jockey Club's London quarters and he should be there about now. You could catch him before he leaves."

"You're coming, I hope," I said.

She smiled for answer and I drove while she gave directions to the rendezvous. It wasn't hard to find but achieving a parking space took up as much time as the journey and I was afraid we'd be too late.

Brose himself was in the bar, talking to a short bald man with a paunch and gold-rimmed glasses. Brose saw us come in, as it was hard to miss Annabel's arrival anywhere, and waved to us to join him.

"Thought you weren't coming," the big man said.

"Parking," Annabel told him succinctly.

"Meet Mr. Higgins," he said, indicating the paunch. "His company insures horses."

We shook hands, completing the introductions. Higgins's attention fastened on Annabel as if mesmerized while she twirled off the cape and rubbed a ruffling hand over her feathers.

"Er," he said. "Oh yes, horses."

I bought drinks for everyone, a bearable pain in the cash flow since Brose, Annabel and I all chose citron pressé, much to the horror of Higgins with his double vodka and tonic. The bar was one of the dark sort, all dim lights and old wood, everything rich-looking and polished and pretending that the Edwardian age still existed, that horses pulled carriages outside in smoke-laden London fog.

Brose said, "Your spot of bother's in the news. I was just telling Higgs about it. Out of hand, isn't it?"

"Pretty far," I agreed.

"What's happened?" Annabel asked. "What spot of bother?"

Brose looked at her kindly. "Don't you watch the box? Don't you read the papers?"

"Sometimes."

He said, "The Hewett and Partners' anesthetist was murdered sometime on Monday night. Didn't the pride of the Foreign Office tell you?"

"I'd have told her this evening," I said.

Annabel listened in dismay to the short account Brose and I gave her. Brose had actually spoken to Superintendent Ramsey, who'd informed him that inquiries were proceeding.

"That means they haven't a clue," Brose said. "I offered any service they needed, and that's where we stand." He looked at me shrewdly. "What do you know about it that I don't?"

The newspapers that I'd seen had printed nothing about hoists or staples and I'd supposed the police had their reasons for keeping quiet. I'd have told Brose then but Higgins was looking at his watch, drinking his vodka and showing signs of leaving, so I said to Brose, "Tell you later," and to Higgins, "I really do want to know about insuring horses."

The paunch resettled itself. I bought him a re-fill, which anchored him nicely.

"Brose suggested," Higgins said in a fruity bass voice, "that I just talk and if you want to ask anything, fire away."

"Great," I said.

"Insuring horses," he began, "is risk business. We don't do it except as a sideline, understand. Agents phone us and we make a deal. Premiums are high because the risks are high, understand?"

I nodded. "Give us an example," I said.

He thought briefly. "Suppose you have a good Derby prospect, it's worth your while insuring it because of the possible future stud value. So we make a deal on how long the policy is to run for and exactly what it covers. That's accidental death usually, but it could include malicious damage, negligence and death from illness. Most horses don't die young from natural causes so that's not as risky as racing. We'd agree to a policy that included death from natural causes but we'd review it every year and increase the premium. After ten years, except for stallions at stud, we might decline at any price, but generally racehorses live well on into their late teens, or middle twenties. That is, if nature takes its whole course. Many people put down their old horses earlier, if it's more humane."

"Or cheaper," Brose said dryly.

Higgins dispatched half his second drink with a nod of sad agreement.

"What about a broodmare?" I asked.

"In foal?"

"In foal to a top stallion."

"Mm. We'd write a policy as long as the pregnancy was definitely established and proceeding normally. It isn't usual, but it could be done, especially if the stallion fee has to be paid whether there's a live foal or not. No foal, no fee is customary. How old a mare?"

"I don't know."

"It would depend on her age and her breeding record."

"I can tell you," Brose said. "She was nine and had been barren one year but had borne two healthy foals, one colt, one filly."

Higgins raised his eyebrows until they rose

above the gold rims of his glasses. I could feel my own eyebrows going up in unison.

"How do you know?" I asked.

"Peter, really. I'm a detective by trade."

"Sorry."

"I obtained the list of mares covered by Rainbow Quest last season and checked them. People with sires like Rainbow Quest are choosy about what mares they'll accept because they need foals of good quality to maintain the stallion's worth, so that the stud fees stay high."

"It makes sense," I agreed.

"So," Brose said, "I phoned the former owner of that mare you were supposed to have in the hospital and asked him how come he had sold her to Wynn Lees. He said his business was going bad and he needed to sell things. He'd sold his mare at the first decent offer. He'd never heard of Wynn Lees before that, he said, and he couldn't remember his name without being prompted. Utterly unbusinesslike, no wonder he was in trouble."

"Was the mare in foal when he sold her?" I asked.

"He says so. Maybe she was, maybe she wasn't. Maybe he believed she was or maybe he was selling an asset he knew had vanished. Either way, he sold her to Wynn Lees." He paused. "Did you get tissue samples from the foal?"

I nodded. "Hair. Also the mare's hair. They've been sent off to be matched. They need some of Rainbow Quest's too."

"I'll get that for you," Brose said. "Which lab's doing the matching?"

"I'll have to ask Ken McClure."

"Ask, and let me know."

I thanked him profoundly. He didn't like fraud, he said.

Higgins nodded, saying, "The temptation to kill an insured horse is one reason for the high premiums. Fraud is a major problem. Some of it is absolutely blatant but if we insure a horse and he breaks a leg, we have to pay, even if we think someone's come along with an iron bar and taken a swipe."

"Did your company," I asked, "insure any horses that died during or after surgical operations?"

"Not recently," he said. "They don't often die during operations. I can't swear we haven't insured one in the past, but I can't recall that we've ever had to pay out for that. Mind you, I'm not saying other companies haven't. Do you want me to ask around?"

"Would you?"

"For Brose, sure."

Brose said, "Thanks, Higgs."

I asked, "Would you ever insure a horse specifically against dying during an operation?"

Higgins pursed his lips. "I would if it was already insured. I would charge an extra one percent premium and pay up if the horse died."

"It's all wicked," Annabel said.

Brose and Higgins, tall and short, lean and fat,

easy together like double-act comics, smilingly agreed with her. Higgins after a while said his goodbyes and left, but Brose stayed, saying at once, "Go on about the murder."

I glanced at Annabel.

"Tell the girl," Brose said robustly, correctly reading my hesitation. "She's not a drooping lily."

"It's fairly horrific," I said.

"If it's too gory, I'll stop you," she said.

"There wasn't any blood."

I explained about the hoist for lifting unconscious horses. Brose nodded. Annabel listened. I told them Scott had been lifted onto the operating table and left with his arms and legs in the air.

Brose narrowed his eyes. Annabel blinked several times.

"There's more," Brose asserted, watching me.

I explained about vets stapling skin together after cuts and operations. I described the little staples. "Not like staples for paper, exactly, though the same idea. Surgical staples are about an eighth of an inch wide, not narrow like ordinary staples. When you put the stapler against skin and squeeze, the staples go fairly deep before they fold round. It's hard to explain." I paused. "The staple ends up like a small squared ring. Only the top surface is visible. The rest is under the skin, drawing the two cut sides together."

"Clear," Brose said, though Annabel wasn't so sure.

"The staples are like unpolished silver in color," I said.

"Why all this about staples?" Annabel wanted to know.

I sighed. "Scott's mouth was fastened shut by a row of staples."

Her eyes went dark.

Brose said, "Now there's a thing," and looked thoughtful.

"Before or after death?" he asked.

"After. No blood."

He nodded. "How was he killed?"

"Don't know. Nothing to be seen."

"Like the horses?"

"Like the mare, perhaps."

"You be careful," Brose said.

"Mm."

"He couldn't be in danger," Annabel protested, looking alarmed.

"Couldn't he? What about all this fact-finding he's been doing?"

"Then stop it," she told me adamantly.

Brose regarded her with quizzical eyes and she very faintly blushed. All the difficult words popped back into my mind unbidden. It's too quick, too soon, insisted common sense.

Brose stood up to his full height, patted Annabel's hair and told me he'd keep in touch. When he'd gone Annabel and I sat on, constantly talking though with many things unspoken.

She asked about my future in the service and I thought I heard a distant echo of an inquisition designed and desired by her father.

"Did you tell your parents about me?" I asked curiously.

"Well, yes. Just in passing. I was telling them about the Japanese." She paused. "So where will you go from this job in England?"

"Anywhere I'm sent."

"And end up an ambassador?"

"Can't tell yet."

"Isn't promotion to ambassador just a matter of Buggin's turn?" She didn't sound antagonistic but I reckoned that that question came straight from the bishop.

"Buggins," I said, "are very competent people."

Her eyes laughed. "Not a bad answer."

"In Japan," I said, "all the men carry things around in bright carrier bags rather than in pockets or briefcases."

"What on earth has that got to do with anything?"

"Nothing," I said. "I thought you might like to know."

"Yes, my life is illuminated. It's overpowering."

"In Japan," I said, "wherever Westerners don't go, the loos are often holes in the floor."

"Riveting. Continue."

"In Japan, every native person has straight black hair. All the women's names end in ko. Yuriko, Mitsuko, Yoko."

"And did you sleep on the floor and eat raw fish?"

"Routine," I agreed. "But I never ate fugu."

"What on earth is fugu?"

"It's the fish that's the chief cause of death from food poisoning in Japan. Fugu restaurants prepare it with enormous precautions but people still die . . ." My voice stopped as if of its own accord. I sat like stone.

"What is it?" Annabel asked. "What have you thought of?"

"Fugu," I said, unclamping my throat, "is one of the deadliest of poisonous fish. It kills fast because it paralyzes the neuromuscular system and stops a person breathing. Its more common name is the puffer fish. I think someone told me it takes so little to be lethal that it's virtually undetectable in a postmortem."

She sat with the pink mouth open.

"The problem is," I said, "you can't exactly go out and buy a puffer fish in Cheltenham."

11

The evening with Annabel, full of laughter despite the grisly scene I'd transferred to her mind, ended like the earlier one, not with a bang but a kiss.

A brief kiss, but on the lips. She stood a pace away after it and looked at me doubtfully. I could still feel the soft touch of her mouth: a closed pink mouth, self-controlled.

"How about Friday?" I said.

"You must be tired of driving."

"Soon it'll be two miles, not a hundred."

If she hadn't wanted me two miles away she wouldn't have arranged it. I wondered if she felt as I did, a shade light-headed but half afraid of a bush fire.

"Friday," she agreed, nodding. "Same time, same place."

Wishing I didn't have to go, I drove back to Thetford Cottage and there slept fitfully with unhappy, disconcerting dreams. I awoke thinking there was something in the dreams that I should remember, but the phantom movies slid quickly away. I'd never been good at remembering dreams. Couldn't imagine how anyone woke with total recall of them. I bathed and dressed and breakfasted with Vicky and Greg.

"You look tired," Vicky said apologetically. "If we hadn't been mugged in Miami you wouldn't have got into this."

And I wouldn't have gone to Stratford races, I thought, and I would never have met Annabel.

"I've no regrets," I said. "Are you happier now in this house?"

"Bored to death," she said cheerfully. "That wedding seems a long way off. I can't wait to go home."

I hung around impatiently for the postman but he brought only one of the reply envelopes and that not the one from Parkway Chemicals. The only envelope to travel out and back in two days contained a whole bunch of invoices for things I'd never heard of. I put them back in the envelope and tried Ken's portable phone number.

He took his time answering. He yawned. "I'm knackered," he said. "I was out at a racing stable half the night with a colic."

"I thought the partnership was defunct."

"So it might be," he said, "but I'm still a vet and horses still get sick, and if I'm the only one available at three in the morning, well, I go."

"You didn't have to operate, did you?"

"No, no. Managed to unknot him with pain-killers and walking. He didn't leave home."

"What trainer?"

"Not one you know. I promise you, this was a regular bonafide uncomplicated colic."

"Great." I told him one reply had come from a pharmaceutical company and, as far as I was

341

concerned, it needed an interpreter. He said to give him half an hour and he would come to Thetford Cottage. Ask Vicky to feed him, he said.

When he arrived I ate a second breakfast with him in the uncozy kitchen, sitting on hard chairs round a white Formica-topped table. Vicky made toast as on a production line.

"You two have the appetite of goats," she said. "It's not fair that you don't get fat."

"You're an angel," Ken said. Vicky sniffed, but she liked it.

Replete, Ken took the invoices out of the envelope and looked through them.

"They've sent a whole year's," he observed. "Let's see . . . sodium, potassium, calcium, chlorine . . . mm, these are the ingredients of Ringer's solution."

"What's Ringer's solution?"

"An all-purpose maintenance fluid. The stuff in the drips."

"Oh."

"I use commercially prepared, ready-made sterile bags of fluid for operations," he said, "but we make our own in-house fluid for the drips out in the stable as it's much cheaper. In the pharmacy, Scott weighs out . . ." He sighed. "Scott weighed out these ingredients, which are white crystalline powders, and stored them ready in plastic bags. When we need some fluid, we add distilled water."

He went on looking through the invoices and slowly began frowning.

"We've certainly used a lot of potassium," he said.

"In the fluids?"

He nodded. "It's customary to add extra potassium for diarrhea cases because they get dehydrated and low in potassium. You can also inject it into ready-made drip bags."

He sat staring into space, hit much as I had been by fugu.

I waited. He swallowed and slowly flushed, the exact opposite of his habit of going pale.

"I should have seen it," he said.

"Seen what?"

"Potassium chloride. Oh God." He transferred his unfocused gaze from the direction of the stove and looked at me with horror. "I should have seen it. Four times! I'm a disgrace."

I couldn't tell whether his sense of shame was justified or not, because I hadn't the knowledge. Knowing Ken, he'd be blaming himself excessively for any error and would take a long time to get over it.

I said, "I always told you that you'd come face-to-face with realization. I told you that somewhere or other, you knew."

"Yes, you did. Well, I think now that I do. I think the four that died on the table died of excess potassium, which is called hyperkalemia, and I should have seen it at the time."

"You weren't expecting the fluids to be wrong."

"Even so . . ." He frowned. "The serum samples from the last one that died were in the laboratory when it burned down. There's no way now of proving it, but the more I see . . ."

"Go on," I said, as he stopped.

"The waves on the ECG, that I told you about, that looked different? There are P waves from the atria of the heart, and they had decreased in amplitude. The heart was slowing down."

"Wasn't it Scott's job to tell you?"

"The captain's responsible for the ship. I always glance at the ECG, even when he's monitoring it. I simply never gave a thought that the slowing was due to excess potassium. I hadn't given them extra potassium."

"Exactly," I said. "Who fetched the bags of drip, and who changed them when they were empty in all those four operations?" He knew I knew the probable answer, but I asked anyway.

After a moment he said, "Scott."

"Always Scott?"

He searched his memory. "Oliver assisted once. He wanted to be there for the tieback operation. He took Scott's place. It *can't* have been Scott that killed them."

"Mm . . ." I pondered. "How much potassium would you need?"

"It's a bit complicated. You'd have to bring the serum concentration to about eight to ten milliequivalents per liter . . ."

"*Ken!*"

"Um . . . well, the serum potassium would normally be four milliequivalents per liter or there-

344

abouts, so you'd have to more than double it. To raise the four to six in a horse weighing one thousand pounds you'd need . . . er . . . Let's see . . ." He brought out a pocket calculator and did sums. "Twenty-three point six eight grams of potassium in powder form. Dissolve that in water and add it to the fluid. When that bag's empty, repeat the process, as the serum concentration is now up to eight. A third similar bag would do the trick. The operation would be well advanced by now so it would seem as if it was prolonged anesthesia that had contributed to the collapse."

He stood up compulsively and walked round and round the table.

"I should have realized," he repeated. "If we'd been using our in-house mixture I'd have tested it for errors, but what I used had come straight from the suppliers and they would never make such a gross mistake."

I thought of all the bags of commercially prepared drips stacked in boxes in the hospital storeroom, one-liter and five-liter bags. For the operation on the mare, Ken had used four at least of the five-liter bags: horses in shock and pain, horses with complicated colic, all had to be given extra quantities of fluid, he'd told me, to combat dehydration and maintain the volume of blood. I'd watched Scott methodically change the empty bags for full ones.

"You gave the mare a lot of extra fluids which were obviously the right stuff as she survived the operation," I said. "How many bags do you usually use?"

He pursed his lips, still walking, and gave me another not-so-simple answer. Perhaps there weren't any simple answers in veterinary medicine.

"In a routine operation on a healthy racehorse—like the screwed cannon bone—the rate of fluid administration would be three to five millimeters per pound of horse per hour, say about four liters an hour. The mare got fifteen an hour."

"So you would use the five-liter bags for emergency colic operations and the single-liter bags for cannon bones?"

"More or less." He thought. "Mind you," he said, "you could also probably kill a horse by giving it too little fluid, or too much. Forty liters an hour of the normal commercial fluid would probably be lethal."

The deadly opportunities were endless, it seemed.

"Well, all right," I said. "You think there was too much potassium in the bags of fluid. How did it get there? How did it get there for those four specific horses and for no others?"

He looked blank. "It can't have been Scott. I won't believe it."

"On the night of the mare's operation," I said, "Scott came to the hospital while you were still on the way and I saw him collect the bags of fluid from the storeroom and I helped him carry them along into the pharmacy room. He stacked them on the shelf there that can be reached from inside the theater by opening the glass door."

"Yes."

"Did he have any routine for which bags he took?"

"Yes. Always in the order in which they arrived. Always the nearest or uppermost."

"So if you wanted to add potassium you could do it in the storeroom, knowing which bags would be used next."

Ken said with relief, "Then it could have been anybody. It didn't have to be Scott."

It could have been anyone, I reflected, who could go in and out of the storeroom, without anyone thinking it inappropriate. That included all the partners, Scott, Belinda, the nurse who'd left in a huff and quite likely the secretaries and the cleaners. In the storeroom there would have been no need to trouble with gowns and shoe-covers and sterile procedures. The clear fluid inside the stiff plastic bags was itself sterile, and that was enough.

"I think we ought to talk to Superintendent Ramsey," I said.

Ken made a face but no demur while I got busy on the phone and ended with an invitation to meet the policeman in the hospital office later that morning.

Ramsey, the farmer-type, listened patiently to the horsedeath theory and how it affected Scott. He came with us into the storeroom to see how the bags of fluid were kept, the nearest to hand being always the next one used. He read the information printed on the plastic; contents and manufacturer.

He followed us along to the small pharmacy section where the bags were stacked on the shelf and he came into the operating room and saw how they could be reached when needed by opening the glass door.

No one actually mentioned the possibility that Scott had discovered who had doctored the bags; it hardly needed to be said.

"The horses are long gone," Ramsey said ruminatively, back in the office. "The last batch of tests was burned before investigation. The empty fluid bags were disposed of. There's no way of proving your theory." He looked thoughtfully at each of us in turn. "What else do you know that you don't know you know?"

"The riddle of the sphinx," I said.

"I beg your pardon?"

"Sorry. It sounded like a riddle."

"A riddle in a conundrum in a maze," he said unexpectedly. "A good deal of police work is like that." He picked up the envelope containing the invoices. "This wasn't a bad idea. Let me have the other answers when they come."

We said we would, and I asked him if he knew yet what had killed Scott. And if he yet knew who had been burned in the fire.

"We're proceeding," he said, "with our enquiries."

I went to see Nagrebb.

Ken wouldn't come with me, but I wanted, out of curiosity if nothing else, to see the man who'd almost certainly cruelly killed two horses, one with laminitis, the other with a dissolved tendon. He and Wynn Lees hadn't cared if their horses died in agony. I'd seen Wynn Lees's mare suffering as I hadn't known horses could, and I'd felt bitterness and grief when she died. I couldn't prove her owner had fed her a carpet needle. I couldn't prove he'd injected his Eaglewood horse with insulin. I *believed* he had, with a revulsion so strong that I wanted never to be near him again.

Nagrebb instantly gave me the same feeling.

I'd imagined him large, bullish and unintelligent like Wynn Lees, so his physical appearance was a surprise. He was out in a paddock behind his house when, following Ken's reluctant instructions, I located his woodsy half-hidden gateposts and turned between them up a stretch of drive that curled round the house until it was out of sight of the road.

The paddock then revealed was fenced with once-white horizontal railings, a tempting path of escape, I would have thought, for any ill-used self-respecting show-jumper. Inside the paddock on well-worn grass a man and an auburn-haired woman stood beside a bright red and white show-jump like a length of imitation brick wall exhorting another man on a dark muscly horse to launch himself over it. The horse ran out sideways to avoid jumping and received a couple of vicious slashes of a whip to remind him not to do it again.

At that point, all three noticed my arrival and offered only scowls as greeting, an arrangement of features which seemed as normal to them as walking about.

The man on the horse and the woman were young, I saw. The older man, noticeably top-heavy with legs too short for the depth of torso, strode grimly towards the paddock railings. Bald, sharp-eyed, pugnacious; a Rottweiler of a man. I got out of the car and went close to the fence to meet him.

"Mr. Nagrebb?" I asked.

"What do you want?" He stopped a few feet short of the fence, raising his voice.

"Just a few words."

"Who are you? I'm busy."

"I'm writing an article on causes of equine deaths. I thought you might help me."

"You thought wrong."

"You're so knowledgeable," I said.

"What I know I keep to myself. Clear off."

"I heard you might tell me about acute overnight laminitis," I said.

His reaction in its way was proof enough. The sudden stillness, the involuntary contraction of muscles round the eyes, I'd watched them often when I'd asked seemingly innocuous questions in diplomatic circles about illicit, hidden sex lives. I knew alarm bells when I saw them.

350

"What are you talking about?" he demanded.

"Excessive carbohydrates."

He didn't answer.

There must have been something about him that transmitted anxiety to the other two, as the young woman came running over and the man trotted across on the horse. She was fierce-eyed, a harpy; he as dark and well-muscled as his horse.

"What is it, Dad?" he asked.

"Man wants to know about sudden acute laminitis."

"Does he, indeed." His voice was like his father's; local Gloucestershire accent and aggressive. He knew, too, what I was talking about. I wasn't sure about the girl.

"I need firsthand accounts," I said. "It's for general public readership, not for veterinary specialists. Just your own words describing how you felt when you found your horse fatally crippled."

"Tripe," the son said.

"Last September, wasn't it?" I asked. "Was he insured?"

"Fuck off!" the son said, bringing the horse right up to the fence and warningly raising his effective whip.

I thought it might be time to take his advice. I'd evaluated Nagrebb, which had been the point of the excursion, making my picture gallery of the old men complete. Ken's opinion of the son I would endorse any day. If the young woman were the daughter, she was the product of the family ethos but not, I thought, its powerhouse.

"Who sent you to us?" Nagrebb demanded.

"Hearsay," I said. "Fascinating stuff."

"What's your name?"

"Blake Pasteur." I said the first name that came into my head; the name of a colleague first secretary back in Tokyo. I didn't think Nagrebb would be checking the Foreign Office lists. "Freelance journalist," I said. "Sorry you can't help me."

"Piss off," Nagrebb said.

I began to make a placatory retreat and that would have been the end of it except that at that moment another car swept round the house and came to a halt beside mine.

The driver climbed out. Oliver Quincy, to my dismay.

"Hello," he said to me in surprise. "What the hell are you doing here?" His displeasure was evident.

"Hoping for information for an article on equine deaths."

"Do you know him?" Nagrebb demanded.

"Of course. Friend of Ken McClure's. Has his nose into everything in the hospital."

The atmosphere took a chilly turn for the worse.

"I'm writing an article about the hospital," I said.

"Who for?" Oliver said suspiciously.

"Anyone who'll buy it. And they will."

"Does Ken know this?" Oliver exclaimed.

"It'll be a nice surprise for him. What are you doing here yourself?"

"None of your bloody business," Nagrebb said, and Oliver answered simultaneously, "Usual thing. Strained tendon."

I tried to see into Oliver's mind, but failed. I guessed I was allied in his thoughts with Ken and Lucy Amhurst, the faithful upholders of Carey Hewett and Partners, the opponents of change. He was eyeing me with antagonism.

"Are you still in the partnership?" I asked.

"The partnership may dissolve," Oliver replied, "but horses still need attention."

"That's what Ken says."

Nagrebb's son, who'd been watching me more than listening, suddenly slid from his horse, handed the reins to his father, then bent down and ducked under the paddock railings to join Oliver and myself outside. At close quarters, the aggression poured out of him, almost tangible. His father twice over, I thought.

"You're trouble," he said to me.

He held his whip in his left hand. I wondered fleetingly if he were left-handed. He more or less proved that he wasn't by hitting me very fast and hard with his fist, right-handedly, in the stomach.

I might as well have been kicked by a horse. I lost, it seemed to me, the power to breathe. I went down on one knee, doubled over, in virtual paralysis. It didn't much improve things when Nagrebb's son put his booted foot on my bent shoulder and toppled me over.

No one protested. I looked some dusty old grass in the eye. No succor there either.

Breath slowly returned to ease the suffocation and with it came impotent rage, some of it directed at myself for having precipitated the fracas. There was no point in trying to attack Nagrebb junior in my turn; I would be simply knocked down again. Words were my weapons, not arms. I'd never punched anyone in anger.

I got to my knees and to my feet. Nagrebb looked watchful and his son insufferably superior. Oliver was impassive. The girl was smiling.

I found enough breath to speak. Fought to keep my temper.

"Illuminating," I said.

Not the wisest of remarks, on reflection, but the only sword I had. The son made another stab at me but I was ready for that one and parried his punch on my wrist. Even that was hard enough to numb my fingers. The only thing on the plus side, I thought, was that I hadn't disclosed knowledge of collagen-dissolving enzymes and wasn't faced with collagenase-loaded syringes.

"Look," I said, "I'm a writer. If you don't want to be written about, well, I've got the message."

I turned my back on them and walked the few steps to my car, trying not to totter.

"Don't come back," Nagrebb said.

Not on your life, I thought. Not for my own life, either.

I opened the car door and eased painfully into the driver's seat. At the moment of impact, I'd felt as if my lungs had collapsed but with passing time the problem was soreness. Somewhere at the lower end of my sternum was an area of maximum wince.

They didn't try to stop me leaving. I started the car, reversed round Oliver's, and aimed for a straight line down the drive in ignominious defeat. Never engage an enemy, I thought, without buckler and shield.

When I got back to Thetford Cottage I sat for a while in the car, and Ken came out to see why.

He folded his height down to look in through the window which I opened for him.

"What's the matter?" he asked.

"Nothing much."

"Something obviously is."

I sighed. Winced. Smiled lopsidedly. Pointed to my midriff.

"Nagrebb's son upset my solar plexus," I said.

He was exasperated. "I told you not to go there."

"So you did. All my fault."

"But why? Why did he hit you?"

"I asked about acute overnight laminitis."

He looked shocked. "That was a damn silly thing to do."

"Mm. But the reaction was informative, don't you think? And by the way, Oliver was there, looking at strained tendons. Nagrebb had called him in."

"Was Nagrebb himself there?"

"He was. Also a fierce red-haired girl who found it amusing that Nagrebb's son had knocked me down. They were all out in the paddock when I arrived."

Ken nodded. "That was Nagrebb's daughter. I warned you the son was poison."

"You were right."

Poison, I thought. I was on the point of telling Ken about fugu but the more I thought about it, the more it seemed farfetched. Not fugu, then. But if one nontraceable poison existed, then so might others. Wait, I thought, for the delivery note from Parkway Chemicals.

I inched out of the car and stood gingerly upright. In every film I'd seen where people got punched six times in the stomach they'd shaken it off like a tap from a feather. As I wasn't accustomed to the treatment, one punch felt like six attentions from a piledriver.

"He really hurt you," Ken said, concerned.

"Oh well, as you say, I asked for it."

We went into the house with my asking him not to embarrass me with Greg, Vicky or Belinda and he, now amused, promising not to.

On Friday morning two more reply envelopes arrived but still not the one from Parkway Chemicals. I phoned Parkway, reached the sales manager and asked if all our copies had been sent.

"Why yes," he confirmed, "they went off to you yesterday."

"Thanks very much."

He didn't understand my urgency and I

couldn't explain. Sending the copies after one extra day must have seemed immaterial to him. More patience required. Terrible.

I reached Ken on his phone and told him that two more pharmaceutical replies had arrived. Be right with you, he said.

When he came, he asked about the punch site.

"Recovering," I said. "What do we have today?"

He read the bunches of invoices, six months' worth from each place. He nodded, raised his eyebrows, nodded and lowered them.

"Nothing out of the ordinary," was his comment on the first lot.

The second stack excited him.

"Jeez," he said. "Just look at this."

He pushed the papers across the kitchen table, pointing to one line with a jabbing finger.

"Insulin! We ordered insulin! I can't believe it."

"*Who* exactly ordered it?"

"Heaven knows." He frowned. "We don't have a separate pharmacist, the practice isn't—wasn't — big enough. We make up various things ourselves in the pharmacy. Scott often did. Any of us did. When we use or take something we write down what it is. There's a column for identifying the manufacturer if it's not something like maintenance fluids, painkillers and everyday needs that we get from wholesale suppliers. The secretary records the whole list in the computer and automatically reorders everything again in due time when stocks are low, unless we add a note not to."

"So anyone," I said, "could write down insulin as having been used, and the secretary would automatically order it?"

"Christ," he said, awed.

"When the orders arrive, who handles them?"

"One of the secretaries puts the parcels in the pharmacy. Any one of us opens them and puts the contents on the shelves. Most things have their regular space on the shelves and are often used. That's things like vaccines and ointments. Anything unusual or risky is in a special section. Was, of course. I keep seeing the pharmacy as it was and forgetting it's gone."

"So if anyone unpacked a parcel containing insulin, that's where it would be put, the special section, available for the person who ordered it to pick up?"

"Dead easy," he said.

He went on reading the invoices and reached something that stopped his breathing almost as effectively as Nagrebb's son had stopped mine.

"It's frightening," he said hollowly. "We ordered collagenase."

"Who ordered it?"

"There's no way of telling." He shook his head. "After the secretary's entered the list in the computer, she shreds the paper as a precaution against anyone removing it from our rubbish bins and using the information to order drugs for themselves. We have to be careful about narcotics and amphetamines and the ingredients, for instance, of LSD."

"Does the secretary know which of you ordered what?"

He nodded. "She knows our signatures. We always initial for what we've used. She queries if we don't."

"I suppose she wouldn't remember who initialed insulin and collagenase?"

"We could ask her, but she'd have no reason to remember." He looked at the lists. "Insulin was ordered six months ago. That figures. Wynn Lees's horse died last September, just after the order for insulin would have reached here. There was no hanging about."

"And the collagenase?"

He looked up the date. "Same thing. It was delivered here a few days after Nagrebb's horse staked itself." He raised his eyes in puzzlement. "No one could have staked a horse in that way on purpose."

"How long do orders usually take to arrive?"

"Not long. A couple of days, especially if we send a special separate order marked 'expedite.'"

"I would think," I said, "that in the week between the staking repair and the disintegration of the tendon, the show-jumper was insured as sound and the collagenase ordered separately at speed."

Ken rubbed his face.

I said, "What's to stop anyone getting hold of a sheet of partnership writing paper, ordering insulin and collagenase, and getting the stuff sent to their own private address? Like I got all those envelopes sent here."

"None of these companies would send any substance anywhere except to the partnership headquarters," he said, thinking. "They would never do it. There are strict rules."

I sighed. We weren't much further forward, except that with every slow step it became more and more certain that someone had been using the partnership's own methods as a pathway to fraud.

"Do all veterinary partnerships follow your ordering procedure?" I asked.

"Shouldn't think so. Ours is pretty unusual, probably. But up to now it's been convenient and no trouble."

"What about atropine?" I asked.

"We use that all the time after eye surgery to dilate the pupil. It would naturally appear now and then in small quantities on the invoices."

In a repeat of the day before, I chased around by telephone until I reached Superintendent Ramsey.

"What is it?" he said, a touch impatiently.

"Answers from pharmaceutical companies."

A short pause, then, "Hospital office, three o'clock this afternoon."

"Right," I said.

In the event, I met him alone, as Ken, notwithstanding the rumpus of rumors zigzagging the neighborhood like wasps, had been called out by a regular racehorse-trainer client who wanted to check the blood count of several prospective runners. He and Oliver, Ken said, were continually busy with this procedure.

The Superintendent too seemed to be alone, his car in the car park the only one present. I parked beside his and walked across the lonely tarmac and into the deserted building: no dogs, no cats, no partners. Ramsey was waiting for me in the office, having apparently unlocked the doors with a bunch of keys as big as Ken's. His thinning hair was windblown: he looked more than ever an out-of-doors man.

We sat by the desk and I gave him the invoices and explained the significance of insulin and collagenase, and the way they could be ordered.

He blinked. "Repeat it, please."

After I had, he looked pensive. For good measure I told him about the carpet needle and mentioned Brose's theory about the paternity of the dead foal.

He blinked again. "You've been busy," he said.

"I set out to clear Ken's reputation."

"Hm. And you're telling me all this now," he said in his blunt way, "because if I discover who killed the horses, I'll know who killed Scott Sylvester?"

"Yes."

"You said you still have the carpet needle embedded in the piece of gut, and you've sent samples of the mare's and the foal's and the stallion's hair to a specialist lab for DNA matching. Is that right? And that mare was owned by Wynn Lees?"

I nodded.

"What else?" he asked.

"Atropine," I said, and repeated Ken's convictions.

"Anything else?"

I hesitated. He bade me continue. I said, "I've seen or been to visit the owners or trainers of all the suspiciously dead horses. I wanted to get the feel of them, to try to know if they are villains or not. To find out if they themselves were involved with their horses' deaths."

"And?"

"Two are villains, one definitely isn't, one probably is, one may be but doesn't know it."

He asked me about the last one, and I told him about old Mackintosh and his fade-in fade-out memory.

"He remembers," I said, "the order in which racehorses in a far-back time stood in the loose boxes in his stable yard. He recited them for me like an incantation. Six, he said, was Vinderman. Well, one of the horses which was probably given colic through atropine was stabled in box number six. I thought perhaps that if Mackintosh were provided with an apple, say, or a carrot—he gives his horses carrots every day—to feed especially to Vinderman, he would trot down to his stable and give it to the horse in box number six."

He said doubtfully, "Are you sure he would?"

"Of course I'm not sure, but I think it's possible. It's also possible that the head lad knows who visited box six—and box sixteen—bearing

gifts. The head lad knows more than he's saying."
I then added, for no reason except that I had
it on my mind, "Mackintosh lives in an old millhouse that used to belong to some people called
Travers."

Even experienced policemen don't have total
control of their muscles. The subtle shift, the involuntary immobility, he could disguise them as
little as Nagrebb. I had really surprised him.

"Travers," I repeated. "What does it mean to
you?"

He didn't answer directly. "Do *you* know anyone called Travers?" he asked.

I shook my head. The Travers I'd played with
as a child was only a name my mother remembered, not anyone I knew.

He thought for a good time but told me nothing. The interview, he indicated by standing up,
was over, the one-way flow of information at a
temporary end. If any further drug lore should
come my way, he said, he would like to have it.

"Where can I reach you tomorrow?" I asked.
"As it happens we found out that Scott went to
a chemical company personally to collect something not allowed to be sent through the post.
Tomorrow we should know what it was. The
company sent the information off yesterday."

Without waste of time he sat down again, wrote
a number on a piece of memo paper and handed
it to me, saying it would get him at any time.

"The postman comes at about ten," I said. "I'll
have to get Ken there to interpret the chemical

names into words I understand. After that I could call you."

"Do it," he nodded.

"Tell me about Travers," I said persuasively. "There was a financial firm of some sort long ago called Upjohn and Travers. The present Upjohn, Ronnie, he's about sixty. He acts as a steward at Stratford-upon-Avon races. He had an injured horse that he wanted Ken to put down a year or so ago. Ken said he could save the horse, and personally bought it from Upjohn, at not much more than a dead-meat price. The horse, since Ken's expert surgery, has won a race, and Upjohn is far from pleased. Illogical, but people are like that. Anyway, Ronnie Upjohn's father had a partner called Travers. All I know about him is hearsay from Ken's mother, Josephine, who described old man Travers as 'rolling' and 'a frightful lecher.' He would be at least ninety now, I should think, if he's still alive."

Ramsey closed his eyes as if to prevent my inspecting his thoughts. "Anything else?" he said.

"Um . . . Porphyry Place."

"That red monstrosity on the way to Tewkesbury? What about it?"

"Old Mackintosh lost money in it. So did Ronnie Upjohn and a lot of other people round here."

He nodded a shade grimly, his eyes still shut, and I wondered fleetingly if he'd been among the unfortunates.

I went on conversationally, "You don't have to be the owner of a horse to insure it. It can be

364

insured without the owner knowing. The payout, sent in good faith by the company, never reaches the owner, who remains in ignorance from start to finish."

His eyes opened. I saw that he well understood the implication.

"It's a big maybe," I said, "but maybe someone came up with a way of recovering their losses in Porphyry Place."

He put a cupped hand over his mouth.

"Could you?" I asked, "get from anywhere a list of the people who lost money guaranteeing those loans?"

"Don't tell me," he said, ironic despite his training, "that you haven't managed that yourself?"

"I don't know who to ask and I wouldn't have much chance of being told."

"True." A smile glimmered briefly. He didn't say whether or not he would obtain a list, nor whether he would show it to me if he did. Police the world over weren't renowned for sharing their information.

He rose to his feet again and came with me out to the car park, carefully locking doors behind him. He seemed avuncular more than forbidding, but then bears could look cuddly. He might listen to me and reckon that Ken had killed the horses himself. Ken had at first been reluctant, if not afraid, to tell me how horses could be killed on the grounds that knowledge could be twisted into a presumption of guilt.

"I'll hear from you tomorrow," Ramsey said, nodding and getting into his car.

"Right."

He waited until I had started my own car and driven to the exit, almost as if shepherding me out. He needn't have worried that I'd go back: there was barely time to scorch the miles to the Fulham Road by six o'clock.

Annabel, relatively conservative in the silver cowboy boots below a straight black dress, opened her door and looked at her watch, laughing.

"Ten seconds late."

"Abject apologies," I said.

"Accepted. Where are we going?"

"You're the Londoner. You choose."

She chose an adventure film and dinner in a bistro. The hero in the film got punched six times in the solar plexus and came up smiling.

The bistro had candles in chianti bottles, red checked tablecloths and a male gypsy singer with a flower behind his ear. I told Annabel about Vicky and Greg's singing. Old-fashioned but great voices. She would like to hear them, she said.

"Come down on Sunday," I said on impulse.

"Sunday I see the bishop and his wife."

"Oh."

She looked down at her pasta, candlelight on her bouncy chopped-off hair, her eyes in shadow, considering.

"I only miss Sundays with them if it's important," she said.

"This is important."

She raised her eyes. I could see candle flames in them.

"Don't say it lightly," she said.

"It's important," I repeated.

She smiled briefly. "I'll come on the train."

"For country pub lunch?"

She nodded.

"And stay for the evening and I'll drive you home."

"I can go back on the train."

"No. Not alone."

"You're as bad as my father. I can look after myself, you know."

"All the same, I'll drive you.

She smiled at her pasta. "The bishop will have to approve of you in spite of your job."

"I tremble to meet him."

She nodded as if trembling were expected and asked how things were going in the practice. "I can't get that poor man Scott out of my mind."

I told her about the results from the pharmaceutical companies, which fascinated and alarmed her by turns. I told her that since Carey had dissolved the partnership, all the vets were rushing around like chickens without heads, looking after sick animals but with no central organization.

"But *can* anyone dissolve a partnership like that?"

"Heaven knows. The legal problems look knotty. Carey's exhausted and wants out. Half the others want him out. They jointly pay the mortgage on the hospital, which is currently shut. God help Ken if there's a middle-of-the-night emergency."

"What a mess."

"Yup. It's a long way from here or now, though."

"Mm."

"So . . . er. . . does the bishop have any other daughters or sons?"

"Two of each."

"Wow."

"I'd guess," she said, "that you're an only child."

"How do you know?"

"You don't need roots."

I'd never thought of my nomadic life in that way, but perhaps it was solitariness that made the go-where-you're-sent discipline easy.

"How strong are yours?" I asked.

"I've never tried to pull them up."

We looked at each other.

"I'll be in England for four years," I said. "After that, a month or so every two years. If I reach sixty, I can stay here always. Most diplomats buy a house here somewhere along the line. My parents have one but I can't live there now because it's leased to a company. When my father retires in four years' time and the lease runs out, they'll come back here to stay."

She listened carefully.

"The Foreign Office pays for children to come

home from foreign postings and go to boarding schools," I said.

"Did you do that?"

"Only for my last two years." I explained about learning the languages in one's teens. "Also I wanted to stay with my parents. I like them and it's a multi-everything life."

A job description, I thought, was an odd sort of way to tell her I was more than ordinarily interested in her future. She seemed to have no trouble understanding. It was also plain that this was to be no lusty rush into uncontrollable sexual attraction and damn the consequences. Annabel wanted to be sure of her footing.

I drove her home and kissed her goodbye as before. This time the kiss lasted longer and was a tingling matter that made uncontrollable sex look totally desirable. I smiled at myself and at her, and she said she would take whichever train on Sunday reached Cheltenham nearest to noon.

On Saturday morning the letter from Parkway Chemicals finally arrived, and to me looked like gobbledegook. While I waited for Ken I read the few intelligible pieces of information supplied with the invoices.

The Parkway Chemical Company was in the business of selling biochemical organic compounds for research, and also diagnostic reagents. The company that had sent insulin and collagenase had had similar headings. Parkway

Chemicals could be ordered by fax and by Free-fone.

I read the few ordinary invoices but the only substance ordered that I recognized was fibrinogen, used to help blood clot.

The delivery note given to Scott had warnings stamped all over it.

"Extremely hazardous material." "For the use of qualified personnel." "Laboratory only." "Hand delivered."

Scott had signed his name in acceptance.

The fuss, it seemed, was over three small ampoules of something called tetrodotoxin.

When Ken saw it he said immediately, "Anything with the suffix toxin is poisonous." He frowned over the details and read them aloud. "Three ampoules one mg tetrodotoxin with sodium citrate buffer. Soluble in water. Read safety sheet."

"What is it?" I asked.

"I'll have to look it up."

Although the owners of Thetford Cottage weren't book people, they did have a row of reference books and a small encyclopedia. Ken and I searched in vain for tetrodotoxin. The nearest the dictionary came to it was tetrode, a vacuum tube containing four electrodes, which hardly seemed to fit the case.

"I'd better go home for my books on poisons," Ken said.

"OK."

As I had the dictionary in my hands, and on

the off chance, I looked up puffer fish. The entry read:

Puffer, also called blowfish or globefish, capable of inflating the body with water or air until it resembles a globe, the spines in the skin becoming erected,

So far, so good. It was the sting in the tail that had me gasping.

of the fish family Tetraodontidae.

Puffer fish.
It was my old friend fugu after all.

12

"*Puffer fish?*" Ramsey said.

The Superintendent had met us alone again in the empty hospital. It was rather as if he wanted to keep his sessions with Ken and me separate from whatever other inquiries he was making.

Ken had been home for his book on poisons.

"Tetrodotoxin," he read aloud, "is one of the most potent poisons known. It comes from the puffer fish and causes respiratory and cardiovascular failure through paralysis of the neuromuscular system. A fatal dose is extremely small; only micrograms per kilogram of body weight. It is very unlikely to be detected by forensic examination."

"Let me read that," Ramsey said.

Ken gave him the book and we waited while he digested the bad news. Then he picked up the delivery note and read through it for the second or third time.

"You're telling me," he said, "that one milligram of this powder will kill a horse? One thousandth of a gram?"

"Yes, easily," Ken said. "A racehorse weighs approximately 450 kilograms. A microgram is *one millionth* of a gram. One of the ampoules would

372

be enough to kill four horses, at a rough guess. So far, we've two dead, Fitzwalter's chipped knee and the broodmare."

There was a dismayed pause while we each worked out that there might still be a good deal of the stuff lying around.

"Would you sprinkle the powder on the horse's food?" Ramsey asked.

"I suppose you could," Ken said doubtfully, "but it would be more usual to reconstitute it in water and inject it, preferably into a vein."

"And wear surgical gloves while you do it," I suggested.

"My God, yes."

"Scott," I said, "must have known who had asked him to travel that distance to fetch the package. Must have known who he gave it to. He didn't necessarily know what was in it." I paused and added, "I guess he found out the hard way."

"Jeez," Ken said under his breath.

"Tell us," I begged Ramsey. "Just say yes or no. Did you find any needle puncture mark on Scott?"

He pursed his mouth. Looked at the question from north round to south. Consulted a mental rule book.

"You've been of considerable assistance," he said finally. "The answer is yes." He checked some more with his inner self and squeezed out a few more sentences. "Four days of tests have revealed the presence of treble a normal dose of soporific, taken in coffee. No other toxic material of any sort has so far been found. The needle puncture was into a vein on the back of the hand."

At least, I thought, Scott had been asleep when he died. I reckoned he would have had to have been. All that explosive muscle power would have presented a daunting prospect to anyone wishing to creep up on him holding a death-laden syringe. Too much possibility of the tables being turned.

The symbolic closing of Scott's mouth, I thought, had been itself an unconscious declaration of motive. I'd never been involved with a murder before and understood little of the overpowering impulse to kill, but in the macabre state of Scott's body a compulsion of extreme magnitude was unmistakably visible. It hadn't been enough just to stop him talking: the raw statement must have sprung from subterranean urges too powerful to combat. In the depths of the psyche, logic foundered, caution dissolved, obsession swept all decency away.

Scott might have been an accomplice who finally objected. He might have discovered irregularities and threatened to reveal them. He might have tried a little dangerous blackmail. The brutality of the staples had been the violent response.

Ramsey, having once begun to divulge, continued. "I see no harm in telling you what will be released to the press later today. We've identified the person burned in your fire."

"You have?" Ken exclaimed. "Who was it?"

Maddeningly, Ramsey answered the question

crabwise. "Usually if someone goes missing it's reported. In this case, the person was not reported missing as his family believed he was away for a few days' fishing and at a trade conference. When he didn't return this Thursday evening at the expected time, the family discovered he hadn't been to the conference at all. They were alarmed and informed us at once. Owing partly to your information and your innuendos, sir," he said to me, "we speculated that the missing man and the unidentified body were one and the same. Dental records have now proved this to be the case."

He stopped. Ken, disgusted, said, "Come on man, who was it?"

Ramsey savored his disclosures. "A man, thirty-two years old, not on very good terms with his wife, who hadn't expected him to phone her from the conference. He was an insurance agent." He paused. "His name," he said finally, "was Travers. Theodore Travers."

I knew my mouth fell open.

Theo, I thought. The Travers I'd played with, the Travers of the millhouse, his name was Theo.

Dear God, I thought. Perhaps one should never go back to the scenery of one's childhood, perhaps never learn the fates of one's friends. To come back as a stranger into the future of one's past life, an adventure that had at first pleased and captivated me, now seemed like a danger best left alone.

It was too late to wish I'd never returned. Since I had, in the most fortuitous unrolling of events, all I could do was try to leave the present state of Kenny's son in better shape than if I'd stayed away.

"Upjohn and Travers," I said.

Ramsey nodded. "We looked them up after you spoke of them yesterday. The firm no longer exists, and hasn't for many years, but in the days of old lecherous Travers it was an insurance agency. It broke up when both Travers and Upjohn died." He looked at me straightly. "How did you hear, sir, of Upjohn and Travers?"

I said weakly, "I don't know."

Ken gave me a sharp-eyed look, trusting still, but ever more puzzled.

I must have heard the old firm's name at Theo's house, I supposed. I simply didn't know why it had stuck in my mind.

"Why," I said, "should an insurance agent be present in the veterinary building late in the evening?"

"Well, why?" Ramsey asked, as if knowing the answer.

"Someone let him in to discuss insurance schemes," I said. "Maybe illicit insurance of horses. Maybe they had an argument which ended either in the accidental or intentional death of Travers. Maybe the place was set on fire to cover it up.

"That's a lot of maybes," Ramsey observed, "though I'm not saying you're wrong."

Toss up the pieces, I thought, and they all came down in a jumble.

Ramsey ushered us out again and locked the doors, although presumably Ken had his own bunch in his pocket and could let us straight in again if he wanted. Ken seemed, however, to find the hospital oppressive and was happy to leave. We stood together by our cars in the car park and Ken said, "What next?"

What happened next was one of those extraordinary flashes of ancient memory, tantalizingly incomplete most of the time but sometimes blindingly clear. Perhaps many different threads had to converge before the right synapse detonated. I remembered my threatening dream and knew I'd once heard my mother say more than she'd told me on the phone.

"Um," I said breathlessly, "how about if we go to see Josephine?"

"Whatever for?"

"To talk about your father."

"No," he protested, "you can't."

"I think we must," I said, and told him in part what I wanted.

He looked upset, but drove to Josephine's home while I followed.

She lived on the top two floors of a fine big Edwardian house situated in a graceful semi-circular terrace in Cheltenham. Her drawing room windows opened onto an ironwork balcony overlooking the wintry public garden in front. It could have been a delight, but Josephine's furnishings were stilted and unimaginative, as if not changed for decades.

Ken having forewarned her by telephone, she was pleased enough to see us. We had bought a bottle of sweet sherry on the way, Ken saying his mother liked it very much but wouldn't buy it for herself, repressed woman that she was. The gift, grudgingly accepted, was nevertheless immediately opened. Ken poured his mother a large glassful and two less exuberant slugs for himself and me. He made a face over his, but I could drink or eat anything by that time without showing dislike.

Disregard what you're actually putting into your mouth, my father had usefully instructed. If you know it's a sheep's eye, you'll be sick. Think of it as a grape. Concentrate on the flavor, not the origin. Yes, Dad, I'd said.

Josephine wore a gray skirt, prim cream shirt and a sludge-green cardigan. There was a photograph in a silver frame on a side table showing her young, smiling, pretty. Beside her in the picture stood a recognizable version of the Ken I knew: same long head, long body, fair hair. Kenny in the picture smiled happily: the Ken I knew smiled seldom.

We sat down. Josephine pressed her knees together: to repulse lechers, I supposed.

Beginning was difficult. "Was Ken's father a good sports man?" I asked.

"How do you mean?"

"Er . . . did he like fishing? My father fishes

all the time." My father would be amazed to hear it, I thought.

"No, he didn't like fishing," Josephine said, raising eyebrows. "Why do you ask?"

"Shooting?" I said.

She spluttered over the sherry, half choking.

"Do listen, Mother," Ken said persuasively. "We've never really known why Dad killed himself. Peter has a theory."

"I don't want to hear it."

"I think you do."

I said, "Did he shoot?"

Josephine looked at Ken. He nodded to her. "Tell him," he said.

She drank sherry. She would be all right once she'd started, I thought, remembering the unlocking of the gossip floodgates at lunch in Thetford Cottage; and so, hesitantly, it proved.

"Kenny," she said, "used to go shooting pheasants with the crowd."

"Which crowd?"

"Oh, you know. Farmers and so on. Mac Mackintosh. Rolls Eaglewood. Ronnie Upjohn. Those people."

"How many guns did Kenny have?"

"Only the one." She shuddered. "I don't like thinking about it."

"I know," I said placatingly. "Where was he when he shot himself?"

"Oh dear. Oh dear."

"Do tell him," Ken said.

She gulped the sherry as a lifeline. Ken poured her more.

If the flash in my memory was right, I knew the answer, but for Ken's sake it had to come from his mother.

"You've never told me where he died," Ken said. "No one would talk to me about him. I was too young, everyone said. Recently, now that I'm the age he was when he died, I want to know more and more. It's taken me a long time to face his killing himself, but now that I have, I have to know where and why."

"I'm not sure about why," she said unhappily.

"Where, then?"

She gulped.

"Go on, darling mother."

The affection in his tone overthrew her. Tears streamed from her eyes. For a while she was completely unable to speak but eventually, bit by bit, she told him.

"He died . . . he shot himself . . . standing in the stream . . . where it was shallow . . . some way below the mill wheel . . . on the Mackintosh place."

The revelation rocked Ken and confirmed my vision. In memory I heard clearly my weeping mother's voice, sometime soon after she'd heard the news, talking to a visitor while I hid out of sight. She'd said, "He fell into the millstream and his brains washed away."

"His brains washed away." I'd stored that

frightful phrase in deep freeze as a picture too awful to summon into consciousness. Now that I'd remembered it, the suppression surprised me. I'd have thought it was just the ghoulish sort of thing small boys would gloat over. Perhaps it was because it had made my mother cry.

"Do you know," I asked gently, "if his gun was in the stream with him?"

"Does it matter? Yes, it was. Of course it was. Otherwise he couldn't have shot himself."

She put down her glass, stood up abruptly and went over to a mahogany bureau. From the top portion she retrieved a key with which she opened the lowest drawer, and from the lowest drawer produced a large polished wooden box. Another key was necessary to open that, but finally she brought it over and put it on the table beside her chair.

"I haven't looked at these things since just after Kenny died," she said, "but perhaps, for your sake, Ken, it's time."

The box contained newspapers, typewritten sheets and letters.

The letters, on top, were expressions of sympathy. The crowd, as Josephine called them, had done their duty with warmth: they'd clearly liked Kenny. Mackintosh, Eaglewood, Upjohn, Fitzwalter—a surprise, that—and many from clients, friends and fellow vets. I flipped through them. No letter from Wynn Lees, that I could see.

Towards the bottom, my heart skipped a bump.

There, in her regular handwriting, was a short note from my mother.

My dear Josephine,
I'm so terribly sorry. Kenny was always a good friend and we shall miss him very much on the racecourse. If there's anything I can do, please let me know. In deepest sympathy,
Margaret Perry.

My poor young mother, weeping with grief, had had impeccable manners. I put her long-ago letter back with the others and tried to show no emotion.

Turning to the newspapers I found they varied from factual to garish and bore many identical pictures of the dead man. "Well-liked," "respected," "a great loss to the community." Verdict at the inquest: "not enough evidence to prove that he intended to take his own life." No suicide notes. Doubts and questions. "If he hadn't meant to kill himself, what was he doing standing in a stream in January with his shoes and socks on?" "Typical of Kenny, always thoughtful, not to leave a mess for others to clean up."

"I can't bear to read them," Josephine said wretchedly. "I thought I'd forgiven him, but I haven't. The disgrace! You can't imagine. It was hard enough being a widow, but when your husband kills himself it's the ultimate rejection, and everyone thinks it's your fault."

"But it was an open verdict," I said. "It says so in the papers."

"That makes no difference."

"I thought there was a fuss about a drug he shouldn't have ordered," I said. "There's nothing about it here."

"Yes, there is," Ken said faintly. He'd been reading one of the typewritten sheets with his mouth open. "You'll *never* believe this. And who on earth told you?"

"Can't remember," I said erroneously.

He handed me the papers, looking pale and shattered. "I don't understand it."

I read in his footsteps. It seemed to be a letter of opinion, but had no heading and no signature. It was shocking and revelationary, and in a way inevitable.

It said baldly:

Kenneth McClure, shortly before his death, had ordered and obtained a small supply, ostensibly for research purposes, of the organic compound tetrodotoxin. A horse in his care subsequently died suddenly without apparent cause, consistent with tetrodotoxin poisoning.

While not accusing him of having himself administered this extremely dangerous material, one had to consider whether the acquisition or dispensing of this substance could have engendered a remorse strong enough to lead to suicide. As it is impossible to know, I suggest we do not put forward the possible explanation on the grounds that it is alarmist.

In a shaking voice Ken asked his mother, "Do you know about this tetrodotoxin?"

"Is that what it was?" she asked vaguely. "There was an awful commotion but I didn't want to hear it. I didn't want people knowing that Kenny had done wrong. It was all too awful already, don't you see?"

What I saw quite clearly was that somewhere among the old crowd the knowledge of the existence and deadliness of tetrodotoxin had been slumbering in abeyance all these years, and something—perhaps the Porphyry fiasco—had awakened it to virulence.

"Kenny!" old Mackintosh had said joyfully when we'd visited him. "Did you bring the stuff?"

Kenny had, I judged. And then presumably had repented and shot himself—or had decided to blow the whistle and had been silenced.

Scott, the messenger with his mouth shut. Travers, the insurance agent burned to the teeth. Kenny, the vet with his brains in the water and his gun with him, washed clean of prints. Tetrodotoxin, arguably, had been too much for any of them to stomach.

"Oh God," Ken said miserably, "so that was why. I wish now that I didn't know."

"You know where," I said, "but not whether."

"What do you mean?"

"I mean, he left no note. So the question is, did he kill himself in the stream, or did someone shoot him on the bank so that he fell backwards into the water?" Mother and son were aghast. I went on regretfully. "For one thing, how do you aim a shotgun at your head if you're knee deep? You can't reach the trigger unless you use a stick. On the other hand, a shotgun let off at close quarters packs a terrific punch, easily enough to lift a man off his feet."

Ken protested. "That can't be right. Why should anyone kill him?"

"Why was Scott killed?" I asked.

He was silent.

"I think . . . " Josephine's voice quavered, "awful that it is, I'd feel he hadn't betrayed me so terribly if he couldn't help it. If someone killed him. It's so long ago . . . but if he was killed . . . I'll feel better."

Ken looked as if he couldn't understand her logic, but I knew my own mother, too, would be comforted.

Ken stayed with Josephine and I spent the afternoon aimlessly driving round the countryside, thinking. I stopped for a while on Cleeve Hill, overlooking Cheltenham racecourse, seeing below me the white rails, the green grass, the up-and-downhill supreme test for steeplechasers. The Grand National was a great exciting lottery, but the Cheltenham Gold Cup sorted out the true enduring stars.

The course, once familiar to me to the last blade of grass, had metamorphosed into an alien creature. There were huge new stands and realigned smoothed-out tracks, and the parade ring had turned itself round and changed entirely. To one side a whole village of striped medieval-looking tents was being erected, no doubt for sponsors and private parties at the big meeting due to be held in less than two weeks. It would be odd, I thought, to walk again through those gates. The long-ago course and the long-ago child were echoes in the wind. The here and now, the new world, would be yesterday's ghost in its time.

I drove on. I drove past the ugly red lump of conspicuously signposted Porphyry Place and on into nice old Tewkesbury. I stopped by the River Severn and thought of Kenny's washed-away brains, and I tried to sort out everything I'd seen, everything I'd heard and everything I'd remembered since I'd come back.

The conviction that gradually emerged seemed to have been staring me in the face all along, saying, "Here I am. Look at me." It was theory, though, more than substance, so I could certainly *believe* but certainly not yet *prove*. Matching the foal's DNA might be helpful. Porphyry Place might cough up a name. Villainous old Mackintosh essentially knew, as I did, things he couldn't always call to mind.

Devising a revealing trap seemed the only solution, but I couldn't so far think of one that would work.

I drove back to Thetford Cottage in the dark and swept Greg and Vicky out to drinks and dinner in the giddy heights of Cheltenham. Vicky, coquettish, said Belinda would be middle aged before herself. Greg smiled amiably. We talked about the wedding plans, which Ken had left to Belinda, and Belinda largely to her mother. There seemed an amazing amount to arrange. When I married Annabel, I thought, we would surely not need so much.

Dear heavens! I'd let that intention slip in unawares. When I married Annabel indeed! Much too soon, too soon for that.

A short while after we'd returned to the cottage, Ken telephoned.

"Where have you been?" he asked.

"Rioting in the town with Greg and Vicky."

"That'll be the day. Look"—he sounded awkward—"my mother's been crying buckets. You let loose a logjam of grief. But by God I thank you. I don't know how you know the things you know, but as far as I'm concerned, my father can rest in peace."

"I'm glad."

"Since I got home," he said, "Carey phoned. He sounded pretty depressed. He wanted to know how things were going in the practice. I told him we needed him, but I honestly think he's stopped caring. Anyway, I told him about the invoices and what we'd been doing."

"What did he say?"

"Nothing much. Just that we'd done well. I

couldn't seem to get him interested. I think Oliver's right after all. We'll have to regroup and work something out for ourselves."

"Probably best."

His voice sounded purposeful. "I'm going to get all the others together to discuss it."

"Good idea."

"Anyway, thanks again," he said. "See you tomorrow, no doubt."

Maybe, I thought, as he disconnected, but tomorrow Annabel would be coming and I wanted a private, not a family, lunch.

She came on the train nearest noon and we kissed a greeting as familiarly as if the eight days we'd known each other were eighty on a desert island. She wore a vast sweater of white stars on black over tight black stretchy trousers. Pink lipstick. Huge eyes.

"I've found a super pub for lunch," I said, "but we've got to make a short stop on the way. A tiny bit of sleuthing. Won't be long."

"Never mind," she said smiling. "And I've brought you a present from Brose's friend Higgins to help you along."

She took an envelope from a shiny black handbag and gave it to me. It contained, I found, a list of three insurance companies that had paid out on horses that had died off the racecourse during the past year. Alongside each company was a name and number for me to get in touch with, and at the bottom Higgins had written, "Mention my name and you'll get the real dope. More to come next week."

"Wonderful," I said, very pleased. "With these, we must be nearly home. I'll start phoning in the morning. It was boring old paperwork that put Al Capone in jail, don't forget. Paperwork's damning, as everyone knows only too well in the service, when we get things wrong."

"Never sign anything," she said ironically, "and you'll stay out of trouble."

We climbed into my car and set off to the horse hospital.

I said, "Vicky took a message from the Superintendent who's in charge of Scott's death saying he wants to see me briefly late this morning. Ken and I have talked to him at the hospital every day lately. It's getting to be a habit."

"How are things going in general?"

"I'll tell you over lunch if you like, though there are better things to talk about. How's the bishop?"

"Cautious."

I smiled. I was growing less cautious every time I saw her. The prospect of the spring and summer ahead, the feeling of life beginning, the shivering excitement deep down, all came together in a fizzing euphoria. Let it not be a mistake, I thought. In a few months we would know whether it would last forever, if the attraction had glue. I'd never come near to thinking in such terms before. Perhaps it was true that one could know at once, when one met the right partner.

Perhaps she knew too. I saw in her the same

glimmering acknowledgment, but also the certainty of her withdrawal if she should judge it a mistake. A mixture of fun, competence and reserve, that was Annabel. I began worrying that when I asked her, she wouldn't have me.

There was only one parked car by the front entrance of the hospital when we got there. Not Ramsey's usual car, not a car I knew.

"I don't think the Superintendent's here yet, but someone is," I said. "Care to come in and look round?"

"Yes, I would. I've only ever seen the arrangements at Newmarket, before this."

We went into the entrance hall and down the passage to the office, which was empty of everyone, not just policemen.

"Let's see how much is unlocked," I suggested, and we continued on down the passage to the door of the theater vestibule. It opened to the touch and we went through, with me pointing out the changing rooms and pharmacy cupboard to Annabel and saying at least we didn't need to bother with shoe-covers and sterility or any of that jazz.

We went into the theater and looked around. Annabel was enthusiastic about the hoist.

"In the place I saw in Newmarket they stand the horse beside a table thing and strap him to it while he is still standing upright, conscious though sedated. Then when they've given the anesthestic they flip the table over to the horizontal position and hey presto, start cutting."

The sliding door to the padded anesthesia/recovery room was wide open to every passing germ. We went through there, Annabel exclaiming over the resilient floor and bouncing up and down a couple of times.

"What's that wall for?" she asked, pointing.

"The vets stand behind that when the horse comes round," I explained. "Apparently the patient thrashes around sometimes and the vets like to be out of kicking range."

"Like bullrings," she said.

"Exactly."

There seemed to be no one about. We went on across the corridor and into the reception room with its array of equipment round the walls, all quiet and ready for use.

"Usually they're so careful about locking everything," I said. "The whole system's coming to bits."

"Poor people."

I tried the door leading to the outside world. That at least was secure.

I began to feel vaguely uneasy. The entire theater area felt wrong, though I couldn't analyze why. I'd grown familiar with the place and it all looked the same. The difference was that I was now pretty sure who had murdered Scott, and felt anxious to tell Ramsey immediately. It was unlike him not to be there already, though the "late morning" of his message hadn't been pinpointedly precise.

Perhaps I should have told Ken, I thought, but

the damage had been done. Perhaps it wasn't such a good idea to be here on a Sunday morning.

"Let's go back to the office," I said abruptly. "I'll phone Ramsey's number and see how long before he gets here."

"OK."

I turned and led the way back through the padded room, heading for the passage. I went through into the theater with all its lifesaving and businesslike equipment and spoke over my shoulder.

"Have you ever been really ill in hospital?"

Annabel didn't answer.

I looked back and was flooded with horror, feeling adrenaline pour hot through my blood like a drench. She was down on her knees, her arms making uncoordinated movements, her head hanging low. Even as I sprinted back to her, she fell forward unconscious onto the spongy floor.

"Annabel!" I was agonized, bending over her, kneeling beside her, turning her, not knowing what was wrong with her, not knowing what help to get her, frenzied with worry.

I heard only at the last minute the rustle of clothes behind me and turned my head too late, too late.

A figure advanced from a bare yard away, a figure in surgical gown, surgical gloves, surgical cap and mask. He carried a syringe which he jabbed like a dagger at my neck.

I felt the deep sting of the needle. I grabbed

towards his clothes and he skipped back a pace, the eyes like gray pebbles over the mask.

I knew too late that he'd been hiding behind the bullring wall, that he'd darted out to inject Annabel, that he'd hidden again and come out of the other end to creep up behind me as I bent over her.

I knew, while clouds swiftly gathered in my brain, I knew as I went to inexorable sleep, that I'd been right. Small comfort. I'd been foolish as well.

The man in surgeon's clothes had murdered Scott.

An old gray man with all the veterinary knowledge in the world.

Carey Hewett.

I was lying on the floor, my nose pressed to the padding, smelling a mixture of antiseptic and horse. Awareness was partial. My eyelids weighed tons. My limbs wouldn't work, nor my voice.

The fact of being alive was in itself amazing. I felt as if awakening from ether, not death. I wanted to sink back into sleep.

Annabel!

The thought of her stormed through my half-consciousness and quickened my sluggish wits towards order. With an enormous effort I tried to move, seeming to myself to fail.

I must have stirred. There was a fast exclamation above me, more breath than words. I realized that someone was touching me, moving my hands, hastening roughly.

Instinctive fear swamped me. Logical fear immediately followed. There was clank of chains, and I knew that sound. The chains of the hoist.

No, I protested numbly. Not that. Not like Scott.

The physical effects of terror were at first an increase of the paralysis already plaguing me, but after that came a rush of useful bloody-mindedness that raced along like fire and set me fighting.

Flight was impossible. My limbs still had no strength. Equine padded cuffs had been strapped round my wrists. He clipped the chains onto the cuffs.

No, I thought.

My brain was one huge silent scream.

My eyes came open.

Annabel lay on the floor a few feet away, fast asleep. At least she looked asleep. Peaceful. I couldn't bear it. I'd brought her into appalling danger. I'd taken the message to meet Ramsey to be genuine. I should have been more careful, knowing that Ken had told Carey how much we'd discovered. Regrets and remorse thudded like piledrivers, relentlessly punishing.

Muscles recovered faster. I stretched the fingers of one hand towards the buckles on the other wrist. The chains clinked from the movement.

Another exclamation from across the room and an impression of haste.

The hoist whined, reeling in the chains.

I couldn't get the buckles undone. Undid one, but there were two on each cuff.

The shortening chains tugged my wrists upwards, lifted my arms, pulled up my body, pulled me to my feet, pulled me higher until I dangled in the air. I shook my head desperately as if that itself would undo the frightful leadenness in my mind and clear away the remaining mists.

Carey stood inside the theater and pressed the hoist's buttons. Raging and helpless I began to travel along the rails towards the sliding door, through that towards the huge operating table. I lunged towards Carey with my feet, but he was out of range of my futile swings and grayly intent on what he was doing.

His mercilessness and lack of emotion were unnerving. He wasn't gloating or cursing or telling me I shouldn't have meddled. He seemed to be approaching just another job.

"Carey," I said, pleading. "For God's sake."

He might as well not have heard.

"I've told Ramsey it was you who murdered Scott!" I yelled it, all at once without control, petrified, pathetic, in shattering fear, believing I was lost.

He paid no attention. He was concentrating on the matter at hand.

He stopped the hoist when I was still short of the table and put his head on one side, considering. It was almost, I thought, as if he wasn't sure what to do next.

I understood as if in a revelation that he hadn't intended or expected me to be awake at that point, that Scott hadn't been watching him and shouting at him, that things weren't going entirely to plan.

The syringeful of what I hoped against hope had been simple anesthetic had been at least half used on Annabel and he hadn't been able to put me out for as long as he'd meant.

He must have been disturbed to find me not alone. I guessed that perhaps he'd intended to lure me into the theater by some noise or other and plump his needle in by surprise. Perhaps he'd thought I wouldn't be alarmed by a surgeon, if I'd seen him. Perhaps anything.

He made a decision and crossed to one of the wall tables upon which lay a kidney dish. He picked up a syringe that had been lying there, held it up to the light and squirted it gently until drops oozed out of the needle.

I didn't need telling that I was meeting the puffer fish.

Time really had come to an end if I just went on hanging there helplessly. He had to reach me with that needle to do any harm. All I had to do was stop him.

Imminent extinction gave me powers I would have said were impossible. As he started towards me, I bent my arms to raise myself and jackknife my body, bringing my knees to my chin, trying by straightening fiercely to get my feet onto the operating table to my left and behind me. The maneuver didn't really succeed but I did get my feet as far as the edge of the table, which gave me purchase to swing out towards Carey and try to knock away the syringe with my shoes.

He skipped backwards, carefully holding the syringe high. I swung futilely in the air, feeling wrenched and furious.

After a moment's thought he pressed a hoist button and moved me a yard further from the table, towards him, towards the sliding door. Instantly, I repeated the jackknife, aiming this time straight at him. He retreated rapidly. My feet hit the wall where he had been and I pushed off from it violently, turning in the air, scything with my legs at the syringe.

I missed the high-held death but connected with Carey's head, by some chance with one foot each side of it. I tried to grip his head tight but the pendulum effect swung me away again. All that happened was that his surgical cap and mask were pulled off. The mask hung round his neck but the soft cap fell to the ground.

In an extraordinary way it seemed to fluster him. He put the hand holding the syringe to his head and drew it hastily away again. He was confused, his expression not venomous or evil, but showing double the exhaustion of recent days. Not plain tiredness, but psychic disintegration from too much stress.

Still as if nonplussed at things not going to plan, he bent down with his back to me to retrieve the fallen cap, and I, still futilely swinging, drew up my arms and knees and launched my feet with total desperation at Carey's backside.

The force of the connection was only slightly dissipated in the cloth of the surgical gown—no gloriously accurate success like Vicky's kick at the mugger—but it was hard enough to overbalance him, hard enough to send him staggering forward, and hard enough for him to crash his forehead against the sharp metal corner of one of the cabinets before he could straighten up.

He collapsed in a heap, stunned.

Feverishly I fought to undo the buckles of the constricting cuffs. I undid the left cuff first without thinking it out, as it was the one I'd tried to undo earlier. That wasn't too difficult, but it left me swinging from my right wrist alone, and undoing those buckles left-handed and up high cost enormous muscular effort. Sheer extreme panic gave me a strength beyond knowledge, a brute force like madness.

I sweated. Groaned. Struggled. Made my fingers overcome the opposing force of my weight.

My hands slid free at last and I fell, landing awkwardly, off balance, staggering, thinking immediately of a weapon, looking around for something to hit Carey's head with if he should stir, something to tie him with if he didn't.

Hurry. Hurry.

The solution was fitting and blindingly simple. I pushed the hoist buttons in my turn, lengthening the chains, still clipped to the cuffs, to their full extent. Then, very carefully, because of tetrodotoxin still a pinprick away, I pulled Carey's arms out from beneath him and bent them behind his back and fastened the cuffs to his wrists, but cross-buckled them so that they were held together, harder than ever to undo. He had a pulse. It throbbed in the wrists. Better, I thought, if he'd died.

I went to the controls and by degrees shortened the chains until they were just tight enough to lift Carey's latex glove-covered hands two or three inches clear of his back. When he woke in that position, he'd scarcely be able to pick his head off the floor.

Satisfied for the moment, but suffocating with anxiety, I ran into the padded room and over to Annabel.

She slept. I felt her pulse too. Strong enough. Alive.

"Oh Annabel." I smoothed her hair, overwhelmed with feeling.

I felt like crying. Heroes who took six punches in the solar plexus and came up smiling never felt like crying.

I stumbled unsteadily back to the office and sent a telephoned SOS to Ramsey to arrive with reinforcements. Went back to Annabel, sitting down beside her weakly with my back against the bullring wall, watching Carey through the sliding door for signs of murderous consciousness.

I held Annabel's hand, seeking comfort for myself as much as to give it.

She was alive. She would awake, as I had.

She had to.

I loved her intensely.

No trap I could have devised would have revealed Carey as conclusively as the one he'd set for me.

Between intuition and probability I'd come to see that it had had to be Carey I was looking for, but until he'd attacked me I'd had no way of persuading anyone else to believe me. Carey was the grand old man, the father of the practice, the authority figure, the one respected and trusted above all others by the clients.

All those old men. His generation. All knowing each other for half a lifetime. All knowing the secrets.

Long ago, Ronnie Upjohn's father and Theo Travers' grandfather had been insurance agents who'd made a fortune, not the average state of affairs.

Long ago Kenny McClure had ordered tetrodotoxin in order to pass it to the iniquitous Mackintosh, who everlastingly played cards with Carey. It was Carey, I judged, who'd persuaded Kenny, a vet but not his partner, to acquire the poison, and Kenny, balking at what he'd done, had got shot for his pains.

Long ago Wynn Lees had stapled an enemy's pants to his privates; had done his time and had gone to Australia.

The present troubles had begun after Wynn Lees's return, and perhaps he'd been the trigger that restarted the engine.

Carey had to have needed money. Not impossible that in the Porphyry crash he'd lost the savings that were to see him through old age. Not impossible to suppose he'd tried to get them back by using his professional knowledge.

Not impossible to guess that he'd somehow persuaded the third-generation insurance man Travers to join him in growing rich, nor that Travers had wanted out like Kenny, and found that out meant dead.

Carey, I thought, had burned the building not just to postpone or avoid identification of Travers, but also to cover all his own tracks. Orders, invoices, all the telltale paperwork had conveniently gone up in smoke, and particularly—I saw with awe—the blood samples taken that day when the cannonbone horse was dying on the table. Those samples would have shown excessive potassium. The unexplained deaths in the operating room would suddenly have been explained. The hunt for the culprit would be on.

No one would ever have questioned Carey's going in and out of the storeroom where the intravenous drip fluids were kept. No one would ever question what chemicals Carey ordered. No one would think it odd if he went to see old friends and their horses, no one would worry if he were seen at Eaglewood's one night, checking on his patients while surreptitiously taking insulin with him.

Carey could go where he liked, do what he liked, unquestioned and unchallenged, unsuspected. After all, no senior veterinarian in his right mind would set out to destroy his chief surgeon's reputation, nor kill off a practice he'd spent a lifetime building. But Carey, I thought, had meant to make his money and go. Events had hurried him: Travers had precipitated the fire. Ken had saved the colicky mare from what should have been curtains. It had been necessary, from Carey's point of view, only to finish off the mare and close the mouth of the man who'd carried the poison. After that there was nothing to keep him and he'd smartly announced the end of the partnership. If Ken hadn't told him how much we'd found out, he would quite likely have been peacefully packing at the moment, rich again and ready to emigrate, not lying flat, facedown in ultimate disaster.

Annabel stirred.

I felt enormous, heart-swelling thankful relief. I squeezed her hand and though she didn't squeeze back I thought that by then she could probably hear.

"Don't worry," I said, "I'm right here beside you. You're going to be all right very soon. Some bloody madman popped a bit of anesthetic into you but you're coming out of it and everything's fine. Don't hurry. Things will improve very soon, I promise you."

I went on trying to reassure her and in the end she opened her eyes and used them for smiling.

By the time Ramsey arrived, she was sitting snuggled in my arms but shivering with apprehension that the still prostrate figure in the surgical gown would come to life, jump up and still do us harm. He had jumped out at her from behind the wall, she said. She'd caught a horrified glimpse of him before he'd jabbed the needle into her neck.

"If he comes to life," I said, "I'll shorten the chains to pull his arms higher behind his back. I'll bend him double."

"I don't like it."

Nor did I. It seemed an age before the burly Superintendent appeared inquiringly through the door from the passage and stared in astonishment at the man on the floor.

I stood and went to meet him.

"What exactly gives?" he asked.

"I think," I said, "that that's your murderer. And be careful, because under him or nearby there's a hypodermic syringe oozing something that may be very detrimental to your health."

A week later, I phoned my mother and told her most of what had happened. Not Russet Eaglewood, not too much about Scott, not my frantic fight for life.

At the end she exclaimed, "I can't believe a vet would kill horses!"

"Vets put down horses all the time."

"That's different."

"Not so very."

"He must have been warped!"

"Oh, yes," I said.

403

I thought of Carey as I'd briefly seen him last, lying securely strapped to a stretcher with a big swelling on his forehead. Eyes closed. Harmless-looking. I heard later that he'd woken up concussed and been bewilderingly calm ever since. "He's relieved, I reckon," Ramsey said in a burst of unusual chattiness. "They're often relieved when it's all over. Funny that."

A syringe bearing traces of anesthetic had been found on the floor behind the half-wall in the padded room.

The syringe, whose needle Carey had tried to stick into me in the theater, had rolled under a nearby table. Wary analysis proved the contents of that one to be indubitably tetrodotoxin. The empty ampoule, bearing the Parkway company's name and batch number in black letters and "Extremely Hazardous" in red, lay in the kidney dish which had held the syringe.

"Smoking gun," Ramsey said with satisfaction.

His search of Carey's house revealed a book on dangerous marine animals, among which puffer fish took a medal.

"Circumstantial," Ramsey said.

Ramsey's list obtained from Porphyry Place showed Carey to have lost a sum that made me wince.

Higgins's insurance friends came up with every dead horse on our list: agent each time, Theodore Travers; recipients mostly fictitious, but also Wynn Lees, Fitzwalter and Nagrebb.

The expedited report on the DNA matching

of the mare and foal with Rainbow Quest came back negative: nowhere near a match, he wasn't the sire, positively not. Wynn Lees, certain to be charged with fraud, had cannily skipped the country.

My mother said, "What about Ken?"

"I had to tell him I'd lived here as a boy. He's wondered all the time how I knew so much."

"You didn't tell him about me and his father?" she asked anxiously.

"No, not a word. It's better not known."

"Ever the diplomat," she said, teasing but relieved.

Ken and Belinda's wedding, I told her, was going ahead as planned. "And that's just the word for it—planned. They're both so *practical* about it. No spark. But no doubts either, it seems."

"Don't you give it much chance then?" she asked, sounding disappointed.

"Fifty-fifty, I'd say. But Belinda's started calling her mother Vicky, not Mother. That might make all the difference."

My own mother chuckled. "You said I would like Vicky."

"You'll love her."

"We'll never meet."

"I'll see you do."

Ken himself, I told her, would emerge with his reputation in most part restored.

"There will be people," I said, "who might say he should have realized sooner why the horses were dying during operations. I can't judge that,

405

not being a vet. But it looks like being all right in general. The partners all met and decided to carry on at once and sort out the legal details later, and the practice is renamed McClure Quincy Amhurst, which should steady the critics."

"Wonderful!"

"And Mum," I said, "your Kenny . . ."

"Yes?"

"I found out why he died."

There was a silence on the line, then she said, "Tell me," and I told her the theories, and that Josephine believed them and was comforted.

"Are your theories right?"

"Yes, I think so."

A little pause. A voice gentle on a breath, "Thanks, darling."

I smiled. "Do you want a daughter-in-law?" I asked.

"Yes! You know I do."

"Her name is Annabel," I said.